THE ISITANT

OTHER BOOKS BY MEGAN CHANCE

Inamorata
Bone River
City of Ash
Prima Donna
The Spiritualist
An Inconvenient Wife
Susannah Morrow

YOUNG ADULT FICTION

The Fianna Trilogy:
The Shadows
The Web
The Veil

THE VISITANT

A VENETIAN GHOST STORY

MEGAN CHANCE

LAKE UNION

PUBLISHING

Published by Lake Union Publishing, Seattle
www.apub.com

Amazon, the Amazon logo, and Lake Union Publishing are trademarks of Amazon.com, Inc., or its affiliates.

ISBN-10: 1503945170
ISBN-13: 9781503945173

Cover design by Cyanotype Book Architects

To my father, Bill Chance, and my stepmother, Alice Vermillion, with much love.

It is a part of probability that many
improbable things will happen.

—Aristotle, *Poetics*, XXV

[Venice] was, indeed, a phantom of the past, haunting our
modern world—serene, inexpressibly beautiful, yet inscrutably
and unspeakably sad . . . a shadow within the shadow . . .

—William Dean Howells, *Venetian Life*

VENICE—NOVEMBER 28, 1884

Chapter 1

Only in my dreams had I ever imagined I might come to Venice. And, given the nature of dreams, I had always pictured the city sunny and warm, with gentle, salt-tinged breezes and melting colors and a handsome gondolier to row me about and serenade me as he declared his undying love.

But I hadn't considered November, a late train, and a storm that had buffeted the city the day before my arrival and blown refuse into every seam and doorway and alcove, where it lay in sodden, half-disintegrated blobs because the combination of the storm with high tide had filled every street and square with water. It still hadn't quite receded from most places, and left behind a slimy accumulation of silty mud and seaweed where it had.

And it was damply, wetly cold, with a breeze that was indeed salt tinged, but not the least bit gentle, and cutting through my layers of clothing until I wished I'd worn my maroon wool gown instead of a lace-edged, sage-and-rust striped silk that I'd thought might impress a man of Samuel Farber's status. A foolish little vanity, and how I was to impress him now, I didn't know. I was exhausted from the two-week journey and cold, hands numb in my gloves, my hair straggling from my pins to fall lankly against my cheeks, and not looking even close to my best.

And worse, it seemed the Casa Basilio, where he was staying, was in the *sestiere* of Cannaregio. Between the ship and the trains, I'd had plenty of time to read the Baedeker guidebooks I'd brought, and I knew it was not one of the most enviable areas. Not on the Grand Canal, as I'd hoped. Not near St. Mark's or any of the places I'd read about, the Riva or the Zattere. As the gondola made its undulating way toward the Basilio, skimming past the Grand Canal, which was gray and choppy under an overcast evening sky spitting rain, the buildings looking as if they were tossing and turning on a windswept sea and ready to tumble into it at any moment, I began to feel a creeping unease. We went into another narrower canal, and then one narrower still, with dank walls encroaching and the smells of old stone and damp and algae and mildew prickling my nose. The buildings were abandoned and boarded up, more than derelict; some had large pieces missing as if a giant had taken a huge hammer to them. The streets in some places were three inches deep with water, and all of them empty, so it sometimes seemed as if the gondolier and I were the only people alive in a flooded city occupied by ghosts.

The gondola stopped. From outside the cabin, the gondolier said in French—the only language we had in common—"Ca' Basilio, mamzelle."

When I looked out the levered windows, I knew I'd been right to be apprehensive.

The three-story palazzo was white stone, and so ruined I thought perhaps the gondolier had got it wrong. No one could possibly live here. It must have been elegant once, but now its white marble was stained black with mildew in great swaths. The decorative red marble medallions set here and there were cracked and missing pieces, some gone entirely. Of the six herringbone-patterned windows in the bricked white stone of the lower story, all but two were boarded. The same herringbone design carved into the thick wooden door, along with the sunburst crowning it, was nearly invisible through its layer of soot. Three balconies adorned each of the two upper floors. There was a tower cupola on the roof, tiles scattered like leaves about its base. The place looked utterly abandoned.

This was the palazzo Samuel Farber's noble friend had offered him? *This* was where I was to spend the next weeks? It seemed to pulse with neglect and misery. A narrow, wet stone walkway ran the length of the front, an extension of the square—*campo*, as the guidebook called it—on its right, which was barren, tiny and triangular, waterlogged and ragged. Another constricted canal bordered the left. Even in the early twilight, it showed a different color than the others, not a deep greenish gray, but a sludgy, olivey brown that looked like sewage and stank of something so tannic it burned my nostrils. I wanted nothing more than to tell the gondolier to row away.

But then I remembered my father's strain, and my mother's grasping hope, and I reached for the cabin door.

The gondolier opened it before I could and leaned in to offer me a hand, pulling me from the sinking leather cushions and out in one motion. He'd already settled my trunk on the edge of the walk, where the water lapped at it. The stairs were submerged, pale stone just barely visible beneath the current. I lifted my skirts to step into water that came to my ankle, the gondolier holding tight to my elbow as he gave me a small shove and boost. I fumbled in my purse for a tip, which he pocketed as he looked skeptically at the palazzo. "Should I wait, mamzelle?"

I glanced back to the forbidding black door. What if this wasn't where Samuel Farber was staying? What if it was all a mistake? *Please, let it be.*

"This is the Casa Basilio? You're certain?"

The gondolier nodded. Well, that was it, then. Out of all the beauties in Venice, I'd landed here. I would have thought it ironic had I the strength for humor. I took a deep breath and waved the gondolier away, and then I reached for the bellpull.

I heard the ring, both far away and very near, as if it were in two places at once, the water and the wind picking up the chime and flinging it into the air, the stone capturing it and sending it into echo. It was an eerie doubling, disconcerting instead of beautiful.

There was no answer. I rang it again, my discomfort growing, and then I heard the clatter of footsteps beyond. The door handle rattled; the door dragged open, squealing as it caught against the floor, revealing a dark interior tinged with red shadows, a cracked and dipping checkerboard floor of black-and-white stone, and a pretty woman probably ten years older than my twenty-four, with so much black hair that the braided corona of it rose about two inches from her head. Her equally black eyes regarded me suspiciously.

"I'm Elena Spira," I said in French, as I spoke no Italian and I doubted she spoke English. Papa had said that French was Venice's second language. It had been true for the gondolier, but I was uncertain if it would be so for a servant. "M'sieur Farber's nurse."

Her expression did not change, and for a moment I thought this wasn't the right house after all. Or perhaps she didn't speak French. I fumbled for what to say as her measuring gaze swept me; obviously her assessment was not to her liking. She said coldly, in French, "You're late."

I was relieved that Papa had been right after all, but that I obviously belonged here and was expected was not that reassuring. "Yes, I'm sorry. The train was delayed. I hope M'sieur Basilio will not mind receiving me at this hour—"

"He is not here," she said. "And Madame is resting now. You will have to call on her tomorrow."

I had not understood that Mr. Basilio was married, but all I really knew about him was that he was Venetian nobility and he owned the palazzo. I was relieved, actually, that neither he nor his wife was available. I was too tired for courtesy. I wanted only to meet my patient and fall into bed.

"Then, if you could take me to M'sieur Farber," I said.

I gestured to my trunk, and she broke into a flurry of shouted words that didn't sound quite like the Italian I'd heard on the way here, though I wasn't certain. Venetian, no doubt. Her calls crashed and ricocheted through the receiving court, which was walled in red marble—the reason for the blood-tinged shadows. A man bearing such a strong resemblance to the woman that he must be her brother came hurrying from a hall beyond a set of white marble stairs that looked like the entrance to a mausoleum. He threw me a smile and pushed past me to retrieve my trunk. The woman did not offer to take my coat or my hat—not that I was certain I wished to relinquish them. It was as cold inside as out.

She fingered a velvet bag at her waist with the familiarity of habit, jangling the keys obviously inside, motioning me to follow her past those marble stairs. A single candle flickered from a hanging chandelier. I'd seen streetlamps on the way here, so I knew gas was available. But I saw no evidence that the house had been piped for it. It was inconceivable in this day and age. Into what primitive place had I landed? The housekeeper took me into a corridor lined with doors. It opened onto a courtyard—perpetually opened, I realized, when I saw how the broad dark door lay at a strange angle.

The courtyard paving was cracked and uneven, littered with stones from a collapsed wall that looked as if it had been destroyed for some time, long enough for a creeping plant to have taken root among the ruins. There was a black marble wellhead, and here and there statues covered with algae and mildew.

The housekeeper sashayed—there was really no other word for it, though she was dressed as respectably as I—across the courtyard and up another set of stairs, these snaking up the outside wall of a three-storied wing. We went up the narrow, slippery stones to the third floor.

She glanced at me—quick and inscrutable—before she opened the door and gestured me inside, into a hallway that was the size of a large room, ending at balcony doors, and I felt as if I'd stumbled into a nightmare.

The speckled stone floor was skimmed with dust, studded with footprints. Twisted skeins of cobweb, laden with so much dust they were heavy hanks of fuzz, dangled from the chandeliers. Bare spots of discolored wallpaper where paintings had once obviously hung, and rough and unrepaired shallows where frescoes had been, dotted the wall. Bits of plaster scattered over the floor from the disintegrating putti and fauns peering down at us.

It looked as if no one had lived here for years.

This was not at all what I'd expected. Not this decrepitude or this isolation. "*He can be difficult,*" Papa had warned me, and I knew from the file in my trunk that it was true. I'd thought myself well prepared, but now I felt a frisson of uncertainty. What had these people seen that made them keep Samuel Farber up here?

The housekeeper turned into a smaller hallway, toward a cluster of open doors showing mostly empty rooms. She paused at one, gesturing, and I had a quick impression of a simple bedroom, a dark wood bedstead, and a window overlooking the courtyard, before she moved on. She said something; her French was difficult to understand, heavily accented, and it was a moment before I understood. "That is yours. It's the only other furnished bedroom on this floor."

The hall ended at a door. She stopped before it, knocking. "Samuel,"—*Samuel*, said as if her tongue could not quite manage the gathered vowels, and an inappropriate familiarity that startled me—"Your nurse is here."

There was a mumbled sound from inside, a deep voice. She smiled; it was both baleful and gleeful. "Your patient, mamzelle."

Then, with a nod, she left me.

Carefully, I opened the door.

The room was nothing like the rest. There was a carpet on the floor, two upholstered chairs, and a tea table bordering silk-curtained balcony doors. A plaster stove was against one wall, though it was not in use; the room was cold. A richly carved bed painted white with gilding wore bed curtains of blue velvet, and there, huddled within, was Samuel Farber.

In the month since he'd been hurt, his face had mostly healed, though the puncture wound near his temple and the laceration on his cheek would leave scars. His broken nose was still swollen into prominence. Thick, dark hair looked as if it hadn't seen a barber in months. I smelled oil and unwashed skin and . . . and laudanum.

Laudanum.

He stared at me as if he wasn't quite certain I was real. "My angel?" His voice was slurred and uncertain. Yes, definitely laudanum. *Damn.*

I tried to smile. "No angel. I'm Elena Spira. Your nurse. My, it's dark in here. Do you mind?" When I turned up the lamp on the bedside table, it only confirmed my suspicions. Within his deep brown eyes, his pupils were pinpricks.

"You're the one they sent? My parents sent you?"

"Yes. My father is Dr. Spira."

"Did they meet you?"

"Your parents? Yes, I met them once. Some time ago, but—"

He began to laugh, but it ended almost immediately on a groan. His hand went to his cracked ribs. Four of them, according to the hospital. He closed his eyes. "Christ."

"How long have you been here?"

A pause. "Uh . . . don' know. Days and . . . days?"

"Who's been caring for you?"

"Giulia. Caring and caring." Another laugh, followed by a wince.

"Who is that?"

"The housekeeper."

"Is she the one who gave you the laudanum?"

"The doctors," he said. "At the hospital. They sent it with me."

I saw it now. A brown bottle on the table, beside a spoon and a glass. "How much have you been taking?"

His hand went again to his head, his face crinkling as if he found it difficult to think. "Don' know. Not enough."

I pocketed the bottle. He was going to hate me tomorrow. "Well, you won't need Giulia's care any longer. I'm here now. I'll start you again on bromide. And no more laudanum. Or wine. No coffee and no tea. You'll be on a special diet as well."

"But I don't want her to go away," he protested weakly.

I thought of that sashaying walk, that insolent glance. I thought I understood it now. "You're no longer Giulia's charge, but mine."

He mumbled something.

"What was that?" I leaned closer. "I'm sorry, I didn't hear."

His voice was barely a murmur. I couldn't understand. He stiffened. "Here she comes now."

I looked over my shoulder. No one.

When I turned back to him, he was fast asleep, lost in opium-laced dreams.

I drew back from the bed and blew out the lamp. I was exhausted, and suddenly the day's disappointments felt insurmountable. I wanted suddenly to be back in my safe little room at Glen Echo, though . . . I would not be there, would I? I would be on my way to Littlehaven, and a different kind of nightmare.

I reminded myself that Samuel Farber was the answer to my prayers. Redemption and salvation. There was no other choice.

The house was eerily silent as I stepped back into the hall. I'd thought myself used to being alone; I was the only child of a loving but ambitious father and a mother who spent a great deal of time wooing society on his behalf. But this was an alone of an entirely different kind. It was a kind of watchful, expectant quiet that raised the hairs on the back of my neck. I looked over my shoulder, half expecting to see Giulia, but the hall held only the dark, gloomy shadows of evening. This place would look better in the morning. In truth, it could not look worse.

A loud dragging, scraping sound made me jump—a sound I knew, a coffin being dragged into a wagon—and I jerked to see Giulia's brother rounding the hall, dragging my trunk behind him. When he glanced up and smiled, I sagged in relief.

"Thank you," I said, hoping he understood French. I pointed down the hall to the room Giulia had indicated. "I think in there."

I was glad when he nodded, obviously understanding, and pulled the trunk inside. I winced at the scraping sound and the marks it left upon the floor, but they were only tracks in the dust.

When he straightened, I said, "I'm Elena Spira."

His dark close-cropped head bobbed. "Zuan Nardi, mamzelle."

"You must call me Elena, else I shall be too lonely here."

He glanced away, a moment of hesitation before he said with another charming smile that wrinkled his eyes, "As you wish, Elena. Should you need anything—something fixed, a gondola, anything—you must call upon me."

His French was as garbled as his sister's, but I was glad of any ability to communicate. "I see. You're a jack-of-all-trades, then?"

"I do not cook or clean. Well, some cleaning," he admitted.

"I should think that best left to the maids."

"No maids," he said cheerfully. "No one but me and Giulia."

"In this huge place?"

"There is no money," he said simply.

"But aren't the Basilios nobility?"

In Venetian, he said, "*Conte che non conta, non conta niente.*"

"I don't understand."

"A count who doesn't count counts for nothing," Zuan explained.

It was hardly a surprise, given the state of the palazzo.

"Zuan!" A sharp voice, a fluent stream of Venetian, and there was Giulia, her dark brows beetled. Zuan's smile and his ease with me died abruptly.

Giulia's flesh jiggled beneath her dress as she strode toward us. Uncorseted, I realized. "There is much for my brother to do. He should not be wasting time in conversation."

It was rare for me to dislike someone on sight, and I told myself I couldn't afford to. I needed her cooperation, and I could catch more flies with honey than with vinegar. "I'm so sorry. I'm afraid that was my fault."

Yes it is, her look said. Not even the pretense of conciliation.

I went on, "But now that I'm here, you'll at least have one less task."

"One less?"

"M'sieur Farber."

"Ah," she said with a coy look. "But you do not look strong enough to contain him alone, mamzelle. You will need my help, I think. He can be very . . . determined."

Determined. My unease returned. Samuel Farber had looked too ravaged to rise from bed. I had no idea when he'd left the hospital in Rome, but he said he'd been here for days. So much could have happened in that time. What had Giulia seen?

Nothing, I told myself. She would be frightened otherwise. She would not be so coy. I said, "I have no wish to put you or your brother out. Thank you for your help, but M'sieur Farber is now my responsibility. I'm certain you must be relieved to get back to your other duties."

Again, that direct gaze, daring me to look away. Though I was not the first to turn, I felt as if she had gained some sort of mastery over me. *She is a housekeeper*, I told myself. *A servant. She is nothing to you.*

But she would be a problem, I knew already. I was glad when she and her brother left, their footsteps stuttering into silence. The moment they were gone, I felt that invisible gaze on the back of my neck, that uncomfortable expectation. I hurried back to my room, trying to banish the fancy, feeling the burden of my task acutely. I would be lucky if this place didn't turn Samuel Farber stark raving mad. I tried not to think it a premonition.

Chapter 2

I dreamed of Glen Echo. Of my father's disappointment and my mother's fear. When I woke, the bitterness of the dream lingered. For a moment, I was lost within it; I didn't remember where I was. I opened my eyes to overcast light and the clank of metal below, the tolling of bells and a voice I didn't know shouting, "*Preme! Preme!*" The splash of water and a bird cackling that sounded like no bird I'd ever heard.

It all came back to me then. Venice. Samuel Farber. But at least I was no longer tired, and the dream's reminder of everything that was at stake made me more determined than ever to succeed.

I was still dressed; last night I'd taken off my cloak and hat and meant only to lie on the bed for a moment before I unpacked, but I'd obviously fallen asleep. Now, I was sore, my corset biting, my feet constricted in my boots, hair wisping and falling, pins tangled into it and dangling in my face.

My bedroom was spartan compared to his. No carpets on the freezing stone floor; only the simple bed with a storage trunk shoved beneath it, and a chamber pot. There was an armoire in the corner, a small mirror above a rickety washstand with a thick pottery basin and ewer. A rusty coal brazier was shoved into one corner, but there was no coal hod or coal. The bedside table held a guttered candle dripping ancient wax over its cast-iron holder. When I opened the drawer, I found a box of matches. Damp and obviously old. I doubted they would light.

I rose and washed, changed into my warmest wool dress, and once I did my hair, I felt more myself. My own trunk was against the wall, and I unlocked it and unpacked, hanging my gowns and petticoats in the armoire. The door creaked and groaned when I opened it; the inside smelled like mold. I left Samuel Farber's file in my trunk for safekeeping, along with everything else but the medicine case, which I set on the bed to check that all had arrived safely. Bromide and amyl nitrate; various herbal powders and ingredients to make pills; blistering liniments and rough-fibered massage cloths and a syringe and needle in a case; a thick, short leather strap—and there, a bottle of laudanum and a smaller one of morphine. "*Just in case,*" my father had said, and I thought of what Giulia had said yesterday. "*He can be determined.*"

I shoved the leather strap into my pocket. Whatever she'd seen I could explain away. First, I must talk to Madame Basilio and make her understand how crucial it was that no one in this house interfere with Mr. Farber without my permission, though I had no real idea how to do so without raising suspicions. I was starving; it was hard to think. Perhaps breakfast would be a good idea before I spoke to her.

Which meant I must find a kitchen somewhere. If there was one on this floor, it would be especially helpful. But a short exploration showed me there wasn't, so I stepped out onto the landing, looking to the courtyard, where smoke from an upended top hat of a Venetian chimney emanated from the one-story wing below.

It must be the kitchen. I hurried down into the courtyard, maneuvering around the scattered stones, wondering that no one had thought to clean up the mess. The door was closed. I steeled myself for meeting Giulia and pushed it open cautiously. Warmth

met me, the bubble of a pot on the cast-iron stove against the far
wall. I stepped inside, assailed by smells of something spicy and
wonderful, some kind of fish. There was a long table with benches
on either side. Pots hanging from hooks in the wall, barrels
beneath. I was stunned at the quantity of food on the table: bread
and wine, a round of hard-rind cheese, a scatter of shimmering
sardines, oranges and a bowl of eggs and a pitcher of milk. Given
the austerity of the rest of the house, I knew exactly who must be
paying for all this food: Samuel Farber's parents.

A dark head popped from beneath the table. I stepped back,
startled, but it was only a boy. In his hand was a slice of roasted
pumpkin, a string of orange flesh clung to his lip. He must have
been about ten. He rattled off something I didn't understand, his
eyes large with alarm, and then he dashed beneath my outstretched
arm, and out the still open door, veering and weaving about the
obstacled courtyard as if he knew the placing of each fallen stone
by instinct. He took a turn and disappeared.

I had no idea who he was. Giulia's son perhaps, or Zuan's. It
was clear to me that the Basilios—or perhaps just Giulia—were
using the Farbers' money to feed the entire household. I would
have to discuss all this with my hostess later, but it made things
easier for me just now. At least I did not have to shop or take the
time to cook. I cut a large wedge of the cheese—dry and salty and
delicious—sliced a hunk of bread, and took two oranges. I tucked
it all into my pockets and fairly ran with my bounty through the
courtyard, determined to avoid Giulia, who was no doubt being
told by the boy this very moment that her guest was raiding the
pantry.

I managed to make it to the third floor without discovery.
Samuel Farber was still asleep, and the room was nothing but
gloom, the overcast morning barely penetrating the drawn curtains. I wished I had thought to put on my cloak. The plaster stove

was unlit, but—miracle of miracles—there was a hod of coal sitting beside it and a block of matches.

Samuel Farber didn't stir as I piled in the coal and lit it. Immediately, smoke billowed out, though I'd checked the damper, and it was open. After a few moments, I realized that this was as efficient as the stove was going to be. I went to his bed, pulling the cheese and bread and oranges from my pockets and piling them onto the bedside table, and then I lit the lamp.

I'd thought him asleep, but his hand shot out, gripping my wrist, his eyes snapping open. This was not the opium haze I'd expected. He stared at me as if I were the answer to a prayer, a dream burst into reality. With longing and a joy so pure it stole my breath.

"You're here," he whispered. "My angel."

I didn't know what to do, and so I said the only thing I could think. "Good morning. I've brought you something to eat."

He blinked as if he'd just awakened, his brow furrowing. His fingers loosened on my wrist. "Who the hell are you?"

"I'm your nurse. Elena Spira."

He sagged into the pillows, covering his eyes. "Ah yes, I remember. Elena with the Titian hair."

"Miss Spira," I corrected. "I've brought you some food."

"I'm not hungry. I hurt. Where's the laudanum?"

"No more laudanum, I'm afraid."

"I *hurt*."

"Here, have something to eat—"

"I don't want food." He lowered his hand from his eyes, glaring at me. "What kind of a nurse cares nothing about relieving pain?"

"The kind who means to treat what's really wrong with you," I retorted.

His expression became stony. "Go away."

"Mr. Farber—"

"I said go away. If you won't help with the pain, I don't want you."

"I cannot imagine it is still so bad. It's been a month."

"If you don't go away I will throw you out myself," he said.

He looked incapable of swatting a fly, but I knew better than to argue with a patient, and I couldn't make him so upset that he refused to have me here.

I took a deep breath and said as calmly as I could, "Your breakfast is there, should you want it."

"Feed it to the rats."

I hurried away, forgetting about my own breakfast in the rush to leave him, and it wasn't until I was in the hallway that I remembered how hungry I was. But I wouldn't go back in there, not now. Samuel Farber knew as well as I the reasons I could not give him laudanum, and I could not have him dismissing me in favor of a more compliant nurse. Giulia, for example. I was here at his parents' behest, after all, not his own, and I knew it was only a matter of time before he remembered that.

But I hoped to have him reasonable and compliant before then, and to that end, I must speak to Madame Basilio. It was time to meet my hostess.

I had no idea where to find her, but my Baedeker had said the second floor—the piano nobile—was traditionally the main residence of the nobility, and that seemed as good a guess as any. With a sigh, I ignored my rumbling stomach, went back outside, and knocked on the door at the landing of the main floor. Before I was ready, the door opened, and I was staring into Giulia's hostile eyes.

"I've come to call on Madame Basilio," I said.

I thought she would refuse me entry, but to my surprise she said, "This way, mamzelle," and gestured for me to follow her into the hallway, which was expansive enough to serve as a ballroom.

Pillars of green porphyry and pale chalcedony ran the length; between them were frescoes. The one directly facing us

I recognized as a muse—Erato with her cithara—though it had crumbled so badly she looked like a pitted mosaic. The gilding had mostly flaked to nothing, the instrument blackened with mildew. As Giulia led me down the hall, I saw all nine muses, and at least half of them looked as if they'd been afflicted by some terrible disfiguring disease.

Giulia took me through a wide doorway bordered by red marble pillars topped with a gilded cornice in the same sunburst design that I'd seen throughout the palazzo, said, "Wait here," and left me alone.

The balcony windows at one end let in a gray and overcast light that threw undulating, watery reflections over an elaborately painted ceiling so damaged that it was difficult to tell what the scene had been. Everything here spoke of genteel poverty. I remembered what Zuan had said about counts with no money. What a godsend rich Samuel Farber must be. No doubt the Basilios would do whatever they could to keep him here, which could only work in my favor.

It wasn't long before I heard the clipped sound of heels on stone, and I turned just as an older woman with elegantly dressed hair—more white than dark—and fine, pale skin stretched too thinly over her bony face paused at the entrance to the *sala*. She wore a gown of deep gray, half mourning, without any jewelry. Her long, slender fingers were clasped before her. Her gaze was as measuring as Giulia's had been, and as unsmiling.

"You're the nurse?" she asked coldly in French.

I was taken aback, but I attributed her tone to the impatience of the elderly. "I am. Elena Spira."

Her gaze flickered. "Spira? That's a Venetian name."

"My father's people were from here. Many years ago." I had no idea who she was. Certainly too old to be the wife of Samuel's friend, but then, perhaps not. I had no idea how old Mr. Basilio was. "And you are?"

"Valeria Basilio," she said. "Nerone, my nephew, is away, but he has left M'sieur Farber in my care."

"I see. M'sieur Farber's parents have asked me to tender their thanks that you've offered him a place to stay while he is recovering. I understand the hospital in Rome was . . . inadequate." I spoke the words I'd practiced on the journey from New York City, though they seemed foolish now given the state of this household. I did not think the Farbers had any idea of the decrepit nature of the place where they had sent their son, and I could not imagine them finding it better than a Roman hospital.

But if Madame Basilio saw the irony in my words, she made no sign. "My nephew is generous to a fault."

Perhaps it was that my French was deficient. Or perhaps it was hers. Like her servants, Madame Basilio seemed to stumble over the slipping consonants. Had she meant to say that Samuel Farber was an imposition? "I don't suppose you speak English, Madame?" She shook her head, and I sighed and went on in French. "As I said, the Farbers are extremely grateful. They understand what a burden it is to have an ailing guest, which is why they've sent me. I have instructions to make certain M'sieur Farber's stay does not inconvenience you in any way."

Madame Basilio made a short, dismissive gesture. "My servants have found him no inconvenience."

"I'm glad for that, but his parents wish him to be under the care of a doctor they know. I'll be cooking and cleaning for him as well."

Madame Basilio frowned. "It seems a great deal of work for you, mademoiselle."

"It's what I've been hired to do. There are also his medications to consider. I must oversee everything he eats and drinks, and no one wishes to add to your household's burdens."

"Are his injuries so serious?"

"Cracked ribs, a dislocated kneecap, a broken nose . . . yes, I would say they were serious. But he was badly concussed too, and that is what worries the doctor most. He fears there may be . . . well, that M'sieur Farber might evidence certain . . . strange behavior, given its severity. You must tell me, have you seen anything odd in him since he's come here?"

She stilled, and that ramrod-straight back went straighter. "Odd?"

"Has he been seeing things? Hearing things? Anything else that seems unusual?"

I did not think I was imagining the shuttering of her expression. "I have seen nothing like that."

I should have been relieved. I would have been, but for how uncomfortable I was in her presence. It wasn't that she was unwelcoming, exactly, though she wasn't welcoming either. I didn't quite believe her words, though why would she lie? I told myself I was too sensitive. I felt out of place in this house, and I was so aware of the real reason I was here that I saw it in everything.

"You must let me know if you do. Though now that I'm here, I hope to make it so you scarcely notice our presence."

Madame Basilio replied, "Of course, mademoiselle. You are from America, yes?"

The change of subject made me falter. "Y-yes. New York City."

I expected another question, an explanation for why she'd asked, but she did not offer it. Instead she said, "Please let me know if I can help in any way."

It was a courtesy only; I had the feeling she would not appreciate my asking, though I had no reason to believe that either. Obediently, I rose. "Thank you, Madame."

I was happy to go. Madame Basilio had not been unhelpful, and I had no reason to believe she would not do as I asked, and, in fact, every reason to believe she would. I hoped for a smooth road to Samuel Farber's recovery, everything falling into place, the path to healing and redemption, my life opening wide instead of closing steadily shut.

The door to Samuel Farber's room was open. I heard a woman's laughter from within and my heart sank. I was not surprised, when I entered, to see Giulia sitting on the edge of his bed.

"Ah, Miss Spira." Samuel Farber did not take his hands from where they rested at the housekeeper's waist. He seemed completely unrepentant. Worse than that, challenging.

I ignored him for the moment and looked at Giulia. "I must ask you to leave."

Giulia's gaze went sly and dark. "Forgive me, mamzelle. I heard him calling, and no one answering, not even his nurse. He is in such pain. I thought only to relieve it."

I felt a stab of alarm. "What have you given him?"

She smiled at him. "Nothing he did not want, mamzelle."

Her meaning was obvious. It was only then that I noticed the disarray of her clothing. "Please, go," I said, not bothering to temper my annoyance. "I've just spoken to your mistress. She has agreed that M'sieur Farber is to be my responsibility completely. You must leave his care to me. I want him to have nothing without my approval."

She ran a caressing finger down his nightshirted chest and rose, and every part of that motion bounced and swayed. I saw how he appreciated it. "I was only trying to help, mamzelle. Should I have ignored his cries?"

"I would like you to go now," I said, gesturing toward the door.

With a sigh, and those jiggling, twisting hips, a lingering look over her shoulder, she went to the door and disappeared.

He said, "A pity."

"You should be resting," I said. "Such things will only make it worse."

"Such things?" he asked.

"You know what I mean."

He regarded me blandly. In the morning light, the healing scars on his face were brightly pink. "I'm afraid I don't."

"You're not to . . . you can't . . . there's to be no"—I searched uselessly for a word that wouldn't have me blushing furiously, but already I felt the heat of it in my face—"congress."

He snorted, and then winced. "The slightest movement causes me pain. If you would please give me the laudanum—"

"I've already told you. You're to have no more of that. And you seem to be much better this morning."

"What about wine? At least let me drink myself into oblivion."

"No wine either. No spirits of any kind. You're on a very strict regimen, Mr. Farber, as instructed by your doctor. I'm to give you bromide again starting today."

"Bromide? There's a reason I stopped taking it before."

"What reason was that?"

"I felt mummified. And"—a half-lidded look that made me think of Giulia's loosened clothing—"it impeded *congress*."

I ignored my embarrassment. "It prevented your seizures." I lowered my voice on the last word, worried that someone might overhear, but then I realized it didn't matter. We were speaking English, which no one in this house apparently understood. "Which is worse?"

"That's still up for debate."

"Mr. Farber, my job is to help you."

"Your job is to fatten me up like a lamb to the slaughter," he corrected. "Miss Spira, perhaps you could tell me—as a woman—if you would appreciate marrying a man under false pretenses."

So he knew the reason I was here. I had not been quite certain. "I don't know what's false about it. As I understand it, your intended bride is trading a respected family name for money. Everyone gets what they want."

"But my parents aren't telling her the truth, are they? You can't tell me that you would want an epileptic husband."

"If you can control your seizures—"

"By becoming a mindless, drooling idiot? Ah, so much better."

"I think you exaggerate." I reached for the bread I'd brought earlier and tore off a piece, handing it to him. "The bromide has helped you in the past."

"But it's only a sedative, and not a cure, isn't it?" he asked. "The seizures still come."

"Less often. My father has some other ideas as well. He's done some research, and—"

"I'm sure it will all be quite pleasant. Just as every other treatment has been." His sarcasm was blistering. He considered the bread, but before he took a bite, his breath hitched. He dropped the bread; his hand went to his chest.

"Do your ribs still pain you a great deal?" I asked.

"Everything pains me. My nose, my ribs, my knee. Fortunately, there is laudanum."

"I'm sorry. I can't."

He sighed; it turned into a breathless groan. "My parents are quite anxious that I begin breeding the Farber dynasty as soon as possible."

I peeled an orange and poked his hand gently with a section to make him take it.

"They say it can pass through the blood," he went on. "I understand that in England, they don't let epileptics marry."

"America is not England."

"What woman would want to curse her children with such an affliction?"

I couldn't answer him.

"You see?"

"It's not my place to make judgments."

"No, I suppose my parents are paying you very well not to. No doubt they're pleased at all this." He gestured to himself. "It gives them the opportunity they're always hoping for."

"What opportunity is that?"

"Getting their claws into me so they can throw me back into your father's clutches."

"You make him sound like Dr. Frankenstein, and you know nothing is further from the truth. He wants only to see you stable. As he's managed to make you before."

"My parents believe he can cure me this time. Is that what he told them?"

"I don't know what he's said." Not quite the truth, but close enough. There was no need for Samuel Farber to know the terms of his parents' agreement with mine. Nor just how much we needed the things they'd promised.

"What about you, Miss Spira? Do you think I can be cured?"

"I shall certainly try."

"You'll fail. Better to just give me the laudanum and some wine and leave me to myself."

"And have you end up as you did in Rome? The victim of thieves taking advantage of a man in convulsions?"

His expression darkened. "They should have killed me."

"It looks as if they tried."

"Wouldn't it be better for everyone if they'd succeeded?"

"I doubt your parents think so."

He made a sound of derision. "All they care about is their dynasty. A glorious future of Farbers cavorting with Astors and Van Cortlandts."

"You don't really believe that."

"You have no idea what I believe. Or what I am. Or what I'll do." The look he gave me was uncomfortably assessing. "How foolish they were to send you."

"My father trained me for this himself, Mr. Farber. I'm very capable."

He laughed slightly. "Oh, I'm certain you are."

Derision, again, but something more than that too. Amusement
and a *knowing* that made me feel soiled and prickly. "We'll have
you recovered in no time. But you must promise to do as I ask.
Your regimen requires abstinence, which you know. Your parents
expect your return at the end of January. If you want to be well
by then, I must have your promise that you will send Giulia away
when she visits."

"Why?" he asked. "Why does it matter to you? It can hardly
make an ounce of difference to you whether or not my parents can
keep the secret of my affliction from my fiancée."

I couldn't tell him how much depended on it.

He must have seen it in my face. His expression tightened.
"What have they promised you besides money?"

"The contract is between my father and your parents," I said
stiffly. "I cannot reveal—"

"What's your stake in it?" he insisted. "There must be one. I
can see it in your face. What are you, a friend of my fiancée's? Does
it matter so much to her?"

"I don't know her at all. I don't even know who she is."

"Neither do I." His expression was darkly resentful, and any
hope I'd had for a quick resolution died abruptly.

Whatever other problems I had expected to encounter, I had
not thought fighting Samuel Farber himself would be one of them.
He had been at Glen Echo often enough over the years that I had
assumed he wanted to gain control of his suffering; who would
not? He was the only heir to his parents' self-made fortune; why
shouldn't he want whatever normal life they might contract for
him?

I had not realized he'd been admitted involuntarily. His file
had not said it. The one time I'd met his parents, they had implied
that he was desperate to control his seizures. But now I knew that
when Papa said that Mr. Farber might be difficult, he was not just
talking about how much Samuel Farber disliked the treatments,

but of something more crucial still: the fact that he had no desire at all to change the way he lived his life. It meant that I would have to use no small amount of persuasion to win his cooperation. But I would not be dissuaded. I did have a stake in this. However Samuel Farber might wish to ruin his own life, I did not intend to let him ruin mine.

Chapter 3

It was one thing to make the resolution, and quite another to carry
it out. Over the next few days, Samuel Farber was resentful and
intractable. I knew what had helped him in the past, and my father
and I had discussed every detail of the plan to help him now, but
I could not start right away. Though his injuries were healing, his
reliance on the laudanum had made him too sensitive. I had to
wait until he had withdrawn enough from the drug that every
touch didn't cause him pain, which meant that I had a great deal
of time on my hands. I was bored and restless, too many hours to
think, to remember everything that had brought me here.

I had nearly memorized his file already; reading it again was
no distraction. I'd thumbed so often through my Baedeker guides,
imagining myself in each of the magical places they described, that
my longing to be done with this, to have my reward, was uncomfortably constant, and delay only made me irritable and short. I
found myself wandering the floor, going from room to empty,
deteriorating room, trying to ignore that sense of enduring watchfulness. I did not like the hallways especially, with the plaster carv-
ings whose empty eyes seemed to note and judge and measure.

Sometimes I felt myself racing down the hall before I realized I was trying to escape the weight of that expectancy.

Casa Basilio was surrounded by canals on three sides: the wide canal the gondolier had named Rio de la Sensa fronting it; the narrow, stinking canal between it and its neighboring palazzo; and a wider one at the rear. I shuddered from looking at the sheer straight drop from the third floor, unrelieved by balconies or dormers but for those of the sala and Samuel's room. After the first day, I tried not to look down at the water, nor to let my thoughts wander there. The canals were too reminiscent of the Hudson River at home, the constant lapping churn of current that only reminded me of how stagnant was my own life, how I had not been satisfied, no matter how I tried. And in that downward sweep too was the memory of what I'd almost done, of what did not, even now, seem distant enough to easily dismiss.

Instead, I strained to see beyond the walls of disintegrating buildings, hoping to see something of the Venice I'd read about. It was called the city of dreams, and I longed to see all of it. But more than that, I wanted the possibility of what I could become within it. Across the back canal was a church that blocked my sight line— brick and arched mullioned windows, a domed campanile—and I stared at its wall as if sheer will could show me the view inside. I searched for movement beyond its high windows, wondering, fashioning, losing myself in the promise of its mysteries. If I were to take a few hours and explore it, could it make me into something else entirely?

Somewhere beyond these walls was St. Mark's. The Piazza. The Grand Canal and the Arsenal and . . . and . . . everything. A world that I hoped would change mine. My eagerness to step into it was almost nauseating.

But without Samuel Farber, I could have none of it. *Not yet*, I told myself. *Soon.* When Mr. Farber was better, when I had delivered him to his parents and he was standing at the altar with his new bride. Then . . . then I would have what I wanted, the only thing left to me. I turned away from the rooms with the view of the church, its temptation too troubling. All I had to do was be patient.

Although it was hard to be patient in a place so uncomfortable. No amount of coal in my brazier or in the plaster stove in his room seemed to make a dent against the chilly, dank decay of the Basilio, and my discomfort only grew when it became obvious that Giulia meant to do everything she could to work against me. I found her—not once, but many times—in the hall, either leaving his room or on her way there. I could hardly leave him alone without her trying to sneak in. "He was calling, mamzelle. How could I ignore him?" The way she looked at me, daring me to contradict her, to call her a liar, and even more than that, an insinuation that I was incompetent, or naïve. I felt like a fool beneath that look, helpless and immature.

But I told myself it was why I felt watched. It had to be her, hiding, waiting to sneak in to see him, though she seemed brazenly unconcerned about concealing her visits.

I'd been there seven days when I decided I had given him as much time as I could afford. Not just because of Giulia's constant interference, but because I could not stand this house. I searched out Zuan, who was in the courtyard, knee-deep in a damp mist that floated ghostlike among the stones. Beside him stood the boy I'd seen before. He dodged behind Zuan's legs shyly when I approached.

Zuan said something to him in Venetian, but the boy did not budge. Zuan laughed and said to me in French, "My nephew, Giovanni."

I frowned. "Giulia's son?"

Zuan shook his head, but before he could answer, the kitchen door opened, and a man I'd never seen before came striding out, followed by a woman. They were each holding a burlap bag, and tucked beneath the man's arm was a wheel of cheese.

"Giovanni!" the man called, and the boy went running to him.

"My brother Tomas and his wife, Caterina," Zuan said, without the least bit of sheepishness or embarrassment at the obvious pilfering of the Basilio pantry. He spattered off a stream of Venetian, and Tomas laughed and touched the cap covering his straight dark hair, sweeping me with an admiring glance. Then he and the rest of his family disappeared through the gate.

I hardly knew what to say. The kitchen door opened again, and Giulia came ambling out, a little girl on either side. She was jabbering away, smiling, until she saw me standing there with Zuan.

"Zuan!" she snapped, and then a string of words I didn't understand, though their meaning was clear enough. *Stay away from her.*

He frowned. "Ciao, mamzelle," he said as he turned away, but I grabbed his sleeve.

"Please," I said. "I came here to find you. Is there a bathing tub somewhere about? Even a hip bath would do. And I need some water brought up to the sala."

He paused, glancing at his sister, who came sauntering over. The little girls ran to the wellhead, which was so shrouded in draping fog that it looked as if they sat suspended on a cloud to chew on their hunks of bread.

"Zuan is very busy," Giulia said to me, and after he told her what I needed, "Oh, I am so sorry, mamzelle, but the stove is not working well today. No water can be heated."

I glanced at the smoke coming from the chimney. The stove was working perfectly well. I had no doubt there was hot water.

"I don't need much of it," I told her. "It isn't to be a warm bath."

"There are public baths," she said. "You can go there."

"Unfortunately I cannot take M'sieur Farber to a public bath," I said nastily and insistently. "I will need a bathtub in the third-floor salon, and water to fill it."

She regarded me coolly. "Ah, but Zuan is far too busy to bring water. And you do not wish for us to be in the way, yes?"

"Giulia—" Zuan began.

She gave him a look that silenced him.

Zuan's gaze dodged to me, and then away. He mumbled something beneath his breath and went off, disappearing into the receiving court wing before I could call him back.

"There is a tub in the storage room," she said. "And buckets."

Given how often I'd seen her flouting my directions, I was not inclined to release her so easily now. "I can hardly cart that to the third floor myself."

"You have said you do not wish our help."

"Yes, but surely you can see my difficulty. There must be someone else here to help me, as Zuan is so *busy*. Perhaps you. Or those girls. Or perhaps you could call back your brother and his wife, who I think owe you a favor given the amount of food they carried away. I see that the Farbers have been very generous. Perhaps more so than they wish to be."

She regarded me coolly. "For only a few centimes, you can live very well in Venice."

"I doubt the Farbers have been told that."

"I am just the housekeeper," Giulia said, not a flinch in those stony eyes, not a bit of surrender. "I do not decide such arrangements. If you have questions, you should speak with the *padrona*."

"Perhaps I will."

"As you wish, mamzelle."

"Or I might be persuaded to ignore it. If someone can help me with M'sieur Farber's bath."

She shrugged. "I am so sorry, mamzelle, but I cannot just conjure up someone when no one is here. Perhaps tomorrow."

Or the day after, or the day after that. I understood the unspoken words. She turned away with a smug smile, spoke sharply to the two girls on the wellhead, and then the three of them headed off in the direction Zuan had gone.

I stared after them in angry frustration. It was all the more enraging because she was right; I had told her I'd wished for no help. I had half a mind to just let it go. There were other treatments, other things to try.

But my father's instructions had been very clear, and I could not afford to fail. I went in search of the storage room and the bathtub.

It didn't take long. The storage room's door was open; within were barrels and small wine kegs, hanging garlic and onions, a few pumpkins. The smell of fish was strong; no doubt one of the barrels held anchovies or some fermenting something. There, in the corner, was the bathtub I'd been searching for.

I had no expectation that I would be able to lift it, but this wasn't like the heavy tubs at Glen Echo. This had been made to move about, and so it was lighter. Not liftable by me, but with a combination of pushing and shoving, I could move it. I pushed and tugged it, scraping over the floor, down the hall, and into the courtyard. I had to pause now and then to move the fallen stones out of the way; it was astonishing that no one had done this before now. At the bottom of the stairs, I paused to catch my breath. I saw movement at a window on the second floor—Madame Basilio— and felt a wash of relief. No doubt she would see my difficulty and summon help. But as I raised my hand to wave to her, she disappeared.

I waited a moment, expecting her to come out, but as the minutes passed, and she didn't, I began to wonder if seeing her had only been wishful thinking. Or perhaps she had merely been heeding my request for no interference. Resignedly, I looked up the stairs. They looked too narrow, the cast-iron railing in the way. And even if I managed it, there would be the water to bring. Buckets and buckets of it.

I cursed Giulia, Zuan, Samuel Farber, and the rest of the world as I lugged that miserable, godforsaken tub up those stairs. It fell upon my foot, cracked my shin, pinched my fingers between it and the cast-iron rail. Bits of plaster came off as the tub smashed into the wall—just let them try to complain about it! It would serve them all right if I destroyed the entire palazzo. And then, as if to emphasize the point, I lost my grip and the tub smacked hard enough on a step to crack it before I got hold of it again.

I never thought I would get it to the top, and when I did, I stood there disbelieving. And sore. With swollen fingers and a throbbing shin, and sweating so hard my bodice was sticking to me. But I had done it.

I scraped it over the floor to the middle of the sala, out of the way of a rat-bitten settee scattered with fraying pillows and a chair whose upholstery had split in the damp.

I heard a pattering sound from the doorway, and turned to see Samuel Farber standing there, holding on to the white marble pillar of the entry as if it were keeping him upright. He was barefoot, wearing only his nightshirt. "What the hell?"

I straightened. "I am fetching you a bath."

"So I heard. Probably all of Cannaregio heard as well."

"Your lovely Giulia declined to help."

"You brought that up by yourself?" He looked vaguely impressed when I nodded. "You're stronger than you look."

"You'll catch your death, standing barefoot on this floor." It radiated cold; I felt it even through the soles of my boots. I moved past him to the hall. "It might take me a while to bring the water."

He nodded, limping to the settee, where he sank as if the journey had exhausted him. I left him there, irritated all over again that he hadn't offered his help either, though of course he was weak as a babe and just as incapable of hauling water up those stairs.

It took me another hour to draw water from the well and bring it up, two barrels at a time. Samuel Farber only watched impassively as I poured it into the bathtub. When it was nearly full, I brought up hot water from the kitchen—there was plenty of it, as

I'd suspected—so the water was cool, but not cold. Then I stood back, took a deep breath, and gestured at it.

He eyed it dubiously. "It's not steaming."

"No. It's supposed to be cool."

"Cool?" Incredulously. "There's no heat in here."

"I'm not cold at all."

"You've just lugged a bathtub and buckets of water up three flights," he pointed out.

"Get in."

"I'll freeze."

"You're supposed to. It's part of the treatment. You know this. You took cold baths at Glen Echo."

"I hated them."

"It quiets your raging humors."

"There will be more than my humors raging if I get into a freezing bath in a cold room."

"I'll put coal on," I said, glancing to the plaster stove, no doubt as decoratively ineffective as the one in his room. "Now get in."

"No."

I glared at him. "Mr. Farber, I have had a very trying morning. I have just spent two hours drawing you a bath. I have a bruise on my shin, and my fingers are crushed. If you don't get in of your own accord, believe me, I shall make you." A strand of hair fell over my forehead and into my eye, ruining whatever semithreatening stance I'd managed. I let it lie, still glaring at him, while he glared back at me. Truly, I was angry enough to try to make him get into the bath, though I had no real idea if I could budge him.

Thankfully, he rose and stepped over to the tub. He didn't take his gaze from mine. And then, before I realized what he meant to do, he lifted his nightshirt over his head and pulled it off, dropping it to the floor.

I had never seen a fully naked man before. My charges at Glen Echo had all been women. My gaze moved involuntarily to the part of him I was curious about before I jerked my gaze upward again in embarrassment, and noticed the mottled brown bruises and contusions crisscrossing his ribs, a deep purple one wrapping around his hip—and then I realized his knee was so rainbow colored and swollen it did not look like a knee at all. Even after a month, the bruises were livid, deep-tissue tears and hematomas. I had not suspected such damage.

"Most women don't look so horrified when I undress," he said.

"Oh dear God," I breathed. "What did they do to you?"

"Well, they wanted my money, and no witnesses, and I was in no state to stop them, as you know." He swayed, grabbing the lip of the tub, and I realized his knee would not hold him for so long. I hurried over.

"Let me help you." I put his arm over my shoulders, taking most of his weight as he got into the tub, forgetting my embarrassment in compassion. He lowered himself into the water, splashing over the marblelike floor.

He shuddered. "Damn, this is cold."

"It will help—"

"Calm my raging humors. Yes, I know." His skin was covered with gooseflesh.

"And it will help with the swelling too. And quite possibly the pain."

"Do you know what would really help with the pain?"

"Mr. Farber—"

"I think you should call me Samuel. Now that you've seen me in my natural state."

"I had no idea they'd hurt you so badly."

"Please tell me that means you've changed your mind about the laudanum."

I shook my head. He was shivering. I felt bad about that too. "I'm sorry. I am."

"This is only punishment."

"It's beneficial—"

"It's torture. Bring me some goddamned laudanum!" He slapped his hand in the water, splashing more onto the floor, onto my gown.

"No. And acting like a child is not going to help."

"You said yourself it looks horrific. Imagine how it *feels*."

"I do. I can."

He opened his mouth to say something, but then closed it again. He said, slowly and with great restraint, "I can't sleep for the pain. I can't bear it when I'm awake."

"The laudanum only makes you more sensitive. Ten more minutes in the bath. Then I'll bring arnica. I think we'll forget about rubefacients today."

"Rube—what?"

"Liniment. And rubbing. You should be familiar enough with it."

"The burning salve, you mean." His chin dipped to his chest, his hair coming forward to hide his face. "Please God, not that. Not today."

The pain in his voice, the resignation . . . it made me want to do whatever he asked. How was it possible to look at such pain and not be moved?

But I'd been so moved before, and look how that had ended up.

"Not today," I agreed. "We'll try the arnica. What was it that made such a mess of you anyway? Did they use clubs?"

He tried to ease his bloated knee below the water, but the tub was small, and he couldn't stretch out completely. The motion brought a rush of pained breath. "I don't know. The seizures . . . I never remember them. Sometimes I don't remember the time before they happen. Sometimes it's after I don't remember. Hours sometimes. I lost a day once."

He was not unusual in that. "What do you remember about that night?"

"Well . . . that's the question, isn't it? That's what my father wants to know. Who I was with. What they saw."

"Have you any answers?"

"I'd been on a binge for at least a week," he said. "Let's just say everything's a bit hazy."

"A binge?"

"Drinking. Opium. Women." A challenging gaze. "From the moment I got the letter from my father about my imminent wedding."

"I see."

"The last thing I remember is a brothel in Rome. A woman with hair the same color as yours and breasts like heaven." He smiled at my discomposure. "I'd gone with a few friends. Nero and I shared the girl."

"Nero?"

"Nerone Basilio. The owner of this palatial residence. A name that goes back five centuries, and money that disappeared a hundred years ago. Rather like my bride. A good pedigree and little else."

"Did he see your seizure?"

"I don't think so, but I was very drunk. I remember leaving the brothel. Nero dodged down an alley to take a piss. After that . . . nothing but a few bits and pieces until I woke up in the hospital. I could have had the seizure then or an hour later. Sometimes I hallucinate before one. I could have been seeing things that weren't there and not know it."

"Mr. Basilio never said anything to you about it?"

"He never mentioned it," he said. "Or maybe he did. I was in and out of consciousness when he visited me at the hospital. I hardly remember it. He telegraphed my parents and sent for Zuan to bring me here. I suppose you'll be able to ask Nero yourself. He'll be here soon. He's just tying up some loose ends we left in Rome."

"Is he the one who brought you to the hospital?"

Samuel shook his head. "They told me I'd been found on the street." His voice turned bitter. "None of my other friends came to see me, so . . . perhaps they did witness it."

I heard again that resignation that told me it was no more than he expected. I wondered what it would be like, a lifetime of facing such repulsion, of friends turning away. But then, the secret had been successfully kept so far, or so the Farbers had told my father, and part of my task was to discover if it remained so. None of his friends supposedly knew, and there was no gossip of his condition in New York. But I'd seen even attendants turn in revulsion from epileptics more than once, and I wondered what Samuel had endured from his own family.

"Or perhaps they didn't see, and they didn't know you'd been attacked," I suggested.

His smile was thin. "Don't tell me you're one of those idiots who believes the best of people."

"Hardly that," I said.

"Yes, I suppose it would be hard to be so optimistic when you look at madmen like me every day."

"You're an epileptic," I said. "Not a madman."

"Of course you're right."

I'd meant to comfort him, but I saw I'd done exactly the opposite. I picked up his nightshirt from the floor and held it out. "You can get out now. I looked for towels, but I couldn't find them. Just put this on and go back to your room. I'll come with the arnica."

He rose, water sluicing off, and I kept my eyes firmly on his face, offering my shoulder for him to lean on as he came out of the tub. He stumbled, his knee giving way for one moment, falling into me, which made him gasp in pain. I grasped his arm to steady him, helping him slip the nightshirt over his head. It clung damply, doing almost nothing to conceal him. I helped him into his room, and onto the bed, and then I left him to get the arnica in my medicine case.

I had to move the bottle of laudanum to get to the ointment, and for a moment I stood there, holding the bottle in my hand, thinking of those bruises and the pain on his face. *"I can't sleep for the pain, and I can't bear it when I'm awake."* What could it hurt, really? A few drops so he might sleep.

But then I remembered. Pleading blue eyes. *"You would not want me to be in such pain, would you? I can see you're not like the others here . . ."*

I put the laudanum back. I took up the arnica and closed the case with a definitive click, and then I started back to him.

I was halfway down the hall when I heard voices coming from his room. I stopped short, listening. Giulia again, damn her. I marched down the hall, furious, pushing open the door with such force it cracked against the wall. He was still sitting on the bed, exactly where I'd left him. He was alone.

"Was someone here?" I asked.

"Why would you think that?"

"I heard voices. Were you speaking to someone? Is Giulia here? Is she hiding?"

"Giulia isn't here." He looked pale and sick, his eyes haunted. Pain, I realized. The bath had been more rigorous than I'd thought.

I faltered. "I . . . I heard someone."

"There's no one here," he said, but there was something in his voice that made me look at him more closely. "Only me."

I didn't quite believe him. But I saw no sign of Giulia or anyone else. I must have been imagining things.

I looked at the jar of ointment in my hands and said, "Take off your nightshirt and lie on your stomach."

He hesitated, measuring, as if he had a question he wanted to ask but was waiting for some sign that it was safe to ask it. "It won't work, you know. I can't be cured, and it's getting worse. Whatever it is you want from me . . . I can't give it to you."

Oh, but he could. If he only knew.

"I am just your nurse," I said carefully. "Now, please. This will relieve some of the pain."

Chapter 4

The next morning, when I came into his room with his bromide and more arnica, he was sitting in the chair by the windowed doors. I was pleased to see him up until I realized the air was strongly perfumed with garlic and piquant spice. He held a bowl of some kind of stew, already half-eaten. On the tea table was a cup holding what was unmistakably coffee.

In dismay, I said, "What is that? Where did you get it?"

"Good morning to you too."

I swooped down on the coffee. "Who brought you this?"

"Wait! For God's sake, don't take it away."

"You aren't supposed to have it. I gave strict instructions. No coffee. And what's that you're eating?"

"*Sguassetto*," he said. "It's very good. Would you like a bite?"

"I don't need a bite to know you shouldn't have it. I can smell it. You were to eat nothing without my permission. Who gave you this?"

Calmly, he took a bite. "Giulia."

Of course. I'd known before I asked the question. I cursed.

Samuel raised a brow.

"I told her to stay away! I told *you* to keep her away!"

"Well, she came bearing gifts. Which, as it happened, I wanted." He set the bowl aside, swiping his hand through his hair wearily, and I saw what I hadn't seen before, shadows that spoke of a sleepless night. I had an idea who had caused it, and I bit back another curse of pure frustration.

"I'll move a bed in here," I said. "As it seems I must watch over you every moment."

His head jerked up. I was not imagining the fear in his eyes. "That's not necessary."

"It seems it is." I mixed the bromide salts into a glass of water and set it before him. "How else am I to keep Giulia from this room? How often must I tell you how dangerous it is for you to indulge in such things?"

He looked at me as if he had no idea what I was talking about. "Indulging in sguassetto is that dangerous?"

"Yes, probably. But I was speaking of your . . . carnal . . . appetites. You know as well as I do that overindulging will only lead to more seizures."

He laughed, stopping in the midst of it and putting a hand to his ribs with a moan. "I wasn't indulging any carnal appetite, much less overindulging."

"Don't lie to me. You look as if you didn't sleep at all."

"I didn't. But not because of Giulia."

Then it dawned on me that his sleeplessness was because of pain. "I've brought more arnica."

"It won't help enough. What can I do to convince you to forget all this? To let me drown myself in oblivion? How much are my parents paying? I'll double it. What is it you want? Tell me what I can give you in return for walking away and leaving me to myself."

"I don't want anything from you," I said.

"Come, there must be something. Why torment yourself with this? I'm not going to get well; we both know it. I assure you that even my parents wouldn't blame you for walking away. God knows they've done so often enough. I'll send you wherever you want to go. Rome? Paris? London? Vienna's lovely in the snow. Wouldn't you like a life away from that cursed asylum? Just agree, and I'll give it to you."

My longing bloomed, just that quickly. "No," I said, trying to pretend I wasn't tempted.

"Perhaps you don't understand what I'm offering. I could introduce you to my friends. With that hair of yours, and those eyes . . . They'd fall over themselves to fete you. I'm guessing you're not augmenting your shape, though one never knows these days— ah, so I'm right? I thought so. Think of it: you'd eat at the best restaurants. Drink and play until dawn. Wouldn't you like to see the lights of Paris? And Rome at sunrise—there's nowhere more beautiful. No more having to give cold baths or force medicine down some poor hysteric's throat. No more worrying about some epileptic's diet or his sexual habits."

"Drink the bromide, please."

"Don't be a fool. Take what I'm offering."

I shook my head.

"Why? Why not? My parents can't offer better."

"Not everyone wants such things."

"But you do," he said, more perceptively than I liked.

I reached to take the bowl of stew away.

He grabbed my wrist, so hard and so unexpectedly that I dropped the bowl. It cracked on the floor, shattering, stew spreading everywhere.

"What are they holding over you?" he asked. "What are you afraid of?"

I pulled away hard. Blindly, I said, "I need a rag to clean this up."

He sagged into the chair, surrendering. "There are handkerchiefs in the top drawer of the dresser."

I hurried to the top drawer, banishing my discomfort and his wretched temptation, shuffling blindly through the dozens of handkerchiefs as if I meant to find exactly the right one until I realized what I was doing and stopped. These were not his handkerchiefs. They were of all different colors and fabrics, designed to match different gowns. Each had a delicate lace hem, and was embroidered in the corner with a rising, rayed sun in silver and the letters *LB*.

I pulled one out, staring at it, fascinated for no reason I could say. A faint scent clung to it. Cedar and iris and something sweet— vanilla. Very feminine. I was immediately suspicious. Perhaps there *had* been a woman here, someone other than Giulia. A mistress, perhaps? "Who do these belong to?"

"They were here when I arrived," he said. "Along with the furniture."

I felt a shift in the air with his words, a deep, sinking sadness fell over me that I didn't understand. I didn't know where it came from; perhaps it was simply the knowledge that whoever had left these handkerchiefs was gone, and had not returned. Her presence seemed to linger in that bit of cloth, in that subtle perfume, so *present*, I felt oddly as if I might turn around to see her standing there.

I pushed the feeling away. "It's a shame to use these. They're beautiful."

"They're handkerchiefs," Samuel said dismissively. "It's what they're meant for."

There didn't seem to be anything else, and so, resignedly, I took several of the older ones and went to the spill. Samuel scooted back, hard enough that the chair scraped over the floor, but not quite giving me enough space, instead simply spreading his legs so that I had to kneel between them to clean the floor. I tried to ignore him, but my shoulder kept brushing his thigh, my arm bumping his calf.

"The stain will never come out."

Suddenly, I felt a rush of cold air. The temperature in the room dropped precipitously. I shivered and glanced up, looking for the source of the draft, and saw Samuel staring at the riffling reflections from the stinking canal below spilling from the ceiling to dance across the walls.

"My angel," he whispered. His voice was strange, disembodied, distant. His hands flexed on the armrest. It was unnerving. I would have called him catatonic except for his expression, because it wasn't blank. He was watching intently, engrossed, and I had the sense it wasn't just the movement of the light he watched, but something within it, beyond it.

The cold seemed to pierce my bones, making me want to hug myself against it. "Samuel?" I whispered.

Not a motion. No sign that he heard. The draft felt almost . . . preternatural. Again I felt the weight of sadness, caught in time, suspended. The press of the Basilio thickened the air; suddenly I could not take a breath, everything constricting, underwater, submerged.

"What is it?" I forced the words. "What do you see?"

The spell—or whatever it was—broke, a clap in the air, and the sorrow was gone, the press, the terrible cold. I could breathe again. Samuel blinked, confusion in his eyes as if he didn't know who I was or how I'd appeared. He jerked away from me, lurching to his feet, too quickly, all his weight on a knee that could not hold him. It failed; he fell. He made a sound of panic and tried to scramble away. He was like a wild animal, frantic with fear.

He climbed to his feet, and I grabbed his shoulder, gripping hard, and he stopped struggling, but his eyes were still unfocused. I realized what this was. He'd had a petit mal seizure. That's what the trance had been, nothing so strange or unusual after all. And now he was confused in its aftermath.

"Samuel, it's me. It's Elena."

"Elena," he repeated, but not as if he recognized the name, or me.

I heard a "Pardon," from the doorway, and spun to see Madame Basilio standing there. I immediately panicked. I tried to think of what to do, how to hide his confusion. But she glanced past me, to Samuel, and said in French, "M'sieur, I had a letter from Nerone this morning. He says to tell you he will be arriving in a few days."

I opened my mouth to answer, but just then Samuel came to himself, his confusion clearing. "Thank you, Madame."

I was relieved, but Madame Basilio's dark gaze sharpened. "You do not look well, m'sieur."

Samuel sighed and swiped his hand through his hair. "Thank you for your concern. I'm fine."

"He is not," I said, finding my voice. "He's recovering, and he needs his rest, and your housekeeper is bringing him food he should not be eating."

"The sguassetto is very nutritious."

"Not for him. He shouldn't have such highly flavored foods. It excites his blood. It will only inflame his . . . head injuries."

Something flashed through her eyes—understanding, yes, but something else that confused me. Her voice, already cold, went almost brittle as she said, "You must forgive me, mademoiselle. I sent Giulia with the stew. It is well known in Venice to cure every ill."

"Not this kind," I said firmly.

"I see."

She backed into the hall, and I followed her, closing the door behind me. "Madame, I thought we had reached an understanding that everything concerning Mr. Farber was to go through me. Giulia has been impossible, and now this stew—"

"Is he still dreaming?"

"Dreaming?"

She regarded me with something that looked like pity. "You mean you do not know?"

It rankled that she knew something about my patient that I did not, and that she'd said nothing of it before, when I'd first asked. But what rankled even more was the realization of *how* she must know it. Giulia. Who had quite obviously been in his room at night, despite what he'd told me.

"Everyone dreams," I said.

"Of course you are right," she said. "He has a fine voice, and it seems to bring him such comfort, which is a blessing for one so afflicted. So sad, is it not? Such a handsome, rich man."

I had no idea what she spoke of, and my suspicion that she'd seen a seizure grew. "What do you mean, afflicted?"

"How brave you are, to stay with him alone. I admire such dedication, but you should not take such risks, mademoiselle. I would never forgive myself if something terrible were to happen under my roof. Let me send Zuan or Giulia to stay here with you, for your own protection."

"Why do you say this? Why did you say nothing of it before? Has he hurt someone?"

"I am only suggesting that if you hear him singing to an angel, to *her*, I would not wake him. Nor would I discourage something that gives him peace."

Then, before I could ask another question, before I could even formulate one to ask, she turned on her heel and left.

Chapter 5

That night, I went through Samuel's file again. I knew he'd had petit mal seizures in the past, but I wanted the reassurance of my father's familiar words. He too had found such seizures disconcerting. It was some comfort to know it, even if I could not stop thinking of the sudden cold and the strangeness that had accompanied Samuel's trance. The cold was no doubt only a draft, but the rest . . . I put it off to my imagination, which had always been a bit too vibrant. The seizure had taken me by surprise. Next time, I would be more prepared.

It was dark outside my window, but I heard laughter in the courtyard below and saw flickering bits of light whenever the kitchen door opened. The entire Nardi clan must be down there now, judging by the noise. How did Madame Basilio sleep? How did anyone? I glanced at the clock. It was nearly midnight.

I thought about going down and throwing them out myself, or at least asking for quiet, but I had already dressed for bed, and the coal brazier had just now managed to take the chill edge off the air, and I knew I would get no cooperation from Giulia or Zuan, and would only end up retreating to the third floor with my tail between my legs.

Then I heard the crash.

It came from down the hall, reverberating and echoing.

I grabbed the leather strap from the desk where I'd left it and rushed to the door, jerking it open. The hall was empty. Silent.

And then, a male voice lifted in song. I didn't recognize the words; it was a moment before I realized he was singing in another language. Italian? Venetian?

No seizure, then. I put the strap in my dressing gown pocket. Cautiously, I went to his door and knocked. "Samuel?"

He kept singing. The song didn't sound like one angels might sing. It was boisterous and loud, probably ribald, or so it sounded. I opened the door.

His bed was empty, the blankets thrown every which way. The washstand was on its side, shards of pottery from the shattered washbasin scattered everywhere in jagged little shadows polished by the glow of moonlight. Standing before the balcony doors, with his back to me, was Samuel, bare chested, clad only in his long underwear.

"Samuel?"

He stopped abruptly, pivoting. When he saw me, he backed up violently, putting up his hands as if to ward off evil. "What now? What angel is this?"

I stepped closer. "No angel, Samuel. It's me. It's Elena."

"Elena?"

"Your nurse." I stepped closer still.

"You're floating." His voice caught in the middle of the word.

I glanced down at my feet, hidden by the flowing hem of my dressing gown, which was long and trailing. I lifted it to show my feet, the low-heeled slippers I wore. "I'm not. You see?" I held one out to show him. "I'm very corporeal."

He swallowed hard; I saw his uncertainty. He lowered his hands. "Is she still here?"

"She?"

"The angel." More of a whisper now, but one that set me on edge.

He collapsed to the floor in one fluid motion, pulling up his knees, burying his face in them. And then again, a rush of uncannily cold air laden with the stink of algae and fetid canal and . . . and vanilla. The perfume from the handkerchiefs. I glanced toward the dresser. The drawer was closed.

He muttered something. His voice was almost demonic, and so quiet I had to strain to hear it. When he spoke again, it was in that other language, but even I understood the threat in it.

I stepped back in sudden fear. The icy cold turned my breath to frosty clouds. I remembered Madame Basilio's words about not waking him from his singing and his angel. I said softly, "You should be in bed."

Samuel looked up, his eyes in the darkness showing the moonlight the way a cat's did—a full and empty reflection—and then they rolled back, only whites. He gasped, a choking gargle of sound, his back arching with deadly force, so that he looked to break in half. He began to convulse. Foam gathered at his lips; I heard the crack of his teeth against each other as his jaw tightened. I pulled the strap from my pocket and raced over to him, shoving it into his mouth to keep him from biting his tongue, throwing myself upon him, trying to hold him down, to keep him from hurting himself as he bucked and twisted beneath me.

It felt as if it lasted forever, but finally the convulsions lessened, spasms instead, and then he went still; only the racing of his heart beneath my hand told me he was still alive. Dear God, how had Papa thought I could do this? I'd gone from finishing school to my father's side when I was sixteen, but my duties had never been onerous. While the other attendants dealt with the rigors of violent patients, I had been relegated to reading soothing texts and doling out medicines.

And I had not even done that well, had I?

"You can do this, Elena," Papa had said. *"And you are our best hope."*

I took courage from the memory. He had done all he could to prepare me, and there was no other choice.

My patient stirred. His eyes opened, revealing a rapturous gaze like a saint's must be in the midst of a miracle. "River," he whispered.

The ceiling did indeed look like a river, flowing across and downward, sparkling in the moonlight, reflections from the canal below playing across the painted blue medallions to create colors of sky blue and lapis and a deep, rich midnight.

I said, "It's beautiful."

He blinked as if he were trying to focus. "Where am . . . drowning." He struggled to say even that, his confusion obvious, words eluding him, sense scrambling.

"Come to bed." I helped him to his feet. He staggered into me, disoriented, stumbling as if he could not completely command his limbs. It took a firm hand to guide him to the bed, and then he fell onto the mattress, flinging his arm over his eyes.

He was unconscious in moments, but I didn't leave, too alarmed by the seizure, afraid of another. I went to close the door, and heard a whish of movement out in the hallway, moving quickly. The white edge of a shroud flicked around the corner.

A shroud?

I stared in surprise. There was the perfume again, borne on a freezing breeze. Cedar and iris, a hint of sweet vanilla, familiar, and with it the rotten scent of the canal.

I lurched back, and nearly slammed the door shut.

Chapter 6

The morning was so beautiful that the strangeness of the night before lost its power. When I brought Samuel breakfast, and his dosage of bromide, he was lucid, though there were circles beneath his eyes. "I feel as if someone's beaten on me."

"Someone did beat on you," I reminded him.

"I mean besides that. And my head feels encased in cotton wool. I had a seizure, didn't I?"

I nodded. "Last night. Don't you remember?"

"No." He drank the bromide, then let his hand and the glass flop to the blanket. The cup rolled from his fingers to settle against his hip.

"What's the last thing you do remember?"

"Flashes of light."

"Angels?"

"What?"

"You spoke of an angel."

"I don't know what you're talking about."

I had the feeling that wasn't exactly true. "It's all right, you know. You can tell me. Hallucinations are a perfectly normal symptom—"

"You think I don't know that?"

"I just need to know how often you have them. And how intense they are. I can adjust your medication. The bromide can cause such things too, you know, if the dosage is too strong. Though I think it's not strong enough, given what happened last night."

"What exactly did happen last night?"

"I heard a crash. Then I heard you singing."

"Singing?"

"In Italian. Or perhaps it was Venetian."

He paled, making the wounds on his face look red against his white skin. "I barely know either. What else did I do?"

"You said something about an angel. Something else too, but it was in that other language and I didn't understand." No point in mentioning how frightening it had been. "Then you had a seizure."

"Was it bad?"

"I think so," I told him quietly. "Though I don't know how bad your seizures usually are. You had one the other day too, though only a petit mal."

He sighed, again sinking into the pillow. "It's getting worse, not better."

"You've only been back on the bromide for a few days. It takes weeks to stabilize."

"What if it never does?"

"It did before, didn't it? It always has."

"They still happened when I was taking it. Just not as often."

"When did you stop taking it? How long before your seizure in Rome?"

"I don't remember. A few months, perhaps. I don't like it. It dulls . . . everything."

"So you lied to me about how long it had been. It had nothing to do with your father's letter about your betrothal."

"Did I say that?"

I sighed at his obvious evasion. "You must be more honest with me. How can I help you if I don't know the truth?"

"Why not just admit that you can't help me?" he asked.

"Because I believe I can." I felt more encouraged now that I knew he had been months without bromide. I had been afraid that it had still been in his blood, which meant it wasn't helping at all. All I must do was build it back to its proper level.

"I'd wish you luck, except that I don't want to be a married man."

"It will be good for you. You need stability. You need a wife to look after you. It will be restful."

"Restful?" His smile was thin and small. "God, I'm tired."

"Would you like me to read to you?"

"Read what?"

"I've a book of poetry."

"Poetry by whom?" he asked skeptically. "Wait, let me guess. Some suffragette poet. Is there such a thing? Or is that an oxymoron?"

"I don't know, but I have nothing like that. I have a book by Elizabeth Barrett Browning. And another by Tennyson."

"Ah. You're a romantic."

"You sound disappointed."

"I suppose I should have expected such things from a virgin. Tales of knights and princesses, true love . . . nothing real."

I went so hot at the word *virgin* I was certain I must have been blistering red. "You don't believe in true love?"

He laughed; it was more just a breath of sound. "No."

"Then I suppose it doesn't matter that you're marrying someone you hardly know."

"*Don't* know," he said shortly. "But you're right; if I don't believe in true love, how can it matter? Except that I'd like to make the choice myself. If I have to marry, I'd prefer it be someone I liked, at least."

"Perhaps you will like her."

"Unfortunately, I won't know that until after the wedding, when I've already carried her off to our bridal bower. Too late then, don't you think? What if she's a shrew?"

"You could take a page from Shakespeare and tame her. Or she could tame you."

"Poor woman. Rather like bearding a beast in his lair."

"You are hardly a beast," I said.

"No?" He lifted a brow. "You've seen it. Don't tell me you weren't frightened."

I didn't want to admit that I had been. I wanted him to think me competent and assured. I didn't want to tell him I'd felt helpless and overmatched and stupid. "I've seen such things before."

"I've seen doctors quake in fear. What makes you different?"

"You say you remember nothing during your seizures," I pointed out. "How could you know how anyone reacts?"

He made a face. "You're very clever."

"You think to frighten me into running. I won't."

"My parents must have promised you something very good indeed."

"You should stop trying to guess why I'm staying and concentrate instead on getting well. Now I think you should sleep. You look terrible."

"I feel terrible," he agreed. "But you did promise to read to me. No poems, though. I don't have the head for it just now. All those 'thees' and 'thous,' and I'll want to throw myself into the *rio*."

"Then what?" I asked, glancing around, seeing not a single book anywhere.

"I have a book. I think you might like it. It's a romance. Of sorts."

"Where is it?"

He lay back again as if the simple motion of sitting up and holding the position for all of a minute had left him exhausted. "It fell to the floor the other night, and I haven't seen it. I think it got pushed under the bed."

I looked, reaching through dust and probably rat droppings to pull out a well-worn, yellow-covered book. A dime novel. No doubt full of melodrama and daring escapes. Papa would not approve of this.

I sat on the chair I'd pulled next to the bed last night, reading the title out loud. "*The Nunnery Tales*. I thought you said you were tired of 'thees' and 'thous'?"

"Surprisingly, there seem to be very few of those," he said. "I've marked the page where I was. Just start there."

I turned to it. "Chapter Two," I began. "We had an extremely good supper, and our snug little party thoroughly enjoyed it. Everything that could tempt and pamper the appetite was there"— here, a listing of foods, including oysters and shellfish; I had not realized nuns ate so well. And then, as if the author were commenting on my thoughts—"if the ladies in the convent lived on such luxurious and exciting viands, it was no wonder that they found their blood a little hotter and their passions more excitable—" I stopped.

"Go on." Samuel's voice was very quiet.

He was falling into sleep already. I didn't think it would take more than a few more paragraphs. I read on as the narrator's aunt told him that she suspected a priest was his real father. I suppressed a snort of disbelief.

"Don't stop," Samuel murmured.

I read on. "'How do you know that, my dear aunt?' I asked. 'Oh, by the simplest way in the world,' she laughingly replied." The aunt explained how she'd paid a visit to her sister and been met instead by her brother-in-law, who complimented her lavishly. "'He proceeded from compliments to kissing, and from kissing to feeling and handling my—'" *breasts and rump*.

I closed the book with a snap.

"What's wrong?" Samuel asked, oh so innocently.

"This is obscene," I sputtered.

"Come, don't tell me it doesn't intrigue you," he said. "It would be good for you to read something about what real people do and how it feels. Perhaps then you'll understand what you're asking me to give up. You want to take away everything that's worth living for."

"You could find other things worth living for," I said, throwing the book onto the bed, where it sprawled open. "Love, for one thing. A family."

He made a sound of disbelief. "You could not possibly be so naïve."

"I am not naïve. I believe life could be better for you. But you'll never know if you refuse to try."

"My God, you're persistent."

"It would be best if you understood that I don't mean to fail."

He was quiet for a moment. I saw a consideration in him I was not certain I liked, and knew I didn't when he said, "Very well, I'll make a bargain with you."

"What kind of a bargain?" I asked warily.

"I'll do everything you tell me," he said. "If you read that book."

"You must be joking."

He shook his head. "No. I want you to understand why this might be . . . difficult. You're a little self-righteous about all of it. It's hard for me to listen to you when you've no idea what you're asking."

I glanced at those open pages, the words that leaped from them straight into imagery, things I'd never seen, that I didn't know. That I didn't *want* to know, and I was angry that he asked it, resentful not only that he had but also that he'd raised my interest. These were not the kinds of books decent women read, not the kind that I should read.

"Romance isn't real," he went on. "But what's in there is. You'd be better off knowing it. You could say I'm protecting you, really. Once you know what's really on a man's mind, you'll be better at judging whether or not he's lying to you."

It was as if he'd seen into my mind.

He closed the book and picked it up, holding it out to me. "Well? Have we agreed? My acquiescence for your learning. Believe me, I think you have the better side of it."

Gingerly, I took the book. The cover was rough between my fingers. I noticed for the first time how worn the edges were.

His smile was smug. "It won't be so bad."

"You should sleep," I said, rising. "I'll be back later this afternoon. Believe me, I will hold you to your promise."

"I'll hold you to yours," he said.

I tucked the book into the pocket of my skirt. It was not thick nor especially heavy, but it felt both things, and I could hardly wait to be rid of it. I left him and dodged into my room, tucking it under the mattress of the bed where no one would come upon it, where I might even forget it was there. I was angry with myself for agreeing, though really I'd had no choice.

Just like before.

Samuel Farber had worked me just as easily, but I pushed the worrisome thought away and told myself that as long as Samuel ended up doing what I wanted, it didn't matter. I would read every filthy book in Venice if it meant I could deliver a compliant and healthy heir to the Farbers.

Still, I was so undone that I was halfway down the stairs to the courtyard before I realized I had no idea what I was doing or where I'd thought to go. Wanting to be somewhere warm, I hurried to the kitchen. Just as I reached the door, it opened, and Giulia stepped out.

She looked surprised to see me, and then her expression settled into insolence. She kept the door from closing with an outstretched hand. "Mamzelle, how can I help you?"

"You can't," I said, trying to push past her. When she didn't budge, I stepped back.

Her eyes narrowed with a satisfaction I didn't understand or like. "Samuel has a beautiful voice, does he not? I think it is a gift, to be so chosen. Do you not think it too, mamzelle?"

"Chosen?" I asked. "Sometimes the medicines affect him strangely, that's all."

"If that's what you believe," she said, dropping her hand from the door and stepping aside. I caught it with my foot before it closed. She leaned close, whispering, "But I would lock my door at night if I were you, mamzelle."

I was so taken aback by her warning that I said nothing as she stepped away, sashaying and bouncing as she went.

Chapter 7

That night, I stood at my bedside, thinking of the quid pro quo Samuel had asked of me. I felt an unwanted anticipation that made me say to myself, *no, you don't have to read it. Just tell him you have.* But I had a feeling he would know if I lied, that he would ask me something I couldn't answer. I wasn't in the habit of breaking promises, either. So I took off my dressing gown and pulled the book from beneath the mattress before I crawled into bed.

It was poorly written, and I winced from the first sentences, and the preposterousness of the conceit: a mother and son needing to hide from the Republicans purging France of all aristocrats, and deciding to take refuge in a nunnery where a relative was abbess, which required that the son be disguised as a girl. I had only skimmed a few pages before they were invited to witness a priest's "punishment" of a nun. I began to squirm. I was fascinated at the same time I was repulsed, my cheeks heating even with no one here to see, *no one but God, who surely must not want me to be reading this.*

The nun disrobed to take her punishment, and the disguised son began to speak of his own arousal in intimate detail, and I felt a corresponding warmth and slapped the book closed, shoving it beneath the thin mattress. I'd hardly read anything, and nothing of any substance. But what had been about to happen teased at my thoughts, and I felt . . . I hardly knew. Something that wasn't quite shame, though I wanted it to be. I picked up my *Baedeker's Paris and its Environs*, trying to forget *The Nunnery Tales*, but when I finally slept, I was restless, my dreams filled with unclothed nuns kneeling on cushions, and a birch rod trembling in an abbess's hands.

The next morning, the book's cover, peeking as it was from beneath the mattress, seemed to mock me, and images from my dreams still chased themselves in my head like fluttering ghosts. I was angry with myself for being so preoccupied with it, and feeling as unsophisticated as Samuel had accused me of being. Then I realized that he meant for *The Nunnery Tales* to distract me from my purpose. I did not want to understand what he was giving up. I simply wanted him to do so. Though his wounds were healing, the epilepsy was no closer to controlled than it had been when I arrived ten days ago, nor was I closer to convincing him of the need to give up his degenerate habits.

It was long past time that I understood exactly what I was up against. Both Madame Basilio and Giulia made me think there was something here I wasn't seeing, and Giulia's comment last night had only exacerbated the feeling. I wanted to know if they had seen a seizure. Or something else? How much was I going to have to explain away?

I went downstairs and knocked upon Madame Basilio's door. There was no answer. It was early; perhaps she was not awake. I had just decided to give up when I heard footsteps, and the door opened to reveal Madame Basilio, dressed as austerely as ever, this time in lavender, another half-mourning color—and one that did her sallow skin no favors.

"Mademoiselle Spira," she said with a chill politeness made even worse by the formality of her French. "What brings you here so early?"

"I'd like to speak with you for a moment, if I could."

"Of course." She ushered me inside, closing the door behind me.

I could not wait even the few moments it would take to get to the sala, nor bear the small politeness of an offering of refreshment. I burst out, "I wanted to ask you a question about M'sieur Farber's dreams. The angels and his singing."

"It has happened again?"

There was an avidity in her that startled me. "H-he . . . the other night, he was singing, and I would like to know how often you've heard him do that. And if . . . if there was anything odd after."

"We first saw it the second night he was here. Giulia witnessed it."

"Did anything strange happen?"

"You do not think singing in the middle of the night strange enough?" Spoken so dryly there was not a speck of humor.

"Yes, but—"

"She tried to dance with him and he woke from his dream and threw her to the floor. When Giulia told me of it, I asked her to inform me if it happened again. Which it did, four nights later."

"You saw it?"

She bowed her head in acknowledgment. "He was a man in ecstasy."

Just as I'd seen before he'd seized. "And then?"

"He sang '*Un Ziro in Gondola*,'" Madame Basilio murmured, her voice soft with memory. "A favorite of the gondoliers. My daughter also had a special fondness for it."

"I didn't know you had a daughter."

Madame Basilio blinked as if to put the memory away. "She has been gone some time."

I thought of the handkerchiefs in the drawer. Perfumed and monogrammed. But just now I cared only for what Madame Basilio had seen that night in Samuel's room. "You said he spoke of an angel."

"Yes, that is what he said. Did he tell you the same, mademoiselle? Was there an angel in the room? Did he talk of her?"

The oddly gleeful light in her eyes unnerved me. "Not really," I said uncomfortably. "Did . . . was there anything after? I told you what his injuries might cause."

Madame Basilio shook her head. "He calmed and Giulia put him to bed. He seemed confused."

It was all I needed to know. Perhaps Samuel had been hallucinating, or perhaps he'd had a petit mal seizure on one of those nights, but if so, neither Giulia nor Madame Basilio had interpreted it as anything more than dreams and sleepwalking. "Thank you, Madame. You've been most helpful."

She nodded and opened the door to show me out. Once I'd stepped onto the landing, she said, "You should be careful of him, mademoiselle, as I said before. I could send Giulia to help you tend to him."

"Please don't. I'm not afraid for myself. The medications I'm giving him need time to work, but once they stabilize him, I think you will see no more singing with angels."

Madame Basilio looked surprised, and displeased, which confused me. "A pity to destroy such beauty."

"It's illness," I said.

"Is it?" she asked, and the way she said it was needling, as if she knew a secret and meant to keep it from me. I was still wondering uneasily about it when she closed the door.

Two days of bright, cold sun passed without incident. Already December 10—time was moving more quickly than I liked, but at least Samuel was as tractable as he'd promised, although still not sleeping well.

Now, it was snowing; heavy wet flakes that melted the moment they hit the carved stone of the balcony's balustrade, a whirling cloud obscuring the buildings across the canal and masking the black shadows of the gondolas, the whole world muffled and cloaked. It was not like snow at Glen Echo on the Hudson, icy, hard pellets that sparkled over the ground, everything pointed and sharp, icicles and jagged ice forming over the river. As with everything in Venice, even the snow felt as if it held ghosts within it, a lacy shroud hiding indiscretions and secrets.

I'd never had such morbid thoughts before, and I didn't like them now. This place preyed upon the mind. Behind me, I heard the splash of Samuel rising from the bath, the heavy slide of his hand on the metal side of the tub. He said, "I'm decent."

He had dug a dressing gown from his trunk. It was heavy, lined with blue satin, paisley patterned in blues and deep maroons, and as I turned from the window, he was securing the belt tightly. His hair curled wetly at the ends. He shivered, glancing past me to the snow, saying, "I dislike it here in the winter so much I'm not tempted to try any other time of year."

"I hear the summer's quite fine," I said.

"Dreaming of romantic rides in gondolas and serenading Venetians?" he asked. "Perhaps mosquitos and stench would be more accurate. Nero avoids summer here like the plague. Perhaps *because* of the plague, for all I know."

I ignored him, taking in the way he stood, a bit straighter now, as if the pain was not so much. I wondered if he was yet able to manage the burning liniments and massage.

"I can see you're debating new tortures for me."

"Only if you can bear them," I said.

"You mean I have some say in it? Then please, not yet. But I'll tell you what I would like, if you wouldn't mind."

"If I can provide it, and I think it won't harm you."

"A long list of *no*s, it sounds like. But what about chocolate? Something warm." He wrapped his arms about his chest and shivered. "I'm cold to the bone. Deeper than bone, if you want to know the truth."

"What about some mugwort tea?"

"What about something *good*? And sweet. I've obeyed your every command, and I haven't once asked for laudanum, though I suspect you have some and I'd give a substantial reward to anyone who could procure it for me."

"You've promised."

"And I'm not breaking my vow, am I? Even though I think you are not quite heeding yours. How much of *The Nunnery Tales* have you read, hmmm? Ah, not much, I see."

"I've been too busy."

"Or perhaps too frightened."

"I'm not frightened."

"Aren't you? Be honest, Elena. You're afraid you'll like it. That it will make you . . . want things."

"I think you've mistaken me for a different kind of woman."

He grinned, the healing scar on his cheek creasing like a dimple. "Oh, I don't think so."

I hastened to change the subject. "If I were to allow you something warm and sweet, what would you like?"

His grin grew, and I realized what I'd said, and how he meant to take it.

I amended it hastily. "To drink, I mean."

"How virtuous you are," he said with a sigh. "The things you make me want to say—"

"If you say them, I'll leave. Now tell me what you wish to drink."

"Wine or chocolate. Either would suffice."

I didn't see how chocolate could hurt, and I had no reason to deny it, so I nodded. "Very well. I suppose they must have some chocolate in the kitchen. God knows there's everything else."

"My parents are paying well for my upkeep," he said wryly.

So he knew. I felt a modicum of ease over the fact that he wasn't being fooled. It meant I didn't have to worry. If he knew he was feeding Giulia's entire family, and did nothing about it, then I no longer had to concern myself.

I left him and went down to the kitchen, huddling against the snow that fell on my exposed neck and melted to trickle cold and wet down my collar. There was no one in the courtyard, and the kitchen was empty too, not even a pot of polenta or steaming water on the stove, though the table was laden with food: peppers and onions and garlic, raisins and eggs, cheese and sausage and a tangle of slippery purple octopi gleaming wetly in a bowl.

But no chocolate, though there was a pitcher of milk capped with a heavy layer of cream. I poured some into a pan and set it on the stove to heat, and then I went in search. I found cornmeal, beans and vinegar, flour flecked with bran. No chocolate anywhere.

I heard a hiss, and turned to see the milk boiling over. I caught it just as the scorching smell filled the air, along with smoke, and without thinking I grabbed the handle with my bare hand, crying out and dropping it, clattering, to the floor, steaming milk spattering everywhere.

I plunged my hand into a bucket of cold water. The burn was not bad, and the pain faded as I set about cleaning up the mess—the burned milk was nearly impossible to scrape from the pan. It seemed to take forever, and when I was done, I was tired and frustrated and cursing Samuel for asking for chocolate. Not that he was going to get it, because there was none anywhere, unless it was in the storage room.

Now that I'd had the idea, I had to look. Muttering to myself about men who should be content with mugwort tea, I went back into the swirling snow. There was no sign of anyone. It was eerie, how deserted it felt. The snow was beginning to stick now, and my smooth-soled boots were no good on it. Twice, I slid, nearly losing my balance the second time. I made my slow, cold, wet way across the short expanse of courtyard between the kitchen and the receiving court with its storage rooms. There, finally, among barrels of fermenting anchovy and kegs of wine and dangling ropes of garlic and drying herbs, I found a package—chocolate wrapped in blue paper. It was very thick, and hard to break. I had to throw it onto the floor before I got a chunk large enough to use.

This time, I watched the milk as it steamed and melted the chocolate. A cone of sugar wrapped in brown paper sat on top of a barrel, but I saw no sugar cutters anywhere. I had to hack at it with a knife and a spoon, cursing, until I had a small pile of it mounded on the table, and even then it wasn't quite sweet enough. It was going to have to do. Already it felt I'd been in this kitchen for an eternity.

I poured the concoction into a bowl and threw the dirty pan into the wooden sink—let Giulia wash it. I was done with the whole thing. I was sweating from the heat of the kitchen, strands of hair escaped to dangle irritatingly against my cheeks and my throat. It was snowing harder than ever as I went back outside; the other wing and the courtyard stairs were just a dark blur. I held the bowl carefully, but it was steaming, and chocolate sloshed onto my skirt, snow melting into it as I tried to make my way to the stairs without slipping.

I spilled probably a third by the time I got to the door. I nudged it open with my shoulder and stepped inside, but with my wet boots, the floor was just as slick as the courtyard had been, and so I was slow. I'd left Samuel in the sala, but now I heard laughter coming from his bedroom.

I rounded the edge of the door, and saw Samuel lolling on the bed, his dressing gown open, a bottle of brandy in his hand, while

Giulia, her hair down and wild, giggled as she licked spilled liquor off his chest.

"What is this?" I cried, stepping inside. Giulia cursed in Venetian, her dark eyes flashing as she jerked away from Samuel, making him groan.

"What are you doing here?" I demanded. I put the chocolate down and said to Samuel, "What is she doing here?"

"I should think it obvious," he said too slowly, as if he were struggling to form his words. I had been gone perhaps an hour and a half, and he was drunk. Blurry-eyed, slurring, unapologetically drunk. I realized too that he'd planned it. He'd tricked me. The chocolate had been nothing but a ruse. Time enough for Giulia to bring the brandy and perhaps, depending on just how long it took, time for other things as well.

I was furious. Humiliated. Hurt. What was wrong with me that I could not see deception, even when I expected it?

He lifted the bottle as if in toast. "She brought me *petrolio*." He brought it to his mouth again, gulping it.

I lunged for it, furious. Samuel jerked the bottle away from me. Giulia was still swearing as she climbed from the bed.

"Get out of here!" I shouted at her as I tried again to grab the bottle.

She spat something at me, and then, much to my surprise, she actually left, stalking from the room like an affronted cat. Samuel rolled onto his side, taking the bottle with him, so I had to climb onto the bed and reach over him to get it. I grabbed for it again and again, and he kept it just out of my reach, laughing at my efforts.

"It's just brandy." Slurred together *ishjusbranny*.

"You promised." I reached for it again. This time, he elbowed me in the stomach, bouncing off my corset, no effect at all, and in the moment he waited for me to fall back, I did the opposite. I planted my hand firmly on his bare chest, and taking advantage of his surprise and his gasp of pain, I grabbed the bottle. I wrenched it from his hands, but before I could get off the bed, he threw himself at me, grabbing my wrists, forcing me back, rolling, until I was beneath him, his weight heavy, his good knee between my legs, pinning me to the mattress.

"Give it to me." His fingers bit into the tendons of my wrist.

With all my strength, I jerked my arm from his grasp, throwing the bottle. It thudded to the floor and rolled across the carpet, what brandy that was left spilling as it went.

He swore, loud and vehemently, as he watched it go. Then he looked back at me. "What the hell did you do that for?"

"You aren't supposed to have it."

"I'd already drunk most of it. You could let me have the rest."

"You *promised*," I said. "You told me you would be good. You broke your promise." I heard the hurt in my own voice and winced. I sounded like a child.

"You broke your promise too," he reminded me.

"I am not going to read that stupid book."

"Then I'm not going to cooperate." He mangled the last word, his tongue not nimble enough to manage it.

I felt ready to cry with frustration. "Why must you make everything so difficult?"

"Do I? Perhaps you should punish me then." The words all running together. "D'you want to whip me?"

The words were a shock, his lowered voice, the sudden flash of interest in his eyes.

"What a pretty little innocent you are," he whispered, and then, before I could do or say anything else, he kissed me. I was so startled I didn't try to stop him when he pressed my mouth open, his tongue exploring, tasting. His hands tightened on my wrists; his hips pressed into mine, and I felt the same kind of stirring I'd felt reading *The Nunnery Tales*, a snaking, sinking *something* that frightened and aroused at the same time.

Before I could think what to do, I heard him moan and then a gasp. He jerked back, rolling off me and at the same moment pushing me violently away. I fell off the bed, banging my elbow hard on the floor. Cold rushed into the room, a freezing, icy blast, there and then gone, and suddenly I was looking at him as if through water reflections, wavery, shifting, and he was staring at me in fear. *Fear*.

"Since when have you taken to pushing women *out* of your bed, Samuel?"

The voice came from behind me, and with it a hand on my arm, gently hauling me to my feet. "Are you all right?" asked a man I'd never seen before. "That was quite a fall."

Samuel blinked slowly, like a man waking. "Nero?"

Chapter 8

It took me a moment to restore myself, to realize that this man who'd helped me to my feet, and who was looking at Samuel with amused affection, was Nerone Basilio, Madame Basilio's nephew and Samuel's friend, and that he was speaking English very well.

Mr. Basilio was Samuel's age, with dark curling hair, olive-toned skin, and dark eyes dancing with amusement. "No need to dream about me any longer, my friend. I'm really here. Only for you would I have left Rome to come to this decrepit, uncomfortable place. Why the hell did my aunt put you in *this* room?"

"You'd have to ask her." Samuel climbed from the bed, misjudging the height of the floor, stumbling, loosening the already very loose belt of his dressing gown further as he gave his friend a quick embrace. "It's good to see you."

"How drunk *are* you?"

Samuel staggered back to the bed. "Quite."

"And who is this pretty thing you kicked out of bed? Given the violence you were doing her, I can only assume she must be a demon."

Samuel's expression darkened, again I saw that shifting fear in his eyes, rapidly dismissed. "No demon. At least not most of the time. My nurse, Elena Spira. 'Lena, Nerone Basilio."

Basilio looked at me and said, "The nurse, eh? I begin to see what all the fuss is about."

Nerone Basilio's curls were, like Samuel's hair, a bit too long, and his coat was of an older style, the fabric shiny in spots where the nap had been worn smooth, his cuffs fraying. There were no charms on his watch fob, no ornaments at all, and one of the buttons on his vest did not match the others. But he was scrubbed and polished, as if to distract from his general air of impoverished nobility. He was also as attractive as his friend. The two of them must have cut a swath through Rome. I tried very hard not to remember what Samuel had said about them sharing the girl with hair the same color as mine.

"I'm happy to meet you," I said, managing at last to fully regain myself, wondering what "fuss" he meant, curiosity bringing me fully into the present. What had his aunt, and Giulia, told him about me, or about Samuel's recovery, for that matter?

"How does your patient?"

"He would be doing better if he obeyed the rules," I said, picking up the abandoned bottle.

Mr. Basilio made a face. "*Petrolio*. You couldn't have found something tastier, Samuel? Like bilge water, perhaps?"

"Wasn't particular," Samuel said.

"I can see that."

"A long dry spell." Samuel put his hand over his eyes. "Told Giulia to bring whatever she could find."

"Ah. Giulia."

I could not read his tone; I had no idea what Nero Basilio thought of his aunt's housekeeper, but I said to him in a low voice, "I've asked her to leave his care to me, but she's very—"

"Accommodating, thank God," Samuel put in with a laugh.

"A little too much so," I said.

"What would you do, my frien'?" Samuel asked. "No laudanum"—stumbling over the words—"No wine. No sex. A veritable purg-purgatory."

Basilio looked at me in surprise. "Really?"

"He'll heal faster without those things," I insisted.

"I would have thought laudanum, at least. He must be in pain. That was quite a beating he took."

"You saw what happened?"

He shook his head. "He disappeared. I found him the next day after searching all the hospitals in Rome. And the taverns. And the morgue. Not something I wish to do again."

"You see, 'Lena? He agrees that I should have laudanum," Samuel said.

"It would be best not. His concussion was too severe," I persisted, clinging to the lie. "And his father wants him well and sober by January."

Basilio frowned, and then, "Oh yes, the wedding. I'd forgotten."

"The reason for the bacchanal." Samuel raised his arm as if he were flagging down wine-bearers. "Dancing and drinking and whoring before the beast is chained."

"*I parenti mal de denti*," Mr. Basilio said.

Samuel groaned. "God save me from your proverbs."

"In this case, a true one," Nerone Basilio said with a thin smile. "Relatives are toothaches. I will say you look much better than when I saw you last, *amigo*. No doubt it's due to your nurse."

Samuel grunted and let his arm fall back to the blankets with a thud. "I'm glad you're here. We c'n be bored together. Have you a liking for cold baths, Nero?"

"*Cold* baths?" Basilio looked confused, and a bit horrified. "In the winter?"

I wanted to strangle Samuel. I could not have Nerone Basilio wondering what cold baths might be for. Instead I said, quickly, "His regimen is very strict. I'm afraid he won't be very entertaining."

"Ah, I see. But kissing you is permitted?"

I stared at him helplessly, chagrined all over again. "I'm his *nurse*, Mr. Basilio. That wasn't . . . what it looked like."

A teasing, knowing grin. "If I had a nurse like you, I might delay healing."

"He is very drunk," I said. "And even with his injuries, he's strong. I'd interrupted him with Giulia, you see, and—"

"She's an innocent," Samuel slurred sleepily from the bed.

Nero Basilio looked at Samuel with a frown. "A what?"

"I would like him to sleep now. If you wouldn't mind . . ." I touched Mr. Basilio's arm to lead him away, and he followed me docilely from the bedroom, waiting in the hall while I closed the door. "It would be best if you consulted with me before you visited with him," I said quietly. "I don't wish to keep you away, but . . ."

"You're worried I might break the rules?"

"No, but . . ."

"Well, I might," he said with a shrug. "It seems a bit cruel, you know, to keep him in pain. And a little drunkenness never hurt anyone. Especially here." His gaze went to the ceiling, the empty, decaying hall. He shuddered. "God, I hate this place. Nothing but ruin. It's enough to drive a man mad."

I was surprised. I had felt such things, but I hadn't expected it of the man who owned the palazzo. "But this is your home."

"Imagine growing up here," he said bleakly. "Everything falling around you and no money to fix it. I'm dragged back here periodically just to make certain it hasn't fallen into the rio, but other than that, I leave it to my aunt. God knows it suits her."

"She seems—"

"Unhappy? Bitter? As if she breathes gloom?"

It was so dramatic—and true, now that he'd said it—that I laughed. "She hasn't been unkind."

"Is that so? But not . . . kind, exactly?"

"I know Samuel has been a burden."

"Perhaps, but you shouldn't be too forgiving. God knows she's happy enough to take his money. He's free to stay as long as he likes, or as long as he can bear it. But you say only until January."

"That's when his parents want him back. For the wedding."

He gave me a sideways glance. "You know he's unhappy about that."

"It's none of my concern."

"His family seems very anxious to marry him off to this woman he's never met."

"She has a pedigreed name," I told him. "Rather like your own. Old for New York, at least. And Samuel's parents are"—I struggled to find the words—"rather too self-made for society's liking."

"Parvenus," he provided.

"Yes."

"Trading money for prestige."

"You understand."

"Marriage contracts here are a way of life, or they used to be. My own was negotiated when I was only eight. But Samuel tells me it is not the same in America."

"When you were *eight*?"

"There's a certain comfort in knowing your destiny. But enough of this. What must be must be. I'm more interested in you."

"In me?"

"Please tell me you haven't spent all your time in Venice hidden away with a foul-tempered invalid."

"I haven't been out of the palazzo," I admitted.

"What?" he sounded horrified. "Surely you don't have to spend every moment with Samuel."

I did, of course, at least until the seizures were under control. "Perhaps when he's a little better," I said.

"You're too young to be shut away," he said. "And it's snowing. You should see San Marco in the snow. I'll take you."

I tried to ignore the tight little longing that came at the thought of St. Mark's in the snow.

"We'll have Giulia watch over him," he went on.

"No!" I said, and then, at his surprise, "I've already told you. She doesn't follow my orders."

Thoughtfully, he said, "Does it matter so much? Granted, the *sciampagnin* is deadly. I would not have suggested it. There's a reason people call it *petrolio*. He'll have a foul head in the morning. But a little wine or laudanum, what could it hurt? Why make his recovery a misery? Let him play a little in these last days before his family marries him off."

"His family wants him sober, and I've agreed to deliver him that way," I said, disliking how prim and proper it made me sound.

"How dedicated you are." He looked at me as if I were an entirely new thing, and one he did not completely understand. "But I'm certain no one wishes you to deny pleasures of your own for Samuel's sake."

"They are paying me to do just that. What kind of a nurse would I be if I abandoned my patient to see a church in the snow?"

"That you can call it 'a church' proves that you must see it."

"You're very kind, but . . . no. Thank you. I—"

The hard, sharp click of heels stopped me. Giulia, returned, and now I was going to have to dismiss her again in front of Mr. Basilio, and look even more like the priggish nurse he no doubt already thought me.

But it wasn't Giulia. It was Madame Basilio who turned the corner and appeared at the end of the hall. I felt Nero Basilio stiffen, and his aunt looked like a fire poker, so rigid was she, everything about her hard and metallic and sharp.

"Nerone," she said, blunt and snapping. And then a stream of Venetian, every word clipped. It was an order and a scold; even I understood that.

I heard him swallow. He said something back to her.

What came into her eyes then startled me. It was hostility of a kind I'd never seen before, almost venomous, and I couldn't fathom why it should be there, not for this easy, charming man.

He turned to me with a thin smile, all amusement gone. Instead, his eyes looked haunted. "Pardon, Miss Spira. It seems my aunt has need of me."

"Of course," I said.

He made a small bow and went toward her, then passed her, the both of them so careful not to brush that they nearly careened comically into the walls. She followed him without a word or a look at me, as if I hardly existed, but in the wake of that stare she'd given him, the hallways felt suddenly frigid with unease and anger. The disease of the Basilio, desolation and despair, seemed to mock me. It was in the very walls. How did anyone escape it?

Chapter 9

I had grown up in asylums, and so one would think I was used to suffering. But my father did not encourage despondency. He held on to his hopes that insanity could be cured long after his peers had started to put such notions aside. And while other asylums had reputations for patient neglect, restraints, and containment—*"like cattle in barns,"* Papa had said disdainfully—Glen Echo was known for its milder, kinder methods. Of course, it helped that it was a private asylum, catering to the rich. Insanity knew no class, after all. Discretion was the order of the day. Few in New York City had ever heard of Glen Echo, though it was only a few miles up the Hudson River, ensconced in woods that were lush in the summer and picturesque in the winter, with the churn of the river our famously soothing lullaby, mentioned in every publication and letter espousing our services. *"A tranquil place of comfort and rest."*

My father had dreamed of having a superintendency of his own from the time I could remember, and my mother and I did everything we could to further those dreams. My mother—from a good family in New York City, with a name that still garnered respect, if not influence or cachet—had a particular brilliance for sniffing out secrets, and a charm that was as important as Papa's skill. It was my mother who won Papa the superintendency at Glen Echo. She had gone to school with the previous superintendent's wife, and Mama had cultivated her for years—teas and luncheons, suggestions carefully couched, so as not to seem as crassly ambitious as they were. When it came to getting what she wanted without obviously wanting it, my mother was brilliant.

Which is why when I was twelve, I was sent to finishing school in the hopes that I might learn my mother's skill. Or, at least, further my father's ambitions. I would never make the kind of marriage that could help him—that was understood from the start. No one in society would marry their son to the daughter of an asylum superintendent. And so, because marriage couldn't actually benefit my family, it was never spoken of. I was to be instead the symbol of the care at Glen Echo—kind, progressive, and genteel. As much as possible, the patients were to be made to feel that they were in their own homes, with all the elegance and sophistication they were used to, and so I had to move about in society as if I were born to it, and I was taught like any rich man's daughter, that I might pepper my speech with French and comment with ease upon art and literature and the latest fashions. It was even more important given that, in those early days, Glen Echo was a bastion of Moral Treatment, that is, the theory that the uncontrollable could be reined in without punishment or medicines, through kindness, gentleness, pleasant social interaction, and productive labor.

You'll notice how well I say that, how perfectly rote it is. No asylum is ever truly such a utopian environment for the mad, though that was what my father said and what he trained me to say at every social occasion, at every dance put on for the families of our patients, at every consultation, where I stood smiling by the door, dressed in the latest fashion, assurances that *yes, all our patients are happy and productive; yes, we believe them capable of being cured*, falling pleasingly from my lips.

Of course, the reality was not so nice. Glen Echo *was* progressive, but even my father began to realize that medicines were a necessity, and he reintroduced restraints when one of our patients bashed in an attendant's skull with a spittoon in the ballroom because he believed the attendant was a gargoyle come to demonic life. The truly unfortunate part was that the spittoon was only a prop—there was no tobacco allowed.

I was the model attendant, dressed and trained so that our patients' families felt comfortable leaving their loved ones with us. If attendants were so well-bred, so smilingly efficient, well, dear Johnny or Frederic or William would think they were at home. I was happy enough to be that for my parents. In fact, I took pride in it. I *liked* being the shining example of our exacting care. I wanted to be perfect for my father, my mother. And as for the part of me that wanted more, that dreamed of romance and foreign places and a life away from madness and pain, it was impossible to do more than dream. My parents needed me. Glen Echo needed me.

But Glen Echo was as full of misery and futility as any other asylum. It weighed upon me. There were nights I couldn't sleep for the hopelessness. I felt everything too deeply, perhaps. I began to long for a life away, a life that could never be, and so I decided to take on more responsibility, to make myself too busy for yearning. I worked in the female wards, hoping activity might dull my longing, but my sense of being smothered grew worse. I began to empathize with my patients too well. I might have my faculties, but I was as trapped within these walls as they were.

And then, a door opening. My mother was growing tired of constantly traveling, and my father began to speak of my taking her place as the voice of Glen Echo in society. I grasped hold of the idea. When Joshua Lockwood was brought to us, it was an opportunity to show my father I was ready to go out into the world. I charmed Joshua's parents so well that they asked that I be involved in his care, and though my father kept a rigid division between men and women—only male attendants for male patients, and women for the women—the Lockwoods were so insistent, and we were shorthanded. There was no one available to read to Joshua, as they specifically requested—*It soothes him so.* Papa reluctantly agreed that I could do so.

I was determined to do well. I knew my future rested upon it. What a fool I'd been. Such a terrible fool.

I remembered too well that last meeting, and the grim, grieving faces of the Lockwoods. I had seen no forgiveness there, and no chance for redemption. And as for my parents . . . even now, the thought of my mother's groveling—my mother, who was never anything but cultured and graceful and self-possessed—was impossible to reconcile, impossible to watch or believe it had ever happened, that it had been she who so desperately begged for clemency. Even worse was the way my father looked, as if he could not bear to see it, not for one moment, as if it broke his heart.

Days later, I'd packed, numb and barely seeing the plain and utilitarian clothes I needed as I put them in my trunk, setting aside my gowns of the latest fashion, which had been bought for those events meant to display patients to their families, ball gowns trimmed in bows and lace, elegant tea gowns. Such lovely things I would never wear again. When I was finished, the trunk was still half-empty. So sad, really, that a life could be compressed to so few things. Three or four books, a photographic portrait of my parents and me. Should someone wish to write my biography, a paragraph would be enough. Whatever hopes I'd had once that it could be different were gone now, my life shrinking down to size, to a future that required no imagination to predict. My own fault. No one else's. What a relief it would have been to be able to assign blame elsewhere.

I went to my window. My bedroom was in the tower wing of Glen Echo, and so had one of the best views. I stared out at grounds that were pristine and barren, only the footsteps of the groundskeeper marking the snow. Trees fringed the perimeter of what was a rolling lawn in the summer, and past them the Hudson River, and I wondered what Massachusetts was like. Littlehaven was such a bucolic, peaceful name for a town. It would be a good one for an asylum. It was so tiny, it was barely noted on maps. There would be a single dirt road dividing the general store from the livery. A tavern, no doubt. Perhaps a milliner's, though I supposed that was too much to hope for.

I wondered if the snow below was as soft as it looked, and whether the jumping or the landing would be the worst part. The jumping, I thought. The will to do it, to acknowledge that it was over, that you no longer wished to try. Or was it possible to simply open the window latch and lean too far out? Leave falling to Fate, no decision made, just looking out and then . . . one more inch, and then another and another and another, until you could no longer catch your balance on the sill, and then letting go, tumbling and tumbling. How easy it would be. The snow sparkled and beckoned. Was that a whisper I heard, welling up from beneath it? A sound so deep and low it seemed to rumble within me, a feeling more than words. *Come. Come to me. Why do you stay? I'm waiting for you.*

I had my hand on the window latch when the knock on the door startled me.

"Miss Spira? Your father wishes to see you."

I was surprised. It had all been decided; there was nothing to do but wait for the carriage to take me to Littlehaven, due within the hour. What more was there to be said?

The maid, Anna, led me down the hall, this one carpeted, though not all of them were so, and tendered a brief smile that I knew was meant to be reassuring. We passed the room that held the medications, and I turned quickly away.

Anna rapped sharply on the door. "Miss Spira, sir," and I saw shadows move behind the frosted glass, behind the blocky black letters reading Superintendent.

My father's office for only a few more days.

"Come in, Elena." My mother's voice. I felt a pang at the sound of it; to me it still held the heaviness of her tears.

I went inside. Usually, the room was full of plush, thick carpets, comfortable chairs, a polished maple desk that radiated confidence and authority, all meant to reassure patients and their families. *Yes, this is where you belong. We can help you.* I supposed that sometimes it was even true. But now, the office was almost barren but for the crates stacked against the wall, books, pictures, framed diplomas packed away, ready to be carted out at the end of the week, delivered to a storehouse until something else could be found, Mama and Papa moving in with her sister. The evidence of what was to come was intolerable.

"There you are," Mama said with satisfaction. She looked composed, her blond hair plaited and woven about her head, her blue eyes calm. There was no sign of the woman who had been in that room with the Lockwoods; the stress that had lined her plump face was gone.

My parents exchanged a glance. "Plans have changed," Papa said. "I received a telegram from James Farber two days ago." He gave me a look as if James Farber were the antidote to a poison, and one I should somehow know to take.

"You're to go to Venice, Elena!" Mama burst out.

I frowned at her, not understanding. Papa smiled tenderly at her, and said, "Patience, Dolly." Then he laid it out: the Farbers' proposal, Samuel Farber's beating, the upcoming wedding, epilepsy and secrets.

I knew of Samuel Farber, of course. I had been with my mother when the Farbers had first come to Glen Echo six years ago, hoping to find someone who could help their son. It was the first of many such commitments for Samuel. He would come, stay for a few months until Papa had him stabilized, and then go out into the world again, only to return when his debaucheries got the best of him.

But there were many patients at Glen Echo, and he had stayed in the male ward, and so I had never met him face-to-face. His last visit had been more than a year ago.

Mama said, "They've promised your father a new position if you succeed. An asylum of his own to run, wherever we like. It's to belong to us." She was glowing, seemingly ready to burst at the thought of our deliverance.

Papa said, "We could leave all this . . . *unpleasantness*"—a sublime understatement—"behind. With their patronage, we can start over somewhere else."

"You would trust me with this after everything?" I asked softly. "The Farbers would trust me?"

"I've convinced them that it was all a misunderstanding. They trust me, and it helps that you impressed them greatly when you met. I've told them I have every faith in your abilities. And I do, Elena. I know you have learned from your mistake."

I could only nod.

"It will mean, of course, that your own wedding must be postponed. But I didn't think you would be upset by that."

"No."

Papa took a deep breath. "I've informed Michael and your aunt that you won't return until July."

"July? But I thought I was to have Mr. Farber back by January?"

"Yes. But . . . with the money the Farbers are providing, I thought perhaps we could afford to give you six months on the Continent. Your French tutor, Madame du Vallon, is abroad. She's agreed to chaperone you. You've always liked her, haven't you?"

I was stricken by the evidence of his love for me, by how well he knew the things I hoped for. In those words I heard everything he wasn't saying, the wish that marriage to my cousin wasn't my only choice, that he understood the yearning that had driven me to make such a terrible mistake. "Yes," I said. "Yes, I like her a great deal."

"It will help that you're away. Your aunt is rather relieved, actually. She has feared that the talk may follow you to Littlehaven, which will do Michael no good. The time abroad will help people forget. You'll be able to start a new life with your husband when you return, unencumbered by gossip."

Because, of course, my work at the asylum was done, and there was no hope of taking my mother's place now. I could not stay with them. Papa would be better able to redeem his reputation and his position if I was not around to constantly remind everyone.

"You know this is not what your father and I would have wished for you," Mama said softly. "But Michael is a good man. I think you'll be happy. And of course, you'll have your memories of your Grand Tour."

Papa said, "*If* you can bring Samuel around. It all depends on that, Elena, mind me now. Everything. It all falls away otherwise. The Farber money and their support. The Continent. All of it."

"When do I leave?" I asked.

My parents' relief was palpable. I realized that they had been afraid I might refuse. How could I, when everything they had toiled and strived for was threatened now, all because of my one careless stroke?

"Tomorrow," Papa said.

"You'll give me instructions, and—"

"And medications, yes. We'll go over everything. If you follow my directions exactly, there should be no need to fear. You've had experience with the female epileptics, so this will be familiar enough. You can do this, Elena. You are our best hope."

I felt Fate's hand on my shoulder, pulling me gently back, whispering in my ear, *Do not fall.*

Nerone Basilio's words brought it all back. Everything I stood to lose. A return in shame and humiliation, my father without a position, being sent off to my cousin to start my future as a farmer's wife. Without even memories of other places to treasure, without anything to tell me I'd ever lived. As forgotten as the Lockwoods wanted me to be. I did not know how to tell them how sorry I was, that their son haunted me even in my waking hours, that when I closed my eyes I saw him, that I heard his voice.

But in spite of all that, I didn't want to accept the punishment they laid out for me. How much did a single mistake require, even one so big as mine? What was fair restitution? My life in return for Joshua Lockwood's? Should my part in it require a lifetime of repentance? Must I bury myself in manure and mud? Be a broodmare to a cousin I had not laid eyes on for years?

Whether I deserved it or not, I couldn't bear the thought of it.

I did not miss the irony that the Farbers wanted me to put Samuel in the same situation I was so anxious to escape. I was sorry for it; I understood how much he hated the idea, because I hated it too. But I had no other choice. I could sympathize and be sorry all I wanted, but in the end, one of us would be making an unwanted marriage, and I did not wish for it to be me. I needed that six months. My parents didn't know it, but I harbored a secret hope of finding a way not to return, not to marry my cousin. In six months, surely I could discover a remedy?

Marriage would not mean a living death for Samuel Farber. He was a man; he was free to find happiness anywhere. He could do whatever he liked, take whatever mistresses he wanted, travel the world without his wife, as long as he provided for her. My future would be quite different. I could consign him to his without guilt. Was it so wrong to wish for something more?

No, it was not. Nerone Basilio could protest all he liked, but I could not afford to allow Samuel Farber any latitude. Which meant I must watch Mr. Basilio as intently as I did Giulia. Not only because I suspected he might sneak Samuel a bottle or two, but because I must keep him from discovering Samuel's true ailment.

But now, my task seemed harder than ever, too many pieces to move about, and the worst of them Samuel himself. That kiss, his violence . . . what was I to do with that? He'd been drunk, I reassured myself. I would make certain he was not again. And as for what I'd felt—that twinge of something I didn't want to look at too closely, that unwelcome, nebulous stirring—I simply would not think about it.

I glanced over my shoulder at his closed door, wanting to leave him alone, but better to check on him one last time, to be sure he'd suffered no other ill effects from the brandy. I turned the knob on his door as quietly as I could, and eased it open, peering around the corner.

He was sitting up, staring into the darkness, his eyes glittering.

"I'm sorry. I didn't mean to disturb you. I just wanted to look in and make certain you were all right."

"Do you see her?" he whispered. "Tell me you see her."

That strange smell in the room—vanilla and rotting canal and algae—was strong enough to sting. The perfume of those hand-kerchiefs seemed to have permeated everything since that drawer had been opened.

"See who, Samuel?" I asked.

He said, a dreamy voice now, singsong and slow, "*Chi comincia mal, finisse pezo.*"

The air in the room seemed to whisper; I felt the brush of hostility over my skin that made me draw back. Samuel did not move from the bed. There was nothing physically there, nothing to be afraid of. Only my imagination, his drunkenness.

But like a coward, I stepped back into the hall, closing the door, leaving him to himself.

Chapter 10

Samuel and I discussed neither the kiss nor his drunkenness, which was what I preferred, though the specter of the incident remained stubbornly—and silently—between us. He atoned by being well behaved over the next few days, though his despondency was evident, and I tried to remain cheerful in its face, though I had to admit I felt as if I were holding on to things with just the barest control.

There was something more deeply wrong here than I understood. I couldn't put it into words; I could hardly order my thoughts. It all sounded so ridiculous and absurd. How was I to seriously say that the air had been hostile that night? How could I explain how avidly Samuel had watched nothing, or how profoundly his gaze had disturbed me? Reason told me I was imagining things. I wanted to believe I could explain it away as a side effect of the bromide. His epilepsy. Drunkenness. But I couldn't quite.

In that time, I only saw Nero Basilio in passing, or from the window of my bedroom, where I found myself standing a bit too often, watching him laugh with one of the Nardi children or unloading barrels with Zuan. He was not like any man I'd ever seen. While Samuel reminded me of Glen Echo, Mr. Basilio seemed of a different world entirely, one romantic and dashing and full of life. Not that I knew him well enough to know anything about him. The most conversation I had with him was one afternoon, as I drew water from the well.

"Miss Spira!" he'd called, and when I straightened, his smile was quick and wide and blindingly alluring. "I've missed you and Samuel. Too many duties to attend, but I'll be up soon, *ai*? As soon as I can."

He said it in a way that made me think it was not really Samuel he was hoping to see. He'd made a face at the bundles he carried and hurried off, leaving me feeling warm at his attention, brief as it was.

I should have been thankful. Given Samuel's condition, it was better if Nero Basilio kept his distance. I could not risk him seeing a seizure, though I wished . . . well, I sensed Mr. Basilio would be a good distraction for both Samuel and me, and one we both sorely needed.

The third morning after Mr. Basilio's arrival, I went in search of breakfast, and hoped for diversion. The air smelled of snow, and the clouds were heavy and a pale whitish gray. The two little Nardi girls were playing in the courtyard, chasing each other and laughing.

When they saw me, they stopped abruptly. I smiled at them, but they didn't smile back, only watched me with big wary eyes as I went to the kitchen. When I pulled the door open, the gust of warm air scented with fish and spices and toasted corn nearly blew me back.

The first thing I saw was Giulia, bustling at the stove, her hips twitching as she stirred something in a great heavy pot. And there, lounging on the bench at the table as if it were a chaise, his back against the wall while he tossed raisins into his mouth, was Nero Basilio. His eyes were sparkling; he was laughing at something she'd said. He was in his shirtsleeves, no tie and no vest, with an overcoat abandoned in a slump on the bench beside him.

"Miss Spira!" he scrambled to sit up, clearing a spot for me to sit down.

His enthusiasm was an antidote to my agitation. He said something quickly to Giulia, and she glared at me over her shoulder and ladled cornmeal porridge into a bowl, sliding it across the table to me, along with a plate of roasted chestnuts.

Mr. Basilio said something else to her, and her glare turned into a smile for him, and one so brilliant I was momentarily taken aback. She shifted her hips and gave him a suggestive look that told me better than words just what Giulia wished to do to Nero Basilio. Or perhaps she already had.

I felt a prick of irritation and sat down, reaching for the bowl.

"Not yet!" He swooped in, grabbing the plate of peeled and roasted chestnuts. He took his knife, which lay on the table by his elbow, a shining blade with a handle of ebony inlaid with ivory in what I now recognized must be the Basilio symbol—the rising, rayed sun that decorated the doors and fanlights, as well as the handkerchiefs in the dresser in Samuel's room. Nero cut the chestnut into pieces, dropping them into my bowl. "Try it with this."

Giulia made a comment, and he laughed shortly and said something back, and I felt suddenly out of place, as if I'd intruded.

I glanced at Giulia. "Am I interrupting?"

He raised a brow. "Interrupting what? Giulia berating me for offering you chestnuts?"

"Is that what she was saying?"

"Among other things." He put his elbows on the table and leaned forward with that charming smile. "I've told her polenta with chestnuts is your favorite, so don't make me a liar."

Tentatively, I took a bite. The polenta was warm and delicious, salty with cheese, and the chestnuts were sweet and nutty, a rich, deep flavor. It was one of the best things I'd ever tasted, and I told him so.

"You see?" He spoke to Giulia in a quick barrage of dialect. She regarded me as if I were a chicken being considered for the pot, and then dismissed me and spoke to him. The only word I understood—or thought I did—was *mericàn*, which could have meant either me or Samuel, or perhaps wasn't what I thought at all. Nero grinned wickedly when he answered. They were obviously very familiar with each other.

I looked down at my bowl and tried to ignore them.

"I've just told her it's very rude to speak Venetian in front of our guest," he translated. "She thinks it rude that we speak English in front of her."

I felt as if he'd only told me part of it. It didn't explain either the way she'd looked at him or his teasing wickedness, but neither did I have any interest in their flirtation. "You speak English very well. Where did you learn it?"

"School in London," he said. "My father felt Venice's future lay with the English—don't ask me why, it makes no sense to me. I think it was only that he still blamed France for the Austrians. In any event, I was glad to go. Better than moping about a house slowly falling into the lagoon. It's where I met Samuel, in fact."

"At school?"

"In a tavern. Where did you meet him?"

I swallowed another bite of the polenta. "Here. When I arrived from New York."

He sat back in surprise. "You came all the way to Venice to mind a patient you'd never met?"

"I knew his parents. My father is Samuel's physician. He sent me as a favor to the Farbers."

"Why not just hire a nurse who was already in Rome? Surely there was one who could care for him well enough."

Carefully, I said, "The Farbers have known my father for a long time. They trust his opinion. Samuel is their only child, and they're very protective." I glanced at Giulia. "He was right to send me, it seems."

He eyed Giulia thoughtfully. "She is my aunt's creature completely. Aunt Valeria took her in—and Zuan too—when they were children. They were beggars in the Rialto. She moved about in society a great deal then, and she needed servants whose loyalty was unquestioned. She taught them French so they could report to her all the gossip. Trust her to always see the angles. To them, she's a savior, and neither will lift a finger against her. Fine for her, but it meant that when my father died, and my mother asked Aunt Valeria to move in, she just took over. My mother didn't have a chance against a housekeeper who would not follow her orders and a gondolier who refused to take her anywhere without Aunt Valeria's permission. But by then Mama was in no condition to care."

The words hinted at tragedy, and I had no idea what I should say and was afraid to pry.

He went on as if it were of no moment. "My aunt has been a Basilio a long time. She feels this all belongs to her. It's good to remind her every now and then that she's only here by my leave, so I try to show up periodically, as much as she despises it. She's doing me a favor though, really. As long as she's living here, I don't have to. We tend to avoid each other."

"I did notice that she seemed unhappy with you."

"Does it trouble you?" A quick laugh. "Don't worry for me, *cara*. It matters little."

"But you said she"—I gestured to Giulia, not wanting to risk her attention by saying her name—"was your aunt's servant in all things, and yet she seems to like you, despite your aunt."

Again that suggestive wickedness in his eyes. "Oh, she's simple when it comes to some things. She likes what makes her happy."

I didn't want to ask, but I couldn't help myself. "And you make her happy?"

"I have in the past," he said honestly. "And sometimes I still do."

His frankness shocked me. How prudish and silly, but I couldn't help it. Here was Nero Basilio admitting unapologetically to bedding his aunt's housekeeper—still bedding her—with a cocky smile that dared me to object. I was blushing, which must tell him exactly how unworldly I was. *Mericàn*, Giulia had said disdainfully, along with something else to make him laugh, and I wondered if she'd told him how I'd rushed into Samuel's room like an avenging shrew to find them entwined, their conspiring exchange of glances that made me feel young and foolish, too tightly laced, as I ordered her to leave and lectured Samuel. I wondered if Mr. Basilio had spent the night with her after he'd left me at my bedroom door, if she'd made him laugh as she told him about Samuel's virginal little nurse.

I pushed the bowl away and rose, saying stiffly, "I should check on Samuel."

"I've embarrassed you."

"No. No, of course not." Though of course he had. "I've lingered long enough. I'll just take him breakfast . . ." I grabbed an orange and reached for the bread.

He stopped me with a hand. "At least bring him something warm. It's cold up there, and the stoves don't work worth a damn." He said something to Giulia, who had stopped her stirring at the stove to look at us, and with a long-suffering sigh, she spooned more polenta into a bowl.

Nero Basilio took it, and sheathed his knife, shoving it into his pocket with a handful of chestnuts. "I'll go with you."

"I checked on him this morning before I came down," I lied. "He's perfectly fine. He'll be hungry, though, so if you'll just give me the polenta—"

"Just to the stairs, then," he said with a quick glance at Giulia, who was still watching us. "The courtyard is slippery. And I want to show you something first."

He shrugged into his coat, grabbing the bowl and motioning me to the door. Together, we went out into the courtyard. The little girls were gone, and it was snowing again, fat flakes, wet and slushy and slow.

"What did you want to show me?" I asked.

He smiled and jerked his head toward the gate. "This way."

"I've told you I can't leave him—"

"This will only take a moment. And we're not actually leaving." He led me toward the gate, dodging the fallen stones littering the courtyard. A gesture toward the waterfall of rock tumbling from the destroyed wall.

"Lovely, isn't it? My father insisted it stay as it is. He wanted us never to forget the Austrian bombardment of '49," he explained. "Not that there were the funds to fix it, either, so his anger was all very convenient. Ah well. *Sempre crolla ma non cade.* Venice is always collapsing, but it never falls down."

He flipped the lever on the gate with a clang; the swollen wood shrieked against the courtyard pavement as he opened it. We slipped into the very narrow triangle of the campo, so empty and derelict it looked as if no one had been there in years.

At the narrowest end of the campo was a bridge leading over the canal with the church on the other side, and for a moment, I thought that here at last was the chance to go inside, but he turned the other direction, to another bridge at the broad end of the campo. This bridge too he ignored, turning instead onto the stone walkway along the front of the palazzo. Bits of garbage bobbed in the gray Rio de la Sensa. The slushy snow was growing wetter, soaking the shoulders of my gown, and I was cold without my cloak. I had not planned to be outside for longer than it took to get to the kitchen. Nero Basilio stopped at the edge of the palazzo, where the small, muddy, and rank rio separated it from the two buildings on the other side. He gestured to the water with a smile.

"If I can't convince you to come with me to see the beauties of Venice, I can at least show you something beautiful here. Look."

The water wasn't muddy olive now. It was the most extraordinary color. It looked like shot purple silk with a green weft, shifting color with the movement of current and light. It was beautiful, shockingly so. I struggled for words. "Oh . . . but, how? Why has it changed? I'd thought it full of sewage."

"A dyehouse," he said, nodding toward the building farther down, a huge copper pot upended on the sinking water steps. "Haven't you smelled it?"

The source of that acrid, steamy stink, the tang underlying the cold scent of snow.

"It's worse in the summer. Unbearable sometimes. But it's worth it for the colors." He grinned at me. "Though it's brown quite often. I think it's a color he specializes in. Sometimes it's brown for days."

His gaze became distant and dreamy as he looked at the water. "Samuel's balcony overlooks it. It used to be my cousin's room. She and I often left the day's fortunes to the whim of the dyer. Mass or a café . . . is the rio green or blue?"

The falling snow, the purple water, the dreamcast of his voice. I felt shivery, but now I wasn't cold. Snow melted in his curling hair, darkening the shoulders of his overcoat. His expression was wistful. I thought he was remembering something sad, and I waited for him to volunteer it.

He didn't. He said only, "I'm not certain which color I like best. Sometimes I think the scarlet, but then . . . this purple is amazing. But no, I think it must be the blue. It looks like something out of a fairy tale."

"I would like to see that sometime."

"Perhaps it will happen while you're here." A flicker of a smile, a mere ghost of the ones he'd given me before. "Now we should go back. I imagine you're worried about your patient, and I'm afraid his polenta has grown cold."

I glanced at the bowl still in his hands, the thick skin that had formed over the mush. It seemed impossible that I had forgotten about Samuel, but for a few moments I had. "I suppose I'll have to get him another."

"Ah well . . . I probably shouldn't have delayed you. But I wanted you to see that Venice isn't all horror and ruin."

I hadn't seen Venice's legendary beauties, but I couldn't imagine that any could compare with this canal, which was one of the most surprising and lovely things I'd ever seen. "Thank you for showing me this. It really is beautiful. I'm glad you brought me."

His gaze was thoughtful, unwavering, too searching. I could not keep it. "I'm glad I did too."

I felt awkward and strange. Nervously, I blurted, "You are right, though. I should be getting back to Samuel."

"Then, we'll go." He eased past me, heading for the door, and before I followed him, I gave one last glance to the dye-colored water, the fog of snow turning it briefly into lavender before my eyes, and then I glanced up, to the balcony of the second floor.

Madame Basilio stood there, and there was no smile on her face, and no kindness. Her hands curved like claws over the balustrade as she stared down at us, a dark and baleful shadow in the swirling slush of snow.

Chapter 11

When I at last came into Samuel's room, it was to find him at the balcony door, staring out at the falling slush, one hand braced heavily on the chair. The stove was lit, and a layer of smoke hovered just below the ceiling, but there was little warmth to be felt. He had his overcoat on over his shirt and trousers, and wore house shoes lined with fleece.

"Do you see the water's purple?" I asked him. "There's a dye-house down the way. Mr. Basilio says you can see it from your balcony."

"It's not dye. It's blood." His voice was quiet, eerily toneless.

I felt the prickling at the back of my neck, that creeping watchfulness. "Don't be so morbid. Blood isn't purple, the last time I looked. Here's your bromide. And some polenta."

"Have you brought restraints as well?"

"Of course not."

"Thank God." He breathed the words. "I can't abide them. I . . . well." He glanced at me, and I felt the presence of the kiss and his drunkenness and had a moment of panic that he would say something now.

Quickly, I said, "I don't even have any, so you've no need to worry."

He said, "I imagine you wish you did."

"I don't think I'll have need of them, do you?"

"Elena, why not make it easier on both of us? Tell my parents whatever you like. That I'm stable, that I'm cured, whatever you need to say. Just give me the laudanum. Everything will be easier. My parents won't even know I'm using it. I've fooled them before. Countless times."

"I can't do that. You know I can't. What happens if I send you back and you have a seizure before your wedding?"

"I won't."

"How can you know that? Can you control them?" I already knew the answer, of course.

A sigh. "No."

"You see? I can't take the risk. And I don't understand why you want to. Wouldn't it be better to not have to worry about seizures?"

"I've spent my life worrying about them. I'm used to it."

"It's only been two weeks. You must have faith that the bromide and the cold baths will have their effect."

"What happens in the meantime?" He turned back to the door. His voice was desolate when he said, "Perhaps I should just throw myself off. I wonder if it feels different to drown in purple water?"

The window. The latch. The beckoning snow. How well I understood. I pushed the memory away.

"You'll never know," I said. "Because I refuse to let you find out."

"Perhaps I'll do it when you're not here to stop me. It would be easy enough. The railing here is much lower than the others." He became thoughtful. "Nero's cousin fell from this balcony. They say she leaned too far over and couldn't catch her balance. She drowned."

"His cousin?"

"Didn't you know?"

"No. How would I?" I thought of this morning, and his wistfulness, my sense that he was remembering something sad. This had been his cousin's room, he'd said. Madame Basilio had said her daughter had been gone for some time. Not gone. *Dead.*

Now that I'd smelled it, the perfume from the handkerchiefs seemed to follow me about. I caught a sudden, strong whiff of it, borne on a breeze, vanilla cloaked in seaweed, and along with it came a sudden rush of brutal cold that turned my breath to fog. Gooseflesh rose on my arms.

"They didn't find her for two days," Samuel said in a whisper. "Crabs nibbled at her eyes."

A shiver raced down my spine. My sense of profound wrongness returned with force. "She had Titian hair like yours. When they found her it was tangled with algae."

His whisper, the horror of his words, as well as the dazed way he spoke, as if he saw something distant . . . I'd seen this too often now. Uncertainly, I said, "Samuel?"

My voice came out too loud, and he started, looking back at me with fear in his eyes. Then he blinked as if I'd roused him from a trance. Another petit mal, or a vision, or something else? The cold and the perfume disappeared so quickly, I wondered if they'd been here at all.

Samuel said, "Nero's always had a penchant for redheads."

After the strangeness of the rest, this comment, coming from nowhere as it did, was even more strange.

"You're saying he was in love with his cousin?"

"He was betrothed to her from a young age."

We had spoken of arranged marriages, his negotiated when he was only eight. *"She and I often left the day's fortunes to the whim of the dyer."*

Samuel eyed me thoughtfully. "You want to be careful of him, Elena."

"Be careful of him? Mr. Basilio? Why? He's been so kind—kinder to me than anyone else here, including yourself. What reason have you not to trust him?"

"I do trust him. We've been friends a long time. But that means I know him very well, and when it comes to women"—Samuel let out his breath—"I'm simply trying to save you from a broken heart."

"How kind of you. But I can take care of myself."

"Perhaps you think you can. But trust me when I say Nero is not what you're used to. And now your hair has caught his attention. I'm not certain he even realizes he's been looking for her in other women. It hasn't mattered before now, because they've all been whores, and to them, he's only another customer. But you . . ."

"Samuel, I'm here to see you healed, and that's what I mean to do. I don't have time for flirtation."

"It won't be flirtation, it will be seduction. He's very good at it. And you, frankly, are a little too ready."

"Ready for what?"

"To be"—clearly searching for the right word, not choosing the first that came to mind—"tumbled."

I felt I might burst into flame. "That was quite inappropriate."

"But true. Any man can see it, Elena. It's like a . . . a perfume. I'm not immune. Nero won't be either."

"I am not looking to . . . to be . . . for that, whatever you think."

"Really? You never imagine it? You never glance at the book I gave you and wonder what pleasures are to be found there?"

"No," I lied, too loud again, too strident, as if my own voice meant to expose me. "And I think you're the one to be careful of."

He tilted his head in acknowledgment. "I haven't denied it."

"Of the two of you, it's not him I'm afraid of."

I hadn't meant to admit it, and when I saw the way he flinched, I was sorry. It was only that I was embarrassed, and angry for being so, and angry at him for seeing that part of me I was afraid of, the dark little secret of my curiosity, that longing that had me twisting and turning in the night, yearning for something I did not want to put a name to.

It was not his fault. It was my own. But I couldn't say that either, and when he turned away from me and stared out again, saying, "I think I might prefer the water red, wouldn't you?" I said, "I'm partial to blue. Drink your bromide."

Then I left. And I forgot what I should not have forgotten, what his provocative talk had distracted me from: his bleak despair, his fear, and the uncanny cold that had come when he'd spoken of drowning, when he'd stared at a canal he'd told me was the color of blood.

That night, I lay staring up at the smoky darkness above my head, jumping at every noise. A door closing, footsteps in the courtyard below, a woman teasing, and a man laughing in response who I was pained to realize I did not want to be Nero Basilio. The coals in the little brazier were banked, but every now and then one glowed for a moment before it died again, startling me each time with the notion that a red eye had flashed to life.

I waited for a crash or singing. I thought of Samuel's searing, invasive kiss and the things he'd said about me today. I remembered how Nero Basilio had looked at me, the snow melting in his hair. I wondered what those silky curls would feel like to touch.

I was not what Samuel Farber said I was. I was not. I was not so innocent any longer. I only had to think of Joshua Lockwood silent and still to remind myself how hard the lesson had been learned.

"He's so much better, Papa. I think he would improve if we took him out of restraints."

The fervent way Joshua had looked at me, the plea in his eyes to believe him, *"I'm not mad—not the least bit. My brother wants me out of the way. My father's ill, and once he dies, I'll inherit everything.*

But if I'm in here, Marcus will get it all. Come, my darling. You must help me. You know me better than anyone ever has. Do you see madness in these eyes? Help me and we'll leave here together. I'll take you away from all this . . ."

I squeezed my eyes shut, banishing the memories, the way he'd kissed me and touched me, the fever he'd raised that I would have done anything to ease. The hope he'd given me—I'd been able to breathe again once he was there to open the door.

But he hadn't. In the end, there had been nothing, nothing, nothing but the lie between us. Only the perfect evidence of his madness. Only a terrible mistake, and my father's long-suffering sigh. *"Oh, Elena, do you not see what you've done? They lie—have I not told you that a dozen times?"*

"And you, frankly, are a little too ready."

I shifted uncomfortably, restlessly, turning onto my side, my hand slipping down, toying with the edge of the mattress, thinking of what was beneath, that yellow-backed novel. I pulled it out— not all the way, still deciding, my fingers teasing the ragged edges of the page—the paperknife had not been sharp enough, and in places had torn scallops. But it had been well read, and I knew from before—*only skimming, hardly seeing, horrified and fascinated at how vulgar and coarse the words were, the kind the stable-boys used when they spoke to each other about their exploits, when they thought no one was listening and did not imagine a young girl eavesdropping at the door, words with hard consonant sounds, c's and k's and t's, words that exploded off the tongue, inflammatory and exciting and provocative, that made my own blood leap and churn*—that many pages were stained . . . I did not want to think with what.

I played the game with myself. *Take it out. Don't.* Like pulling petals off a daisy, *He loves me, he loves me not* . . . a back-and-forth that tormented and shamed. I would not read it. I was not that kind of woman. I'd already had it a week, but I could not bring myself to meet Samuel's challenge, no matter that I knew my life with him would be easier if I did. Here, in the darkness and my loneliness, I could admit that I was afraid to read it. I was afraid of what I might discover. I was afraid of what Samuel would see with that epileptic vision that revealed what was hidden to everyone else. A knowledge I both wanted and didn't want. Or . . . wanted and didn't wish anyone to know I had.

"It's like a perfume. I'm not immune. Nero won't be either."

I pulled away, my fingers flailing for nothing in the darkness, another game—*don't touch it. Forget it's there. Don't think of it.* But I found the way back to it again, the rough cover a temptation, the worn edges of those pages almost silky, my fingers aching to rub, to fondle. I told myself: *If that man who is not Mr. Basilio laughs again, I'll take it out. I'll read five pages.* I waited, breath held, my heart beating in my ear, not knowing whether I wanted to hear that laughter or was afraid to. Waiting. Waiting.

He did not laugh, and the night grew quiet, my own breathing the only sound, and gradually the temptation fell away, banished by weariness, and I brought my hand up to rest beneath my cheek and surrendered to dreams. *The Nunnery Tales* stayed beneath my mattress.

Chapter 12

I did as Samuel asked and kept my distance from Nero Basilio. When he came to visit Samuel, I stayed in my room, pretending to be busy, reading the travel guides I was growing increasingly convinced I would never use, imagining views I would never see. I listened to the rumble of their voices down the hall, nervously waiting for anything that signaled a seizure, so tense my muscles were sore whenever he left.

Giulia did not stop trying to sneak in, but I managed to stop her before she could get to him, and was more satisfied than I should have been at her obvious frustration. Though even without her interference, I was making little progress. Often I came into Samuel's room to see him staring sightlessly in the distance, while that tickling, eerie watchfulness was so present and strong that I wanted to cover the eyes of every painted creature on the ceiling. I'd scoured my father's notes for any mention that might help me, something I may have overlooked, but I saw nothing to suggest that Samuel's case was odd or unusual, nothing to show he was more prone to hallucinations than any other epileptic. Perhaps his concussion had been more severe than I had thought.

I considered writing Papa for advice, but I couldn't bring myself to admit the task was too hard for me. Papa had believed I could do this. I must believe it too.

Three days after Mr. Basilio had shown me the dyer's canal, there was a knock on the outside door just as Samuel was emerging from his cold bath, and a call from the hall, "Samuel? Miss Spira?"

Nero Basilio. Samuel, who was cursing and shivering, tightened the belt of his dressing gown and glanced at me, a warning in his gaze. "In the sala!" he called.

When Mr. Basilio appeared in the doorway, tousled and good-natured, a breaking smile, I could not help smiling in return.

"Ciao," he said, then glanced at Samuel's state of relative undress, and his smile became teasing. "Am I interrupting something?"

"Only torture," Samuel replied. "Do me a favor, will you, and tell my nurse that cold baths in a freezing palazzo in the middle of the winter are more likely to cause my death than speed my healing."

Mr. Basilio made a face. "*Santa Maria*. Torture indeed."

"It helps ease the pain of his ribs," I said, saying only part of the truth. "And it takes down the swelling of his knee."

"So I can greet my bride without looking like Frankenstein's monster," Samuel added.

I caught his glance, his tease. I said only, "Your wounds are healing as they should. You're beginning to look like yourself again."

"Since you've only ever seen me misshapen, I've no idea how you can know."

"It's done nothing to improve his personality, I can tell you that," Mr. Basilio offered. Like the other day, he wore a coat. Apparently the second floor was no warmer than the third.

"Well," I said. "I'll leave the two of you alone."

"Please don't," Mr. Basilio said. "I've come to see you particularly. Though you've been avoiding me, I think. Have I offended you?"

I couldn't look at Samuel. "No, of course not."

But Mr. Basilio didn't believe me, I saw. His expression was faintly chiding as he reached into his pocket and pulled out a piece of paper, holding it out to me. "For you."

I took it warily. "What is it?"

"My aunt invites you to tea this afternoon," he said with a grimace. "Which should be delightful for you. *Cafè* too strong to drink and *baicolo* too dry to swallow. Add to that bitterly nasty conversation and gossip about people you either don't know or don't remember, and my aunt's teas are truly a shining example of Venetian hospitality."

"Oh," I said, opening to the letter to see the invitation—in French. "I suppose there's no delicate way to refuse."

"No," he said with insouciant cheer. "I am afraid not. It's rather a royal command. Now that I'm here, she wants to be certain to warn you of my black heart."

Samuel said lightly, "Word of your debauches in Rome has undoubtedly arrived."

"Rome has nothing to do with it." Mr. Basilio leaned against the wall, casually brushing away the plaster dust that sifted to his shoulder. "She's never lost an opportunity to disparage me to anyone who will listen, and now—voilà!—she has a new and impressionable ear. I am sorry, cara, but I tried to dissuade her. I know you've better things to do than spend an hour listening to a choleric old widow. I only ask you to remember that my shortcomings have long been a source of repellent fascination to her. I try not to deprive her of her only entertainment."

"Will you be there?" I asked.

"I've been expressly forbidden," he said with a thin smile. "All the better for her to impugn my character with ease. I can't defend myself. But I promise you that I am really not so irredeemable that it requires daily prayers for my soul."

"She still hasn't forgiven you for the bacchanal you threw in her sala," Samuel said, undoubtedly for my benefit.

Nero winced. "I was nineteen. And how was I to know she would arrive from Milan a day early, with my cousin in tow?"

"That perhaps had something to do with your betrothed's irritation." Samuel's voice was wry. He made his limping way to the settee and sat down, easing his hurt knee. "She can't have liked walking into the room to find two whores draped all over you."

"Well, yes," Mr. Basilio admitted. "It was a shock for her. What can I say? *Amor sensa barufa fa a muffa.*"

"I have no idea what you're saying half the time," Samuel complained.

"Love without a fight grows moldy. But I did what I could to make it up to her. A man can change."

"Can he?" Samuel laughed. "Did you?"

Nero Basilio's dark gaze slid to me. "You'll frighten Miss Spira with your stories. Is this why you've been avoiding me, cara? Has he despoiled my character and made you think I haven't properly atoned for my sins?"

I said, "Your atonement is between yourself and God and none of my concern."

"You see, Samuel? Not everyone is so judgmental. My cousin had a bit of the puritan about her sometimes, though I did my best to rub it out. Does no one believe in redemption these days?"

Who understood better than I, whose own mistake threatened to demand a lifetime of repentance? "I do," I said fervently. "I believe in redemption."

His gaze met mine, quick interest flaring in his, curiosity, and I realized I'd spoken too intently, and glanced away only to see that Samuel was watching me as if I'd given something away.

Nero Basilio said softly, "Ah, an ally at last. So you won't believe the stories my aunt tells of me?"

"I will at least allow you to tell me your side," I said.

"I had never hoped to find an understanding ear. You will forgive me, won't you, if I bend it too often?"

"She won't have time for all your stories," Samuel said abruptly. "She's too busy tending me."

I glanced again at the invitation and said to Samuel, "I hate to leave you alone. I'll give you some valerian while I'm gone, so you'll sleep."

Mr. Basilio pulled away from the wall. "As it's on my account you must go, I offer myself as Samuel's nursemaid."

I had not anticipated this, and it made me nervous. "You must have other things to do."

"As it happens, no. Unless you wish for me to show you more of Venice's beauties"—here a look that reminded me of the purple rio, the snow in his hair—"I have little else to occupy me today."

"He should be resting after his bath."

"I'm right here, you know," Samuel snapped. "The two of you make me feel like a child. You don't need to guard me so well, Elena."

I couldn't explain the real reasons for my objection, at least not with Nero Basilio in the room. It was impressive that, after all their time together, Samuel had managed to keep his affliction from his friend.

I frowned at Samuel. "I would feel better—"

"I'll be fine," he said firmly. "Go to tea. I'll be in good hands."

I turned to Mr. Basilio. "He must have no laudanum and no liquor of any kind. No coffee or tea. Nothing spicy. And please no . . . nothing to excite. No talk of . . . of debaucheries or . . . or anything like that."

"You blush charmingly," he said with a grin. He flicked his fingers at his own high cheekbones. "A very delicate pink. No Italian woman blushes so sweetly."

"No Italian woman blushes at all, that I've seen," Samuel said.

"You see only whores, so how would you know?" Mr. Basilio teased. "But I *do* know, and I promise you I've never seen anything so delightful."

"At least it keeps her warm," Samuel said. "Which is more than I can say for anything else in this place."

I knew I was not delicately pink. I felt as if I were lobster red. I could not even look at Nero Basilio. But it seemed he understood that his compliments embarrassed me, because he adroitly followed Samuel's lead, giving me time to recover. "Better than the summer, amìgo, when you'd be eaten alive by mosquitos and suffocated by the stink."

They talked back and forth, ignoring me for the moment, for which I was grateful, and then Mr. Basilio took his leave with a final word to me. "You will want to hang yourself before tea is over, but I promise it won't last beyond an hour. Impatience is a Basilio trait."

"I'll remember that," I said, unable to help my smile as he gave me that quaint little bow.

"Ciao, then. Until later."

When he was gone, Samuel sighed. I heard in it the whole of his warnings.

"I haven't forgotten anything you said," I told him.

He said sourly, "He's already got his tongue halfway down your throat."

Distracted again. But it wasn't Samuel I was thinking of as I dressed in the striped silk I'd worn the day I'd come to the Basilio and went to meet Madame Basilio for tea. I was thinking instead of the things Nero Basilio had said, the warnings about his aunt, and when I was shown into her salon, I was already bristling with the urge to defend him, with righteous indignation—*I think you misunderstand him. Do you not believe that men can change? He has been nothing but kind to me.* I remembered the last time I'd seen her, staring down at us with disapproval from the balcony, and the time before that, the dislike I'd seen for her nephew.

But I saw no signs of either now. Her greeting was polite, if stiff, as disconcerting as always. She rose from a table that had been set with coffee and a plate of sugar-dusted fritters and another of honey-colored nougat, and said, "Mademoiselle Spira, thank you for accepting my invitation. Please, sit. I hope these things please you. It is not often I have company."

I sat in the chair opposite hers, and she moved with grace to her own and poured the coffee, asking me if I preferred it with milk.

I took the tiny cup of coffee, so black and strong it looked syrupy, and undoubtedly as bitter as her nephew had predicted.

"*Mandorlato?*" she asked, nudging the plate of nougat toward me, and politely I took a piece and nibbled upon it. It tasted of honey and was studded with almonds.

"Thank you for inviting me," I said, sipping at the too strong coffee and putting the delicious candy aside.

A thin smile. "I am not used to having guests. It's been many years since my husband died, and I have been perhaps a bit too content in the silence he left behind."

I had no idea what to make of that, and so I said nothing.

"And I have had no wish for company since my daughter's death," she went on. "But M'sieur Farber's arrival—and yours—has been a . . . change."

I could not tell if she found that a good or bad thing.

"How does your patient?" she asked.

I hesitated, uncertain what to tell her. "He's progressing daily."

"Not well, then."

"He is healing. His parents expect him back in New York in January, and so we won't be impinging on your hospitality for long."

"January?" She seemed surprised. "So soon?"

"He's due to be wed."

Madame Basilio sipped her coffee, that black gaze as uncomfortable as ever. "Is he still having nightmares? Sleepwalking? Does he see things?"

"Less so now," I assured her, which was an overt lie, though it seemed best to prepare the ground for an explanation in the event I needed it. "But I don't think such things are gone for good. His head injury was significant."

She nodded thoughtfully, putting a fritter onto a plate with a pair of silver tongs. She passed it to me. "My nephew felt M'sieur Farber might find the Basilio restful. It seems he does not find it the least bit so. A pity."

"It's a beautiful home." It was partially the truth.

"It is a ruin," she said with a shrug. "And it can be uncomfortable. M'sieur Farber is in one of the best rooms in the house, which is all I could do. It was my daughter's when we moved to the upper floor for the summer months. Fortunately, many of her things were still there."

Carefully, I said, "Yes. I heard she died. I'm so sorry."

"It was devastating," she said simply. "But I still feel her here, and so am loath to leave. Her spirit lingers in the hallways. Sometimes I fancy I can hear her voice. Do you believe in such things, mademoiselle?"

"I have never thought much about it."

"Venice is full of ghosts. A whisper in your ear that comes from nowhere. A cold breeze where there should be none. Furniture that moves without agency."

Her voice had lowered, raising a shiver that was as much from her tone as her words. I found myself thinking of the icy cold, the scent of iris and vanilla.

But, a ghost? No, I didn't believe that. It was only this house: drafts from nowhere, a perfume that still lingered in a room that had belonged to her, Samuel's hallucinations feeding my own imagination.

"There is a chair in Laura's room that moves, though I have no maid and Giulia claims not to have done it. I must believe her, as no one goes there but me. At least, no one did until M'sieur Farber. Do you know it? The blue one near the window?"

"I haven't seen it move."

"Ah, I wondered. Perhaps he has seen it do so?"

"He's never said anything of it."

"She liked to sit on the balcony and look at the changing colors in the water from the dyer. You've seen the colors, I believe?"

She knew I had. She had been watching. "Yes. Very beautiful."

"The water was red the day she died," Madame said, her gaze going briefly distant, then a blink and back to me. "She loved the Venetian scarlet best. She could not keep away. It was an accident. The balcony was slick from the rain, and the rail too low. She slipped and . . . Ah, you must forgive a grieving mother her stories. I think sometimes I want her back so badly I have conjured her. Perhaps the voice I hear is only my longing. Perhaps the chair moving is a mirage born of grief."

"It must be a comfort to know she is with God now."

"But then I know it is not my imagination," she went on as if she hadn't heard me. "I know these are messages from her. I know there is something she wishes to tell me, but she hasn't the strength to come to me."

Her eyes glittered. Such talk as this, such grieving. I knew where it could lead if not relieved. I'd seen it too often in the asylum.

I said quietly, "Perhaps a doctor could help you."

"A doctor?"

"Or perhaps the church—"

She laughed bitterly. "The church believes ghosts can only be evil. My daughter is not a demon."

"Of course not. I'm certain she is with God, and content. You should think of that. It would give you some measure of peace."

"She is an angel. She is trying to show us the truth."

God's truth, no doubt. Madame Basilio had the look of one who attended mass daily. "Yes, of course."

She seemed to crumple before me, her proud expression sagging, the steel of her spine bending. She looked defeated, exhausted, even ill.

"Madame, are you all right?"

She rose. "I think it is time that you return to your patient."

What had I said? I set down the coffee and the fritter. "As you wish."

She followed me to the doorway, nostrils flaring, high points of red on her pallid, sallow cheeks, and then snapped out "Giulia!" and the housekeeper emerged from another room so quickly I suspected she'd been eavesdropping.

"Show Mademoiselle Spira to the door."

An impudent, smug smile crossed Giulia's lips, and she gestured to the receiving hall. "This way, mamzelle."

"I can find my own way out." I turned to Madame Basilio, still uncertain, feeling I should apologize and not knowing why. "Thank you for the coffee, Madame."

She only waved her hand at me and turned away. I felt I'd insulted her, though I had no idea how.

When I stepped out, the outside was somehow warmer than the sala had been, though still cold and wet. The snow from yesterday was already mostly gone; the sky was overcast, but it wasn't raining. I hurried up the stairs, wanting to speak to Mr. Basilio about the things his aunt had said. He had said she wanted only to impugn his character, but she had not done that at all. What had been the reason for this tea? To talk of ghosts? To speak of Samuel's well-being?

I reached the third floor and opened the door. Inside, it was quiet; I heard no talk or laughter, which I'd expected. Perhaps Samuel had fallen asleep. I immediately quieted my own steps, not wanting to wake him, and headed toward his bedroom, thinking to peek in, expecting to see Mr. Basilio sitting in a chair at his bedside, perhaps reading.

But as I passed my room, I saw the door was ajar. Which was not so unusual, except . . . I slowed at the sound of rustling from within. Someone was inside.

I heard a quiet bang. A whispered curse. Carefully, I opened the door.

I took it in in a glance. The medicine case was on my bed, opened, bottles and boxes and paper-wrapped bundles scattered over the coverlet. And standing beside it, a bottle of laudanum in his hand, was Samuel.

Chapter 13

"What are you doing?" I demanded.

Samuel jerked around, panic on his face, and then when he saw it was me the expression changed to relief—*relief*, when I had just caught him in *my* medicine case; why should it be relief?—and then to pleading. "Elena, please." His voice was low, almost hoarse. "You don't know. You couldn't know. Just a few drops. Please."

I stepped toward him, holding out my hand. "Give it to me, Samuel."

He clutched the bottle of laudanum more tightly and stepped back. "Elena, listen to me. It's only for today. Just today and then I'll give it up. I promise you I will. My head . . . you don't know. Please."

"You know I can't."

"I know you won't." Resentment and anger. His fingers were white where they gripped the bottle. "But think about it. What could it harm, really? I'm not sleeping. I see things."

"Where's Mr. Basilio? I suppose he was part of this plan too?"

"No. I've no idea where he is. He never showed up."

That was one good thing, anyway. "Give it to me, Samuel."

"I'll do whatever you want." His tone changed, wheedling now. "You've a half dozen Baedekers here. Choose one and I'll send you there. Hell, choose all of them. I can give you the money to disappear, to be whatever you want, to do whatever you wish."

It was as if he saw inside me.

"I'm a rich man," he whispered, taking a step toward me. "You want more than this. I can give it to you. All for the price of this bottle."

"Just a few drops. Enough to help me sleep. I'm not mad. You know I'm not. You believe me, don't you? We'll run away together. I'll give you everything you've ever wanted."

The words tangled in my head, the past and the present knotting, trapping me. I looked at Samuel and I saw Joshua. Those same intense eyes. The lies I wanted to believe.

You want more.

Yes, that was the truth. And here he offered it, anything I wanted. Anything at all.

They lie.

My father's voice. Everything I already knew. Joshua Lockwood's casket in the middle of the great hall, waiting to be carted away. My mother's tears.

"No," I whispered. "Give it to me, Samuel."

The incipient triumph on his face crumpled. His eyes flashed with sudden rage. He threw the laudanum onto the bed, where it bounced and dropped against the pillow. "Why the hell are you so persistent?"

"Because I made a mistake." The words flew out before I could stop them.

Samuel stilled. "What mistake?"

It was none of his concern. I did not want him to know more about me than he already did. I felt my vulnerability like a wound—I knew he would see it, that he would poke at it.

"What mistake, Elena?" His rage was banked; still there, but controlled. "One that will take your whole life to redeem? If I have to suffer, at least tell me why."

"I believed someone I shouldn't have believed."

"How did that bring you here?"

I struggled to find a way to call back the words, to unsay them, but it was too late, and I reluctantly realized that he would not forget my indiscretion. He would keep prying and needling until I told him everything. I could not withstand him forever, and perhaps, if I told him now, he would understand why I wouldn't walk away and he would stop tormenting me with his bargains and his quid pro quos. Perhaps he would even help me. I clung to that possibility as I told him all of it: Joshua Lockwood, my unwanted marriage, the six months promised me, my hopes to find within that time a way to escape my fate.

He laughed shortly. "My God, the irony is staggering. My forced marriage frees you from yours."

"I hope so."

"You feel as trapped as I do."

I raised my eyes to him, my heart racing with hope of his sympathy. "Yes."

"But you'd rather ask me to give up my freedom than lose your own. You'll understand that I don't feel inclined to make such a sacrifice."

"It's not just me," I whispered. "My father . . . my mistake has cost him. The scandal . . . He was forced from Glen Echo. Your parents have promised him his own asylum. They've promised to restore his reputation."

"I don't care."

"But it wasn't his fault! He didn't do anything! He's worked his entire life for a place like Glen Echo. He's a good superintendent and an excellent doctor—you know this. It's not fair to take that away from him because I was a fool."

"He put his trust in you, and you failed him," Samuel said coolly. "A captain goes down with his ship. A leader never deserts his men. Use any trite saying you like. The end result is that he misplaced his trust. He's paying for a lack of judgment. That seems deserved to me."

"Samuel, please!"

He sat heavily on the bed. The bottles and jars rolled into his hip as the mattress sagged beneath his weight. "I think we're at an impasse, don't you? I don't want to go back and neither do you. I'm sorry for your father, but whatever happened had nothing to do with me. I don't want to pay the price for it."

"You'd rather we fight one another constantly?"

"That's not necessary, Elena. We could each have what we want. All you have to do is say yes to what I'm offering."

I shook my head, my throat tight. "My parents . . ."

"You'd sacrifice your life for them?"

"Wouldn't you?" I asked. "For your parents?"

"No," he said bluntly. "Why should I? They've been ashamed of me since my affliction first showed its ugly head. My whole life has been one of secrets and lies. I wonder if you can imagine the burden of it?"

"I have some idea," I said. "These last two weeks, keeping it from everyone . . ."

"Imagine a lifetime of it. It would have been easier if I'd had a brother or sister, I think. Someone else to inherit, to give them grandchildren and ensure the Farber name is on Mrs. Astor's invitation list." He snorted. "They would rather that, you know. It frightens the hell out of them that I might pass this flaw to another generation, but they can't bear the thought of everything ending with me."

"Perhaps you won't," I said. "It might not be hereditary in your case. It can also be caused by—"

"Licentiousness. Yes, I know. Do you know how old I was when I had my first seizure?"

I shook my head.

"Ten. I hardly knew what my cock was for." He laughed at my shock over his vulgarity. "Please God, you *are* something. Nero was right about your blushing. Very pretty. Like a tea rose."

"Don't try to flatter me. It won't change my mind."

"A pity." He sighed and rubbed his brow. "God, I'm tired. I'm so tired. What I would give to sleep without nightmares . . ."

"The laudanum would only make your nightmares worse."

He looked at me hopefully. "I can think of something else that might help."

"What would that be?"

"Come to bed with me. Let me fuck you until we're both exhausted."

I backed up so violently I hit the wall.

He laughed wryly. "Well. It was only a suggestion."

"I am not . . . I would not . . . to say such things—" I broke off when I saw his gaze jerk past me, to the doorway. I looked over my shoulder. There was nothing there. When I looked at him again, his expression had changed. His eyes were almost black with fear, and something else too. As if he couldn't look away, as much as he might want to. As if he were compelled to stare.

It was a look that frightened me, because I did not see him in it. Which sounds absurd, I know, but that was what I felt. And then . . . cold. Icy cold surged into the room with such intensity my skin felt rimed with frost.

"Samuel," I whispered urgently. "Samuel."

He didn't move. Only stared. It was as if he were listening to something beyond us both. An indicator of another seizure, or another petit mal.

Or something else completely. *Dear God, what? What was this?* It was all I could do to touch his shoulder.

He jerked, and I started, yanking my hand back, hastening away, adrenalin rushing hot. He blinked, and then . . . then he was there again. The cold eased as suddenly as it had come. I could no longer see my breath. No more reflections, or tingling unease.

"Are you all right?" I asked.

He looked at me as if he didn't understand who I was or what I was doing there. Then, his vision cleared. He buried his face in his hands, a quiet moan of distress.

"What is it?" I asked. "What were you looking at? What did you see?"

"She was only in my dreams at first." His voice was so low and muffled I had to strain to hear it. "But now . . . now I see her everywhere."

"Who? Who do you see?"

"I think it's Laura Basilio."

Madame Basilio had said her daughter's ghost roamed the halls. What had she told Samuel in the days before I arrived? A man who had visions before his seizures, a man whose mind was so sensitive to other stimuli that it often turned on him, should never have been brought here.

But where else was I to take him? Back to New York? In this state? He was not close to stable. Everything would be over then, any hope of reward or redemption. Perhaps there was another place to go here in the city. Another palazzo, one not so dank and sinking, one where we could actually be comfortable. A healing place.

Yet that was impossible too. To be alone with him with no chaperone. I could hire no one to help without risking his secret. His epilepsy made him unpredictable. He was dangerous not only because he could be violent but because of how intimately he challenged me. Here, at least, there were people who could help if I needed it. Madame Basilio's presence made it all very respectable.

No, we couldn't leave. What then was I to do with this?

My father used to say that science could explain everything. I believed it was true. There must be a reasonable cause for what was happening to Samuel. All I must do was find it.

I went to the bed, pushing aside the medicine chest and the medicines, sitting beside him, a bottle between us, digging into my thigh. I put my hand on his arm, and when he looked at me, I said, "None of this is real, Samuel. I know it feels that way, but it isn't. It's only that you're so impressionable. It's not your fault. The disease makes you that way. As you know, the bromide can make you see things too. You must remind yourself that it's not real. None of it."

"You don't understand—"

"You've hallucinated before," I pointed out. "Your file says it. This isn't different, is it?"

The bleakness returned to his face. "It *is* different. These visions are more real than anything I've seen before." He twisted, grabbing my hand, his fingers digging into mine. "I'm afraid I'm going mad."

I struggled to hide my apprehension and fear. "No. It isn't that. You must have faith that it isn't."

"Elena—"

"There must be something I can try. Galvanism or . . . Papa spoke of magnetism. Perhaps a mesmerist."

He was silent, searching my face, his hand still holding mine so tightly it hurt.

"I'll find a way," I said. "I promise it."

He released my hand, looking at me now as if I were something foreign and surprising. "I wonder if I would have been a different man if I'd had someone like you."

His words surprised and saddened me, but I don't know what I would have said to him in response, because just then the sound of the door opening and closing echoed, along with rapid boot steps striding down the hall. A shadow rushing past my bedroom door and then stopping, turning back, and there was Nero Basilio in the doorway, his gaze sweeping me, the scattered medicines, Samuel rising, anchoring himself on the bedpost to ease his knee.

"I'm sorry," Mr. Basilio said, looking distressed. "I meant to be here earlier, but I was delayed. I hope I'm not too late. I'll apologize to my aunt on your behalf. Probably she's still waiting for you—"

"Tea's over," I said, rising, the strain of the last moments turning to irritation. I began collecting the medicines. "I went without you."

"You did?"

"No doubt it was better that way. I suppose you were planning on bringing Samuel some wine. Or perhaps something stronger? I'm so sorry to ruin your plans to ruin him."

Mr. Basilio looked uncertain.

Samuel said, "I've disappointed her. She's taking it out on you."

"*You* should have been here," I snapped, jabbing my finger at Nero Basilio, forgetting that I hadn't wanted him alone with Samuel, more annoyed than I should have been over his unkept promise. "You told me you would be."

"I'm sorry." Then, to Samuel, "*Santa Maria*, what did you do?"

"He tried to steal the laudanum," I said.

"That may have been the least of it." Samuel let out his breath, wavering, clutching the bedpost more tightly. "I think I should lie down."

"Yes, you should," I said.

"I'll help you," Mr. Basilio said.

I said nothing more as the two of them left the room. I focused on setting the medicines back into their case, everything fit just so, no room for deviation, and with every bottle and package put into its place, my distress eased a bit more, order restored. If only life were so easily arranged.

I half hoped that Mr. Basilio would stay with Samuel, even as I feared the vision Samuel had seen might turn into a seizure. I wanted a few moments to restore myself. But he returned before

I was ready, angling himself in the doorway, his arm bolstered on the frame above his head, hand dangling.

"You're upset with me," he said.

"I'm not," I lied. "I understand you might have had other things to do than play nursemaid."

"All I can say is that I tried."

"Who delayed you?" I heard myself saying. "I suppose Giulia had some pressing need for happiness?"

He lowered his arm. "I should not have told you that."

"You said you would be here. I had not expected you to take the promise so lightly."

He closed the door.

At its soft click, I spun from the bed. "What are you doing? Leave that open."

He held up his hands as if to ward me off. "I only meant to keep Samuel from hearing."

"From hearing *what*?"

He leaned back against the door and ignored my question. "What else did he do, other than try to steal laudanum?"

"Isn't that enough?" I put the last of the bottles in the case and closed the lid.

"There's something you're not saying. You're fluttering like a bird. He disturbed you in some way. I can see it."

"It's only that I'd thought I could trust him."

"He's desperate."

"As am I. Desperate to help him."

He crossed his arms over his chest and watched me as I shoved the case beneath the bed. "A good hiding place," he observed. "It might take him all of a minute to find it."

"I don't think he'll be trying it again," I said.

"Oh? Why not? What did you threaten him with?"

"My disappointment."

"A potent threat."

"I wish you would open the door. Anyone could note it."

"Anyone?" He raised a brow. "Giulia? Zuan? My aunt? Does what they think matter?"

"Perhaps not, but I—"

"How was tea?"

I sighed, surrendering. "Short, as you said."

"What stories of my bad behavior must I explain away?"

"None, as it happens. She wanted to know how Samuel was doing. I think. It was strange. She spoke of spirits. And your cousin. And then she asked me to leave."

"Why?"

"I don't know. We were talking of your cousin's death and she became upset."

His frown grew. "What did she say exactly?"

I sat on the edge of the bed, trying to remember. It seemed so long ago already, though it could not have been more than an hour. "I said I was certain your cousin was with God, and she said Laura was an angel, and then she told me to leave."

He pushed off from the door and came over, seating himself at the foot of the bed, a safe distance, clasping his hands between his knees. "She's always been odd when it comes to Laura. I think you shouldn't worry over it."

"I can't help it. She is hosting us."

"She's not. I am. And I say it doesn't matter."

"Well." I took a deep breath. "Your aunt is quite unsettling. I don't know if I like her. I know that's not very Christian of me."

"I don't like her either," he admitted with a smile. "So we can go to hell together. It's probably more interesting, anyway."

I couldn't help a small smile in return. "How blasphemous."

"I don't want you to be distressed. Laura died two years ago, and still Aunt Valeria keeps her room a shrine. I was surprised she put Samuel there."

"I suppose losing a child might do that to anyone."

"She was impossible before that. Laura spent half her life trying to escape her mother."

"It was Laura you were betrothed to."

"Yes. Another of my aunt's great disappointments, that I wasn't the godly man she hoped for her daughter. I think Laura didn't mind it. Which would you rather have, a tirelessly good and godly man? Or one with a touch of wickedness?"

"A godly man," I teased, because it was not what I knew he wanted me to say. "One for whom I can be a helpmate."

He grinned; it was infectious. "You break my heart. I'd wager I could change your mind on that score, but unfortunately, I promised my aunt I'd accompany her to mass. All those prayers for my soul, you know. But if you have need of me . . ."

"I'll call if Samuel becomes troublesome," I promised.

"Not really what I'd hoped for," he said. "But I'm happy to oblige. For that or . . . anything else you might think of."

His flirtation was a balm; I felt it soothe and caress. I lowered my eyes and said quietly, "I'm sure I don't know what you mean," and when he left with a light chuckle, I felt much better.

Chapter 14

The next morning, once I'd measured the bromide, I pushed the medicine case under the bed until it couldn't be seen. Mr. Basilio was right; it wouldn't stop Samuel if he decided to come after the laudanum again, but at least it was out of sight, and therefore I hoped not a temptation.

When I went to his bedroom to give him the bromide, he was curled beneath the blankets, sound asleep, and I mixed the medicine quietly and left the cup on his bedside table. I didn't want to disturb him, but I couldn't resist going to the balcony—soft steps, holding my skirts to keep them from swishing—to peek at what color the canal was today. A rather sickly yellow. Nothing to impress. Still, it astonished me to see the water change so completely, and I stood there for a moment, watching the dye tangle in the gentle current, before I left to get breakfast.

The air was cool and wet, the courtyard stones dark with moisture from a morning shower. Gray-tinged clouds floated languidly against a pale blue sky, darker ones hovering in the distance. The little boy I hadn't seen for several days now leaned against the wall outside the kitchen, looking bored. When he saw me, he tensed in alarm, but he didn't run off or leave his post, though he looked as if he wanted to.

I said, "Bonjour."

His eyes widened, fingers clenching. He ducked his head, muttering something.

I opened the kitchen door to warm air and the rich scent of roasting pork, something briny and fishy. Giulia and Zuan, along with the man I'd seen the other day—a Nardi brother, the boy's father—sat around the table with bowls of polenta and shrimp in some reddish sauce. They had been talking and laughing, but they stopped short the moment I stepped inside.

The bounty on the table was astonishing. *Not my concern*, I reminded myself. Samuel didn't care. But I couldn't help my surge of annoyance, not just because of the food, but because of Zuan's immediately lowered eyes and Giulia's glare that made me feel my intrusion acutely, though the Nardi brother stared at me with unabashed, and rather too ardent, interest.

I glanced away, and it was only then that I noticed Nerone Basilio standing in the corner. My heart gave a little jump—how had I not seen him immediately?

He said, "Good morning, Miss Spira," and I smiled a hello.

"I didn't mean to interrupt. I've just come to get some breakfast for Samuel."

Mr. Basilio motioned to the table. "Help yourself. In fact, I believe this is all for him."

I felt the gazes of the others, and I tried not to meet them as I stepped forward to see what was on the table that would be appropriate for Samuel. The Nardi brother said something, and Giulia snapped something back—obviously not complimentary—and the brother's gaze swept me with impudence. He ran his fingers over his mouth suggestively before he muttered something that made Giulia laugh and Zuan smirk.

Mr. Basilio set the cup he held on the table with an audible thud, speaking with a clipped, hard tone. Whatever he said wiped the insolence from the Nardi brother's face. Giulia's mouth tightened, and Zuan's chin dipped nearly into his chest.

Nero Basilio smiled grimly and said to me, "Would you like some coffee? I've made it, so at least it's palatable."

"*You* made it?"

"It was either learn how or be subjected to Giulia's," he said. "Which I believe you've tasted."

Giulia's dislike of me seemed to corrupt the very air. But with Mr. Basilio standing there, that slight smile on his lips—not grim now—I felt in no hurry to leave.

He said in a low voice, "Is he waiting for you?"

"He's not awake yet," I told him.

"So you've time to have a coffee with me?"

I hesitated. I remembered too well Samuel's warning. He would not be pleased. But Mr. Basilio's expression was so hopeful I could not disappoint him, and I found myself nodding and smiling. "Yes, but I don't have long."

That slight smile grew. He poured a cup of coffee and handed it to me, and then stole two sugar-dusted fritters from the table while the Nardis watched, and it was as if they'd disappeared, so well did he ignore them. He gestured me to the door, and we went out, but now the cool air felt good upon my skin. The little boy was still there, but his eyes lit when he saw Mr. Basilio, who gave him a small salute.

Nero Basilio's coat flapped about his legs as he led me into the courtyard, the coffee steam curling in a thin wisp above his cup and my own. "Have you been to the cupola yet?"

"The cupola?"

He glanced upward, and then I remembered the cupola on the roof settled among missing tiles. I shook my head, and he motioned for me to follow him up the stairs. I paused at the third floor, feeling guilty at the thought of Samuel waking to find me gone, remembering yesterday. I should *not* be leaving him alone, but Mr. Basilio said, "No, no, no, cara. No changing your mind," and I followed him up the last flight, very narrow and steep, the stones slick with moss as if it had been some time since they'd been used.

They ended at a slate walkway at the flat part of the roof that skirted the edge, the canal gurgling threateningly below, a dizzyingly long way down. Nero Basilio negotiated it as if he had done so a hundred times, without hesitation or pause, not seeming even to notice the drop, nor the loosened red tiles that skittered from the vibration of our steps. The slate walkway broadened into a kind of terrace surrounding the cupola. He pushed on one of the windowed doors, which didn't budge, not until he handed me his coffee to hold and braced his shoulder against it. It squealed open, making me wince as he shoved it far enough for us to enter. If Samuel had not yet been awake, he would be now.

Mr. Basilio stepped back to allow me to come in, apologetic as I handed him his coffee. "It's been years since I came up here, and I doubt Aunt Valeria has ever stepped foot in it."

When I was inside, he closed the door again, more squealing, sounding even louder than before. The cupola was bigger than it looked from the outside. All four sides were windowed, with fanlights styled as the rising sun symbol of the Basilios; three walls were lined with padded benches with cabinets beneath. The cushions had once been pale blue, but were now stained with mildew, stuffing spilling from where they'd been gnawed at by mice or rats, droppings scattered about the floor. There was a table in the middle of the room, a settee—water-or-piss-stained, again with gnawed-at cushions—against the other wall. It stank of wet and neglect and rodents.

"It's worse than I remember it," Mr. Basilio said with a grimace. "But it's worth it for the view."

He was right; the view was stunning. It was the one I'd longed for. Hard to believe only a single floor made such a difference. From the front, tiled roofs and campaniles reached against the expanse of the pied Venetian sky. On one side, in the distance, you could see the train station, the deep blue water beyond; on the other, tiled roofs and a misty blue horizon that must be the lagoon. I spun around, taking it all in, stopping short at the sight of the gothic brick and pilastered church across the canal, the whole of it now before me. Arched, mullioned windows, a domed campanile, a campo of stone in red and gray before it, and the water beyond, breathlessly lovely.

He came up behind me. I felt the warmth of his breath against my neck as he spoke. "The Madonna dell' Orto. Tintoretto's church. His paintings grace the altar. His tomb is there as well. I'll take you to see them sometime, if you like. If you can pull yourself away from your patient for an hour. It's only just across the bridge." He pointed to the left. "And over there the Sant' Alvise. Not so pretty from the outside, but inside . . ."

Oh, it was everything I'd hoped for. Tintoretto's church! "It's beautiful," I breathed. "If I'd known this was the view I would have been up here every day."

"You sound like my cousin. She would sit up here for hours when she was young. Reading. Staring. A daydreamer."

"It would be easy to get lost in daydreams here."

"It's not as old as the rest of the house," he said. "Quite new, in fact. They built it to watch the Austrian bombs during the Revolution."

"They came up here to watch *bombing*? Weren't they afraid?"

"Not until one of the bombs took out the wall," he said, disdainfully amused. "Then I understand that my grandfather forbade the women the view."

"But the men took the risk themselves."

"It was something Venice had never seen, and what Venetian doesn't love novelty?" He handed me a fritter, still warm from his hand. "Try it. Tomas is a fritterer by trade."

"Tomas?"

"Giulia and Zuan's older brother. The one who couldn't take his eyes from you."

"Oh." I remembered now; Zuan had mentioned his name before. I took the fritter, biting into it. Crisp outside, chewy inside, sugar clinging to my lips.

"He's married, but as I said, Venetians like novelty. I think he's never seen an American woman before."

"This is very good," I said, taking the last bite. "But if Tomas didn't come around again, I wouldn't mind it."

"You've nothing to worry about. He won't trouble you now."

"What did you say to him?"

"That you were my guest, and one to be treated with respect," he said.

"Giulia didn't like you defending me," I noted.

"I don't care about Giulia." He sat down. The cushion expelled dust and more stuffing. "Or my aunt. Or anyone in this place."

I sat down on a cushion against another wall, keeping a respectable distance. "Do you miss your cousin very much?"

He laughed. "Do you know what I like about Americans?"

"What?"

"How forthright they are. Just asking questions outright that are none of their business."

"I'm sorry—"

"No, that's not what I mean. I'm not offended. It's refreshing. Venetians are just as curious, but they'd never think of asking. They'd rather sneak about, spying, gossiping"—he made a sound of disparagement—"everything out of sight, so you can't grasp it. It's our history, you know. The Council of Ten, the *bocca di leone* for people to drop anonymous notes about their neighbors . . . no one in Venice actually tells you what they're thinking. Everyone lies constantly. You have to parse everything. But Americans . . . you wear your curiosity like a badge of pride. Samuel's like that too. It's why we've been friends for so long. He keeps no secrets. He always says exactly what he thinks."

I felt suddenly uncomfortable. I wondered what he would say if he knew exactly how big a secret Samuel and I kept. Nero Basilio seemed the kind of man who *could* keep a secret like that. It suddenly seemed absurd that Samuel had not told him.

But it wasn't my place to say anything. To resist temptation, I changed the subject. "You've nicely deflected my question, I notice. But I'll understand if you have no wish to answer it. You're right; it's none of my concern."

He set his cup on the table. "Yes, I miss her. She was everything to me. We'd been betrothed since we were children. The world is uncertain, but the fact that Laura would be my wife, that was something constant. Something I always knew waited for me. Nothing else might go as I wished, but there was always Laura." He sat back against the window. "There's a very wise saying: *I morti verze i oci ai vivi.* The dead open the eyes of the living. I didn't realize until she was gone just how much I took her for granted. I was out traveling the world, trying to make something of myself, while she became a pretty wrapped package awaiting my dispensation. I could go anywhere, while she must stay here, where the history of despair is in the very walls."

Trapped. I understood too well how she must have felt. "A history of despair. How poetic. And sad."

"It's the truth. My father inherited a ruined palazzo and nothing else. He sold every painting or pilaster he could, but he could not bring himself to touch the piano nobile. Not even to keep it from ruin. The worry that the noble house of Basilio might be reduced to one of *poverinos* . . . his pride couldn't bear it. It drove him to suicide. My mother drank herself into oblivion." He stopped suddenly, as if he'd surprised himself. "I never tell anyone those things. What are you, cara, a witch to pull my secrets from me?"

The marveling way he looked at me was exhilarating. "Not a witch, no, but it does seem to be a talent of mine. It used to happen with my father's patients all the time. He would send me in to talk to them when they were reluctant to say the truth of what ailed them. They would tell me anything." *And I would believe it.* "He said I had a calming presence."

"I don't think I would call it calming, exactly." His voice was bewitchingly soft and deep. "There's something about you that makes me wonder . . ."

"Wonder what?"

"Ah, perhaps nothing. In my heart, I'm too Venetian; I see mysteries and tragedy in everyone. I come from a long line of troubled souls. You should take care. This house is full of ghosts. Truthfully, I should have taken Laura away long ago. Perhaps she would still be alive if I had. But it never occurred to me. Not until it was too late. Then again, it would have required money, and as you see"— he spread his hands—"*Conte che non conta, non conta niente.*"

I recognized it. "A count who doesn't count, counts for nothing," I translated quietly. "Zuan said it too. I'm so sorry."

Nero Basilio shrugged again. "Every Venetian has a similar story. Hopelessness is in the air. Don't you feel it? It's almost as if God *wants* us to abandon the city. I'd like to accommodate him."

"Why don't you?"

"Lack of funds—what else? And obligation. This place is all that remains of the Basilio fortune. Do you see how proudly I hold it?" His tone dripped sarcasm. "I don't think I would care if it fell. It would be good to have all reminders of the past gone. All encumbrances."

"Yes," I agreed, thinking of my own encumbrances. "I understand that. The past can be a burden."

"Spoken as one who bears burdens of her own," he said. "How can it be so? You're so young—"

"Not young. Twenty-four."

"Ah then, let me guess: an engagement gone awry? A scandal?" His eyes twinkled when he said it, a tease. It was obvious he didn't believe it could be that. He could not possibly know how close he came. "Please tell me yes. I like scandalous women."

"That hardly surprises me," I said.

"I've told you my sad past. Now you must tell me yours."

"You've just said Americans are too forthright."

"I also said I liked it."

But there was too much I couldn't reveal, too much that was knotted with Samuel's secrets. I was uncertain what I could say that wouldn't lead to more questions, and so I kept it as simple as I could. "My past is not sad, nor very interesting, I'm afraid. My father trained me to work by his side. He could not leave his patients so precipitously when the Farbers asked him to tend to Samuel. So he sent me."

"And when you deliver Samuel to his bride, what then? You'll return to your parents? Or perhaps . . . to a lover?"

His question encompassed everything, didn't it? Everything I must do, the price I must pay if I could not bring Samuel to heel.

"You *do* have a lover," he said.

I forced myself to look at him. "I'm to have six months in Europe to spend as I will."

He raised a disbelieving brow. "A woman alone? What did you do, cara, to make them so eager to destroy you? I would no sooner send my sister abroad alone than I would drown myself."

"You don't have a sister, do you? And I won't be alone. I have a chaperone. My widowed French tutor. She's to meet me in Paris when this is all over. I'm so looking forward to it. I've never been *anywhere*, and I want so to see all the museums and the theater, and music and . . ." I trailed off, hearing the frantic yearning in my voice, realizing too late how much I revealed.

"Everything," he finished quietly.

"Yes. Yes. I want to see everything."

"And perhaps *do* everything." There was something in his voice that made me think of the book beneath my mattress, Samuel's words about the perfume of my desire. "Before you go back to New York City and marry whoever is waiting for you and live the quiet life you're destined for."

I started at his perception.

"It's not so hard to guess, cara. You're a pretty, well-bred woman. To not have someone waiting to marry you would be the surprise. And your longing to see the world before you're caged, that's obvious too. The only real surprise is that your betrothed would allow you such freedom."

"I'm hoping he won't *be* my betrothed in six months," I said quietly.

"I see. Does he know this?"

"It's not a love match."

"Just your parents wishing to find someone to take you off their hands?"

I nodded. Not quite true, but close enough.

"Perhaps I can be of some service to you then. I can show you all the best places."

It was appealing; too much so. "I told you, I have a chaperone. If I gave her up to go with you, it *would* ruin me."

He eyed me, a smile playing at his lips. "I have the idea that ruin is your intention, Miss Spira."

"*Knowledge* is my intention," I said firmly.

The smile grew. "As you say. I wonder if they're not the same thing."

"I cannot allow them to be." How prim I sounded. Priggish even. I wished I hadn't said it, and I waited for him to mock me, but he only laughed, and it was so charming, so irresistible, and suddenly I was remembering Samuel's words about broken hearts and my naïveté, and . . . and . . . *Samuel*.

I had forgotten about him completely.

I gasped. "I've been away too long. I must be getting back."

"And just when things were getting interesting." Mr. Basilio rose languidly. "Very well, as you wish. Though I don't think Samuel deserves such dedication."

I went to the door, nearly trembling in my haste, pulling at the handle. The door did not budge.

"Perhaps we're locked in. That happened to Laura and me once."

When I turned to look at him, his expression was wistful, tender with memory. He stared out at the roofs checkerboarding the view before us. From somewhere I heard the coo of doves, and it seemed to mirror his mood, which had been teasing only moments before. How quickly he'd changed. His expression pulled at my heart.

"We were here for hours before someone found us," he went on. "You know, you remind me of her, Miss Spira."

"No doubt because we have the same color hair," I said, tugging again at the door.

He looked bemused. "How do you know that?"

"Samuel told me."

"He mentioned the color of her hair?"

I jerked harder at the door. "This won't open at all."

He seemed confused, uncertain.

"Please, Mr. Basilio," I said.

He blinked, obviously shaking away his thoughts. "It's only stuck." He came up beside me, his hand on mine, curling around my fingers so I was trapped between him and the handle. I felt the heat of him at my back. "Last chance. Are you quite certain you wish to return to your patient? Or would you rather stay here and see if there isn't some kind of *knowledge* to be found?"

I didn't know whether to be tempted or afraid. Nervously, I shook my head, thinking of Samuel, of what I could not afford to lose. "Please," I managed.

Nero Basilio's sigh sent a loosened strand of my hair bouncing against my ear. "Very well." I felt the flexing in his chest and arm as he pulled the door. It didn't budge, didn't budge, and then, suddenly it did, so quickly that I stumbled back, fully into him. He caught me, a settling hand on my shoulder, and I stepped away, skin tingling, and suddenly I wished that I had said *yes, let's stay. Let's see what there is to discover* . . . oh, how stupidly dangerous.

The door screamed as he dragged it fully opened. I stepped out, moving quickly to retrace our steps.

"Not so fast. Some of those tiles are loose."

I stopped short, though it was all I could do not to run. He came up beside me, moving past me. "Follow me," he said, and together we went down the stairs.

He left me at the third floor. "Ciao, cara." At the bottom of the next flight, he paused, looking up at me with a grin that turned into an exaggerated grimace before he opened the door. I could not help but laugh.

When he was gone, I opened my own door. I stepped inside and heard a noise, a shuffling, and there was Samuel, coming around the corner of the doorway of the sala, bracing himself on the frame. He took one look at me, and I knew that he'd heard us in the cupola. He knew exactly where I'd been, and when he turned away in disappointment, I hurried after him.

Chapter 15

"I'm sorry I wasn't here when you woke," I said, following him into the sala.

"It was you who woke me," he said, which of course I'd known. "What were you doing up there with him?"

"He wanted to show me the view."

"No doubt."

"That *was* what he wanted," I insisted. "He's proud of it, even as he says he'd like it all to fall into the lagoon."

"He can thank his aunt that it hasn't," Samuel said wearily.

"I don't think he's very grateful."

"No, he wouldn't be." Samuel snorted, and then, at my questioning look, "She's his burden and his curse."

"She doesn't like him. I thought I was imagining it, but—"

"I don't think you are. Nero's spoken of it before. He thinks she resents him because she's so beholden to him. Nero's father made him promise to take care of her. She was always a bit fragile, I take it."

"Fragile?" I laughed in disbelief. "She's like steel."

"Yes, well, perhaps that is the fragility. In any case, Nero's father also made him promise to keep the art on the piano nobile intact."

I remembered Mr. Basilio telling me how his father feared their noble name sinking into poverty, and how it had led to suicide. I remembered the flaking gilding, diseased muses. "What has that to do with his aunt?"

"The place is falling apart, but Nero can't fix anything, because there isn't the money. To get the money, he'd have to sell something, which he promised his father he'd never do. You see the dilemma? But it seems that, over these last few years, Madame Basilio's been selling off pieces. A canvas here, a fresco there. If she hadn't done it, the whole palazzo would be crumbling worse than it is about our ears. They would have starved to death. Nero's angry with her for making him break his promise, and I think he's heartbroken too. She's angry at him for . . . too many things. I don't know them all. They're bound together in ways they can't get free of, which always makes for trouble."

"Laura's accident must have made it all so much worse," I said.

Samuel stiffened and glanced away, a little too quickly, as if he meant to hide something.

"What is it?" I asked.

"Nothing." He looked at me again, and I noticed the deep lavender shadows beneath his eyes, his pallor that only made the scars on his face more evident. His hair was lank and tangled, unbrushed. I remembered what he'd told me about his dreams trespassing into his waking hours. I remembered my own resolution to help him.

"Did you have nightmares again last night?" I asked.

"They never leave me," he said.

I said firmly, "Meet me in your bedroom."

"Oh? That sounds promising. Have you been reading? Do you mean to take me up on my offer?"

I must learn to control my blushing. "Liniment. I think you're ready for it."

"So you intend for me to be in excruciating pain."

"I hope not excruciating."

Samuel sighed, and I went to my room and gathered the things I needed. When I returned, he stripped off his coat and shirt and flannel vest to reveal the edge of the bruise still lingering on his hip, lying on his stomach on the bed. I rubbed in the burning liniment down either side of his spine. I had gloves on, so I couldn't feel his skin, but I was acutely aware that he was lean and powerful, and I felt his every gasp, every twitch of his muscle, every dip and valley in his spine. I tried not to think of how it had felt to be trapped in his embrace.

Suddenly I was freezing. Icy fingers touched my neck where it was bared above the collar of my gown and below my chignon. His skin turned blue, then white beneath the pink irritation of the liniment. He was a statue carved from ice beneath my hands, hard and slippery and cold even through the fabric of my gloves. I shivered, drawing away, confused and disoriented, my breath only frost. He was no statue, but a man trapped in ice. Dying, freezing—*No, not dying. Not ice.* I stared at him, blinking, trying to right my vision— for a moment my imagination had been so vivid—until he turned his head and said, "Are you finished?"

Whatever daydream I'd slipped into slipped away. Madame Basilio's words about ghosts manifesting in cold breezes taunted. I didn't believe it, of course, but I couldn't help shivering. The smell of the liniment was dizzying, nauseating. Pungent and piney, sharp and peppery, nearly wiping away the constant, acrid scent of the dyer's canal. And beneath it all . . . Laura's scent, that haunting perfume that clung to everything in this room.

I covered him with a blanket and told him to stay still for a time, then left him to put everything away. The vision of him dying in ice had shaken me, the wintry kiss on my neck, that plunging cold . . . I needed a breath of fresh air to clear the stink of the liniment from my head. I needed a moment to gather my thoughts. I went to the sala. The sun had beaten back the clouds of morning, though a line of heavy gray still threatened in the distance. Sunlight shone brightly through the balcony doors, slanting in glowing panes across the floor, sending rippling, dancing shadows and reflections over the ceiling, so it looked in constant motion. But as beautiful as it was, it did nothing to alleviate the uncomfortable, moist chill that breathed from stone and plaster. I unlatched the balcony door, which was nearly as swollen into its frame as that of the cupola. It had to be dragged open. I opened it only enough to ease out onto the stone balcony.

The breeze was cold and laced with the scents of salt and wet stone and the tannic stink of the dyer, along with something rotten. My gaze felt dragged to the canal below. For a moment, I suffered that nauseating rush. The canal was choppy and dark, bobbing with bits of fast-moving flotsam, at one point a broken crate and several drowning, dancing lemons following it like ducklings. Something that looked like a shirt, bloused by the water and the breeze, lost laundry tumbling in the current. A dark, furry dead thing that made me wince.

The glancing of the sun off the white stones of the palazzo across was almost blinding. I gripped the balustrade, the chill of it radiating into the fine bones of my hands as I leaned over. The narrow walk below was hidden by the balcony of the second floor, the railing of which was just visible. From this vantage point, I could not see onto the balcony at all. The water of the canal rippled and sparked, sun glinting on shadow, deeply blue. I found myself mesmerized by it, entranced, staring at the currents and the constantly changing surface, the sun piercing the depths fleetingly and then withdrawing, leaving it mysterious again. So beguiling, beckoning, singing *Come to me. Come and let me take you.* Cajoling. *Come to me now.* I knew this song, and how to answer it. All I must do was lean out just a little bit, like this, loosening my grip, a bit more, off balance, and I would fall into air, into water, plunging below, deep and deep and deep, until all light was gone, all air, nothing but darkness, and it was where I should be, where I wanted to be, to drown, to sleep, all mistakes forgotten, nothing to redeem or remake, oh, how peaceful, how perfect and right, impossible to resist.

A seagull dipped and cawed, so close and loud that I started, feeling as if I'd awakened from a dream. I was on my tiptoes, at the edge of my balance. I clutched the balustrade, and jerked back, disconcerted at the too familiar turn of my thoughts, the past mixing with the present. I stepped to the middle of the balcony, safe again, shaken by memory—my hand on a window latch, snow shining like diamonds, the song in my head. I thought of Laura Basilio falling just as I almost had. What had she been thinking as she leaned to look at water churning a Venetian scarlet? Wrapped and waiting like a pretty package, her life closing in, doors slamming shut, no other choices. But no, that was me. She had only slipped. It had been an accident.

I shuddered and hurried back inside.

I did not go back to Samuel. I went to my room and busied myself emptying the medicines from the case and then putting them back in their careful order, concentrating on the puzzle of it until my mind had settled, and I could put those thoughts back into their own boxes and shut them tightly away.

That night, I was sound asleep when the light woke me. A sudden blaze, blinding and painful, inches from my face. I cried out, covering my eyes with my hand. When I lowered my hand, I saw it was a lamp turned very high, and behind it stood Samuel Farber, bare chested, barefoot, his shaggy hair falling into his face.

I sat up, pulling the blankets with me to cover my nightgown. "Samuel?"

He blinked and stepped back, but his gaze was blank, he was not there. Sleepwalking again, but he'd always kept to his own room before. I didn't like that he'd found his way to mine. Giulia's warning to lock my door returned, bringing with it a twinge of panic.

I swallowed my fear and got out of bed slowly, and cautiously, not wishing to alarm him, remembering the seizure that had overtaken him when he'd awakened the last time. As soothingly as I could, I said, "You're dreaming. Come, let's get you back to your room."

He stared down at his hand, opening it, flexing it, as if he'd expected to find something there and was surprised that it was empty. "I don't want to," he said in an anguished whisper, not to me, but to someone in his dream.

Gently, I took the lamp from him, my hand at his back, guiding him to the door. "It's all right. Just a dream."

I maneuvered him into the hall. The lamplight bounced over the floors, clambered up the walls in swinging reflections, making the cracks in the plaster look wide and gaping and the long, curling shadows of peeling wallpaper drip eerily. "You'll feel better when you're back in bed."

We were nearly to his door. He stopped short, jerking back. "No."

"*Shhh*. It's all right."

His eyes were wild, but he wasn't looking at me. He was staring at the open door of his bedroom. "No. No! I won't do it!"

"Samuel—"

He wrenched away from me, spinning around, tearing back toward the sala, disappearing around the corner before I knew what he was about. I had not thought he could move so quickly, not with that knee, even in a dream state.

I hurried after him into the sala, the lamplight careening crazily over the walls. The moon was setting, its fading light chased by clouds. Samuel looked like a ghost where he stood at the windowed doors, his skin glowing palely, his hair disappearing into darkness. His breath pulsed in puffs of frost, as did mine. The floor was a sheet of ice beneath my bare feet. *"A whisper in your ear . . . a cold breeze where there should be none . . ."*

I pushed the thought away. Madame Basilio's inanities.

"Samuel," I said, stepping up beside him. "It's time to go back to bed now."

He stared blindly out the window. He didn't seem to hear me.

I touched his arm. "Come along now."

He turned on me suddenly, grabbing my arms. I dropped the lamp. It crashed to the floor, shattering, shards of glass everywhere, oil scattering, little flames across the stone. Samuel propelled me backward, slipping through the oil. Tiny bits of glass stabbed into my feet. I cried out in pain, "Samuel, please!"

But he didn't release me. He pushed me against the wall. His gaze searched my face; I didn't know what he was looking for, but it wasn't me he saw. He was still in his dream, and he was so close his clouded breath was warm and moist on my face, his mouth inches from mine. If I had not been afraid before, I was now. More so when he brought up his hand, when his fingers lit upon the pulse beat in my throat, a soft, soft touch.

I froze. He smiled, but it was cruel, nothing to reassure. "How fast your little heart is beating," he said, and there was mockery in his tone, a nasty edge. *"Corexin de conejo."*

It was not his voice, and yet it was.

He said, very softly, *"Mé viscara,"* and then words I could not distinguish; I felt only the malice in his intention.

He gripped my shoulders, pulling me toward him, then slamming me back against the wall. Little bits of plaster crumbled over my shoulders.

"Samuel," I gasped, no longer trying to wake him slowly, no longer caring about anything but getting free. His grip was so tight, he was so much stronger than he should be. "Samuel, wake up! Wake up!"

He was deaf to me, pushing, shoving, the wall a barrier he could not budge. I don't think he even saw it. I don't know what he thought he was doing. And his eyes, what I saw in them terrified me. Ill will, aggression. Anger.

"Let me go!"

I saw behind him a flash of white, the shroud I'd seen before. Stars burst before my eyes, tangling in Samuel's hair, in the air all around him, scattering as he slammed me back again.

I couldn't breathe. The air had been sucked away. I was suffocating, and the stars were dancing all around, so beautiful and terrible, spinning and twirling in a mesmerizing rhythm set to the drum of my racing little heart.

Chapter 16

"What the hell?"

The voice came from the doorway. The stars blinked away; my vision cleared in time to see Nero Basilio slide to a stop. He took in the flames across the floor, the glitter of glass, Samuel and me.

I tried to cry for help, but Samuel slammed me into the wall again. Mr. Basilio raced across the room, launching himself at Samuel. I was caught between them, unable to get free, my nightgown tangling around my legs and Samuel's, their arms locked about me.

Basilio grunted, Samuel pulled back to hit him, and I grabbed his arm to stop him, throwing him off balance. His weak knee buckled; we all went tumbling to the floor, a knot of arms and legs.

The fall seemed to release Samuel from his dream. He stilled, and then shook his head as if to clear it, blinking, frowning. "What?"

I was lodged firmly between them, the warm solidity of Nero Basilio at my back, my hands pressed to Samuel's bare chest. I tried to sit up, but my nightgown was caught beneath Samuel's legs, and I couldn't move.

"How familiar," Mr. Basilio said drolly. "Except I believe the last time we were so entangled, you weren't trying to kill the lady involved."

"I was what?" Samuel moved now, freeing my nightclothes as he sat up.

I scrambled away. "You were sleepwalking."

The tiny fires of the shattered lamp were flickering out, one after another, as they consumed their drops of oil. "I was sleepwalking and I . . . I tried to kill you?" Samuel slid back until he sat against the wall. He looked terrified and confused and so bleak that I forgot how frightened I'd been only moments before.

"You came to my room," I told him. "You said something about not wanting to do something? I don't know what exactly. I was taking you back to the bedroom when you bolted. Do you remember any of it? Any of what you were dreaming?"

He looked away at the question, but I felt the tension that came over him. "No."

I thought he lied. But then, perhaps it was better not to question him now, not with Nero Basilio here to witness anything he might say.

Mr. Basilio sat up. His feet were bare. He was in his shirtsleeves, the placket unbuttoned as if he'd thrown it on hastily, untucked and hanging to his trousered thighs. "I heard a crash. The lamp, I suppose. When you do something, you do it well, my friend."

One of my feet began to hurt. I reached down to feel, my fingers slipping through either blood or oil—probably both—brushing away prickling shards of glass, nothing large, but it smarted enough that I knew I'd been cut. I thought I should ask Samuel if he was hurt. I thought I should check his feet. But I was reluctant to touch him, even though he was obviously himself again.

Samuel buried his face in his knees. "Christ. I am a madman."

I threw a quick glance at Nero Basilio. "No, you were—"

"You certainly looked to be," he said.

"—sleepwalking," I finished.

"That excuses nothing," Samuel said.

"For once, I agree with him. When I came up here he was trying to pound you into sausage." Mr. Basilio rose, offering me a hand, hauling me to my feet. My cut foot stung. I pulled away and braced my hand against the wall. "Has this happened before?"

"His head injuries. And the medicine sometimes has this effect," I said. It was both the truth and a lie. The bromide and epilepsy could cause visions. But what I'd seen in his eyes was like nothing I'd seen before.

"Medicine? What kind of medicine would do this?" Mr. Basilio asked.

"It takes weeks to stabilize."

"Weeks where he's trying to throw you off a bed or through a wall? There must be something else. Something that doesn't cause him to sleepwalk, or to hurt you."

"Laudanum?" Samuel suggested hopefully from his place on the floor.

"No. And I'm all right now. I'm used to such things."

Mr. Basilio looked horrified. "*Used* to such things? How could that be?"

I cursed myself inwardly at my carelessness. *Yes, by all means tell him about all your epileptic patients at the asylum.*

"You should leave, Elena," Samuel said softly. "I've told you before. I'm not fit for—"

Firmly, I said, "I'm not leaving. There's no point in discussing it."

Samuel said, "I promise I'll do what I can to . . . to help you."

I was aware of how intently Nero Basilio was listening. Samuel Farber was ostensibly healing from a beating and being readied for a wedding he didn't wish to attend, and that was all. But Basilio must hear the deeper currents of what was being said. All I could hope was that my comment about the medicine's side effects would stop him from asking questions I couldn't answer.

"I find I must agree with Samuel," he said. "He meant to hurt you."

"He didn't know what he was doing," I said, and though I believed that, it didn't make anything better. I had seen the menace in his eyes. I'd heard it in his words. I'd felt his hostility, that same hostility I'd felt before, I remembered. That evening in his bedroom, as he'd stared at whatever vision assailed him.

And then I felt a deeper fear. Nightmares moving into his waking hours, he'd said. Visions. *Caused by the medicine*, I told myself.

Or ghosts.

Or madness.

I didn't want to follow either thought. The first was just ridiculous. Had Madame Basilio not said it—a woman still deeply grieving her daughter—it would never have occurred to me. But the second . . . empty eyes and restraints and men who shouted at things that were not there. Those at Glen Echo who had been beyond hope. Beyond help. Keeping them quiet and placid was the most anyone could do.

"That makes it even worse," Mr. Basilio said. "Tell me you weren't afraid just now."

I insisted—as much for myself as for him—"Once the medication is stable—"

Samuel laughed bitterly. "It won't matter."

"It helped before," I said before I thought.

"*Before?*" Basilio's voice was sharp.

Another misstep. I didn't know how to explain. I was too rattled to come up with a lie. "I have to sit down."

"You're hurt," Mr. Basilio said.

Samuel's head jerked around. "Are you? How badly?"

"My foot," I said. "The glass. It's nothing, I'm sure."

Nero Basilio was at my side in a moment, taking my arm to help me to the settee, skirting the scattered glass and oil. "Is there another lamp?" he asked.

"Hanging near the doorway."

He released me to the settee and went to get the lamp, the flame flaring to life, gilding the planes of his face as he brought it over. He set it on the floor at my feet, kneeling beside me, taking up my foot in a gentle grip. He leaned close, one hand moving up my ankle to hold my foot steady, his curls brushing my bare calf as he looked for wounds. I struggled to keep from jerking away. His touch seemed far too intimate. Even more intimate than Samuel's kiss, though how that could be, I didn't know.

"Not that one," I said, and he set my foot down carefully and picked up the other, sliding his fingers over my heel, the arch of my foot.

"It's not bad. Not deep, though you're bleeding like a stuck pig. Have you any bandages?"

"There's a roll in my medicine case."

"Fetch it, will you, Samuel?" he asked. "Unless you're unable to stand."

The laudanum. The morphine. Samuel had already proven himself untrustworthy. "No," I said. "No, it's fine. I can do it myself. If you've a handkerchief or something to stop the blood . . ."

Basilio frowned, a questioning look, and then I saw him remember why I objected, what Samuel had done. He reached into his pocket, pulling out a handkerchief and wrapping it around the wound, tying a small knot to keep it in place. When he was finished, his hand slid down my calf, a bit too lingering.

I drew my foot away with a shiver. I could breathe again, though my heart pounded. *How fast your little heart is beating.* "Thank you."

He sat back on his heels, glancing at Samuel. "You shouldn't be alone with him."

"You aren't the only one who thinks it," Samuel said.

I said, "I won't have Giulia here, and she forbids Zuan to help me."

"In that, she's right," Basilio said. "Zuan is useless. He'd only stare at his feet and mumble while Samuel was beating your head against a wall."

Samuel made a sound of defeat.

Basilio's lips thinned, a moment of hesitation and then, "I'll move my things up here."

In sudden panic, I said, "Mr. Basilio, you cannot possibly—"

"Why not?" he asked reasonably. "Samuel's my friend. I'm the one who sent him here. And please, I'd prefer it if you would call me Nero. I've seen you now in your nightgown, after all."

"Nero," I said uncomfortably, too intimate again. I crossed my arms over my breasts and saw his tiny smile at it. "Surely you must see that it would be completely inappropriate. I . . . I cannot be here alone with you and . . . and only an ill man to chaperone . . ."

"She's right," Samuel said. "You'd only compromise her."

"Ah, I see. You want her to yourself. To kiss and bash about without interference."

Samuel glared at him. "Don't be ridiculous. I'd prefer it if she would leave me completely."

"But as she won't, she needs protection."

"Is protection all you're offering?"

"Would I be getting in the way of your plans?" Nero asked nastily. "Or did you mean to do a little seducing before you beat her insensible?"

"Please," I said quickly. "Enough of this. I'm sorry, Mr.—Nero, but it won't do. There's no place to put you even so."

"I can have a bed hauled up here quickly enough," he said. "Zuan's good for that, at least. I ask you to think about how my aunt and I would suffer if something happened to you here. Let me make certain it doesn't."

"Perhaps you could sedate me," Samuel suggested. "That would make it easy for all of us."

"No," I said, though just now it did not seem a bad idea.

Samuel took a deep breath. Dawn light eased the darkness, making visible his pain as he slowly stood, sliding up the wall for support, testing his knee before he put weight on it, grimacing when he did. "I'm going back to bed, if you don't mind. Discuss it without me if you like. Just know that I agree with Nero that you need protection from me, and I agree with you that it shouldn't be him."

He staggered from the room, waving me off when I started to rise to help him.

When he was gone, Nero said, "I'd feel better if you'd let me help."

"He was dreaming. The medicine makes such dreams more . . . intense."

"Why would you continue it? It makes him a danger."

"I know what I'm doing. Truly."

It wasn't true. I was anything but certain. Samuel had frightened me badly, and I wanted someone here to help me. To save me if I needed saving. The burden of my task seemed unbearable suddenly. What was I doing here? How had I agreed to this? How could I possibly fulfill the bargain I'd made? No one had known Samuel Farber was this ill, had they? My father had not known it. He would never have sent me otherwise.

I was so caught in my agitation that it was a moment before I realized Nero was quiet. He had drawn up his knees, folding his arms across them, and his head was bowed so I couldn't see his face.

"I should go to bed." I grasped the armrest and rose, favoring my foot.

When I stumbled, he was on his feet, gripping my arm. "Let me at least help you to your room."

I didn't refuse him. The pain was not so much, but I wasn't ready to be alone. There was no help for it, of course, and once we were back in my bedroom, I drew away. "Thank you. For everything tonight."

"Why are you really staying, Elena?"

My heart stuttered at the sound of my name on his lips. "What?"

"There's something more here, isn't there? You're staying when he's hurt you. No one would do that unless they had to. Or unless . . . are you in love with him?"

I was so surprised at the question I could only gape at him.

"Are you?" he asked again.

"No. No, of course I'm not. You've mistaken it. You've mistaken everything."

"Oh?" He was intent, insistent. "This isn't just about the beating he took in Rome, is it? What's really wrong with him?"

I struggled to calm my growing panic. "He's—" I foundered, searching for a suitable excuse—"he abuses himself with alcohol and . . . and opium. I'm trying to break him of the habit. Of . . . debauchery. That's what the medicine is really for."

I felt him measuring, weighing. I didn't know if he believed me, but finally, he nodded. "Will you at least do me a favor and lock your door tonight?"

I tried to hide my relief. "Yes. Yes, of course."

"Then good-night." That courtly half bow. I had the feeling he'd learned it as a child and it was so rote he hardly realized he was doing it. He backed away from the door, leaving me. I heard the patter of his bare feet down the hall, and I stood there listening until the stairway door opened and closed, and he was gone.

I locked the door, as he'd asked. My head was throbbing now, both from tension and the release of fear. The white sheets of my bed gleamed. I stumbled to it, relieved and exhausted. But then I only lay there, staring into the darkness, my fears chasing themselves. Samuel's distant, dangerous eyes. Nightmares and visions.

A madman. A beast.

What really was wrong with Samuel Farber?

Suddenly, the key in the lock did not seem protection enough, and I wished I had not asked Nero Basilio to go.

Chapter 17

I watched the dawn grow into morning and listened to the sounds in the courtyard, the dragging creak of the pail at the well, Zuan calling to someone to fetch coal, the clang of metal on stone, gurgling water, a splash. Church bells, the ones from the Madonna dell' Orto across the canal loud, along with others more distant—perhaps those from the other church Nero had pointed out, the Sant' Alvise. A veritable chorus of bells, all with their different tones, blending and weaving, separating to echo among the stones, some lingering, others fading quickly. Someone laughing, muffled and misty. I thought of Laura Basilio with algae in her hair, stuck in a cupola with her teasing cousin, watching rainbows in the water. Samuel's black eyes as he whispered, "*How fast your little heart is beating.*"

I was still weary as I finally roused myself, washing and dressing slowly. The cut on my foot smarted, but it was small and not bleeding as I rewrapped it, and it didn't bother me to walk on it. Once that was done, I sat aimlessly, reluctant to see my patient. I no longer trusted myself to know madness from sanity. I'd been wrong before, and Samuel's visions and nightmares could be explained—couldn't they? They were more intense than I would have expected, but still manageable. I told myself that last night was the worst it would get.

And so, finally, I made myself go to him.

The balcony door was open, and he stood staring down into the canal. I went to stand beside him, following his gaze down three stories to the narrow strip of water, which was bright green, fantastical and looking even more so in the clear, bright light. The sky was intensely blue, no clouds today, and the colors of the buildings were vibrant, every streak of rust and mildew in high contrast, shimmering silver salt stains the only evidence of a morning fog.

I touched his arm, not liking him there, where it was too easy to jump, to fall as she had. "Come inside."

He let me bring him into the room, watching as I closed the windowed door.

"I remember some of it," he said softly, though I had not asked a question. "My dream, I mean. There's an angel . . . I can't really see her. She's . . . just light."

"*He's speaking to an angel,*" Madame Basilio had said. I wanted to strangle her. All her talk of ghosts and angels—it affected even me, and I did not have Samuel's troubled, impressionable brain.

"She shows me things," he went on.

"What things?"

He was quiet for a long moment. "Sad things. A woman I don't know drinking herself into a stupor. A man putting a pistol to his temple."

The words burst from my mouth before I knew I was thinking them. "Nero's family."

Samuel gave me a puzzled look.

"Nero said that his father committed suicide, and his mother drank. Who else could it be? This house is so full of sadness. It feels as if it's always . . . watching. As if it wants to pull you in."

He turned to me quickly, hopefully. "Yes, you understand. It *is* this house. It's putting things in my head. It's making me see things."

"I only meant that it's depressing. These aren't hallucinations, they're memories. Nero told you how his parents died, and you're imagining the scenes."

"No, I"—he put a hand to his head in frustration—"No. I don't remember that. I never knew any of that. Only that they died."

"You've known each other for years. Don't you think it possible that one drunken night he told you, and neither of you remember? That's the only rational explanation for what you're seeing, Samuel. Things don't just appear out of nowhere."

"They do for me. All the time. Out of nothing."

"Because of the epilepsy," I said.

"Yes," he agreed with a sigh. "Buildings and people that rise from thin air. Ground dissolving before my feet. Trees turning into ladders. Roads disappearing into grass. I know they're not real, but they *are*. They *feel* real. You tell me: How can I trust anything? How can I believe in anything?" His voice was so soft I had to strain to hear it. "I've always hallucinated, but it's only come with seizures before. But now . . . now I'm seeing things all the time. I don't know what to think. I'm afraid."

"You're seeing things all the time," I repeated. "When did that start happening? Was it before you came here?"

"No," he said. "I see that woman drinking and falling unconscious. I hear her neck break. And the man . . . the crack of the shot, the cloud of powder . . . there's blood on the walls—"

"Oh, Samuel."

"I see them drag Laura from the canal. She leaves puddles on the floor where she walks. It's so cold I wonder why they don't turn into ice."

"It might be that the bromide dose is too strong. I'll lessen it."

"It's not the medicine, Elena. You know it. The bromide's never had this effect on me before. It's made me sleepy and . . . it's sometimes made the visions more vivid. But it's never done this." He turned to me, again with that bleak gaze, the fear within it. "I was sleepwalking last night, as you say. I was in a dream, and in it, the angel wanted me to hurt you and then . . . then I wanted that too. I wanted to push you over . . ." he trailed off as if he couldn't bear to say the words.

Carefully, I said, "Push me over what?"

"I don't know. I only knew that I wanted you to fall. This is why you should sedate me, Elena. There's something wrong with me. It's never been this bad. I'm *becoming* my visions. I think I'm going mad."

"No," I said, because I didn't know what else to say. My worst fears realized, everything falling from my grasp. "I won't believe it. Together we can—"

"Don't be a fool! Don't you understand? I'm *afraid*. Every time I touch you"—his fists clenched—"I hear—Christ, I don't even know. That cursed angel? Or maybe a demon. Whatever she is, I can't make myself believe she's not real when her voice is in my head. She's angry with you, and I'm afraid of what I'll do about that. Is that madness enough for you? Or would you like me to be more specific?"

"No." I was backing away without realizing it. "No, that's quite enough."

He half turned, watching me, his eyes dark and intent. "You're running away. Good. You should run. Tell your father you couldn't save me. Tell my parents I won't come home to terrorize a woman whose only misfortune was to have the right name."

"I'm not running away," I said, though I was still moving to the door. He was not seeing visions now, not sleepwalking, and his words were more frightening for that.

He made a bitten-off sound—discouraged, hopeless, amused . . . I could not tell which.

I needed time to think. Time to decide what to do. I was at the door. I said, "I'll draw your cold bath."

"Wonderful," he said. "Bring it to me naked. I want to see if your body is as lush as I imagine it."

His crudity fell between us like a stone. I fled without thought to the only safety I knew.

I was outside and halfway down the stairs before I realized where I was going, but I didn't stop. When I reached the landing of the second floor, I rapped loudly on the door. It wasn't until then that my panic eased enough to hear what I hadn't before: shouting from inside, gone suddenly silent.

But then Giulia opened the door, and it was too late to retreat, not that I truly wanted to. Where would I go?

"What do you want?" she asked in blunt and almost accusatory French. To say *Go away, you are unwelcome* would have been to soften it.

"I'd hoped . . . is Mr. Basilio in?"

I knew he was. It was his voice I'd heard shouting, along with Madame Basilio's, and not only that, I heard him now in one of the rooms beyond, speaking rapidly and insistently in Venetian, voice lowered but still touched with anger.

I remembered what Samuel had told me about Nero's relationship with his aunt, and I stepped back. "Never mind. If you could just let him know I called . . ."

"Do not leave," Giulia said. "I am certain he would wish to see you." That look of hers, slightly amused—or, no, as if she anticipated my discomfort—could mean nothing good. When I hesitated, she motioned for me to step inside, saying "Please, mamzelle," and so, warily, I did, following her down the length of the hall. Nero and his aunt were still arguing.

"Truly, I don't wish to interrupt."

She ignored me. We were at the entrance to the sala. She announced, loudly, "Mademoiselle Spira."

The talk stopped dead. Nero and his aunt stood facing one another, each bristling, on either side of the settee. Nero's expression was dark with anger. When he saw me, his hands, raised in gesticulation, fell to his sides. Madame Basilio twisted to look over her shoulder, her eyes narrowed, back stiffly straight. The silence was explosive.

I could not have felt more uncomfortable.

"Pardon me," I said, turning around before I'd finished the words. "I don't wish to interrupt. I'll go—"

"No!" Nero said, too loud, and then, more quietly, "No. You're not interrupting. We were just finished." He dodged around the settee as he spoke, crossing the room to me. "What is it? What happened? Did he hurt you?"

That he'd seen something was wrong even through his own anger made me forget my discomfort. His concerned sympathy made me glad I'd sought him out.

"No." I shook my head. "No, I'm just . . . forgive me. I shouldn't have come, but I thought . . ."

"You thought what?"

I tried to smile. It wobbled into place and fell again. "Nothing. I just needed to escape for a moment. I'll go back upstairs."

"I think you're not ready to go back," he said, taking my arm. "Come with me."

I saw Giulia's satisfaction crumple. However she'd thought to disconcert me had not worked as she'd intended. I wondered what she'd meant to do, but mostly I felt vindicated as Nero escorted me from the sala without a single backward glance at his aunt or his housekeeper.

He pulled me with him down the darkened interior stairwell that led into the receiving court, the white marble steps only partially illuminated by the ambient light from above. He said nothing,

and I felt the argument with his aunt churning in him, making him
go too quickly for me, who had not traipsed these stairs a hundred
times in the dark. I stumbled after him to the bottom, where we
emerged into the red-walled room made more oppressive by the
sunlight struggling through the algae-skimmed glass of the only
two unboarded windows.

It was there I stopped, pulling from his grasp. "I know I interrupted you, and I truly don't wish to take you from anything
important—"

"I'm thankful you did," he said, "You've saved my sanity,
though I fear only wine and your company can fully restore it."

"It's too early for wine," I said.

He laughed shortly. "It is never too early for wine, cara. I can
see there is a serious dearth in your education if you believe that."

"I—"

"Call it one more lesson in your quest for knowledge," he said,
grabbing my hand this time, taking me with him again, down the
open hallway lined with storage rooms and servants' quarters, to
the kitchen.

We stepped into warm air and the yeasty scent of bread, the
ripe, pungent aroma of the cheese on the table. There was no one
else there.

I felt a twinge of nervousness, which I tried to dispel. I'd been
more alone with Samuel, and I was in more danger from him too.
Which reminded me of why I'd sought Nero out.

I'd never had wine so early in the day, and I could almost hear
my father's voice in my head, warning of the dangers of excess—
but I said nothing as Nero grabbed a pitcher and two glasses and
sat beside me on the bench, not across, as I'd anticipated he would.
I felt a little jab of pleasure, and fear too.

Nero poured the wine and took a deep gulp, sighing when he
brought the cup away again, saying, "My aunt would drive a saint
to drink." He tapped my cup with the back of his finger. "*El vin fa*

gambe. Ah, forgive me, how to say it? Wine gives you legs. Go on, drink it."

Obediently, I took a sip. It was young and a bit sour, but not unpleasantly so.

Nero gave me an amused look. "You'll have to do better than that. How are you ever going to gain the ruin you wish for without indulging now and then in decadence?"

"It wasn't ruin I was wishing for."

"What happened? What has Samuel done so early in the day to send you running to me?"

He was as perceptive in his way as Samuel. It surprised me, but unlike with Samuel, it didn't make me feel uncomfortable. Instead, I felt a relief that startled me, and before I knew it, everything Samuel and I had spoken of this morning spilled out, tumbling over my lips so quickly I was unaware of forming words or thoughts.

Nero listened silently, and when I stumbled to a halt, he said, "But you said it was caused by the medicine and his injuries. So . . . it's all temporary, yes?"

My own words, thrown back at me. Then I realized how impossible this was. What had I thought to tell him? How could he possibly help? I couldn't explain anything, not without revealing too much. How to say that Samuel believed these visions different from those he'd had before without telling Nero about the epilepsy?

I couldn't. I had been a fool to search him out. I took a gulp of wine, too much, too fast, burning down my throat and into my stomach. I would have to work this out on my own, and I was so ill suited to the task. I could not even tell when a man was lying, much less when he was mad. I said, "I'm sure you're right."

"I've disappointed you," he said. "That wasn't the answer you wanted."

"No, it's fine. It's . . . you're exactly right. I shouldn't be worried."

"It didn't look like it was caused by medicine to me," he said. "But you could stop giving it to him and see if he gets better. Isn't that the way to tell?"

"You're right." I tried to smile. "Yes, of course."

"Elena." Nero twisted on the bench to face me. "What is it you want me to say?"

"I . . ." I could not tell him the truth, and so why was I disappointed when he told me the only solution he could know?

He went on, "I've told you I'll stay with you upstairs. You won't let me. Samuel tells you to leave. You won't. You won't stop the medicine, for whatever reason. What can I say that hasn't already been said? I don't know why you're so insistent about the laudanum and the wine, frankly. Take him to his parents and let him fool them the way he always has. He's happy, you get whatever it is they've promised you, and"—a snap of his fingers—"all is right with the world."

I raised my gaze to his. "Before the beating . . . did he . . . did you ever . . . had you any reason to think he might be . . ."

"Insane?" He drank the rest of his wine, poured more; the *glug splash glug* filled my ears. "Perhaps now and then. But then, when we were together, well . . . let's just say there were usually other things involved as well."

"Laudanum, you mean. Or drink."

"Yes. And opium. Absinthe, which would turn the sanest man into a lunatic. Cocaine. Hashish. Wine, women, and song." He lifted his glass in tribute and drank again. "Shall I go on?"

"I believe I have the general idea," I said.

Again that amused glance. "You sound disapproving. Tell me, cara, have you ever done what you knew you should not just for the sheer joy of it?"

"I sneaked into the kitchen once to eat cake when I shouldn't. Does that count?"

"Not good enough," he said. "Have you ever been drunk?"

I shook my head.

"Have you ever taken laudanum until you were stupefied?"

"My father is a doctor. He would never allow it."

"And you never sneaked any on your own?"

The hallway, quiet but for my shuffling. No lamplight to give myself away. The creak of the door, swiftly silenced. The quick look around to be certain I hadn't been discovered, my heart pounding in my ears, my breath too fast. The bottle in my hands, shoved into my pocket. "I would not," I said quietly.

"No cocaine, then," he said.

"I wouldn't even know what to do with it," I told him.

"Tobacco?"

"It's vile."

"What about lovemaking?" he asked.

I went hot, again, with a longing that frightened me. I saw the way he noted it, the small smile on his lips, the way his eyes did not leave my face though I willed him to look away.

"Well?" he went on. "Have you ever kissed someone just because you wanted to? Only because you were hungry for it, and you didn't care what else might happen? You weren't thinking of love, or marriage. You just wanted to appease a desire."

"Once," I said. *His hand cupping my chin. Leaning in. Feeling his breath against my lips.*

"Not that kiss I walked in on?"

"That wasn't my doing."

His gaze was probing. "I think you're lying. I think you've always expected something from a kiss. A future. Perhaps love. I think the kiss you speak of had all those things wrapped up in it. It wasn't only about desire."

"We'll leave together, you and me. We'll make a future together. I'll show you the world.

We'll be married at that little church down the road."

"Ah," Nero said. "I'm right. I can see you haven't risked everything for a momentary pleasure."

"I'm not . . . I'm not that kind of woman."

"What kind of woman is that?"

"A . . . a woman who is not respectable."

"A whore, you mean? But I'm not talking about whores. Desire has nothing to do with them, only money. I'm talking about decadence, which I'm trying very hard to lead you into. But you won't even drink your wine, so it's much more difficult than it should be."

"I've told you ruin is not what I'm looking for."

"I don't want to ruin you, Elena," he said with a smile. "I'm trying to get you drunk enough that you forget this mess of a world. I'm trying to get you to relax, because after last night, you look as if you need it. I'm trying to get you to forget your patient, who has an intimate enough knowledge of decadence and ruin that it's no doubt rotted his brain, though it may look like madness to you."

My hand tightened on my glass. "I'll lower his dosage. You're right; it needs a change."

He looked at me as if he were trying to decide whether or not to believe me. I glanced away, taking refuge in wine. One sip, another. That burning I was starting to enjoy, the growing warmth in my stomach. The wine tasted better with every mouthful.

He said, "Let me stay up there with you."

I shook my head.

"Then I want you to take this." He reached into the pocket of his coat, pulling out something dark, laying it on the table. It was a moment before I recognized it: his knife, sheathed, the Basilio rising sun on its handle.

I stared at him stupidly.

He slid the blade out, turning it so it caught the light. He touched the edge with his thumb, barely pressing. It raised a thin line of blood. "It's very sharp, so you should be careful. Keep it sheathed, but within reach. It will dissuade him, I promise you."

The thought of taking the knife, of using it, was unfathomable. "I can't. I couldn't. I wouldn't even know how."

"I'll show you, though it won't take much finesse to put him off. Slice. Or stab. One or the other will do."

"I couldn't hurt him."

"You'd let him hurt you instead?" He slid the knife back into the sheath and held it out to me. "Take it. Please."

I shook my head. "I don't need it."

He made a sound of frustration. "Elena. Please. There's too much unhappiness is this house already. It's burden enough. I would not be able to bear it if he hurt you or . . . or worse. I'd feel responsible."

"You shouldn't. You've been so kind. No one would blame you."

"I would blame myself. Take the knife. I'll sleep better knowing you have it."

I didn't want it. I didn't want the responsibility of it. I didn't want to admit what taking the knife forced me to admit—that Samuel was dangerous, that he might be mad, that he had hurt me and frightened me and would do so again. I didn't want to acknowledge the danger I'd felt in the air. The way his eyes had darkened. *How fast your little heart is beating.*

I took the knife reluctantly, turning it over in my hand.

"Like this," Nero said, leaning close. His hands were much warmer than mine, which lately felt perpetually cold. His fingers were as gentle as I'd remembered them last night, when he checked the wound on my foot. Again, so intimate.

He guided my hand to slide the knife out. "Hold it like this." Turning my hand to press the knife handle against my palm. Heavy and lethal. "Like this"—a quick stabbing motion, a slice. "Or this"—he brought it to his throat—"see here? A flick of the wrist, and it's all over. But I would prefer you not take it so far. Probably just the sight of it will put him off." He released me, sitting back, smiling grimly. "Keep it with you at all times. Don't hesitate to draw it on him if you need to."

"But what will you do without it? And it's obviously a family heirloom. I can't just take it."

"You're only borrowing it. I'll expect its return when the medicine starts to work and he's no longer a threat. As you keep telling me, it won't be long."

Carefully, I slid the knife back into its sheath. I was not as optimistic as he thought.

"Just try not to stain the carpets, will you? They may be the only things in this house actually worth selling." His grin was quick, as sharp as the blade in my hand, slicing through my tension.

"Thank you. I'm . . . very grateful. For everything."

The grin slipped away. His eyes, so intense, caught mine. I did not know how to look away. The moment stretched, and then he shook his head lightly, as if recalling himself. Another quick smile—not so easy this time, pensive instead. He reached for his wine, downing the rest of it. "What do you say, cara, shall we finish the wine? Will you get stinking drunk with me?"

I rose. "I should be getting back. But I appreciate what you've done. You've comforted me immeasurably."

He cocked his head, glancing up at me, again that melancholy smile. "What I meant to do was make you forget. The wine will do that, you know. Make it all go away. At least for a few hours. The world will seem very different then. Better."

"I don't want to forget," I said, and it was true. It was only remembering my own mistake and how I must atone for it that gave me the courage to go back to that room, to try to think of a way to save Samuel.

"Ah, well then. Perhaps another time." Nero looked away, splashing more wine into his cup, and yet there was a studiousness in it that told me he was measuring his every move, his every word. "I'll come up to see him later this afternoon, if you like."

"That would be good for him."

"And you, cara? Would it be good for you?"

Before I could stop or think I said, "Yes."

He turned a teasing smile on me, and it was all I could do to mumble a good-bye and open the door, and when I stepped outside, I leaned back against the wall, needing to gather myself, feeling stunned and undone by his attention, by the things I wanted. To stay, to get drunk, to forget. To let him lead me where he would. To learn whatever it was he had to show me.

I took a deep breath and started back to the third floor, and Samuel, and it wasn't until then that I realized that I'd never discovered what it was Nero and his aunt had argued about, or why he had wanted to get lost in a pitcher of wine.

Chapter 18

Samuel was asleep when I returned, which was a welcome reprieve. If my years at Glen Echo had taught me anything at all, it was that madness couldn't be cured. It could be lulled into obeisance, babied with laudanum and cold baths and calming words, enough so that patients could return to their families—at least for a time, with everyone pretending that all could be normal again, that all that was needed was a nice rest in the country, and *oh, how pink your cheeks are now! How rustication becomes you!*

But most came back to Glen Echo, every year or so surrendering to voices or hysteria or melancholia, come to nurse invisible wounds out of sight of society, out of mind.

How often I'd heard bitterness in the voices of the women I'd tended at the asylum. How much they'd feared and hated having to hide the pieces that did not quite lock together. I'd heard it in Samuel's voice too. Living a lie. The strain of a lifetime of keeping secrets. I had not understood before. Not really.

And perhaps I didn't understand now, either, but I began to wonder if perhaps it was time to write to my father and tell him what I suspected. I suppose I even wanted him to tell me it was all right to give up, to leave Samuel to himself and the Farbers to their quaint little delusions that he could be the son they wanted. *It will be all right, my dear*, he would say. *We will find another way to survive this.*

I wondered what Littlehaven would be like, and whether my cousin would expect me to bake bread, or clean out stalls, or milk cows, and . . . and I felt only a swift and debilitating desperation. *No. Not yet.*

I racked my brain, trying to remember my every interaction with other epileptic patients. I studied my father's notes with renewed vigor. There must be something I'd missed, something that could help me. I was not ready to admit defeat.

I heard a scraping sound, like something heavy being dragged over stone, and I looked up in alarm. Then I heard someone racing down the hallway. There was a frenzied rap on my door.

"Mamzelle! Mamzelle!"

My heart froze. I dropped the pen and jerked to my feet, unlocking the door and pulling it open to find Giulia standing there. Her hair was down, volumes of hair, thick tangles to her waist, and her eyes were wide and frightened.

"Please, mamzelle." Her gaze darted toward Samuel's door, which was wide open.

I pushed by her, running to his room, stumbling to a stop just inside. The first thing I noticed was the thick and spicy smell of the sguassetto. The second was the mess. The chair was on its side, halfway across the room—the scraping sound I'd heard—and handkerchiefs were strewn everywhere as if someone had grabbed them from the dresser and tossed them into the air. The drawers were wide open. Sguassetto spilled in an ugly brown pool on the carpet, next to an upturned bowl. The room was frigid, that uncanny cold again. I did not see Samuel anywhere.

But then I heard him. From the other side of the bed came gasping; when I rounded the bedstead, I saw him flat on the floor, and at first I thought he was having a grand mal seizure, but no. He was still but for his breathing, which was staggered and harsh, bursts of icy clouds, only half dissipating before he expelled another.

"Samuel?" I asked.

Nothing. No response. I stepped closer. His eyes were open, but he was staring into space, that distant, faraway look. Whatever he was seeing was not me.

Madness. I fought the urge to run. This was only a petit mal, wasn't it? Nothing to be afraid of. I knelt beside him and forced myself to touch his shoulder.

"Samuel," I said again.

He jerked away and flung out his hand at the same time, a backhanded blow that caught me so hard I fell back, tears stinging my eyes at the pain.

He sat up, enmity in his eyes, nostrils flaring. He began to speak. It sounded like Venetian. Like his singing the other night, it seemed fluent, and I found myself scrabbling away, trying to get beyond his reach, crashing into Giulia's feet. I'd forgotten completely about her.

She stood watching, her face white, her eyes wide and dark, staring at him as if she could not believe what she saw.

No, no, no.

"Get out of here!" I shouted at her. "You shouldn't be here."

She backed away, but not because of my words. It was him she was frightened of, and whatever it was he was saying. It was him she fled, her hair flying out behind her as she turned and ran from the room. I was glad when she was gone. Or at least I was until I realized Samuel was getting to his feet, clutching the bedcovers to help him rise, bringing them and the pillows to the floor in a cascade of fabric. He hadn't stopped speaking, and now there was an intensity that frightened me, spittle on his lips, his gaze not here but somewhere else. I didn't understand the words, but I understood the venom in them.

He stumbled, catching himself again, advancing on me where I sat like a helpless bundle. I reached into my pocket for the knife Nero had given me, but it wasn't there. I'd left it in my bedroom. *So very stupid.* Samuel stared beyond me and spat what sounded like invective. Then his tone changed to a plea, his eyes full of fear. He fell to his knees.

"Samuel," I whispered, half afraid to call his attention, remembering too well what it had cost me the last time. But that look in his eyes, that raw anguish—I couldn't let it stay. "Samuel, please. You can make it stop. You can. You must try."

His gaze jerked to me. "Elena," he breathed. For a moment, I saw him, a fleeting glimpse of Samuel, and then he was gone. His expression darkened. He got to his feet. I should not have called to him. My instinct to say silent had been right. Why didn't I have the damn knife? Or morphine. I could sedate him. If I could just get to my room.

But he was coming toward me, angry and menacing.

I scrambled to my feet.

"Elena!"

Nero's voice came from the hall.

I called, "In here! The bedroom!"

He was there in moments, Giulia running in behind him. She had obviously gone to fetch him, and I felt a rush of gratitude before Nero said sharply, "Samuel!"

Samuel's head snapped around. Nero came in slowly, raising his hands, palms out. "It's all right, amigo."

Samuel's entire body stiffened. He lunged at Nero, falling on him so heavily Nero crashed into the wall. I heard the thunk of his head against the plaster, and then they were grappling. Samuel was shouting, garbled words now, no language at all.

"I've got morphine," I said, making for the door.

Nero's only answer was a terse, "Hurry!"

I pushed past Giulia, who stood wringing her hands, as I rushed to my bedroom. I fumbled to open the medicine case, everything spilling in my haste to find the morphine. *There.* I pulled it out, along with the needle and syringe in its small, hard leather case.

Giulia shouted, sounding panicked.

I opened the case and took out the pieces, screwing the needle to the plunger with trembling fingers. The cork of the bottle was stuck; finally, I pried it loose, set the syringe to it. The plunger froze. I could not get it to move. *Careful. You can do this.* I had done it a hundred times, calming hysterics.

I heard a crash. Giulia shrieked.

Finally, I had the syringe loaded, and I grabbed the knife for good measure, shoving it into my pocket as I ran back. Giulia had not moved. Nero and Samuel were on the floor, rolling, Samuel fighting him in earnest, meaning to do damage while Nero was working to avoid his blows and keep him contained at the same time.

"Try to hold him still!" I directed.

"I can't," Nero grunted.

I grabbed for Samuel's arm, and he threw me off so violently I nearly lost the syringe. I jabbed the needle into his shoulder. He pulled away, dislodging it before I could get the morphine into him. He jammed his arm against Nero's throat.

"Now," Nero ordered in a strangled voice. "Do it now!"

I jabbed again, pressing the plunger in the same moment Samuel twisted away, but not before I got most of the drug into him. The syringe went flying, scattering droplets of morphine everywhere.

Nero was choking. For a moment I thought it wouldn't work. It hadn't been enough. But just as I thought it, Samuel shook his head, blinking, easing up. Nero gasped a breath. Then Samuel collapsed, unconscious.

I sat back in relief.

Nero pushed off Samuel's limp body and sat against the wall with a heavy sigh, his curls falling into his face. "What was that?"

I glanced at Giulia, my gratitude gone now in my suspicion that she had caused his fit. "Why not ask her?" And then, before he could, I asked her in French, "What happened?"

She looked at Nero, a look heavy with some hidden import, before she answered. Reluctantly. "He likes sguassetto."

"I told your mistress he wasn't to have it."

She shrugged as if my orders were of no moment. "You keep him like a child. He is a man."

I ignored that. "What happened then?"

"The chair moved across the room."

"The chair *what*?"

"Moved." She walked her fingers in description.

I remembered Madame Basilio's comments about Laura's spirit moving the chair, wanting to be heard. I realized then that I would not get a straight story from Giulia, who was no doubt so encumbered by her mistress's tales that she would not be able to say what she'd really seen. Nero had said she was his aunt's creature through and through. I didn't doubt it. "I see."

"Then the drawers opened, and the handkerchiefs flew"—she raised her arms, fluttering her fingers with a meaningful glance at Nero, though I had no idea what meaning it was, and he did not even look at her—"and his eyes rolled back in his head and he began to sing. That is when I came to get you."

I glanced at Samuel, his chest rising and falling steadily now, at peace—or as much as he could be in dreams.

Nero's expression as he looked at his housekeeper was a mix of contempt and dismay. "That's quite a tale."

She shrugged again, staring at him insolently, as if daring him to contradict her.

"What was he saying?" I asked.

"He spoke Venetian," she said smugly, again that challenge to Nero. "He sang '*Un Ziro in Gondola.*'"

Nero stiffened, his expression melting into one of incredulity. The name of the song sounded familiar, and I remembered that Madame Basilio had mentioned it. A favorite of her daughter's. I understood then what Nero must be feeling, and my heart ached for him.

"He wasn't singing when I saw him. And he can't speak Venetian." I looked at Nero. "Can he?"

"Not that I know," he said.

"Of course. It was only babbling," Giulia said, but there was something in her manner that told me she lied. "Nonsense words. Like a baby. Silly rhymes. Poems the washerwomen say."

Nero stared at Samuel as if my patient held some confusing mystery.

"We should get him to bed," I said, rising.

Nero nodded. He got to his feet, saying something in Venetian to Giulia, who frowned at him, but, thankfully, stalked off.

"Take his feet," Nero directed, and the two of us lifted Samuel. He was very heavy, and I was breathing hard before we had deposited him on his mattress. I glanced about the room.

"I suppose I should clean this up," I said.

Nero shuddered. "I'll help."

The two of us began setting things to rights. I was glad he was there, though we spoke little. The room seemed to discourage it with its oppressiveness. I felt almost as if it were pushing me to hurry, to finish, to leave. As if it could not wait for me to be gone.

I glanced at Nero, wondering if he felt the same. He squatted among the mess of handkerchiefs, which were blown about as if by a sudden wind. Squares of fine linen dangled from his hands, and he was staring at them with a heartbroken expression.

As if he felt me watching, he looked up. He gave me a tiny quirk of a smile, and held up a handkerchief. "Laura's. I hadn't realized Aunt Valeria kept them."

"She had one for every gown, it looked like," I said softly.

"They smell of her. She was the only woman in Venice who wore this perfume. They made it for her in this stinking little shop over on the Merceria. I could barely stand to go inside, but she loved it."

"The scent is in everything. I get whiffs of it all the time."

His expression turned quizzical. "Do you? This is the first time I've smelled it since she died."

"Perhaps my nose is too sensitive. You should keep one with you. As a reminder."

"A reminder of what?"

"Her death was so sudden. Her perfume must be a comfort."

"I've never liked the scent. Too sweet. I found it cloying. And I don't want to be reminded of her death."

"No, of course not. Such a terrible accident—"

"It was no accident."

I wasn't certain I'd heard him correctly. "What?"

"It wasn't an accident." He gathered up the handkerchiefs, one great ball of them, and shoved them almost violently into the open drawer of the dresser. "An accident is what we tell people."

"I don't understand."

"She took her own life."

He spoke the words so simply, bare fact, no embellishment and no emotion. But I saw in his eyes the same sorrow I'd seen when he'd shown me the purple canal. The same I'd seen in the cupola.

"Oh, I'm so sorry."

"She threw herself off the balcony," he said.

"Dear God. How terrible. Why?"

He shrugged. "My aunt believes it's because I didn't try to make her happy."

"Is that what you think?"

"I try not to think about it." He closed the drawer with emphasis, as if he were putting a period on a sentence. "She was despondent. I was gone. There's nothing else to say."

Suddenly, I remembered the canal's beckoning song as I'd stood on the balcony, my thoughts of falling, of drowning, my memories and my despair called back as if I'd smelled some truth in the air, as if understanding could exist in a whiff of perfume.

I realized he was watching me.

"I'm sorry," he said. "I should not have told you. It's only that . . . those handkerchiefs . . . I was not expecting them."

"It's all right. I understand."

"Do you? We had to tell the church something, or they would not have allowed her to be buried in consecrated ground. My aunt could not bear the thought of Laura bearing such a mortal sin."

It made sense now, how upset Madame Basilio had grown at tea. Our talk of her daughter as a demon or an angel, my innocent words that she was with God. "Of course."

"Samuel knows, but few others."

"He does? He told me she fell. He said nothing of it being a suicide." But now I remembered the careful way he'd worded it. *"They say she leaned too far over and couldn't catch her balance."* They say. Not really a lie, but not the truth either.

"I've asked him to be discreet. As I am asking you. My aunt's distress . . . you understand."

"Of course."

His expression softened. He glanced about. "I think it's clean enough, don't you? How long will Samuel be unconscious?"

"I don't know. Some time, I think."

I followed him into the hallway. When the bedroom door was closed behind us, Nero said, "You didn't use the knife I gave you."

"I'd left it in my room," I admitted. "I won't do that again."

"You should let me stay, Elena. If not for Giulia—"

I had forgotten all this in his story of Laura. Now my helplessness returned. The reasons to keep Nero away had not changed, but . . . but now, what did it matter? Samuel was mad, and I could not fix him, and everything I'd hoped for must now be given up.

"I think perhaps Samuel's right," I said softly. "Perhaps I should keep him sedated for a time. Until I can arrange to . . . send him home."

"Send him home? So soon?"

"I don't know what else to do," I admitted. "I've done all I can. I think it's just best to tell his parents he's . . . not himself."

"Not just the medicine then," Nero said.

I shook my head. "I've never seen a patient react this way to it before."

I started back to my bedroom. Nero followed me. At the door, I turned to him. "Thank you for your help. I won't subject you or your aunt to any more of this. If you'll just give me a few days to arrange things . . ."

"What happens then?" he asked.

"I suppose that's for his parents to decide. He belongs in an asylum."

He said, "Or . . . you could just let him go. It's his life. Let him make the choice. In any case, you'll be well compensated. He'll give you whatever his parents have promised. Plus more. I'll make certain he does."

"He's already offered that. I refused him."

Nero frowned. "Why? Did you not believe he had the means? He does. He's paid our entire carousing way for years, much to my embarrassment."

I sighed. "It's not the money that matters to me. Well, it is, but not for the reason you think. The other day, in the cupola . . . you asked if I was running from a scandal."

It was so quiet I could hear his breathing. He was standing close, close enough that I should have stepped away. But it was reassuring to have him near. I wanted someone to understand. Samuel had not cared. Perhaps Nero would. I could tell him my story without revealing the truth of Samuel's. There was no need to mention Glen Echo at all.

"One of my father's patients promised to show me the world, and I wanted so to go . . . I convinced myself that I was in love with him."

"So he seduced you and it was discovered. A familiar tale." His voice was rough; I didn't know why.

I shook my head, swallowing the lump that was suddenly in my throat. I could not look at him. "He had a weakness for opium and wine, and so he wasn't allowed those things. My father was trying to break him of the habit. But he was in such pain, and he promised me he would not abuse it. He wanted only a few drops. I didn't see the harm."

"Elena, you don't have to tell me this." Nero's hand came to my arm, fingers opened, lingering, tingling.

"I want to. You've told me your secrets. It seems only fair that you should know mine. The next day, they found him dead of an overdose. He had taken nearly the entire bottle."

"*Santa Maria*," Nero whispered, obviously shocked.

I told him the rest, finishing lamely with, "It was my fault, and I should be brave enough to take the consequences, only I'm not. I can't bear the thought of it. There's not even a *shop* in Littlehaven. I'll be buried alive there. Everything I've always wanted, gone."

"Everything you've always wanted," he repeated slowly. "Which is what? Ruin, perhaps?"

I looked up and fell into his gaze.

He whispered, "Come here."

But I was already there, wasn't I? A bare step away. His hand still on my arm, that caress turning me into liquid. My mind was a muddle; I was mesmerized, entranced.

"Come here," he said again, the barest movement of his lips, and it was as if he commanded himself, because he was the one who took the step closing the distance between us. Then his fingers were beneath my chin, tilting my face to his. He kissed me as I gasped, my lips already parted, sucking the pulse of my breath into his mouth. But before I could really respond, he drew away. I nearly fell into him before I caught myself.

"I'm sorry," he said. "I shouldn't have done that. But I couldn't resist."

"Why shouldn't you have done it?"

He laughed lightly. His finger swept my jaw. He brushed my lips with his own, the flicker of his tongue, a taste only, and then pausing only a breath away, so I felt the concussion of his consonants as he said, "I'm not a good man, Elena. Not like Samuel. I'm no prize. You should run from me."

"I don't want to run." It may have been the bravest thing I'd ever said. Certainly, I felt a kind of vain and bubbling courage, a recklessness that felt very like the night I'd sneaked the laudanum for Joshua, such heady excitement, as if I were jumping off a very high cliff into the unknown, falling and falling without end and not caring, wanting only to keep falling, to be lost in ruin.

His expression became wistful again, and held too a kindness that made me understand that he was going to walk away. He was going to save me, when I had no desire to be saved.

"No," I managed. "Please."

"You'll thank me for it," he whispered, stepping back, into the hallway again. "Lock your door, Elena."

I didn't know who he thought a locked door would save me from. Himself, or Samuel.

Chapter 19

I sedated Samuel again before I went to bed, locking the door and putting the knife Nero had given me beneath my pillow. Still, I jumped at every little sound and settling, every echo from the streets or the canals. I could not get comfortable, and it wasn't just the danger of Samuel or my uncertainty that made me so restless, but the things I'd felt with Nero, which seemed to squirm beneath my skin.

I must have fallen asleep eventually, because the last thing I remembered was the sky lightening with dawn, and then suddenly I opened my eyes, and the morning was full on. I heard laughter in the courtyard—male voices, muffled. No doubt Giulia's family again, and Tomas, with his hard-edged stare that had seemed to see beneath my clothing. I rose and readied for the day, pausing at the sight of the morphine and the needle and syringe, and then deciding to bring them with me. I put the knife in my pocket, reassured by its heaviness against my thigh.

But Samuel was not in his room. Nor was he in the sala or anywhere else on this floor. Rising panic had me rushing to the door, out onto the landing of the stairs, and there he was. Below, in the courtyard, sitting on the wellhead beside Nero. The two of them were talking and smiling. I realized they had been the source of the laughter I'd heard earlier. There wasn't a Nardi in sight. The sky was clear and blue, the chill, moist air smelling of salt and mud and smoke. They sat in a shaft of misty sunlight, which glinted on their dark hair, bringing out the red in Samuel's, making Nero's look even blacker.

I was stunned to see Samuel looking so like himself. After last night, I had thought to find him completely surrendered to madness. It seemed impossible that he should be otherwise today, that he should be sitting in the courtyard laughing with his friend, completely at his ease. At the asylum, patients had good days and bad ones, and I supposed that was all it was. I could not bring myself to interrupt the moment; it was such a blessing. Instead I pressed against the cast-iron rail and watched them, thinking how different things would be if Samuel were only healing from a beating, if there were no secrets, if this house were truly as bright and inviting as the courtyard looked in that moment.

I heard a door open and softly close below me, and glanced down to see Madame Basilio emerge from the piano nobile. She looked at the courtyard, her expression tightening, and then she glanced at me. It surprised me when she came up the stairs to stand beside me, so much so that I could not answer her "Good morning" with anything more than a nod.

"Look at them there," she said quietly. "The whole world thinks them perfect, but one needs a priest and the other only God can help."

I only stared at her—what could one say to that?

"Has he spoken of what he saw?" she asked.

"Pardon?"

She had not turned to look at me, but remained staring at Nero and Samuel. "Yesterday. Did he tell you what he saw?"

Giulia must have told her what had happened. For what seemed the hundredth time, I silently cursed the housekeeper. "No."

"He saw *her*." She looked at me slowly, with a burning gaze that froze. "My daughter."

"He's very impressionable now. Nero's told him about the tragedies in your family and—"

"Her spirit moved the chair. She threw her handkerchiefs all over the floor."

"You cannot truly believe that," I said.

"He sang her favorite song. He spoke to her."

"Nursery rhymes, Giulia said. Nonsense. Babbling."

Madame Basilio's gaze was pitying; I realized then that Giulia had, in fact, lied to me about what he'd said. Which should not have been a surprise, given that I'd suspected it. But it made me feel beaten and manipulated, even more ineffectual.

"Then what? What did he say?" I asked.

"You should be careful, mademoiselle. She will not stop until we understand the truth."

I was too exhausted and undone to be kind or patient. "Yes, yes, you've said that before. She is God's messenger. She is the truth and the light and the way—"

"You should be careful," Madame Basilio said again.

"Of what?"

She motioned toward the courtyard. "Nerone can be very appealing. My daughter found him irresistible."

I was surprised at what she'd perceived. And discomfited. It was a moment before I managed, "She was lucky, then. Not all women are delighted with an arranged betrothal."

Down below, Samuel laughed, a deep, rich sound. Nero answered with a flurry of talk, his hands moving, extravagant gestures, so perfectly foreign. I knew no one in America so animated and alive. He seemed to glow with energy and joy.

"I did not favor the match," Madame Basilio said.

I was surprised at that—not only that she had not approved, but that she was telling me this at all.

"His father was prone to melancholia," she went on. "His mother I did not like at all. A foolish woman, easily corrupted."

Nero had told me his aunt would try to impugn him. I should not be surprised. "Your nephew seems unlike either of them," I noted. I could not help thinking that perhaps it had been Laura who inherited the melancholia, given how she'd ended her life. It seemed too cruel to say it, even to a woman I didn't like.

She turned on me so suddenly I jumped. "You understand nothing. Believe me when I tell you that Nerone is not for you."

"You have misjudged me. I'm interested only in my patient."

It was clear that she did not believe me. Her stare was measuring; I saw a debate within it. "If you will not heed my warning, I can do nothing more. But you should leave my nephew alone."

Nero's laughter rose as if to punctuate her remark. She turned from me and went down the stairs, back inside, letting the door close hard behind her. The sound clapped in the air, bouncing against stone. In the courtyard, the two men looked up.

"Elena!" Samuel called, smiling. "Come and join us!"

I should have been warmed by how well he looked, how glad he seemed to see me, but I was too shaken by Madame Basilio's words, and I saw too the way the smile died on Nero's face when he saw me. My longing pinched. It was all I could do to call down, "I don't think so. But you should not stay out too long. It's cold."

"Warmer here than inside," Samuel said, bracing his hands behind him, lifting his face to the sun.

Nero looked away and said nothing. No plea to change my mind, no disarming smile to make me rethink ruin.

I rushed back into the house I'd been in such a hurry to leave only a short time before. How cold it was inside. I felt frozen to my very center. All this talk of ghosts. *She will not stop until we understand the truth.* "Nerone is not for you. You should leave my nephew alone."

I took a deep breath, pressing my fingers to my forehead to stop my thoughts, shaking away the frigid air and its accompanying hopelessness. Madame Basilio's warnings had got beneath my skin; Nero's indifference made them prick. That was all it was. If there was any ghost at all in the Basilio, it was the wretchedness that infused the very walls. Probably it was what had led Laura Basilio to kill herself. Such sorrow. Such despair. Hadn't Nero said it?

I would not give in to it. And as for Nero . . .

I would not embarrass myself further. There was still a chance I could leave here with my dignity intact, and that was what I resolved to do.

Chapter 20

It was an easier promise to make than to keep. I was in my bedroom, mending a tear I'd just discovered in my nightgown, when I heard them come in. The two of them together, stomping and making all manner of noise as if they meant to alert the whole city to their arrival. I bent more closely to my sewing, concentrating on making perfectly tiny stitches in a tight row. I would stay here. I would ignore them completely.

But I hadn't closed the door, and a shadow crossed the opening, and when I looked up, there was Samuel, his eyes clear and a smile curving his wide mouth.

"What are you doing?" he asked.

I bent again to the gown. "Mending. I should think that evident."

"I feel rested today. Better than I've felt in weeks."

"Good."

"Nero said you gave me morphine."

"You needed to be sedated."

"It worked. I didn't even dream." His voice rang with wonder, which changed quickly to fear and trepidation with his next words. "But . . . Nero couldn't tell me what I need to ask forgiveness for."

"Nothing. You didn't hurt me. Nor did you insult me."

"Elena, look at me."

Obediently, I raised my gaze.

"I . . . don't remember much. Only that I saw the angel again. I thought it was a dream. She was singing, and then . . . she was angry, which means, I suppose, that I was. What did I do?"

I didn't know how to explain it. I only said, though I didn't believe it, "I think you had a seizure. A small one. A petit mal."

A look of such relief came over his face that I wished I hadn't said it. I understood why he felt it. The incident could be explained away. It wasn't madness.

But it also wasn't the truth.

"Did I frighten you?" he asked.

"You always frighten me, Samuel," I said bluntly, then wished I hadn't been so honest when he flinched. "I wanted to send you home last night. Nero convinced me otherwise. I hope I don't come to regret it. Where is he? I heard him come in with you."

"In the sala," he said. "Waiting for you."

My pulse jumped. "Waiting for me?"

"We were hoping you would come with us to the Rialto."

I looked at him in alarm. "You're in no shape to be walking about."

"I don't intend to walk. We'll take a gondola. There's a café there Nero knows of. He says there will be street performers."

"A café? Coffee? All that stimulation? No, Samuel, I'm sorry, but I must forbid it."

An exasperated sigh. He gave me a cajoling look from beneath his lashes—very pretty. "Don't tell me you wouldn't like to see the market."

"What if you have another seizure?"

"I can't breathe here, Elena. I need to get out, just for the day. When I was sitting in the courtyard with the sun on my face, I felt *myself* again. Please. I want to hold on to that feeling for just a bit longer. Please."

It was all said so sincerely, and I saw the fear in him and knew he told me the truth, and I could not deny that I too wanted to be away from the sad gloom of the palazzo. I longed to see more of Venice. Why not?

I put the sewing aside. "Very well."

His face lit. "Excellent. Meet us at the water stairs."

He disappeared from the door. I hesitated, for the moment thinking better of it, but then I let my worries go, or as much as I could, at any rate. I kept the knife, the bottle of morphine, and the needle and syringe in my pocket, and grabbed the leather strap for good measure. Then I put on my cloak and hat and gloves and went to the water stairs to meet them.

The door was open; for once the receiving court did not seem dim and bloody, and I noticed for the first time that the red marble was veined not just with black and white, but with gold that glittered in the sunlight. It was easy to see now how elegant it all might have been once.

Nero waited on the walk. He smiled at me as if he could not help himself, and I smiled back, pulling up the hood of my cape against the cold, tucking back a stray curl, and the strangest expression crossed his face. His smile died, and his eyes darkened, gleaming with something I didn't understand. He masked it quickly, glancing away, saying, "Come aboard."

I told myself not to be disappointed, to think nothing of it. The door to the cabin was open; Zuan took my hand to help me into the boat, and then tucked me inside. Samuel was already there, sinking into the black leather cushions—worn and creased white in places—and I sat beside him, noting with dismay that there was no place for Nero to sit but on the side seats. He ducked inside, taking the one next to Samuel. The cabin door closed, and the gondola swayed into motion.

The cabin was dimly lit with a single oil lamp, casting us all in sickly brown shadows. Samuel relaxed against the cushions, but I could feel Nero's tension. He sat hunched, arms braced on his knees, jiggling his leg as if he could not keep still. Now and then I thought I felt him looking at me, but when I glanced over, his gaze was always averted.

"Have you been to the Rialto before?" I asked Samuel, forcibly brightening my voice, keeping to my resolution not to let Nero Basilio affect me.

"Not for a long time," Samuel said. "I think I was last here five years ago, and then only for a few days."

"It won't be different," Nero said. "Everything is always the same. Nothing in Venice ever changes."

"Some people might find that comforting," I ventured.

"The city has lost her will to live," he said, still not looking at me, lightly contemptuous. He glanced out the open levers of the window just over his shoulder. "Those with money and a name revel in past glories. The rest are too poor to leave. Venice belongs to the tourists now. The artists, especially. They want it to stay as it is so they can continue to paint their pretty scenes of dereliction and melancholy and pay the girls a centime or two to pose and then hopefully bed them later. Venice loves to oblige. Centuries of power and riches, reduced to a stage set for poets to moon over."

The bitterness that came into his voice was intriguing; I had known that he despised the city and that he longed to be away, relieved of obligations he had no wish to carry. But now I heard something else too, a regret for things lost, a lingering pride in an ancient history, sorrow over Venice's abasement.

"Careful, my friend," Samuel said. "You sound as if you care."

Nero laughed shortly. "It was just an observation. I'm no nostalgic, mourning a life I've never known."

"You can see her past glories in her bones," Samuel noted. "There's an elegance here still. The city might yet find her way."

"Long after we're both dead," Nero said.

"How your optimism cheers me."

This time, Nero's laugh held amusement. "Forgive me."

"You were perfectly well earlier today."

"I saw something that reminded me of . . . a past sorrow."

"Well, forget it, will you? We're here to enjoy ourselves. I don't want to cry over anything today." Samuel turned to me. "Look out the window, Elena, and see the city as we pass. It's truly beautiful enough to make you forget Nero's dreariness."

"Oh, I think he protests too much. I can hear in his voice how much he loves it here."

Nero's gaze came to me, quick and fleeting, but long enough to show his surprise that I'd understood him. I felt a warm satisfaction, and then I reminded myself that I wasn't supposed to be feeling anything.

Obediently, I did as Samuel directed. I watched the city roll by, swaying with the motion of the gondola so the buildings themselves looked set upon waves, soft pink and white and ochre that seemed to have risen fully formed from the canal, still stained with the algae of their submersion. The light dazzled off the buildings and water, casting the city in brilliantine.

"Beautiful, isn't it?" asked Samuel from beside me. "The view never gets old."

Beautiful was not quite the word. *Magic* was the word. *Unreal* would have been another. I had been nervous when I'd arrived in Venice, and the cloudy day had not set it off to advantage, but now the city cast its spell, much as it had the day Nero had taken me to the cupola.

The scenery changed; we were in the Grand Canal now, and it grew busy, the waters wide and choppy and blue, filled with watercraft: gondolas, small steamers, barges and fishing boats, along with some very large gondolas holding several people standing— the *traghetto*, I remembered. I watched, enthralled, barely listening to Samuel and Nero's intermittent comments—directed at each other—as we traveled.

Then we were there, the Rialto with its broad, arched bridge, the profusion of boats of all kinds. Our gondola slowed, and then stopped altogether, and Zuan was opening the door to sunshine touched by water vapor, a brumous, luscious light that made everything look richer and more lovely, and made me realize how stuffy the cabin had been and how badly the oil lamp smoked. Zuan took my hand, pulling me out. I stumbled, blinking, and then stared at the profusion of people and stalls, noise and smells. Impossible to take it all in at once, to pull anything apart, to measure. The Rialto hit me as a wealth of noise and color, all at once, as if fireworks had gone off unexpectedly right before my eyes.

Samuel laughed as he came up behind me. "It's something, isn't it?" He grabbed my arm as the gondola rocked in the gently splashing waves. Then Nero came out, and steadied Samuel with a hand. Nero nodded toward the market. "Ghosts walk every *calle* in Venice," he said. "But here it's so crowded it's hard to feel them."

Samuel smiled and said, "Lead the way."

It was nothing but chaos, a cacophony of shouting and talk, fishwives hawking their wares and the crab soup man cajoling us to come and taste and the fruit and vegetable sellers calling over each other. We wove our way through women with baskets and men carrying kegs and heavy bags over their shoulders, boatmen unloading and loading wine and beer, barrels of flour, bulging sacks, haunches of pork, and baskets full of wriggling fish.

The aromas from dozens of cookhouses and stalls mingled in a confused, delicious mess—sausages and onions, garlic and polenta, fritters and crab. A pretty brunette, red-cheeked from the heat of the grill, turning sections of eel as she flirted with everyone who passed, glanced our way. I saw her immediate interest—two attractive men—and she sent Nero a coquettish glance, a smile that he returned, and my heart squeezed.

It was the only bad moment. The yellow and white awnings reflected the misty light; the bright purples and greens and blues of bolted cloth seemed to glow, as did the pyramids of pumpkins and squashes, pears and cabbages. It was six days until Christmas, and everywhere were the jars of fruited mustard and mandorlato that Nero told us were traditional gifts. In one shop window, brightly colored glass gleamed, in another lengths and coils of serpentine gold chain. We passed men and boys lingering in shadows, and girls with beseeching eyes, men sleeping on heaps of garbage as if the whole world wasn't shouting around them. Nero and I were on either side of Samuel, who had started to limp, but we had to go slow enough with the crowds that he was doing well with only Nero for support. Nero warned in a low voice, close. "Watch out for pickpockets. They're everywhere."

But even with such a warning, and the reminder that all was not as perfect as it seemed, I felt restored, the energy of the market pulsing in the tumult of peddlers and street performers and men and women laughing and bartering, and the lonely shadows of the Basilio seemed very far away.

The café Nero had spoken of was near the end of the market. When we reached it, I wondered why he'd brought us. There seemed to be nothing to recommend it. The tables and chairs outside were shaded by an awning; only two people had dared to sit there, a couple who sat shivering over their coffees as they watched a desultory juggler, who exclaimed in a pained manner every time he dropped his pins as if he had surprised himself, obviously making excuses in a flurry of Venetian while the couple nodded in sympathy, their gazes vaguely curious as they watched us go to the door.

I eyed the facade dubiously—peeling paint and crumbling plaster and brick.

"It's better than it looks," Nero assured us.

He opened the door, and we were immediately assailed by scents of garlic and sausage, frying fish and sweat and wet wool. The place was tiny, clouded with tobacco and coal smoke, and so long and narrow we brushed up against people sitting at tables as we came inside. The floor was made up of little tiles in gray and black and white, cracked at the doorjamb to show the Istrian stone of the foundation, then slanting down and suddenly up again as if meaning to trap the unwary.

It was hot, both from bodies and from the brazier smoldering in the center of the room. Nero paused, glancing about, and then he nodded toward an empty table in the far corner, and we pushed our way to it. He grabbed a passing waiter by the arm before we'd even reached the table, growling out a long string of Venetian, and when we sat down at a shining ceramic tile–topped table, he said, "I ordered for us already. Otherwise we'd be waiting all day."

It was only a few minutes before the waiter returned bearing three glasses and a jug of wine and hurried away again. Nero took up the jug and splashed wine into two glasses. When he went to pour the third, I put my hand over it.

"You don't want any?" he asked in surprise.

"None for Samuel," I said.

Samuel let out a frustrated sigh. "Can we please just forget about your strictures today and enjoy ourselves?"

Nero glanced between us. "He's a grown man, you know. He can decide for himself what to drink."

"Exactly," Samuel said.

"Of course." I lifted my hand from the glass. "You *do* know best, I suppose. And I imagine Venice is safe as houses, is it not? There are no cutthroats and thieves here waiting to rob you and leave you for dead in an alley." Deliberately, I held Samuel's gaze, willing him to think of Rome, of the drunken seizure that had led him to such a pass before.

He sighed again. "Only one glass then. I promise, Elena."

Even allowing that was too much, but I also didn't want to spoil the day, and the truth was that it didn't seem important. I rejoiced in how clear were his eyes; no shadows lingered there now. The Rialto had worked wonders upon him. Here, I could almost believe he could be cured. I could almost pretend there was nothing wrong with him, that we were only three friends on an excursion. The future, his parents, and my mistake all seemed very far away.

Nero pushed a glass of wine toward each of us and lifted his in a toast. "To friends," he said.

"And nurses who have at last learned to compromise," Samuel added.

I made a face, but I raised my glass with theirs, and drank the wine, which was rich and fruity and good.

"Does he not look well today, Elena?" Nero asked. "Not the least bit insane."

Samuel's gaze leaped to me. "You think I'm insane?"

"No, of course not," I lied, glaring at Nero, who looked unabashed.

"My aunt thinks you need a priest," he said to Samuel. "What she thinks a priest can do for you, I have no idea. Beyond deliver last rites. Are you even Catholic?"

"Yes. Nominally, anyway. I was raised Catholic. It was the one thing my parents stayed true to, even faced with a sea of Episcopalians." Samuel pressed his glass to his lips, sipping slowly, obviously meaning to savor and make it last. "It only made it harder for them to break into society, of course. I imagine my bride-to-be is horrified at the thought of it. Among other things."

I rushed in to change the subject before he could move on to beasts and chains. "I'm surprised Madame Basilio has any faith in priests. She seemed angry with the church at tea."

"Angry?" Nero asked in surprise. "Why would you say that? She's the most devout woman I know."

"She said the church believed that ghosts could only be demons. Given that she thinks her daughter's ghost is an angel moving chairs about and tossing handkerchiefs, it's not hard to imagine she might be annoyed."

Samuel went quiet and stared down into his glass. Nero reached convulsively for the jug, though his glass was still half-full, pouring so carelessly it splashed onto the table.

Just then, the waiter returned, bringing a plate of fried minnows, piled high, and another of sardines in some shiny sauce that smelled of vinegar, studded with raisins.

"You are speaking about a woman who also believed my father spoke daily to the devil." Nero dangled a minnow into his mouth, crunching with satisfaction. He poured more wine into my glass, though I'd only drunk a little. "Every time I think of coming home, I think, *God, no*. The house breathes melancholy—who can bear it? But then I return and I realize the sorrow comes from my aunt. It was not Laura's natural state, despite how she died." At Samuel's quick look, Nero explained, "I've told Elena the real story."

"You're spilling all sorts of things these days."

"I know. I surprise myself. Or perhaps I'm just weary of secrets." Nero took a sip of wine. "I would prefer to think of Laura as she lived, not as a specter haunting rooms she despised. What a terrible fate. I would not wish it on anyone."

"It's better, I think, to not always be sad," I agreed.

"Oh, I'm sad too. Often. But I know Laura wishes me not to mourn her, but to live."

"I've no doubt of it. Isn't that what any of the dead would want of the living?"

I said it because I hoped it was true, for Nero and for myself. I didn't want to believe in ghosts, lingering spirits full of resentments and angers that hid in every shadow to punish us, damning us with their eyes, demanding penance. I wanted to believe in for-giveness and peace.

"*A morir e a pagar se fa sempre in tempo*," Nero said.

"That one I know," Samuel said to me. "God knows I've heard it often enough. There is always time for dying and paying."

Nero said, "It's true, yes? Life is short. One must dive in."

I smiled because I could not help myself, because again he was so unlike anyone I'd ever known, and when he looked at me, he smiled too, and for a moment the rest of the world fell away.

His gaze was so intense that I dropped mine and took a bite of sardine, and as the sweet and vinegar flavors bit and sang on my tongue, I felt a stare. Samuel's, thoughtful and heavy. A slight shake of his head, and I remembered his warning, and Madame Basilio's, and Nero's own. One thing they all agreed on was that I should keep Nero at arm's length. But I was no longer certain I could. Or that I wanted to.

Chapter 21

We lingered while Nero and Samuel regaled me with tales of their exploits in Paris: an absinthe-fueled club that catered to contortionists; a night walking along the Seine that neither of them could quite remember except that they were alternately terrified and elated by hallucinations caused by something they were loath to reveal; a masquerade ball they'd attended dressed as sheep, where they followed any Bo Peep they happened upon—"There were six or seven," Nero said. "Ten," Samuel corrected. "And one was Robert Pennington." Nero winced. "I'd prefer not to remember *that.*"

By the time the wine and food were gone, we were all laughing, and Madame Basilio's ghosts were long forgotten. When I rose, the floor tilted slightly beneath my feet before I caught myself on the edge of the table. The café windows—small, shaded—had muted the sunlight, and the day seemed too bright when we stepped out into it, the afternoon sun starting to dip. We made our way back to the gondola, both Samuel and Nero steadier than I, in spite of the fact that Nero had drunk most of the wine. A street performer singing Verdi jumped in front of us, following us persistently, bellowing "*Libiamo ne' lieti calici*" at the top of his voice, making me laugh and Nero make faces until Samuel finally palmed him off with a few centimes.

I did not want to go. It had been one of the best days I'd ever spent. As we approached the gondola, Samuel stumbled. I caught his arm, and when he looked up, his gaze leaped beyond me, distracted, tense. His brow furrowed. I followed his gaze, but there was only the gondola, its toothy prow bobbing, Zuan waiting.

"Samuel," I whispered.

His gaze cleared. "It's nothing," he said quickly, but his smile was thin and troubled, and I didn't believe him. The day had fooled me into thinking he was finally getting better, but now I realized it had only been a brief respite.

Nero was at the gondola. He had seen nothing, and his mood was still joyous as he settled into the cabin. Samuel was tense as he sat beside me.

I said, "Let's never go back."

"Agreed," Samuel said, and I knew he was trying as hard as I to regain our earlier pleasure in the day.

Nero said, "Your wish is my command. Let's just tell Zuan to keep going, shall we? Out in the lagoon and past the Lido and into the sea until we end up in . . . where would we end up?"

"Listen to you. You'd wander blind across continents if not for me," Samuel said affectionately, relaxing into the seat, stretching out his arm so his hand brushed my shoulder. I saw the almost jealous way Nero tracked the movement, and could not help my joy at it. "Depending on the direction, Athens. Or Constantinople. Algiers. Barcelona."

"Let Elena decide," Nero said.

"I don't know. I don't know which is best."

"Perhaps Samuel's parents will pay for you to try each one."

"Indeed. They're very generous. Especially when it comes to getting what they want." Samuel's words were bitter. "I used to think my father could read minds; he was so *very* good at using what people wanted against them."

"We'll find a way out for you, amìgo," Nero said fervently, and I had the impression it was a long-standing conversation. He looked at me. "And Elena will help us, won't you, cara?"

I felt the lure of his persuasion. He knew already how bound I was. I had no idea how to change things. I almost resented him for his words. Almost. But there was a look in his eyes, too, that reminded me suddenly of the book beneath my mattress, the way his lips had brushed mine, and my mouth went dry. I wanted to do what he asked of me. But I didn't know how.

Samuel slid a glance to me. "Is that so?"

"No one wants you to be unhappy," Nero said.

"Really? I'd thought Elena had no real care for my happiness."

"That's not true," I said quickly. "I *don't* want you to be unhappy. It's just—"

"It seems we are in negotiation," Samuel finished. "About who should be doing the sacrificing."

"It's unfair of you to ask it, when you know how important it is to my family," I said quietly.

"You're a grown woman who should be looking at a life away from her family," Samuel said, equally quiet.

"As an only son, you have a responsibility to your parents," I retorted. "When do you intend to stop being a spoiled child and become a man?"

Samuel let out his breath in surprise.

Nero made a sound—a strangled laugh, I'd thought, but then, when I looked at him, I realized it wasn't that. He was looking at Samuel and me as if he'd suddenly noticed something he'd never seen before.

We all went silent as the gondola made its sure and steady way toward the house where none of us wanted to be. As it approached the water stairs and the peeling, leaning mooring posts, dread was the only thing I felt.

Little wisps of mist already formed on the water, heralding evening, ribbons of fog tangling and dipping, dissipating only to re-form. The receiving court felt ominous and dead, the red-tinged shadows creeping with evil intent. The hazy light held ghosts within it. Samuel had one hand on the wall for support and was walking quickly, even with his limp, as if he meant to be away from me as soon as he could.

He rounded the mausoleum-like entrance of the stairs, disappearing ahead of me down the hall. I paused, turning to say good-bye to Nero, who would go up those stairs.

He was closer than I expected, nearly on my heels. Before I could say the words, he grabbed my arm, pulling me close, up against his chest, his hips to mine. I looked up at him in surprise and question, only to find him studying my face as if he meant to find some secret in my eyes. His were dark and intent, raising an answering desire in me, a terrible yearning. He was going to kiss me, I knew, and I waited for it, wanting it, my heart pounding.

A soft crack echoed down the hall, a rock, dislodged by Samuel's foot, rolling across uneven paving.

Nero released me, backing away. His lips thinned, his expression changing from desire to something so barren and desolate it took me aback. What could cause that look in someone's eyes? In his?

"Nero," I whispered.

He turned away. He was on the stairs even as he was saying, "Good-night," taking them two at a time in hasty retreat, and I was left to hurry after Samuel as if nothing had happened. Though in truth, I had no idea if anything had.

The day had been spoiled; there was no doubt. Samuel went to his room and closed the door quite definitively, and I closed my own too, leaning back against it, thinking of that look in Nero's eyes, reliving the moment until it took on the quality of a dream, until I wasn't sure I hadn't made it up.

I went to the window and stared down into the courtyard, the smoking top-hat chimney of the kitchen, the fog from the canals on three sides beginning to coalesce, still formless and searching, easily blown apart by a breath or an air current. From below, a door closed; there was Giulia, hurrying across the cracked paving stones to the kitchen, and behind her, head bowed, his step slow and thoughtful, was Nero.

He did not look up. He followed Giulia to the kitchen and disappeared within, but I wasn't certain she'd known he was behind her.

Or perhaps she did. Perhaps they meant to meet. Perhaps he was on his way to make her "happy."

The thought tormented; I turned away from the window, and still the thoughts came. *How long has he been with her? What are they doing?* And then, *of course he has gone to her. She knows what to do. She knows how to satisfy him. What do I know? Nothing.* What was it Samuel had said to me? That I should know what it was I asked him to give up.

I glanced toward my bed. There it was, peeking out, that ragged yellow cover. It was absurd to think of reading it. How could it possibly help me now? Still, it seemed to tempt me like some ancient devil.

Perhaps it was time that I learned what it was I was longing for.

Before I could think about it too much, I strode to my bed and reached beneath the mattress, pulling out the tattered book, opening it to the place I'd left off. My gaze fell upon the line, "Now I think, Father Eustace, that poor girl has been on her knees waiting her penance long enough," and I took a deep breath and began to read.

Chapter 22

I read until very late, and my dreams were the words on the page come alive. I woke exhausted and drenched in sweat even in the cold, the blankets tangled about me. My skin felt too sensitive; I longed to be touched, for more than that. It had been a bad idea to read *The Nunnery Tales*. Now I felt worse than ever, more unsettled, plagued by thoughts that would not leave me, no matter how I tried to distract myself.

Worse, I did not know how I would look Samuel or Nero in the eye without thinking of the book. I felt embarrassed already, and I had not even left my bedroom. Nero knew nothing about it, of course, and so perhaps he would notice nothing untoward, but Samuel would take one glance at me and know I'd read it, and that troubled me as much as anything.

But I couldn't avoid him all day. He was my patient; I had a responsibility. Finally I forced myself to go to his room. Samuel stood at the balcony door, staring down at the canal.

"What color is it today?" I asked.

"Muddy brown. There's yellow too." He turned to me, and I steeled myself against his gaze, but I realized immediately that he was in no shape to notice anything. The clarity that had been in his eyes yesterday was gone. He wore that haunted, distracted expression I'd grown used to, jaw clenched as if he struggled for control, a gaze that darted beyond me and then to the wall as if he expected to see something there and dreaded that he might.

"You didn't sleep," I said.

He raked his hand through his hair. "I can't think. I'm so tired. All I do is see things that aren't there. Yesterday helped, but"—his gaze shot to mine—"I could use some distraction."

I thought of the last time he had asked for distraction, "*Let me fuck you until we're both exhausted.*" And the time before, when I'd ended up with the book that would not leave my thoughts now. I felt a sinking churning in my stomach. Lower. No, distraction did not seem like a good idea. "A cold bath first."

"They aren't working, Elena. Why must you torture me with them? Even you believe I'm going mad."

"No, I—"

"Don't lie to me. Nero said it yesterday. I know you think it. I don't blame you." He sank onto the chair, throwing his head back to stare up at the ceiling. "I feel it myself. Every day, a little worse. Yesterday I thought . . . well, it doesn't matter. I can barely remember the day already. Christ." He swept his hand over his eyes.

I did not say, *You aren't mad*, because I couldn't bring myself to lie.

He went on, "I always knew this might happen. Your father told me the epilepsy destroys the brain a little at a time. But this is sooner than I expected. And I didn't expect to be so aware of it happening. I thought . . . I don't know what I thought. That I would be older and half-senile already. I thought it would be a blessing. But this"—he closed his eyes—"this is a nightmare."

"Perhaps it's time to go home," I said quietly. "Back to your parents."

He opened his eyes and frowned at me. "That's what you said yesterday. But then you told me that Nero convinced you to stay."

I tried to ignore the flutter at the sound of his name. "Yesterday you seemed to be fine. But today . . ."

"You're giving up."

"No, I . . . I . . ."

"Be honest with me, Elena," he said, straightening. "Tell me the truth, whether or not you think it will upset me."

His gaze compelled honesty, so I told him what I thought. "I don't know how to help you. This is beyond me. I wonder if you wouldn't be better served by returning to"—I lowered my voice—"Glen Echo."

His expression didn't change. "This is what you want. For me to go back there."

"The bromide isn't helping. You said yourself the cold baths aren't. Nothing I try . . . your wounds are getting better, but your hallucinations are worse than ever, and you've had two seizures since I've been here."

"Three," he corrected. "The petit mal the other night. That's three."

I only looked at him.

"It wasn't a petit mal," he said tonelessly.

Reluctantly, I said, "No, it wasn't. Not like any I've seen."

"So it's true then. I am going mad."

"I don't know, Samuel. I haven't enough experience—"

"Don't tell me you don't know madness when you see it."

"I could be wrong. It *could* be the medicine. And the epilepsy."

"You don't believe that. If you thought there was any hope at all, you would keep trying. Otherwise you lose everything and so does your father."

I could not bear to think of that. I had been attempting not to.

He snorted derisively. "You'll have to marry your cousin. The Rialto will be all of the world that you ever see."

I flinched. "I wish you wouldn't paint such a vivid picture."

"It's no better for me," he pointed out. "I'll be locked up and surrounded by attendants who are a little too fond of restraints. I can't even ask you to run off with me. I can't trust myself not to hurt you."

Running off was not really a choice, of course. I could not just leave my parents to the wreck I'd made. And he was right; I couldn't trust him. More than all of that: when I dreamed of touring the world, he was not the one beside me.

"There's still time," I said. "It's only the twentieth of December. There's no need to return until January, if you don't want to. We can see what happens."

"And if it grows worse?" he asked. "If I *do* hurt you?"

"We'll decide what to do then."

"What if I don't want to take the risk?"

"Then we'll return now," I said, more confidently than I felt. "I'll tell your parents we couldn't help you. I'll marry my cousin. The Rialto will be all of the world I'll ever see."

He laughed—short, explosive. "My God. You are something. You truly want to take the risk of staying?"

I was afraid for him and for myself. Yet there was still a chance for this to end how I wished, wasn't there? To spend a few more days hoping that Nero Basilio might look my way. I thought perhaps I could face my wedding with equanimity if I had a kiss to remember, a touch to hold close in the deepest parts of the night.

"Yes," I said. "I'm willing to stay. Until we cannot."

"Very well. How do we decide when that will be? I think it best that we agree. I wouldn't be able to live with myself if I hurt you. So I say you take me back the moment I become violent."

"You're often violent. I have morphine."

He sighed. "Then you tell me. What would be more than you could bear?"

When you frighten me, I thought. But no, because he pushed, he prodded, he was too intimate and too insistent, and all those things frightened me. His violence frightened me, but if I just kept the morphine with me, and the knife, I thought I could manage that. Finally, I said the thing that frightened me most. "When I can no longer find you in your eyes."

His face fell. "Christ. Elena."

"I won't let you forget who you are," I promised.

"You may not have a choice."

"If I can't bring you back, that's when we return. Are we agreed?"

"If I'm that far gone, I won't know to agree."

I put my hand on his arm. "I won't leave you, Samuel. I promise. I'll make sure you're taken care of. I won't leave you to restraints and sedation. Whatever happens, even if you don't know who I am, I'll see you through to the end. Maybe a part of you will remember that, and find comfort in it."

He said in a whisper, "You don't owe me that."

"I want to do it. I want to make the promise."

"I never thought to meet anyone like you." He put his hand on mine, his fingers curving, holding me in place. He bowed his head, his hair falling forward to half hide his face. Then he raised his eyes to me, and I saw within them an admiration that startled me, and beneath that, a starkly evident hope. He pulled me closer; the sun touched his hair with honey, a misty, luminous fog around his head like a halo, and I became lost in that as he bent his head to kiss my throat, the throb of my pulse. His mouth was moist and warm, the touch of his tongue sent a shiver coursing through me. He moved to my jaw, and I thought, *stop this*. My own breath came fast, a cloud of fog, and then a rush of brutally icy cold, my skin pimpling with gooseflesh, the hair on the back of my neck rising.

Her perfume teased my nose. Samuel made a sound deep in his throat that made my heart falter. *Stop him*. But I felt helpless to do so, held in place, confused and disoriented. I could not tell—was that his breath I heard, rushing and short, or my own? His hands skimmed my breasts. He murmured something against my skin; I felt him tense, a broken breath, and then, before I knew it, before I had time to react or to stop him, his hands were around my throat, a gentle touch at first, and then he began to press, and I realized numbly that he was strangling me. In panic, I pushed at him, but he was immoveable. He was no longer kissing me, but staring at his own hands. Spellbound. I pried at his fingers, trying to break them loose.

"Samuel," I gasped. "Stop!"

His eyes were black, and fathomless. I did not see him behind them. He squeezed; I began to see stars.

He whispered, "*Chi comincia mal, finisse pezo.*"

The stars turned black. His breath was a frosty cloud. It was freezing. The scent of vanilla, fetid canal water, and acrid dye filled my nose.

His eyes flickered. I didn't see Samuel within them, but someone else, not the dead look of madness but *someone*. Consciousness and intention and jealous anger. But that was absurd and I couldn't breathe, and everything took on dark edges, and he was still squeezing as I scrabbled at his hand, scratching now, digging my nails in. He was so strong. I was going to die, and so soon after I'd made him the promise to save him, and where was someone to save me now? Where was Nero?

The knife. I had the knife in my pocket. Desperately, I pawed at my skirt, trying to find it within the folds of fabric. Samuel's teeth were clenched, his expression intent and furious. *Not Samuel.* Everything exploded before my eyes, red and black. Finally, I felt the knife, the hilt. I gripped it and tore it loose, the dagger sliding from the sheath, in my hand, and I couldn't think what to do with it—*what was I supposed to do*? I couldn't make my thoughts obey, or my hand. It was only instinct now, only the pure will to survive that brought my hand up and then down, and I heard his cry of pain, and he jerked away.

I gasped for breath, nearly swooning as air rushed into my lungs again, choking, scrambling away even as I struggled to breathe, dropping the knife, everything going white before my eyes, the world spinning and then, finally, settling, and I could see again. Samuel with his hand pressed against his shirt, his ribs, red seeping between his fingers, staining his shirt. He looked at me in disbelief, and there—there he was—Samuel again, and I thought how strange it was that he should be there when before he had been someone else entirely.

"Elena," he said, a wretched sound, torn from his lungs, horror and fear. He reached for me.

I wrenched away. "Don't touch me."

"Elena, my God . . ." How terrible he sounded, racked and hopeless.

Blood dripped over his fingers. He took his hand away to look, and then grabbed the edge of the chair as if he might faint. He pressed his hand back again.

Warily, I rose to my knees. He looked so lost, like a child who had done something wrong without knowing what it was. His eyes glistened.

"Samuel," I whispered, my voice raw; I could not make it louder. "Look at me."

Whatever I had seen in him was gone, but I was still cautious as I went to him, and I felt the way he held back too, his reluctance to let me touch him, even as I pulled his hand away from his chest so I could look at the damage I'd wrought. It was not so bad as it looked. A slice, but not deep, bleeding profusely. "I'll have to get bandages," I said. "Wait here."

He grabbed my hand before I could leave. "Don't. Don't come back. Stay in your room. Lock the door."

"Not until I wrap this," I told him.

But when I was in the hall, I thought about doing what he asked. My throat ached; I had trouble swallowing. I knew there

would be bruises. And what about my promise now? He had not
wanted to hurt me, and I had told him I would not condemn him
until I saw madness in his eyes. Surely that was what I'd seen.
Hadn't it been? Samuel Farber gone, and someone else in his place.
Someone else . . .

But no. He'd been strangling me. Who knew what it was I'd
seen in him? Or if it had been anything at all? I ran to the bedroom
and grabbed my medical case. When I returned, he was at the balcony door, struggling with the latch.

I went cold. "What are you doing?"

"It's calling me," he whispered. "Don't you hear it?" He jerked
open the door. The chill air rushed in, that molten, misty sunlight.
He stepped out.

I stared at him in horror.

"Good-bye," he said.

I dropped my case and rushed over, grabbing him around the
waist. "No, Samuel. No. Stop!"

He struggled to get free. "Let me go."

I felt the wet, warm stickiness of his blood on my hands. I dug
my fingers into his wound. He gasped, crying out in pain. I dug
harder, and it was enough to weaken him, enough so I could drag
him back inside. He crumpled onto the floor, and I closed the door
and locked it, leaving bloody fingerprints.

I was trembling when I turned to face him, sick with what he'd
tried to do, not just to me, but to himself. "No. You won't do this.
Promise me you won't."

His hair fell into his face. "My fingerprints are on your throat."

"You won't do this."

"I can't be in restraints again. I'd rather be dead than in an asylum. At least give me that peace."

"No," I said again. "No."

"I just tried to kill you. I *wanted* to kill you. I would have done it too, if not for that knife." He looked at it where it lay on the floor. "Nero's."

"He gave it to me in case I needed to use it against you," I said.

Samuel buried his face in his hands. "We'll return to New York tomorrow. Pack your things. Perhaps I can convince Nero to come along. To keep you safe."

Yes, I thought, and then *no*. What I'd seen in Samuel's eyes nagged at me. It had been so strange. Not like any madness I'd seen before. "I brought you back, Samuel. You're here. We agreed. We don't have to leave yet."

He looked up. "All I had to do was lean out too far over the railing." His voice lowered; he spoke as if in a trance. "To dream, to sleep, all mistakes forgotten . . ."

I froze at the echo of my own thoughts. *Not just mine.* Laura Basilio too had felt such temptation. Had surrendered to it.

"Nothing to redeem, nothing to remake," he went on. "Only peace."

I did not believe in ghosts. Damn Madame Basilio for even suggesting it. *I do not believe.* But I heard myself ask, "Samuel, did you see your angel?"

He frowned as if trying to remember.

"Just now, when you were . . . kissing me and then . . . did you see her? What do you remember?"

"I wanted you, that's what I remember. I was—*am*—mad for you." A bleak look.

I ignored the tiny thrill I felt, wrapped as it was in regret and a wish not to disappoint. "And then?"

"And then . . . yes, the light. Her. I felt this rush and . . . I wanted to hurt you. I wanted to kill you. Then everything went dark. I didn't come to myself again until you stabbed me." He looked down ruefully at his chest. "Well done, by the way. It hurts like the devil."

"Not like a petit mal."

"No, nothing like."

I grabbed my medicine case and moved closer, reaching to unbutton his shirt. Samuel jerked back, paling, raising his hands. "Don't."

I rolled my eyes and pushed past his hands, feeling the warmth of him beneath my knuckles as I unbuttoned. A long cut, crossing browning bruises, stretching from below his nipple, slashing diagonally across his ribs. I cleaned it, ignoring the harsh jag of his breath.

"Tell me about this rush you felt," I said, wrapping the bandages around him.

He hesitated. "It was like morphine when it's injected. Like a surge in the blood, I suppose, but one you don't cause or control."

I finished tying the bandages and sat back. It all battered about in my head, things locking together now, beginning to make a sense I did not want to contemplate. Laura Basilio's favorite song and her handkerchiefs flying. Samuel lunging for the balcony and Laura's suicide and Madame Basilio's belief that her daughter's spirit had returned to deliver a message. Demons. Angels. Ghosts. In New York, I never would have countenanced any of this. But here, in Venice, everything seemed possible.

The preternatural cold. Her scent. My sense of being watched and the shrouded figure. That consciousness I'd seen in Samuel's eyes that wasn't his own, but wasn't emptiness either. Hatred and jealousy. Not his, but someone else's.

Laura's?

Ridiculous. Impossible. Madness even to think it, wasn't it?

"Why are you asking these things?" Samuel asked. "What are you thinking, Elena?"

"I don't know." I put the bandages back in the case and closed it. "Not yet. But I think it's time I asked some questions."

Chapter 23

I was a rational being. I'd never believed in ghosts. But I had no other way of explaining the things I'd seen here, and my questions and rationalizations snarled into an impenetrable knot. I was afraid to leave Samuel alone now, so I did what he asked and sedated him. The morphine had become a blessing; when I left him, he was safe in bed and sleeping, and I went in search of Nero.

There was no answer when I knocked on the door. Zuan was in the courtyard below, cleaning out a barrel, puddles of murky water about his feet and the sleeves of his coat dark with wet. When I called to him about Nero, he jerked his head to the kitchen. "There, mamzelle."

I hesitated. The chances that Giulia would be there too were high, and I had no wish to speak with her or to interrupt whatever they were about. I had no right to feel jealous over that either, I reminded myself. What mattered now was Samuel.

But thankfully, when I went into the kitchen, I saw no sign of Giulia. Only Nero, lounging on the bench, drinking wine and idly mangling a piece of bread into a pile of crumbs. He looked louche and lazy and lovely, those tousled curls, the coat over his shirtsleeves, no collar or vest or tie. When I entered, I said, "There you are," but I got no welcoming smile from him.

He frowned. "What's that on your throat?"

I tried to cover the forming bruises with my hand, wondering how bad they were. "Isn't it a bit early in the day for drinking?"

"I told you before, in Venice it's never too early. What happened? What are those red marks?"

"They're nothing. I need to talk to you about your cousin."

His hand tightened on the glass. "I've no wish to talk of Laura."

"I think you need to. I know this will sound bizarre. I don't know if I believe it myself, but I can't quite discount what your aunt says about her ghost."

I expected laughter. Outright disbelief. Even scorn. Instead, he rose from the bench in a fluid motion and grabbed the pitcher of wine, the glass. "We can't talk here. Anyone could come in."

"Wherever you say," I told him.

"The cupola. No one will find us there."

I nodded and followed him out, neither of us speaking until we'd gone up the stairs and skirted the tiles of the roof, wet with mist, and slippery. Once we were inside, door safely closed, he poured wine into the glass and turned to me. His gaze went directly to my throat. When I made to cover it, he brushed my hand away, his expression one of horror and fear—for me, I realized gladly. "*Santa Maria*. He tried to strangle you."

"He wasn't himself. And I'm perfectly fine. I used your knife. He's asleep now. I sedated him." I took a breath, then, "I've promised to stay."

"Elena, don't be a fool."

"He's not himself," I said again. "He says an angel tells him to do things."

A flicker in his eyes. Terror, I thought, and something else, a dawning awareness that told me he was going to believe me. But he shook his head. "An angel? Do you hear yourself?"

"He sees a man putting a pistol to his head. A drunk woman falling. I think they must be visions of your parents' deaths, but I don't know. Is that what happened? Is that how they died?"

Nero frowned. "Yes, but—"

"Did he know any of it? What did you tell him about them?"

"I don't talk about them as a rule."

I gripped his arm hard. The wine splashed in his glass with the force of my movement. "Try to remember. Did you tell him any of it?"

He pulled away. "He knew they were dead, but I never told him the details. I never tell anyone. It tends to cast a pall, and what does any of it matter?"

"You're certain?"

"I don't know how he would know." He gulped the wine.

"He says he sees Laura. He sees them dragging her from the canal—"

"Please." A wince, a lifted hand to quiet me. "I understand."

"The handkerchiefs, things moving . . . He tried to hurt me because she told him to. Because she's jealous."

"Jealous?" he asked sharply.

"I don't know what else it could be. I don't know what any of this could be."

He paused as if he didn't want to speak the next words. "Madness, perhaps?"

"Before you didn't think it was."

He met my gaze. "I know. I didn't want to believe it. But a ghost? Tell me the truth now, Elena: That medicine you give Samuel, what is it really for? There's no remedy for debauchery that I know, and I've never heard of cold baths being a cure for it either. You said such treatments helped him before, but if you mean he became sober and changed his habits, I assure you that has never been the case in the years I have known him. And that rich man with the weakness for opium, the one you stole for . . . What kind of doctor is your father?"

There was no way around it. I needed him to understand completely. I needed his help. "He's an asylum superintendent."

Nero nodded as if he'd suspected it. "So Samuel has a history of madness. He was in that asylum."

"Yes, but not for madness."

"Why else would he be there?"

"I couldn't tell you this before. No one's meant to know."

"Know what?" Nero asked warily.

"Samuel is an epileptic."

Nero went still. I felt things dropping into place for him, questions he'd perhaps had about his friend, things that had not made sense before.

"I see."

"His parents have kept it a secret his entire life. They're desperate that no one know. Samuel *can't* tell people. The things they would think . . ."

"Of course. Of course."

He was so quiet. I wondered if he thought it a betrayal. I might think it so, had I a friend I'd known most of my life, whose greatest secret had never been told to me.

"I'm to stabilize his seizures," I explained. "That's what the medicine is for. And the baths. His fiancée isn't to know until after the wedding. They're afraid she would refuse to marry him."

Nero made a sound, a small laugh, a rush of breath. He stared into his wine. His voice was low when he said, "Too many secrets."

"I don't disagree."

"I wonder if everyone has something too terrible to admit to the world," he mused, running his finger around the rim of his glass. He spoke as if to himself. "I loved Laura. I thought she felt the same. And I was so *certain* of her."

I tried to ignore the tightness in my chest. *You have no business feeling this.*

He went on, "We ran around like wild things when we were young. She was my first kiss. We were ten and playing at being husband and wife. It was only a quick buss. Even though we were betrothed, anything more was discouraged. Rather fiercely"—a half smile—"in fact, my father beat me once when he caught me trying to kiss her in the *portego*. She was *not for trifling with*. His words exactly. 'A wife is a sacred duty, son, and that she is family makes her doubly so.' And so I was good. Very much the courteous cavalier. No more kisses except on the hand. When I went away to school, I sent her letters full of admiration and regard. I did not let myself speak of passion or desire. I sent her gifts, all carefully chosen so as not to offend. Perhaps I took my father's words too seriously."

"Why do you say that?" I asked.

"I spoke of our future life together, but not of love. I didn't try to woo her—she was already won, wasn't she, and I thought she felt as safe and happy in that as did I. But I should have known. I *did* know. It wasn't as if I were chaste in those years. *Santa Maria*, I'm no monk. I have spent a hundred thousand pretty words and gestures on women I wanted for nothing more than a moment's pleasure, but Laura, who was meant to share all my pleasures . . . I did not think that she might want the same."

I heard his disappointment and regret.

Nero let out his breath in a long hiss. "I was not ready to settle, and so I put off our marriage. One year, two . . . there was no money and I didn't want to think of what I must do to support a wife. All this noble waiting, and for what? What did I intend? I thought I was looking for a way for us to live, but I was only playing. I thought she would wait, but in that I misjudged her. No, I did not speak to Laura of love, and so she looked for someone who would. She found it in the son of another Golden Book family, whose name is as old as our own. Impoverished, just as we are. Filippo Polani. No money and no skills beyond writing poetry, which apparently he did extraordinarily well." A harsh laugh. "I've read some of his poems to my betrothed. They're quite beautiful. And passionate. She must have blushed to the tips of her toes. Ah well, what can I say? She fell in love with him. It went on for months before Aunt Valeria discovered it and put an end to it. She forbade Laura to break our betrothal. It would have dishonored my aunt, you see, for the world to see her own daughter so disobedient. Had Polani been rich, it might have gone differently, but he was not."

His expression was miserable. "Laura wrote to tell me she no longer wished to marry me. She expected Polani to fight for her. That is one reason my aunt is angry with me. Perhaps the biggest one. Because I did not try to win Laura back after her betrayal."

"Why didn't you?" I asked quietly.

"Imagine, if you will, that you have spent a lifetime watching everything that belongs to you fall away. Bit by bit. Piece by piece. There is nothing you can do but cling to the one thing you do have. That one thing becomes your anchor. A tether from your heart to heaven. Then it is snatched away. And the truth was that I was angry with her too. I didn't want to see her. I did not want to admit to myself that she had not felt our bond as I had. I loved her deeply, and I thought she felt the same. To give to him what was mine by rights . . . I was hurt, and jealous, and angry. I did not want to forgive her."

"So you lost her."

"More completely than I expected," he acknowledged.

"Do you forgive her now?"

He shrugged, a gesture of helplessness, remorse, sorrow. "How can I not? The question, cara, is, does she forgive me?"

"You said she wanted you not to mourn, but to move on," I reminded him.

"That's just what I tell myself. Who knows if it's true?"

"I think we must all tell ourselves something, mustn't we? Else how would we live with our regrets?"

His gaze was puzzled, admiring, searching. I felt the deep, reaching tug of it. He said, "How is it that you have the power to draw my secrets from me?"

"Perhaps it's only that no one else listened."

He set the empty wineglass on the little table, along with the pitcher of wine. Such deliberate movements. "Do you listen to Samuel this way?"

I didn't allow myself to hope it was jealousy I heard. "I suppose. I think when burdens are shared they are easier to carry."

"Like a modern-day sin-eater," he said thoughtfully. "I wonder if it could be enough."

I frowned. "Enough? For what?"

He stepped closer, reaching out to touch the marks on my throat, the gentlest of touches, a flutter I barely felt, but my heart set up a frantic beat. I felt as if I surged to his touch, though I was frozen in place. "To save me," he whispered, the words breathed more than spoken.

I hardly knew how it happened. I was not aware of moving. We met each other openmouthed, hungry, overwhelmed. I threaded my fingers through his hair, keeping him there, tugging on his curls when I thought he would pull away, and he made a small cry of pain and then laughed into my mouth, his hands tightening, jerking me close, anchoring me against him. I felt his need; my own was like drowning, my bones liquid, everything in me urging him on. It was only a kiss, but it felt like more; it felt like I'd been ravaged, flayed alive, images from Samuel's book playing through my head, and I wanted it all. I wanted Nero to do each of those things to me, but I had no words for it, none that I could say, and when he finally did break away, breathing as hard as I was, his dark eyes black, I felt I might become the ache that had lodged inside me, just one big bruise of longing. I could not bear to let him go.

He was smiling; he brushed my lips again with his own. I grabbed at him, but he did not let me keep him. His fingers were at my jaw, a gentle stroke. "We could do this right here," he whispered to me. "But it's all windows."

"I don't care," I said.

"I think you would, when the priests at the dell' Orto began giving you lecherous looks."

"How would I know it? I don't go to church." I put my hand on his chest, wishing to touch his skin, wishing I could bring myself just to unbutton his shirt, taking control like the women in that wretched novel, but I was too aware of myself, of everything I didn't know. As much as I wanted it, I was afraid.

"Heathen," he whispered, kissing the forming bruises on my throat, and the image came into my head of Samuel doing the same thing, that same kiss. "Your heart is racing. *Corexin de conejo.*"

I stiffened. Those words. Just what Samuel had said. But then, they were friends. They spent so much time together. They'd shared women—not a comfortable thought—and it made sense that they might say the same things. "What does that mean?"

"Little rabbit heart," he whispered against my skin.

I was disconcerted, though I shook it away. I did not want to be disconcerted. I wanted to keep feeling that urgency in my blood, that singing yearning.

He must have felt my hesitation, because he raised his head, a light frown in his eyes. Before he could ask, I forced myself to be bold; I attacked the buttons of his shirt—how clumsy I was; I could not make them work. He glanced at my hands, covered them with one of his own, stopping me. When I looked at him in question, he said, "Elena, I know you've never done this before. I want to be gentle with you. And I don't want to bed you here, where all of Venice could see."

The words sank into all my darkest, deepest places. "Then where?"

He laughed. "*Santa Maria*. So impatient."

My face went hot. He laughed again, but more tenderly now, brushing my cheek with his fingers.

"I'm moving to your floor, as you insist upon staying. I'm not leaving you unprotected, whatever is going on with Samuel—no, I don't want to hear your protests. It's either that or I put you on the next train, regardless of how much I want you. Now: Shall I have Zuan bring up a bed, or will yours suffice?"

Now I was burning. I could barely manage to say, "Mine."

He backed away; I thought he meant to say something to delay, that he would see me tonight, or that he must go pack his things, and I wondered how I would bear the hours until then, but then I saw how he looked at me, as if the sight of me was painful, and he said hoarsely, "How long will Samuel sleep?"

"Hours yet." My own voice sounded ragged. "Hours."

He grabbed my hand and yanked open the door, pulling me with him out onto the roof, the slippery tiles, but he was surefooted, his coat flapping back against my skirt as he nearly dragged me with him down the stairs. Neither of us had any care for noise as we went to my bedroom—he nearly threw me into it. He closed the door and locked it, and the look in his eyes made me dizzy. He came to me, and although I felt his impatience with every moment, where I expected ravishment, there was tenderness. He didn't give me a chance to change my mind. Perhaps he was afraid I would. He need not have been, no matter that my own fears nagged. I had wanted this too long—without even knowing what I wanted—to turn back now. I tried not to think of what it would mean for my future, or how it would be another secret I must keep. I tried not to think of anything at all as he took the pins from my hair so it fell loose over my shoulders. He unbuttoned my bodice with care, peeling me out of it, my skirt and my petticoats following, sure fingered as he took off my corset.

He did not even kiss me, but undressed me with something almost akin to reverence. I was trembling as he urged me to the bed, as he lifted my shift to undo my garters and roll down my stockings. It wasn't until I wore only my chemise and my drawers that he leaned to kiss me again, and I clutched him like a wild thing. He didn't break the kiss as he shrugged off his coat, then only long enough to take off his shirt and throw it to the floor, and my hands touched taut, warm skin. I heard the thud of his boots, I felt him struggle with his trousers, and then I felt the lean heat of him against me, the solidity of his weight, his desire.

I struggled to be free of the chemise, but he stopped me with a whispered, "Let me." His fingers at my shoulder, lowering the sleeves, his mouth following, his tongue. My throat and my collarbone, lower, baring my breasts. I gasped and arched against him, again tangling my hands in his hair, bucking against him, mindless and breathless, and then there was nothing between us and he was moving lower, parting my legs, an intimate kiss that shocked me into stillness. I had read about this, but I had not expected it, and I tried to close my legs in embarrassment. He would not let me, and then, suddenly, I didn't care. I had been titillated by this without knowing why, without suspecting . . . *oh dear God*, I could not think. I could only gasp and moan, and then he was rising up, plunging, and the pain shattered me, along with the pleasure, so I cried out—half a scream, silenced by his kiss, and after that, I realized why Samuel had said he could not give this up. I understood at last why he would risk seizures to have it, because I would have risked anything.

Chapter 24

"I hate these," he said afterward, kissing the bruises on my throat. "They're turning black-and-blue now. I should kill him for hurting you."

I ran my hand down his back, muscled and smooth and warm. I never wanted to stop touching him. "He didn't want to. It was as if"—my breath caught as his mouth found my breast—"Oh. Oh. Stop doing that. I can't think."

"I don't want you to think," he murmured against my skin. He brought himself up to kiss me, deeply and erotically, and I lost all sense of where I was and what I'd meant to say. He seemed to fill every space in my head; I felt only him moving against me. I felt only pleasure. I heard only our moans, the faint slap of skin against skin, his broken cries, mine. I was nothing but sensation, feeling things I'd never thought to feel, doing things I did not even realize I'd known how to do, and then I was crying out, splitting apart, and yet miraculously still whole, spiraling down and down until I was only a gentle throbbing, every part of me thrumming like water lapping gently on a shore.

His face was buried in my throat. I did not want to move, but only to luxuriate in the feel of him, and it seemed he felt the same, because we were quiet for some time. I tangled my fingers idly in his hair, so shiny and soft, feeling his warm breath on my skin. Then he kissed my throat gently and rolled off, putting his hand to his eyes as if the world were too bright for him. "*Santa Maria*. I thought you were a virgin. Where did you learn to move like that?"

The Nunnery Tales flashed into my head. "I don't know."

He laughed lightly. "It must be that I inspire you."

"Yes." I touched his chest, running my fingers down to the edge of the blanket where it wrapped about his hips.

His breath skipped. "Cara, give me time to recover."

"How much do you need?"

He laughed again, rolling over, pulling me to him, brushing a strand of hair from my cheek. "You have the most beautiful hair."

I felt a pang at that, a stinging vulnerability. "I think you would like any redhead."

"I do," he said unapologetically. "Most are very passionate."

"Most? How many have you had?"

"One or two," he teased. "Fourteen or fifteen. Twenty perhaps. I've lost count."

I was not very good at teasing, and I couldn't help my dismay. "Is that the only reason you're here with me? Because of the color of my hair? Not all redheads are the same you know, so if you wish to relive the past, I'm afraid you're doomed for disappointment."

"Or perhaps it's only that I'm looking for a cure," he said. "I'm beginning to think I might have found it."

"A cure?" I couldn't modulate my voice. That self-doubt took up center stage. "Oh, but . . . I've never . . . I can learn to be better—"

"Elena," he said gently. "You've bewitched me. I've dreamed of you since the moment I saw you. Many sleepless nights. It's been all I could do to keep my hands off you. I think the whole house knew it."

"The whole house?"

He nodded, nuzzling my jaw.

I thought of the angel that told Samuel to hurt me. *Laura's ghost.*

Nero sighed, rolling again onto his back. "I see what you're thinking, cara, but Laura no longer loved me, if she ever did. There would be no reason for her to want you hurt, even if she did exist."

"I know. I know. But I wonder . . . your aunt said Laura's spirit lingers because there's something she wishes to say. Do you think that possible? What do you think it could be?"

"Probably 'leave me in peace, you evil shrew.'"

I hit his shoulder. "This is important, Nero."

"I know. Believe me, I know." He rose to one elbow. His gaze was darkly, insistently compelling. "Now come and kiss me. I've rested long enough."

It was dark when I woke again, the courtyard clouded with mist as I crawled from bed, sore and sticky, and lit the lamp, turning it to a dull glow, startled to see streaks of blood on my skin. My virtue, most effectively gone. I could not bring myself to miss it, whatever complication it might raise in the future.

Nero slept on as I washed and put on my dressing gown. It was long past time that I checked on Samuel. I wondered if it was possible to hide what I'd been doing from him. I felt I should. I would be just who I had always been—how hard could that be? After all, only one thing about me had changed.

I put the knife and the morphine in my pocket and cast a last glance at Nero—dark lashes on cheeks made golden by the lamplight, the black shadow of his head against the pillow. I could not quite believe he was mine, that I had touched him the way I had, that he had touched me. I was loath to leave him, but I had a duty. I closed the door softly, not wishing to wake him. If I were quick, I could return before he knew I was gone.

Samuel's door was cracked open, which surprised me, because I was certain I had closed it. I tapped softly, pushing it at the same time, stepping inside. Samuel was not in his bed, but no lamp had been lit. Then I saw him at the balcony door, clad only in his robe, his feet bare. It was too early for the moon, but the mist had grasped hold of the light of the streetlamps and that in the windows of other palazzos and flung it back, softly reflective, luminous and smoky, and Samuel was a shadow within it.

He turned. "I've been waiting for you."

"I'm sorry. I should have been here earlier. How do you feel?"

"How is your throat?"

"A bit sore. But I think no harm was done."

He snorted. "Christ, what are you, a saint?"

"Samuel—"

"You've been with him, haven't you?"

I was too startled to lie. "How do you know?"

"I've never seen your hair down. You're naked beneath that robe. You would never have come to me this way."

"I fell asleep—"

"You're not blushing at the word 'naked.' You feel ripe and heavy and satisfied. You are, aren't you? Satisfied?"

He was too perceptive. I should have remembered that. I heard the edge in his voice. Jealousy and anger. Pain. "Samuel, I'm sorry. I—"

He waved my words away. "She hates you. Right now, so do I. Just a little."

I stepped back.

He laughed, it was bitter and short. "You're going to leave me, aren't you? For him. Despite your promises."

"No, I'm not. I'm not."

He slammed the ball of his palm against his head. "The visions never stop. I keep seeing them over and over."

As inconspicuously as I could, I felt for the hilt of the knife. "Seeing what?"

"That woman falling, breaking her neck. Blood and brains splashed on the wall. A letter. Poetry. A man—Laura had a lover, did Nero tell you that?" He took a deep breath. In it was distress. "It's her life I'm seeing, I know. She's falling and I'm falling with her, and the water's cold and red, and she's so *angry* . . . Christ, I can't bear it. I swear to you that one day you'll walk in here and I'll have thrown myself off that balcony, just as she did."

I hurried to him without thinking, understanding the temptation far too well. "No, Samuel. No. Please. You must fight it. Until I find a way—"

He held up his hands before I reached him, backing fiercely away. "Don't touch me. I don't want you to touch me."

"I can only agree with him, cara."

Nero's voice. I looked over my shoulder to see that he had thrown on his trousers and his shirt, but he was barefoot too, and the moment he entered, the temperature dropped, the floor became ice, cold even through the carpet. My thin dressing gown was no protection; the cold was so intense I gasped.

Nero did not seem to notice as he came over to us. He put his hand to my back possessively. I saw Samuel note it, the hard look that came into his eyes. "I see you've stolen my nurse."

Nero was equally tense. "She came to me trembling. You left a ring of bruises around her throat."

I hugged myself against the cold. "Please. Let's not speak of it."

"I'm moving my things up here," Nero said to Samuel, ignoring me. His fingers crept to my waist, curving round. "To Elena's room. I mean to protect her."

"Somehow I doubt that's your only motivation."

"Would you prefer I leave her to your rages?" Nero asked quietly.

Samuel glanced away. "No. But . . . who's to protect her from you?"

"You're so certain she'll need protecting?"

They were both bristling. The room was freezing. "None of this matters now. I've told Nero everything, Samuel. He needs to know the truth."

"What truth is that?"

"She told me of your epilepsy," Nero said.

Samuel stiffened. "It wasn't her secret to tell."

"I wish I'd known it before," Nero said. "I could have helped you."

"I don't need your help," Samuel said indignantly. "I kept it from you for a reason. I would have preferred it remained so." He turned to me, his eyes blazing. "I trusted you. My parents trusted you. How long did you wait to tell him? A minute after he kissed you? Two? Or did you wait until he made you come?"

I pulled away from Nero, uncomfortable and freezing, the room prickling with ice crystals, sharp and pointed. "You have no right to speak that way to me. I was trying to help."

"Perhaps next time you should let me jump," Samuel said, advancing on me, hands working at his sides. "That's the kind of help I need."

"Enough." Nero shoved Samuel in the chest. "Don't come closer to her or I'll be forced to hurt you."

"You've already hurt me." Samuel grimaced with pain and shoved him back. Pushing, the darkness in his eyes flickering. "You should have taught her how to use the knife better, and I'd be dead. It's what you want, isn't it?"

"Don't be a fool," Nero snapped. "Why would I want that?"

"You tried, didn't you? You left me in that alley in Rome."

Nero's expression hardened. "*You* left *me*. You disappeared. And I found you, didn't I? I didn't abandon you."

They were chest to chest, glaring at each other, their breaths ghostly in the scant inch between them. I felt Nero's temper rise; I saw his eyes flash, the tightening of his jaw as if he worked hard to control it. But then everything went wavery and strange. I could not see or focus, that scrim of watery reflections again, forming a wall between me and them. I felt paralyzed as they faced each other, mesmerized by the anger between them. I could only watch helplessly.

"You hated me," Samuel breathed. "Admit it. You were jealous. Tell me, did you hire those men to rob me and beat me?"

"Of course not," Nero ground out.

"You did. I know you did. I know it was you. I know you better than anyone else. I know what you're capable of." Samuel's eyes were glowing. He shoved.

Nero stumbled back. I saw fear in his eyes in the moment before he caught himself and then that fear was gone, in its place a rage that surprised me as he lunged at Samuel. Suddenly, I knew how this must end. The two of them fighting while I stared impotently. It all played out before me, the future already done. Samuel's hands around Nero's throat, strangling, and then Samuel in a seizure as Nero lay cold and still, his skin blue and those lovely lashes grizzled with frost. No more breath or winsome smiles. Nothing and nothing and nothing—No, this wasn't real. It was just this house.

Not a ghost.

Not her.

I shook it away and lurched between them, pushing them apart. "Stop this now. This isn't you, Samuel."

Samuel faltered, blinking. Nero grabbed me, pulling me into his chest. He looked shaken. "Get out of here. Go."

I wrenched loose, going to Samuel, who put his hand to his temple. "You don't think these things. You don't believe Nero tried to kill you."

Samuel exhaled heavily. He backed away from me, nearly collapsing onto the chair.

The cold dissipated with an almost palpable burst.

"*Santa Maria*," Nero said. "I begin to believe my aunt is right, and only a priest can help you now."

I was unsettled and desperate enough to grab at any suggestion. "Do you really think one could?"

"I was joking," he said. "A prayer and a wafer, that is all a priest can do."

But Samuel lifted his head. "Perhaps a prayer and a wafer would help. God knows I'll try anything now. Why not a miserable priest? Go ahead, Elena, bring one. If all he can do is last rites, I'm ready."

I winced at the desolation in his voice. "We won't need that, I'm certain. But I'll at least ask Nero's aunt about it." I reached into my pocket, taking out the morphine, the case with the needle and syringe. I did not want to use either, but then I saw the way Samuel's eyes lit at the sight of them.

"You *are* a saint," he said softly.

I gestured to the bed, and he went without hesitation, lying down and pushing up his sleeve in the same motion. I went to him, lighting the lamp on the bedside table to better see as I assembled and filled the syringe. When I leaned to inject it, Samuel wrapped his fingers about my wrist, bringing me close enough to hear him whisper, "Be careful, Elena. Promise me."

I nodded, but I didn't say the truth: that he was the one I must be careful of. And after what I'd seen tonight, I was more shaken and afraid than ever, because it wasn't only myself I knew I must worry about. It was Nero too. My vision had troubled me.

When Samuel was asleep, I turned to Nero, who leaned against the wall near the door, arms crossed over his chest, watching me with an expression I could not decipher—it was too thoughtful, too quiet. I blew out the lamp and went to him. He pulled me close, wrapping his arms about me, kissing the top of my head. His heart was racing. *Little rabbit heart.*

"He belongs in an asylum," he whispered to me. "We should send him back to New York, as you wanted. You and I can leave all this behind. We'll make love in every city on the Continent."

"With what money?" I asked softly. "And I can't abandon him. I can't believe you would abandon him either. You said you wanted to help him."

I felt the current of his sigh. "Yes, of course. Of course you're right. Go speak with my aunt then. But Elena, please, she is half-mad herself. Do not believe anything she tells you."

"I won't," I said. "I promise."

Chapter 25

I did not get much sleep the rest of the night. Nero said nothing more to me about abandoning Samuel and running off, but I felt he tried to convince me with every touch and every kiss. In the morning, he watched me dress with that same quiet thoughtfulness I did not like, but he did not try to stop me.

I gave him instructions for Samuel and went to the piano nobile. Giulia answered the door. She glared at me as if she meant to flay me alive with her stare, and I realized that of course she must know where Nero had spent the night. She knew everything. Resolutely, I said, "Is Madame Basilio in?"

I thought she would close the door in my face, but just then Nero's aunt stepped into the receiving hall and said something sharply in Venetian, and Giulia stepped back mulishly to let me in.

Madame Basilio gestured to me to follow her. Her heels clacked ominously on the floor; her back was rigid with disapproval, and I remembered Nero telling me that the whole house knew of his interest in me. I could only assume that Giulia had spoken of us, and Madame Basilio knew how well I'd disregarded her warning.

It was disconcerting knowing that such private things had been fodder for discussion. Disconcerting and humiliating. I had not yet even accustomed myself to what had happened between us; I did not know how to defend it or ignore it. I did not even know what it *meant*.

We went into the sala, and she turned to stare at me, those dark, birdlike eyes unblinking and cold. "I asked you to leave my nephew alone."

It didn't help that I'd expected it. "Perhaps you should have asked him as well."

She pressed her hand to the nearby lamp table and sank into the chair beside it as if she'd suddenly lost her strength. "Why have you come?"

"I want to know why you think M'sieur Farber needs a priest."

Her chin jerked up. Her expression changed to pure self-satisfaction. "You have seen her?"

Uneasily, I thought of the shroud and the perfume. *Nothing. My imagination.* "No, I haven't. But M'sieur Farber believes he has, and I wonder what you think a priest can do."

She murmured something in Venetian that sounded like a prayer and rose. "We must go to Padre Pietro immediately. Come, mademoiselle. We will speak to the priest together."

It was not what I'd expected, but there seemed no good way to excuse myself, and I had set this in motion, hadn't I? I supposed it would be best to discover what Madame Basilio was telling the world about my patient, to see what she really believed. So I followed her out of the palazzo, through the courtyard, to the gate leading into the campo. She led me to the narrow end, across a rail-less bridge whose stones were slick with a morning mist that still scrimmed the canal, on the other side of which was the Madonna dell' Orto.

The gray stone and brick campo was quiet. We were the only ones in it as Madame Basilio hurried us across. It felt odd; the church was so beautiful I expected that visitors would flock to it. Its sloping sides were topped with arches of white stone, each containing a statue of an apostle. Looming over all was the brick bell tower, square-sided with an onion dome. At the summit was a white marble statue of the Redeemer.

Madame Basilio barely spared a glance as she walked quickly through the door. Inside, I blinked in the change from bright sunlight to the soft, dim light from the arched windows. Pillars of swirled gray and white marble, a double aisle, pews softly glossy. The pentagonal apse held gorgeously illuminated, richly colored paintings on either side of the altar. Tintoretto, I remembered Nero saying. This was the artist's parish church; his tomb was here. I wished for the chance to look at it, but when I paused, Madame Basilio hissed, "Mademoiselle," the sibilant echo ricocheting among the archways, and gestured urgently for me to catch up.

There, near one of the front pews, was a deacon, the only other person I'd seen in the church or the campo. I'd begun to have the creeping sense that we were alone in the world. He looked up as we approached, starting slightly when he saw me. I saw when he realized I was not whomever he'd thought me to be, and he turned to Madame Basilio with a bow. The same kind that Nero had made to me. A Venetian specialty, it seemed.

"Ciao, Signora Basilio," he greeted.

She sputtered something to him in Venetian; I recognized only the words *Padre Pietro*. The deacon nodded and led us into the back rooms of the church, a hallway lined with doors. He stopped before one and knocked, speaking swiftly. I heard a muttered answer from within, and the deacon opened the door to usher us in, and closed the door behind us.

The office was small, with an arched and mullioned window, the scent of gas almost nauseating. A gaunt, balding man with a fringe of closely shorn gray hair was bent over a ledger. His hands were stained with ink, his back hunched as if he had held that position for so long he had grown into it. His nose was hooked, his eyes bleary as he looked up at us. He looked like a hidebound academic, not at all what I had pictured Madame Basilio's savior to be. But when he saw us, those eyes sharpened. The redness in them seemed to clear away; they became a pale and icy blue.

He rose. I had the impression he was not used to moving. He said, "Signora Basilio," and then proceeded to spout a long string of Venetian that of course I didn't understand. What was clear, however, was that he had expected her, and that this was the continuation of a conversation that had obviously been going on for some time.

Madame Basilio sat in one of the chairs facing the desk. I took the other. He sat again, and glanced at me in question, and Madame Basilio made a curt gesture toward me, speaking what I assumed was an explanation, and then Father Pietro was saying to me in French, "You're an American?"

I nodded, and his gaze became assessing; I felt I was being studied like an ant or a curious species of butterfly. His gaze left me the next moment, dismissive, finished—*I have learned all I wish to know.*

"How can you help?" I asked bluntly in French. "What does God have to say about ghosts?"

His interest bounced back, those sharp eyes. "Souls, mademoiselle. They are souls who have returned to relay His message."

"I don't know that I believe in such things, Father," I answered. "But I cannot explain what I have witnessed, or what my patient claims to see. I had hoped you might have an answer about how to help him."

"What have you witnessed? What has he seen?"

I told him, stumbling over the words, struggling to say what I meant in a language not my own. The complexities here I could not master. But the priest listened attentively, and when I was finished, he looked at Madame Basilio in surprise.

She said, "What does this stranger know? She comes into our house and thinks she understands. But I am the one who knows my daughter best. She is an angel come to render the Lord's judgment."

"That's what Samuel calls it," I said. "He says an angel shows him things. But do angels do things like this?" I reached for my collar, undoing the tiny buttons at the throat, peeling it back to show him the bruises.

Father Pietro frowned.

"She shows Samuel visions as if she means to drive him mad. She makes him want to hurt me. Perhaps she's jealous, but—"

"What did you say?" the priest asked.

"Did I use the wrong word? Let me think . . ." I searched my memory for the correct French term.

Madame Basilio leaned forward, her arm on his desk, her fingers brushing the leaves of the ledger as if she could not keep them still. "Jealousy? Bah! *He* was always the jealous one. Not her. I tell you, my angel—"

"How can she be an angel when she took her own life?" I had spoken impatiently and unthinkingly, and Madame Basilio's expression went stony.

"That is a lie. Where did you hear such talk?"

I realized my misstep. I should have remembered what Nero had told me, the story they'd circulated, the "accident" with no hint of mortal sin for priests and neighbors to judge. Even in New York, with Joshua, his suicide—if it had indeed been that, instead of an accidental overdose, which was just as bad, both ends unspeakable—had been covered up. *He'd been so very ill. He had a fatal reaction to a medication. Perhaps it was God's mercy that he was called to Heaven now. The disease could only have grown worse.*

My father had lied for the Lockwoods, giving them the face-saving excuse they'd needed, and I wondered if the priest was doing the same for Madame Basilio now. His expression was bland; I had no idea what he believed. Quietly, I said, "Forgive me. I'd heard a rumor. I should not be repeating such hurtful gossip."

"No," Madame Basilio said. "You should not."

Father Pietro said to me, "The room grows cold, you say? And you see strange things in his eyes?"

"He is not himself," I said, trying again to find the words to explain. "He tried to take his own life. He's afraid and impossible to control. He's so strong, too, much more so than he should be, and . . ." I faltered as Father Pietro's expression slowly changed from one of polite sympathy to horror.

"What?" I asked. "What is it?"

"She is trying to tell us something," Madame Basilio jumped in. "She wishes to show us the truth."

She'd said that before, and I'd thought she meant God's word, but now there was something about the way she said it that made me think it wasn't that at all. "What truth, Madame? What do you mean?"

Father Pietro's raised hand stopped her from answering me. "I would like to see him. Tomorrow, at noon. I wish some time to pray for guidance."

I still didn't know how he felt he could help. Prayers and confession, I felt, would be useless here. But then again, ghosts and demons were beyond my expertise. *How strange that I should even be considering this.* "Thank you, Father. Perhaps you can find the answer to this puzzle."

"I already know the answer," Father Pietro said.

"You do?"

Father Pietro said, "I begin to think that your patient is no longer just a man."

I frowned. I felt Madame Basilio stiffen beside me.

Father Pietro pressed his fingers to his lips thoughtfully. "I think we are dealing with a demon. What do you know about exorcism, mademoiselle?"

Chapter 26

Madame Basilio's sharply indrawn breath was too loud in the silence that followed the priest's words.

"Exorcism?" I asked in disbelief.

Nero's aunt began muttering in Venetian—a prayer, I thought. The priest frowned and said something to her, and she snapped back at him before rising abruptly, saying to me, "We must go now."

I looked at Father Pietro uncertainly. I had no idea what had passed between them, nor whether I should follow her lead. He said quietly, in French for my benefit, "I am not saying that your daughter has turned from God, Madame. I do not know that she is the demon who possesses M'sieur Farber."

"It *is* my daughter," Madame Basilio insisted. "She is trying to tell us something. She has answered my prayers. And she is no demon, but one of God's holy angels."

"We shall see," the priest said. "I shall be there tomorrow at noon. May God be with both of you."

Madame Basilio nearly ran spitting from the room. I followed more slowly. An exorcism. Possession. I would have said I didn't believe in it. But what I'd seen in Samuel's eyes, the way he spoke of her—in his head was her voice, her memories, her anguish and her anger. Singing her favorite song, speaking a language he did not know.

Possession.

The priest believed in it, and I had certainly heard of such things. My father would have said it was only madness, and until now, I might have said the same. But I knew it wasn't insanity I saw in Samuel, and this . . . well, I supposed it didn't matter what I believed. I wanted some kind of answer, as I had none of my own. I wanted someone to *do* something before I ended up having to make excuses to a grieving family again, before I had to find a way of making Samuel's end acceptable to a society already too prone to despise him.

Once we were out the door, and onto the abandoned campo, Madame Basilio turned to me in a fury. "God has not abandoned my daughter."

"Of course not," I said, placating.

"Laura did not take her own life. She would never have done such a thing."

My pity for her grew. "Perhaps she hid her despair from you."

"You come here and think you understand."

"I haven't meant to trouble you. I'm only trying to take care of my patient."

"Is that all?" she asked meanly. "I did not realize that bedding my nephew was part of M'sieur Farber's treatment."

What I would have given to be able to control my blushes.

Madame Basilio made a sound of satisfaction. "You are a fool. Ask Nerone what happened the night Laura died. I should dearly love to know what he says."

We were at the gate. She hurried through so quickly it nearly slammed shut before I could follow. I rushed after her.

"I don't understand. Are you accusing him of something?"

She stopped. Her expression set with displeasure. "I accuse him of nothing. But he will not answer my questions. Perhaps he will answer yours."

My thoughts were racing and dodging, everything dancing just out of my reach. I glanced up at the third floor, catching a movement in my bedroom window as if someone stood there watching. I gasped; the memory of the shrouded figure flashed back. It was her, that whisper of movement, that flicker of light. Laura Basilio's spirit. What else could it be?

I felt a moment of panic before I remembered that the room was not just mine anymore, but Nero's too. All this talk of ghosts and possession . . . It was no shroud I'd seen, but undoubtedly Nero moving about. Suddenly all thoughts of Laura's ghost, of Samuel and the visit with the priest, fled, and I was awash in the shame I'd felt beneath Giulia's gaze and at Madame Basilio's words, aware suddenly of my intense feelings for Nero, and how quickly I'd succumbed, how right it had felt to be in his arms.

The wantonness of my character troubled me. I was so easily seduced. Were other women so undone by desire? I'd felt the same kind of excitement in Joshua Lockwood's kiss, in Samuel's, that I'd felt in Nero's. What kind of a woman was I that I could let a man make love to me without the promise of a future? What was wrong with me that it was so easy?

I went up the stairs to the third floor with a heavy step. I had been incautious, but then again, what were the chances that word of this would get back to New York City, to my parents and my aunt and cousin? None perhaps, especially if I stopped it now.

The third floor was quiet. No laughter, no talk. I felt a flurry of fear: Where was Samuel? Again I thought of him opening the balcony door, stepping out, leaning too far over the rail. I hurried down the hall, but when I got to his room, he was in bed, sound asleep. Nero was nowhere in sight.

I went to my bedroom, thinking to find him there, but it was empty, the burning lamp the only evidence that he'd been there recently, the flickering light I'd seen from below. But when I stepped back into the hallway, the air felt prickly, charged, the way it did before a thunderstorm in New York, but softer, blurred and unfocused. *Laura's ghost*, I thought, and shivered, startled at how impressionable I was now, how much I wanted to believe something, anything, that seemed to explain Samuel's behavior, no matter how ludicrous. I wanted the priest to be right. I wanted to believe in possession, because that would mean Samuel wasn't mad. It would mean he could be cured.

The charged feeling didn't ease as I went to the sala, and I was reassured to see Nero there. He was half lounging on the settee, an open book on the cushions beside him. At the sight of him, I felt a surge of desire, the need to touch and be touched, a rush like adrenalin, but lower and deeper.

"What are you reading?" I asked.

He started. It was obvious that he'd been involved enough that I'd come upon him unawares. He didn't smile when he saw me, though. Slowly, he sat up. "A book I'd given to Samuel. I've read it before."

I could not read his expression, but it made me nervous in a way I couldn't explain. "It must be engrossing, if you've read it before and I could still sneak up on you."

"You would know, I imagine."

"I would?"

"I found it in your room." He flipped the cover closed. Yellow paper, worn and ragged. "Beneath your mattress."

"Oh. Oh, I . . ."

"I'm curious to know how it came to be in your possession." His tone was flat; I heard no emotion at all.

"Samuel asked me to read it."

"Really?" He rose, slow and languid. "For what reason? No, don't answer that. I can guess. The same reason any man gives a woman such a thing."

Now I recognized what I was seeing. Jealousy. I said quickly, "It's not what you think. He gave it to me because . . . because he wanted me to understand what I was asking him to give up."

"I see." Nero's voice was deceptively mild. "Did you read it with him?"

"Only a few paragraphs, and then I couldn't go on. He meant to tease me, that was all."

"Only to tease?" Nero stepped forward.

"Yes. He laughed at how embarrassed I was."

"Did he kiss you again?"

He advanced. Involuntarily, I stepped back. The wall was just behind me; there was no place else to go. I raised my chin and faced him—I had nothing to be ashamed of. *Except for the way you felt at Samuel's kiss. The way you liked the feel of him. How easily you respond to a touch.* "It wasn't like that."

"He wanted it to be like that, though, didn't he?"

I couldn't deny it; Nero knew already that was true.

He pressed closer, his body against mine now, pinning me there. "He meant to arouse you, didn't he?" His voice was hoarse; his eyes darkening, glittering, a danger I recognized, and a part of me thrilled at it, at how reckless he was, how passionate.

The air became electric; my breath turned to fog. The temperature dropped precipitously, and I tried to catch my breath. "Nero, this is ridiculous—"

"Did it work? Did he seduce you with the book? Which part did you like best, hmmm? The interlude with the priest? The one with the aunt? Did you like the whipping? Or the two women together—"

"N-none of those."

"Which part then?" His words materialized as frost. He pushed his hips into mine. "Come, cara, which appealed to you best? The toys? The two men with the virgin? The carriage ride? Which would you like to try? Did you tell Samuel?"

"Please, Nero." The images his words conjured . . . that flutter again. *What is wrong with you, that such perversions excite?* I felt ashamed and embarrassed, and below it all, aroused, and his jealousy aroused as well. "I'm not that kind of woman. I would never—"

"But you were that kind of woman with me, weren't you?" His voice was needling, as icy as the room. "All it took was a touch and you were mine. When I kissed you, you only wanted more. Why shouldn't I think it would be the same with any man?"

My own thoughts. My own fears. I struggled against them, and suddenly they were gone, and in their place were my desires manifest, a vision of him arching above me, pressing into me, rough and hard, his curls falling into his face, and the gleaming of his eyes, the snarl on his lips, his anger coalescing into something dark and dangerous and painful too, his jealousy raw and potent and terrifying, and suddenly I wanted that. I wanted him to feel how dangerous I was too. I wanted to hurt him. I could not resist it. I wanted him in my power. I wanted to see him crawl.

Before I understood what I was doing, I gripped the knife in my pocket; I drew the blade, bringing it up, pressing to the point just below his ribs.

He went very still, his eyes widening, jealousy giving way to wariness, and yes—yes, there it was. The fear I craved. I pressed harder.

"What are you doing?" he whispered.

I pressed harder, twisting my wrist so the flat of the blade was against his shirt.

"*Santa Maria*," he murmured.

But oh, I loved that look in his eyes. Fear and desire, anger and wariness and arousal. His nostrils flared; I felt the leap of intoxication between us. I wanted to see more. My skin felt too sensitive; I felt as if I were fashioned of ice, with a heart of fire, and within that heart my satisfaction burned. I saw him still and pale, on the floor. I could do that, I knew. Reduce him to nothing. One quick stab, and he would be at my feet, crawling in blood. Lifeless. Breathless.

I dug the knife a little deeper, raising a spot of blood. His gasp was hard and broken.

I could do it now. *Skin blue. Eyelashes crusted with frost. Beautiful and cold and still for eternity. One thrust of the knife and how ironic it would be. Stabbed through with his own blade* . . . how tempting it was.

"Elena," he whispered. His hand came to mine, gripped as it was about the hilt. His fingers were warm—so warm. How did my own become so cold? I felt the blood moving into them at his touch. His eyes burned. I was mesmerized by the working of his throat, the muscles, the bobbing of his Adam's apple.

Skin blue. Nero crawling on the floor at my feet. Supplication and pleas, begging for mercy only I could give . . .

"Cara. Elena."

I blinked, trying to think, my thoughts like mist snaking through my head, twining and hard to manage, hard to take hold of. It wasn't me. It didn't feel like me. I knew who it was. Laura Basilio, her spirit restless and angry and vengeful. A demon, Father Pietro had thought. *And if it were true? What then?*

I felt Nero's hand firm on mine. I felt the rapid rise and fall of his chest. I felt him watching, and Laura Basilio's desires snapped; I felt the loss of her, a clenched fist suddenly loosened, releasing, impotent in the wake of my claim. My mind was my own again, but now I'd felt the power I had over him, and I liked it. I wanted more. My arousal spiraled; I didn't know where such longing came from. *The Nunnery Tales*, perhaps, or perhaps it was only that the book fed something already within me. I didn't stop to consider; I only accepted it as mine. I pulled my hand with the knife gently from Nero's, and then I flashed the blade at him and said, "Take off your clothes."

My own boldness surprised me. But once I said it, I felt an exhilaration that was almost terrifying in its intensity. I felt . . . otherworldly. Not myself, but something stronger, better.

He frowned; I saw him measuring me through his uneasiness. "Here? Anyone could come in."

I gestured with the knife. "I don't care. Take off your clothes."

"Cara—"

"Or should I do it for you?" I asked.

I put the knife to his chest again, and he didn't move, but only watched me, his own breath hitching as I sliced one button from his shirt, opening the collar, and then another. I heard them ping to the floor, bounce and roll. When I got to the bottom of the placket, I simply sliced, straight through the fabric, splitting it neatly, exposing his skin. I gestured again.

His smile was dark and dangerous; I saw the way my hunger fed his. He said nothing, only slipped out of his coat, his shirt, letting them both fall to the floor. The light in the room flickered as if touched with a gasping breath. I ran the point of the knife lightly down his chest, not making a mark, but pressing enough that he must feel it. His breathing was shallow and fast. I rested the knife at the waistband of his trousers and looked up at him. "Now these."

I didn't take my gaze from his as he stepped out of them and his underwear, and he stood naked before me. I had never wanted anything as I wanted him in that moment. His smooth, olive-toned skin and the hardness of him and the gleaming blade. I pushed him back to the settee, the edge at the back of his thighs, and he sat down hard. *The Nunnery Tales* bounced to the floor, splaying open. Nero reached for me then, but I held up the knife in warning and shook my head, and his hands fell back.

I was trembling with the strain of waiting. I lifted my skirts, unfastened my drawers and let them fall, and then I straddled him. I knew I could put the knife down now, but there was a power in it I relished, a brutality and cruelty that called to me, that made me want to answer. Nero's gaze was coiled and watching. I dug the knife into his flesh, not hard, just another nick, a tiny bit of blood. His pained inhalation made my head spin with excitement and anticipation. I could wait no longer.

He looked at me in question, and I nodded, giving him permission. A single, quick movement, and he was inside me, and I was so ready I sighed in relief. I kept the knife at his chest, that little cut, his blood trickling. His hands were on my hips, and soon I was panting, and then breathless, and then mindless. The knife fell from my grip, clattering to the floor, and I was so lost in pleasure I didn't care.

He pulled me down to meet him in a kiss, and then his mouth slid to my cheekbone, my jaw, biting my earlobe gently, and then his hot breath on the tender skin below, his tongue, and I came unexpectedly and powerfully, crying out and bucking against him. He moaned and arched his hips, lifting us both from the settee. His hand came to my throat, tearing at the collar, revealing the bruises on my skin, his fingers dragging against them, evidence of Samuel's desire, and there in Nero's eyes was that jealousy again, and there was something so unbearably carnal in it I could not look away. He jerked from me with a cry, and I felt him throbbing between us, hot and sticky and wet. His hand fell from my throat, and it was as if his hold had been the only thing that made me solid, and now there was nothing to prevent me melting into nothing. I collapsed upon him, feeling his soft kiss on my shoulder, and on the floor the knife gleamed in the reflected light, sending its blinding shine into my eyes.

Chapter 27

He murmured against my hair, "What a surprise you are. Usually my jealousy only provokes women into calling me foul names and throwing things."

"Jealousy is a terrible fault," I whispered, trying not to feel shaken at what I'd just done, or how much I'd liked it.

"I know. I try to control it, but as you can see"—a wince, as if it pained him—"I am not always successful."

I picked up the blade and held it to his throat. "I understand. But if you ever accuse me of preferring Samuel again, I will use this on you. I promise."

"Don't tempt me," he said, that dark desire flashing through his eyes, his hand flexing on my hip. "I ask you, what was I to think when I found that book in your bed?"

"Perhaps not what you did."

"I gave it to him two years ago, and I've seen him use it many times. I know his intention."

"It might have been so once. Not anymore."

Nero laughed, short, disbelieving. "He can't take his eyes from you any more than I can."

I brushed my lips against his ear. "You should have more faith in your powers of persuasion."

"*Ai*, a mesmerist is what I am," he said self-deprecatingly. "This is why my betrothed left me for another man."

"I think she couldn't have known you as I do."

He cocked his head, again there was something in him I couldn't quite grasp—sadness, I thought. Something more than regret. "You should be careful, cara."

"Are you telling me not to fall in love with you?"

His hand traveled my thigh, fingers easing beneath my garter. "Truthfully, I wish you would."

"I'm halfway there already."

"It's only because you like what I do to you." He sighed. "I'm good at this, Elena, but not much else."

"Then you can keep doing this to me all across Europe."

He smiled ruefully. "How? As accommodating as you are, I can't think you'd like sleeping in the streets and scavenging for food."

"Perhaps it won't come to that after all."

He went suddenly attentive, all the soft languidness of after-math gone. "Yes, of course. You're very distracting. I forgot. What did the priest say? What happened?"

I moved off him, sitting beside him on the settee. He reached for his trousers as I said, "I hardly know where to start."

"Start with my aunt," he directed, pulling on his trousers, no underwear, and grabbed his shirt, pulling it on too, as ruined as it was, flapping open to reveal his chest. He sat down again, resting his elbows on his knees, leaning forward, his whole stance begging me to continue, a fiercely directed interest I could not resist.

I told him all of it. The priest's words, his aunt's anger, and the exorcism. "He's coming tomorrow at noon."

"What?" Nero looked thunderstruck. "An exorcism? Now I'm beginning to believe you're all mad. Don't tell me you believe a demon is possessing Samuel."

"I don't know. Whatever it is, perhaps Father Pietro can find out what it wants."

"Or perhaps we'll find it's only a figment of a fevered imagination."

"I have to admit that I hope Father Pietro is right. Then at least this would be over. I wouldn't have to worry about Samuel jumping off the balcony or anything else."

"Such despair doesn't have to come from a ghost or a demon, Elena. Sometimes it is only despair."

"I know that," I said, remembering my own. Then I heard what was in his tone, and I looked at him in surprise. "You've tried it yourself. You've thought about suicide."

He said, "I've thought of jumping off this balcony a hundred times. It seems to be a family trait. We are all prone to self-destruction."

"You mean . . . because of this house. When you're here."

"Unfortunately, it's not just here. If not coming here helped me to escape my thoughts, I'd never return. But no, they follow me everywhere. Laura hated my 'black moods,' as she called them. Ask Samuel. He's seen them a time or two. Everyone does. Fair warning. I suppose I shouldn't have told you that. I'll frighten you away."

"No."

He hesitated. "Here is something else I should not tell you. You won't think well of me."

"I suppose I should know the worst, shouldn't I? If we mean to . . . continue."

"Do we mean to?" he asked quietly.

I looked away, forcing myself to say, "You don't want to. I understand—"

"I'm falling in love with you, Elena." His voice was so soft. When I looked at him again, his gaze seemed to penetrate; I felt it in every part of me. "But you should know what I am before it's too late."

"Too late for what?" I managed.

"It's unfair of me to ask you to help me be a better man if I don't tell you what I've done."

That unease again, along with a searing little joy, an unsettling mix. "What have you done?"

"I killed him. Laura's lover. I shot him."

Involuntarily, I jerked away. Whatever I'd been expecting, it wasn't that.

His expression became deprecating. He made to rise. "Perhaps I was expecting too much—"

"No!" I grabbed his arm before he could move. "You surprised me, that's all. You can't just walk away without explaining."

He took a deep breath. "You know I had reason. I challenged him to a duel."

"A duel? That's against the law."

"This is Venice," he said. "Murder and vengeance are our traditions. Though, actually, it was in Milan where I caught up with him. I told you, jealousy is a fault. I had been in Paris with Samuel, and he got me drunk and stupid enough that I calmed down, at least when it came to Laura. But the thought of *him* . . . I tried, but I couldn't get past what he'd stolen from me. I couldn't just let it lie. When I heard he was in Milan, I left Paris to challenge him. He accepted. It was a fair fight. He lost. I suppose . . . I didn't have to kill him. But I did."

"This is why your aunt told me to ask you what happened the night Laura died."

"Did she?" A short laugh. "Another old refrain. She wants so much to believe that Laura didn't kill herself that she's convinced herself I must have played a part in it. But I don't know what happened the night Laura died. I wasn't here. I was bribing authorities in Milan. After that, I returned to Paris. Still, my aunt is right to blame me. I blame myself. Laura might have forgotten her suffering. She might have grown to love me again. But when she heard what I'd done . . . you know the rest. It's my fault she jumped into that rio, Elena. No one else's."

I stared down at his hand over mine, fingers that had been so gentle. I wanted to be able to say that I could not imagine him so angry that he'd killed a man. But today . . . I'd seen his jealousy, the volatility that had frightened me.

Still, I could not stand for him to take the blame when there were other things I saw as well. He was too ready to be thought terrible, but I knew he was right; I *could* make him a better man. I would start with changing his perception. "You said Laura wrote you that she expected Filippo Polani to fight for her. Did he? Did he try to change your aunt's mind? Did he write to you and ask you to step down?"

Nero shook his head. "No, none of those things. He gave her up and left for Milan. Another reason I should have let him live. But to think of her pining away for him . . ."

"She *was* pining. That was why she jumped, Nero. Not because you killed him but because the man she loved didn't fight for her. He walked away. That would have been the bigger hurt." Her lover gone, leaving her a prisoner in a house of madness and bitterness and sorrow. I thought of what might happen to me if my life became what I dreaded. A lifetime of wanting more and never having it. A time when a maid's interruption might come too late to keep me from opening a window latch.

"She'd misjudged him. How could she live with that? She'd dreamed of a life different from the one she had, and it was gone because the man she'd chosen was not what she'd imagined him to be. She had only the mess she'd made and no way to repair it. The future seems unendurable. How do you go on, knowing you'll be watched every moment because of your indiscretion, that you'll be married off, only to wonder forever what you might have had if you hadn't been so stupid as to think you were different from every other woman. What a fool you were, to believe that you were special—" I stopped short, realizing what I was revealing, seeing the way Nero stared at me—was that pity in his eyes?

I looked down, banishing the past, regrets, everything Laura's story brought back. We had much in common, and that was frightening too, that I had felt such pain, that I understood why she had jumped.

Nero lifted my chin so I was forced to look at him. He kissed me gently, a brush of his lips that sent every nerve tingling. He whispered, "I've changed my mind. I think I'm the one who should be careful. You will shatter me."

I tried to smile. "I haven't the skill for shattering."

"What is this, a bacchanal? Why was I not invited?" Samuel said from the doorway.

I jerked away, and Nero let me go. "I didn't want the competition," he said, smiling, looking every inch debauched and languid, his shirt spilling open, hair falling across his brow. "It's not often that a woman has eyes only for me."

Samuel smiled, but it was pained. "You look cold."

"No buttons. Elena has a way with a knife," Nero said, taking up the edges, letting them fall again. "As I think you know."

"She was a bit more zealous with me." Samuel's hand went to his chest, to the wound I knew was there. "I wish it had been only my shirt that suffered."

I did not miss the edge in their banter. I ignored it, and my embarrassment, and rose from the settee, going to Samuel, who looked terrible, drawn and tired, as he limped into the room. He was not the kind of man whom pale listlessness flattered.

He said, "The morphine is only making my dreams worse."

"Did you sleep at all?"

"I kept hearing noises. Moaning. Panting. The settee creaking."

I blushed. Nero grinned. "A pity you had not been only a few minutes later."

"A fault of mine. I'm always too early or too late." Samuel sank onto the settee beside Nero, his foot kicking the edge of *The Nunnery Tales*, which had slid beneath. He leaned over to see, and raised his brow at me. "Putting it to good use, are you? Though not really as I'd intended."

"Always the teacher," Nero said with deceptive lightness. I saw the way his hand gripped the carved wood of the armrest. "I am happy to inform you that your pupil has learned *very* well."

"I still have the knife," I said mildly, trying to pretend I wasn't horribly chagrined. "Perhaps you'd like a wound to match Samuel's?"

Nero looked surprised.

Samuel laughed. "Careful, my friend, she has a sting." He turned to me; again I saw his hurt, limned with anger. "Did you find the priest you went looking for? Or have you been too distracted to remember me?"

"I spoke to him, along with Madame Basilio."

Nero made a sound of contempt. "According to Padre Pietro, God's armies are waging battles inside of you. The priest wishes to be a general leading the charge."

Samuel looked at me in question.

"He wants to do an exorcism," I said. "Tomorrow at noon."

"A *what*?"

I told him what had transpired with the priest. When I was finished, Samuel asked, "You believe I'm possessed? You agreed to this?"

"It's your decision, of course. But I don't know how else to explain what's happening to you."

"Why not just admit that Nero's right and I'm mad?"

"Is that what you want? Because if it is, we can arrange for you to return to Glen Echo, though my father won't be there to see to you. I can't vouch for whoever will take over. But if you wish it, say the word, and I'll see it done."

Samuel was quiet for a moment. Then, "If I do this exorcism, and it doesn't work, what then?"

"Then we'll try something else. I promised I wouldn't leave you, and I won't."

Samuel got to his feet woodenly. I could only watch as he came up to me. His hand brushed my arm as if he searched for comfort, and then fell away again. He leaned close, his breath hot against my ear as he whispered, "No restraints, Elena. Promise me."

"I promise."

"Thank you." His relief was obvious. "And Nero—you'll be here tomorrow, won't you? You'll witness?"

"Of course," Nero said.

"Then . . . don't let me hurt her."

Nero was quiet, hooded, contemplative in a way I hadn't seen. "I'll see to it."

Samuel left. I heard his heavy, halting step into the hall, and I felt sick, the decision I'd made untenable and somehow wrong, though I could not think of any other way. I wished I could take it back. I wished I knew something else to do. I felt alone and vulnerable—and then I looked at Nero and saw his affection for Samuel in the lines on his face, a worry that matched my own. I wasn't alone. He was here with me. It was enough to comfort, for now.

Chapter 28

Father Pietro arrived with the ringing of the noon Angelus from the Madonna dell' Orto, the echoes and murmurs of Venice's other church bells wafting and lulling in chorus, music that seemed ominous and eerie and bodiless, suspended as it was in the fog that shrouded the city. That morning I'd gone to Samuel's balcony, needing to see the color of the dyer's canal. It seemed important to know what it was. *Not red*, I prayed. *Please, not red*. But all I could see was a thick layer of fog below, as if it meant deliberately to hide the color. I hoped it was not a portent.

Both Giulia and Madame Basilio accompanied the priest to the third floor. He was vested in surplice and purple stole, wearing a large cross around his neck and bearing a heavy leather bag and a Bible, and the moment I saw his serious expression, I wanted to send him back to the church, to cancel the rite. It all seemed too much for this . . . this was not so large a problem, was it, that it required God's mediation?

We were in the sala. Samuel lay exhausted on the settee, eyes closed; Nero leaned against the wall, arms crossed over his chest, surveying the scene with thinly veiled contempt. When his aunt entered, he gave her a look of such accusatory scorn I was surprised that she did not wither beneath it. It had the opposite effect: her already ramrod-straight spine went rigid, her chin jutted out, bristling as if at any moment she might start spewing a stream of poison. The dislike between them was so palpable that even Father Pietro felt it. He frowned at them, though he said nothing.

Giulia leaned over Samuel, brushing his hair back from his forehead. He did not respond, not with a look or a smile, and I felt a thin satisfaction when she drew her hand away, clearly annoyed.

Father Pietro gestured to Samuel. "This is the afflicted one?"

I nodded.

The priest clutched his Bible more tightly. "If I could ask you some questions, m'sieur."

"As you will," Samuel said tiredly.

Father Pietro peered down at him as if he could see into Samuel's soul. "Have you had a loss of appetite?"

"No."

"Have you tried to harm yourself? Cutting, biting, scratching?"

"I tried to throw myself into the rio. Does that count?"

The priest frowned. He held out the cross around his neck, brandishing it in Samuel's face. Samuel only stared up at him blandly. Father Pietro stood there for a moment, measuring. I wondered if he'd expected Samuel to burst into flame at the sight of a holy object. He seemed disappointed that Samuel didn't.

"Have you entered a church recently?" Father Pietro asked.

"No."

"Because you could not?"

"Because I would not," Samuel responded. "I haven't been to church in years."

"Then I would hear your confession, my son."

"I've nothing to confess. Or too much. It comes to the same thing. I committed sins with deliberation and purpose. I have no wish for God's forgiveness."

Father Pietro turned to me. "Have there been strange bodily postures? Frenzies?"

Samuel's gaze jerked to mine, a warning. I willed Nero to say nothing about Samuel's epilepsy, and said to the priest, "He's attacked me, as I said. I would call it a frenzy."

"Does he speak an unnatural language? Or one he's claimed no knowledge of?"

"Venetian," I said. "He's spoken it in trance but says he doesn't know it."

"I don't," Samuel said. "Beyond a few words—mostly curses. And some of those ridiculous proverbs Nero's always spouting. *Fra Marco e Todaro*, things like that. That's the extent of it."

"But your nurse says you're strangely strong," the priest went on, half murmuring, as if he spoke to himself. He glanced about. "Cold in the room."

"It's always cold in here," Nero said. "Just as it is everywhere in Venice in the winter. The dell' Orto is frigid—you should tend to your own house, padre. By the way it feels, the church is swimming in demons."

"Nerone," Madame Basilio said sternly.

Giulia dipped her head with a little amused smile.

I felt a stab of irritation and said quietly, "It's a different kind of cold. An unnatural kind."

"Then I think we have enough proof that it is not just madness."

"Have we?" Nero asked. "Are we really so certain?"

The priest ignored him. "We will proceed." He reached into his bag and pulled out a tangle of thick leather straps—it was a moment before I caught Samuel's look of horror and realized what the priest meant to do with them.

"No," I said quickly. "No restraints. He won't be a danger."

"He attacked you, mademoiselle."

"He won't be a danger."

"I'm afraid I cannot take the risk." But Father Pietro did not look sorry as he approached Samuel.

"No." I turned desperately to Nero.

He pushed off from the wall, striding to the settee. "Leave him be, padre. I won't let him attack anyone."

Father Pietro looked uncertain, but he nodded and dropped the restraints to the floor, though within arm's reach. He said to Samuel, "Kneel before me."

Samuel obeyed, sliding off the settee and falling to his knees, but it was clear it was a position he could not keep for long. He swayed with exhaustion and pain, his hair falling into his hollowed eyes, the pink of his new-made scars the only color on his face. The priest reached into his bag again, taking out a bottle of what I assumed was holy water.

He gestured for us all to come closer, and then he made the sign of the cross over Samuel, over himself, and then the rest of us, sprinkling everyone with holy water. He knelt before Samuel and bowed his head, closing his eyes, murmuring a prayer I had no familiarity with, calling for us to repeat after him, which I did without really listening, *Lord have mercy, Christ have mercy . . . Christ graciously hear us . . .* on and on, seemingly forever, a listing of saint's names *Michael and Gabriel and Raphael . . . Benedict, Bernard, Dominic, Francis . . . Mary Magdalen, Lucy, Agnes . . .* a stupor of names.

Samuel's swaying became more pronounced; Nero watched him with half-lidded eyes, taut with expectation—he would be on Samuel in a moment if he fell, I knew. Madame Basilio mouthed the litany along with the father silently, almost ecstatic. Giulia stood with her hands clasped before her, looking . . . afraid. I wondered what she feared, and then I remembered that she'd seen Samuel in a frenzy.

From the window, sunlight glowed through the fog, sending a current of rippling reflection over the ceiling.

The priest switched to Latin, the droning rhythm of which sent me into a near trance. I saw Samuel's eyes close, his head droop forward, shoulders down. Nero started toward him, but then Father Pietro said, "Amen," and Madame Basilio and Giulia echoed him, and Samuel roused, starting when the priest raised his voice, booming, reverberating, made the sign of the cross and then: "*Praecípio tibi, quicúmque es, spíritus immúnde . . .*" on and on, his voice seeming to fill the room. He placed his hands on Samuel's head and raised his own, speaking again, and then traced a flurry of signs on himself, on Samuel's brow, over his heart. Samuel leaned his head back, staring up at the ceiling, that mesmerizing, rippling light, sparkles of sunlight chasing now, bursting through the fog in little flashes—

Flashing lights.

Samuel twitched, a quick flex of his fingers.

No, oh no.

The priest raised his arms. "*Exorcizo te, immundíssime spíritus, omnis incúrsio adversárii, omne phantasma—*"

"Samuel," I said urgently, not caring that I interrupted, ignoring Father Pietro's frown, the shake of his head. "Samuel, look at me. Look at me."

It was too late. Samuel shouted—a short, piercing shriek, hands up as if to ward off an approaching specter, and then he fell as if something attacked him. His head cracked upon the edge of the settee, his eyes rolled back, and he was convulsing, jerking and contorting, teeth gnashing. Father Pietro started, his eyes widening. Giulia dropped to her knees, babbling in terror. Nero nearly threw himself over the settee to get to Samuel, looking to me in desperation. "What do I do? Tell me what to do."

I ran over, shoving the settee to keep Samuel from hurting himself on it.

"Hold him as best as you can," I ordered, fumbling in my pocket for the bit of leather to shove between his teeth that I should have been carrying—and wasn't.

Father Pietro yanked me away, nearly throwing me to the floor behind him. "Stand back!" he shouted. "The demon is come!"

"It's no demon—"

"*Vade retro satana!*" he cried, brandishing his crucifix, repeating it again, once more, leaning over Samuel, wielding the cross like a weapon. Nero tried vainly to still Samuel's flailing arms. Madame Basilio watched almost rabidly.

Saliva foamed at Samuel's mouth. He struck out; the priest dodged, and the blow landed squarely on Nero's cheek.

"*Vade retro satana!*"

"Quiet!" Nero choked. "You're not helping, padre. Can't you see it?"

"*Exorcizo te, immundíssime spíritus, omnis incúrsio adversárii . . .*"

I tried to push my way back in. Father Pietro forced me away, his face sharp with concentration, religious conviction giving him a strength I didn't expect.

Then I felt it: the freezing draught, burrowing into bone, sending shivers over my flesh, swirling, a whirlwind of feeling, fury and distress. Madame Basilio felt it too, I realized. She looked up at the ceiling, and the ecstasy that burst over her face was almost obscene in its intensity. She looked like a saint in the throes of orgiastic revelation, skin stretched too tight, cheeks hollowed, the bones of her skull defined and set—terrifying.

Samuel gave a cry. His back arched, raising his hips violently from the ground, and he muttered Venetian words. Ones he'd said before: "*Chi comincia mal, finisse pezo.*" Then he began to choke. He tried to pry away fingers at his throat, throttling fingers that weren't there. Red marks began to form on his skin, though there were no hands to make them, the tendons in his neck collapsing, his breath strained and gasping as we all watched in horror.

He was being strangled, but not by anything we could see.

He gasped, ". . . *lasagnone . . . garbatìn . . .*"

Nero sprang back in shock, his gaze leaping to his aunt. She stared at her nephew as if he had become a monster before her very eyes.

I lurched forward, pushing Father Pietro with all of my strength, surprising him so he let me through, and fell upon Samuel. I pulled away his hands. The bruises on his throat were still forming. I screamed, "Help him! Someone stop her!" and no one did anything but stare. "Samuel, come back to me. Come back. Fight her. Please."

He shuddered; I felt his attention like a terrible, wicked thing, intention and determination. He made a horrible gurgling sound, and his hands clasped my throat, curving round, squeezing, squeezing, the power and strength of him impossible to dislodge, Father Pietro's voice in my ear, his hand with the crucifix at the edge of my vision. *"Vade retro satana!"*

I couldn't breathe, those black stars now, the cross and the priest's hand blurring, and then someone was pulling at me—Nero—and Samuel opened his eyes to stare at me, and they were black too—she was there again. *"Mé viscara,"* he murmured, a small, dreadful smile on his lips, satisfaction and victory, his strength something prodigious, a necklace of linked reddened marks about his neck, matching mine—Nero pushed between us. I heard the thwack of bone against flesh, and the pressure on my throat eased; pain and air rushed in, dizzying. I fell back, gasping, and then I realized that Samuel was unmoving, unconscious. Madame Basilio's eyes shone; I did not miss the vindication in her expression when she looked at me. Nero pulled me into his arms until I was cradled against his chest, muttering a stream of Venetian into my ear, his English having completely deserted him, kisses in my hair, his heart racing against my cheek—or was that my own?

I collapsed into him, tears blurring my eyes, the shock of everything numbing, horror still buzzing. It was some moments before I could bring myself to lift my head from the comfort of his chest, the soft linen of his shirt, and I saw that Father Pietro was busy strapping an unconscious Samuel into restraints.

I wrenched away from Nero. "What are you doing?"

"We cannot risk that the devil will still be inside him when he wakes," the priest said grimly.

"But it's not the devil. Don't you see? It's—"

"Quiet," Nero whispered, dragging me back. "Cara, quiet. Let him do as he will for now."

"Samuel hates restraints."

"I know."

"You don't understand. At—"

"Quiet, cara. *Shhh*. Not now."

He held me close, pressing my face again into his chest. Madame Basilio and Giulia and the priest spoke tersely to each other in Venetian. Now and then Nero interjected something in a curt voice, and I thought he sounded tense and frightened and angry. But I could not blame him for that. The image came to me again, bruises being made by invisible hands, and I was horrified all over again. But as I began to calm, questions came too. The otherness in Samuel's eyes and his smile of victory reminded me a little too well of the vindication I'd just seen on Madame Basilio's face. Whatever had happened, Nero's aunt had wanted it to be so. Whatever had happened, I thought that she understood it.

Perhaps she did. I didn't.

The priest said something to Nero, who nodded and drew gently away. He peered at my throat, pushing aside strands of my fallen hair to see. "Are you all right?"

"Shaken, that's all."

He was as well, I knew. He kissed me in full view of his aunt and Giulia, and I heard Madame Basilio's hiss of disapproval. Then he said, "I'm going to help the padre take Samuel to bed."

I nodded. "I'll get the morphine."

"I think he has no need of it now. For how long will he be asleep? What's usual?"

I tried to think. My thoughts were a shamble, everything jangling and twisting.

"Elena," he prompted.

I turned my attention back to him. "I don't know. Minutes. Hours. It can be either. He won't remember any of this when he wakes."

Nero looked thoughtful. He squeezed me reassuringly and rose, turning to help the priest lift Samuel from the floor, his arms bound to his sides with leather straps that wound to his thighs.

I said, "Take those off him when you put him to bed."

"He asked me to keep you from harm, Elena. He would want it."

Knowing that was true didn't make it more bearable. Nero and the priest struggled with Samuel's limp body to the doorway. I saw the way Nero glanced at his aunt, not scorn now, but something else, something pointed and sharp. Dread. Or fear. He said to me, "Come with us. You'll want to check him over."

But I understood that what he really wanted was for me to be away from his aunt, who stood watching, seeming nearly to twitch with a kind of half-suppressed emotion—I couldn't tell what it was. Satisfaction or grief. Horror or malice. I liked nothing about her. I was afraid of her. I had no idea why I felt that what had happened here today had been exactly what she'd hoped for—and more than that, that she was confused now as to what to do with it. How did one put the specter that had arisen today back into its box?

The last thing I wanted was to be alone with her. And so I followed Nero and the worried-looking priest from the sala, and when we were in the hallway, Father Pietro said, "We may have to do this again. I am not confident I have expelled the demon."

"It's not a demon I'm afraid of," I replied.

Chapter 29

Father Pietro had gone. He asked us to send for him when Samuel awakened, but the moment I heard the close of the door, I said quietly to Nero, "I don't want him back here."

Nero only nodded. He seemed distracted, unsettled; we both were. He pulled the chairs over to Samuel's bedside, and we sat there, watching him sleep, rigid and straight beneath the blankets, bound about with leather straps.

For a very long time, we were silent. Then Nero said, "What happened?"

"I don't know. It was a seizure, but . . . something else too. Did you feel it? How cold the air became?"

He shook his head. "No, I didn't. I've never seen him do that before."

"It's unnerving, I know."

"How often does it happen?"

"When he's taking his medicine, they happen less often. My father felt he had it nearly controlled the last time Samuel left Glen Echo."

"Does he always try to throttle himself that way?"

"Throttle himself?" I asked in surprise.

"He had his hands around his own throat. His bruises will be worse than yours."

I was stunned. "Nero, Samuel didn't make those marks."

Nero's brow furrowed. "Of course he did. I watched him."

"Something else did. The ghost." I believed it fully now. There was nothing else to explain, nothing else that made sense.

Nero's voice was sharp with disbelief. "Elena, do you hear yourself? A ghost strangled Samuel hard enough to leave bruises? How is that even possible?"

"I know it sounds absurd. But what else could it be?"

"I saw Samuel put his hands around his own throat."

"He was trying to loosen her hold."

Nero let out a rushed breath of exasperation and raked his hand through his hair. "You're as bad as Aunt Valeria. She planted the idea in your head the moment you arrived. There's a ghost, she says, and suddenly you're believing it must be true. Don't you see how she's manipulated you? She has no peer when it comes to that. Believe me, I know. If Laura were here, she would tell you the same."

"I think Laura is here," I said steadily.

Nero bit off a Venetian curse. He rose restlessly, pacing from one end of the bed to the other.

I went on, "The look on your aunt's face when it was over . . . did you see? I think she understands Laura's message, whatever it is."

Nero stopped short, pivoting to face me. "There is no message, Elena. What my aunt saw was a man in a seizure, and a ludicrous priest only making everything worse."

"She said Laura didn't kill herself," I pushed on. "That's what she told me. She said it wasn't in Laura's nature. Do you think that could be true?"

A short laugh. "No, I don't. Aunt Valeria closed her eyes to Laura's sorrow. She can't accept her own guilt in refusing to break the betrothal. Another reason for her to hate me—because I remind her that she too is to blame. She'd rather believe the story we told everyone. I think she's convinced herself it's true. But the answers don't change just because my aunt wishes them to."

"You're certain it wasn't an accident, that she meant to jump."

"It was no accident. Laura was unhappy. She hated this house. She was angry at the world. She wrote me all of those things in her last letter. She told me she wished to leave it all behind, that there was no place for her. By the time the letter arrived, it was too late to help her; she was already gone. Yes, she meant to jump."

"Then why?" I asked. "If she did take her life, why would her spirit return? What does she hope to tell us?"

"What if it's only Samuel's imagination?" he asked. "Some lesion in his brain that tells him to hurt you and himself? Those seizures must cause damage."

"My father believes they do, eventually," I admitted. "But it doesn't explain that strange cold."

"This place is full of drafts. A board on a window has come loose. Or the damper on the stove isn't closed. Elena, there are a hundred ways to explain all this."

My father had been a scientist with no faith in the unseen, and now Nero's words reminded me that I had been Papa's best student. My certainty faltered. The palazzo was falling apart. There were holes in the plaster; the ceilings were spiderwebbed with cracks; boarded windows everywhere. It could have been only a draft, and my imagination and fear had run away with me. And as for the marks around Samuel's throat . . . had I really watched them form before my eyes, beneath the pressure of invisible hands? Or had Samuel's own fingers made them? Suddenly, I could not quite remember exactly what I'd seen.

Perhaps what Nero said was true, and the answers could not be different than they were. Perhaps I would achieve nothing by speaking with Madame Basilio. But I could not rid myself of the belief that what had happened today had answered a question for her.

I could not just let it lie.

I rose. "I'm going to talk to your aunt. I want to ask her what she thought she saw today."

Nero started and grabbed my arm, his distress evident. "Elena, please. Don't pursue this."

"How can I not? I want to know if she saw what I did."

"Think of my family. We've been hiding this a long time. You'll only raise questions that are better left unasked, when it's all easily enough explained by Samuel's illness. My aunt isn't well either. You'll only make things worse. Did you not see her when we left? She looked ready to swoon. She was crying, Elena. Talk to her if you must, but not right now. Give her some time. She's a grieving old woman who believes she saw her daughter's ghost today. You'll get no sense from her. And I don't want her more upset than she is already."

His concern for a woman who treated him so badly lodged a soft spot in my heart. I remembered the confusion of emotions playing over her face. I had not thought of it from her point of view, but I realized Nero was right. Madame Basilio had been undone. It would be more compassionate to wait.

"Very well," I said. "Tomorrow will be soon enough."

He released my arm gratefully. "I should go see to her. But I don't want to leave you alone here. If he wakes—"

"He's bound so tightly he can't move. And I have the morphine and a knife." I patted my pocket. "I'll be fine. Go see to your aunt. It does you credit that you want to."

He made a face and then smiled softly. "I don't want to. You see? Already you're making me a better man."

"I'll see you're a saint before the year is up."

"Perhaps not a saint," he said with a wicked smile, pulling me against him. "That would be boring for you, I think. Ah, I love your blushes. Are you pink all over? I should like to see."

"I thought you meant to look in on your aunt."

"Perhaps later. In an hour. Do you think that enough time?"

"Enough time for what?"

"To see just how pink you are." A kiss on the tip of my nose. "I want to explore every inch of you."

From the bed came a rustling, a restless movement.

I pushed Nero gently away. "Samuel's waking up. Go. I'll be safe enough."

He glanced over his shoulder at Samuel. "Are you certain you'll be all right?"

"Shall I show you the knife?"

Again that smile. "I wish you would. But probably it would be inappropriate just now."

I gave him a little shove. "Go."

"Very well. But, cara, be careful, yes? Shout if you need me?"

I promised, and he left, looking back as he did so, clearly worried, and I felt warm and protected.

I sat back down just as Samuel roused again. A murmur, a movement, quickly stifled by the restraints. His eyes flew open. He blinked at me, obviously confused, and then frowned as he tried to move his arms. The panic that leaped into his eyes made me want to loosen the straps immediately. But I was wary now, my throat throbbing again.

"Elena?" he said my name uncertainly, testing his memory.

"Don't try to move," I warned.

The panic didn't lessen. Now it was joined by fear. "What did I do?" His voice was gravel; the bruises on his throat seemed to pulse brightly.

"What do you remember?"

He closed his eyes; I saw his struggle for memory. "Umm . . . Nero's shirt. You cut it."

"That was yesterday," I soothed. "Do you remember anything more recent?"

"Water. Cold, and . . . and struggling." He opened his eyes again, frowning, perplexed. "I drowned." Another movement, as if he tried to raise his arm, a hushed sound of frustration. "My throat hurts."

"You didn't drown," I said calmly. "The priest was here to do an exorcism. Do you remember?"

He struggled against the bonds. "I can't breathe. It hurts."

"I know. Be still or you'll make it worse—"

More struggling, another flare of panic. "Catch me! I'm falling—someone catch me!"

I put my hand on his chest. "You're not falling. Do you feel my hand? I'm right here. You're in bed. You're not falling."

"It hurts. It hurts . . . afraid . . ." He twisted, tossing his head on the pillow, hair falling in his eyes, which were full of pain and fear, but he was not here. Not with me, but in some other memory. "So much . . . red." A garbled, ratcheted breath.

I hated this. It was not unusual for patients after a seizure to not know where they were, to make no sense. All I could do was comfort and reassure and wait until his mind caught up with him again.

"Stinks. So cold." A shudder that racked his whole body. He looked at me, only bewilderment in his eyes, and then I saw awareness sneak back, recognition. "I remember. Falling and drowning, and I was afraid. You saved me."

"You were never falling or drowning," I said. "There was a priest. Father Pietro. He said some words, a few prayers, and you had a seizure. You never left the sala."

Frowning confusion. "But I remember. I didn't want to fall. I knew I was going to drown and I didn't want to. My throat hurt.

There was so much red." He jerked, trying to escape the restraints. "Take these off. Please. You know how much I hate them. Take them off."

"Everyone feels you'd be better—"

"Get them off me!" He flailed, bucking against the mattress. "Get them off!"

I leaned over him, both hands on him now, pinning his shoulders. "Samuel, look at me. Samuel. You're only making it worse."

"Get them off!" Stricken with terror, his eyes beginning to roll—and all I could think was that he was going to send himself into another seizure, and I couldn't stand to see him this way. "You promised! You promised!"

I felt sick and helpless. "I'll take them off. But you must be still, can you do that? Be still. Tell me you won't hurt me."

He nodded. "I can't breathe. My throat hurts."

I peeled back the blankets. The straps had been wound tight. Carefully, I wrestled with the buckle of one of them. "I can't get this without pulling it a bit tighter."

His face was white, but he nodded. I pulled the strap, trying to push the prong back through the leather hole. I felt Samuel tense, the rapid rise and fall of his breath.

"Almost there." I pushed it through. One strap loosened. Samuel relaxed infinitesimally. "Now another one."

There were four, one just below his shoulders, another across his chest, above his hips, and the last at his thighs. It took me a long time to undo them; the priest had been overzealous, especially given that he'd been shackling an unconscious man. I was on the strap that kept his hands well at his sides, and Samuel clenched and unclenched his fists so forcefully I said, "You must be still or I can't do this."

"Your throat," he said. "It looks worse."

I focused on the buckle, which was very tight, the strap so firmly lodged in the buckle frame that I could hardly budge it. "It's nothing."

"There are new bruises there."

"They match your own," I said, managing to ease the leather back.

"I tried to strangle you again."

"Samuel, be still." I pushed the prong through. Success. Another one loosened.

But Samuel grabbed the strap as I tried to pull it away. "Don't."

"Don't what?"

"Untie me."

I sighed in exasperation. "You've just been begging me to do so."

He flinched; I saw how much it cost him to say it. "Undo the restraints, but tie my hands to the bedposts. Loosely, though, so I can move, but tightly enough that I can't reach you."

"You're in no condition to hurt me."

"Do as I say, dammit." His voice went hard, an order. "And tell me what happened. Exactly."

I explained it all to him as I did as he asked, looping one strap to his wrist and tying it to the bedpost, and then doing the same with the other before I addressed the final strap binding his hips. He sighed when I finished both the explaining and the buckle.

"I would have sworn I drowned," he said. "I can still see it. I can feel it. Like a memory. I know—I think I know—that it never happened, but it's confusing. It feels like it belongs to me."

Slowly, I began to understand, to make connections that had eluded me before. "The dreams you had of Nero's family felt like your own memories too. That's what you said."

He closed his eyes. "Christ, so sad. I felt . . . so sad. I still can't quite believe I didn't see them myself."

How strained he looked, shadows highlighting the fine chiseling of his long face. He'd lost weight since I'd been here; there were hollows in him where there had not been before. I studied him—arms stretched, hands dangling from wristbands of the heavy leather leashing him to the bedposts, the darkening bruises mottling his throat. I felt in him a surrender, a painfully acute exhaustion, and I ached so for him that I found myself dangerously near tears. He could not bear much more of this, I knew. I had to find an answer, and quickly, before he gave in completely, before he did go as mad as Nero believed he was, or worse, before he answered the call of the canal.

I leaned over him, brushing his too-long hair from his face, and he turned his head, easing into my hand. "Don't stop," he whispered.

I cupped his cheek and said quietly, "I won't."

Such a small promise. Only a comforting touch. Something I could do without thought or consequence. But I realized in that moment that I was no longer here for the reasons I'd thought. I was no longer here for the reward of a Grand Tour, or to redeem the mistake I'd made, or to salvage my father's name.

This house had done nothing but wish me ill from the moment I'd set foot within it, and yet I recognized its pleas for help. I felt how they colored Samuel's visions and his dreams like the dye in the canal. I felt them in the watchfulness of crumbling statues. And I knew, as I stroked Samuel's hair, that to save him I needed to understand the house too. I needed to understand the secrets its walls had seen—Laura Basilio's secrets—and somehow find a way to make all this misery a dream of the past.

Chapter 30

I roused when Nero returned that night. As he came into the room, I heard voices in the courtyard nudging through my half sleep, Madame Basilio calling, "Giulia!" and then a chatter of dialect, followed by the clang of metal against stone.

Nero smelled of cold. His hair was flecked with icy droplets. "It's snowing again," he whispered as he crawled naked into bed beside me, fingers already at the buttons of my nightgown, drawing the muslin from my shoulders, pushing it down to nuzzle my breasts. "Warm me up, cara."

Which I did, with enthusiasm, until we were both sweating and languid, and then I fell back into sleep touched with disturbing dreams—wisps of spirit floating through the air, twisting in the currents, walls crumbling at my touch to reveal deeper, darker shadows that stretched so far back into time and terror I could not see the end, a canal pulsing red and churning with algae and flotsam, a woman falling from a balcony, chestnut-colored hair flying upward, white gown tangling about her bare legs, arms flailing.

I woke in the middle of the night, gasping and frightened. I reached out to touch Nero, certain he was dead, panicked until I felt the steady rise and fall of his chest. I laid my cheek against him to hear his heartbeat, burrowing close; his arm came around me in sleep, and after that, I dreamed of nothing.

But everything felt different when I woke to gray morning light and snowflakes falling intermittently and slow, melting the moment they hit the stones below. A seemingly benign scene, and one that should have been lovely, but the world felt weighted and somehow off, wrong, as if the snow were just a pretty stage set that hid something dark and dreadful behind the backdrop.

I glanced away from the window. Nero was still sleeping, on his stomach, the blankets to his waist, his arm flung over his head. The light cast him in grays, dark hair and ashen skin against white sheets, so he looked like a portrait someone had drawn and put upon my bed. Nothing real. I could not quite remember the feel of his touch; last night came to me in bits and pieces, images against lamplight.

I looked back to the courtyard and saw Giulia hurrying across to the kitchen, carrying something wrapped in paper. This was as good a time as any to speak to Madame Basilio. With Giulia in the kitchen and Nero sleeping, there was no one to stop me. I thought about waking Nero to ask him how his aunt had been, but I didn't need him to tell me. I would know upon seeing her whether yesterday had affected her for good or ill.

I closed the bedroom door quietly behind me, and went to check on Samuel. He was asleep as well, the straps jumbled together in a pile beside the bed—I had untied his hands immediately upon his falling asleep. There was truly nothing to stop or delay me, but I found myself wishing there was. That strange uneasiness. I forced myself to ignore it and went downstairs.

When I knocked at Madame Basilio's door, there was no answer. I knocked again, harder, and looked over my shoulder, half expecting to see Giulia racing up behind me. The courtyard was abandoned. I rapped again.

Again, no answer. No sound of footsteps within. I wondered if Madame Basilio was ignoring me deliberately. Carefully, I tested the lever, expecting it to be locked, surprised when it gave way. I pushed the door open—only a few inches, not wanting to offend— and called softly, "Madame Basilio?"

My voice fell on marble and stopped dead as if the house had absorbed it. I pushed the door open a bit farther. "Madame? Madame Basilio, are you here? It's Elena Spira. I'd wondered if I could have a word?"

Still nothing. The silence was profound, as if the floor was abandoned and had always been so. I stepped inside, closing the door softly, giving in to the impulse to not make a sound, careful, quiet footsteps, the hush of my breath. "Madame Basilio?" I tried again as I went down the hall, a whisper really, anything louder felt unnatural. I checked the sala. The room was empty.

I heard a shuffle, a breath, and I started, spinning around, but there was no one there, and I realized I'd heard only my own movements. It was eerily quiet; the watchfulness from upstairs descended, needling. I knocked quietly at each closed door before peeking inside. The dining room held a massive table but only three chairs clustered at its end. The bedrooms were spartan; the beds simple and unadorned, velvet bed-curtains replaced with looped swaths of cheap yellowed mosquito netting.

Again, I was aware of the ruined artwork, rotting, mildewed. The floor must have been beautiful once. As I went through the rooms, I realized how much was missing—like upstairs, there were empty spaces on the walls, shallows where frescoes had been removed. I remembered Samuel's story about Nero's promise to his father, his aunt's steady whittling away at it, his resentment and his broken heart.

But Madame Basilio was nowhere. When I emerged into the courtyard, Zuan was drawing water at the well.

"Have you seen Madame?" I asked, and he frowned and shook his head.

I hurried past him, into the kitchen. Giulia was the only one within. She was up to her elbows in some large fish, filleting it, her forearms dotted here and there with silver scales like sequins on a costume. She pursed her mouth, her brow furrowing in disapproval and dislike when I entered.

"There is no polenta today," she said defiantly. "Take him some cheese."

"Where's your mistress?" I asked.

"She is too tired to see you. Yesterday was very trying. She is sleeping."

"No, she isn't. I've been looking for her. I can't find her anywhere."

"You were in her rooms? Alone?" Giulia's dislike turned to startled alarm. She withdrew her hands from the fish, wiping them madly on the apron about her waist, leaving flecks of scales and bits of grayish, translucent flesh. She pulled off the apron and flung it onto the bench. "I will ask Zuan where she is."

"I already did. He hasn't seen her."

"She would not have gone somewhere without one of us."

Giulia hurried from the kitchen. I followed her to the courtyard, where she stopped before Zuan, her words a flurry. Though I could not understand them, I didn't mistake the fear in her voice, nor the way Zuan froze, his face going pale beneath his black hair.

Giulia turned to me. "Does Nerone know she is gone?"

I said, "Perhaps she went up there, and I simply missed her. I'll look."

I ran back to the third floor, but I knew the moment I went inside that Madame Basilio was not there. It was as quiet as I'd left it. I reached the bedroom just as Nero stepped out, shrugging into his coat. His smile of greeting died the moment he saw my face.

"What happened? What's wrong?"

"I went to talk to your aunt, and she has disappeared. Giulia and Zuan are worried."

"I haven't seen her since last night," Nero said.

"Perhaps she's with Samuel," I said, but Samuel was alone, sitting on the edge of his bed, wearing only trousers and rubbing his face tiredly. He looked over his shoulder, frowning when I asked, "Has Madame Basilio been here?"

"Why would she be?" he asked in a low, dull voice. "She was there yesterday, wasn't she? The exorcism." He shuddered, his skin pimpled with cold. "I've been remembering. Only bits and pieces."

There was no time to worry over that now. My sense that something was wrong grew.

Nero said, "She's no doubt gone to see Padre Pietro to arrange another bout of torture for you."

"Giulia said she wouldn't have gone anywhere alone," I said.

"Giulia wants to believe she is indispensable. Aunt Valeria will return soon enough, I promise you, and all this worry will be for naught."

I could not banish mine.

"You don't think that's where she's gone, do you?" Samuel asked me in a quiet voice.

"I can't help it," I said. "Something's not right. Don't you feel it?"

"Yes." Samuel's gaze slid to the corner of the room.

"Perhaps . . . don't you think we should at least go to the church and see if she's there?"

Nero frowned. "Why are you so concerned, Elena? You don't even like her."

"But she's your aunt," I said. "I know you would care if something happened to her. And I just . . . I can't explain it."

He studied me for a moment, and then he nodded. "Very well. If it will make you feel better, there's no harm in looking."

"You're going to the church?" Samuel rose. "I'm coming too. Let me get dressed."

It didn't take long for Samuel to finish. When he put on his overcoat over his suitcoat—no vest, no tie or collar—Nero said, "The two of you look like a matched set."

Because of the bruises, I realized. Samuel's were now dark and spreading, large purple pearls ringing his throat, obvious without the collar or tie. I knew from looking in the mirror this morning that mine looked the same, though more livid, because beneath the darker thumbprints were also healing bruises, mottled green and yellow.

We followed Nero to the courtyard gate. Giulia came flying after us, her voice rising. Nero said something brusque to her, and gestured for us to follow him out into the campo, closing the gate again firmly in her face. "She's sent Zuan for the police."

Neither Samuel nor I answered, though I was somewhat relieved. Our worry had become contagious; Nero's mouth was set, anxiety chiseling his face as he led us over the slick bridge to the Madonna dell' Orto.

The snow began to fall more heavily, though it was still little more than a soft sprinkling of cold. The dell' Orto was not so quiet today as it had been when I'd visited it with Madame Basilio. People—mostly women, heads bowed beneath black shawls— dotted the pews. I heard the soft whispers of prayers, a murmur I found vaguely comforting.

Several glanced our way, their prayers paused by curiosity, and I couldn't blame them. Nero strode down the aisle with purpose, and Samuel and I scurried like acolytes behind him. What must we have looked like—neither man wearing a hat or a tie, Nero's face set like stone, Samuel limping as he tried to keep up, I too would have wondered what such urgency could mean.

Nero went to the archway leading to the offices, where we were stopped by a priest. Nero spoke to him impatiently. The only words I understood were *Padre Pietro*.

It became clear that the priest was not going to let us through, and Nero's words became shorter and more clipped. Samuel limped up beside. In French, he said, "Please. If you would inform Father Pietro that his . . . patient from yesterday is here, and I am sorely in need of his aid. It is all I can do to hold the demon at bay. I am terrified for my soul."

It was evident that the priest knew of the attempt at exorcism. He drew in his breath sharply and stepped back.

"Please," Nero said, tense with strain and impatience and worry.

Nervously, the priest nodded. Now it seemed he could not let us through quickly enough.

Nero didn't bother to knock at the office door. He opened it so quickly Father Pietro started, dropping the pen he held. It rolled across the floor.

"Signor Basilio! And Signor Farber—"

Nero interrupted him, each word in his question bitten off.

The priest shook his head, looking puzzled as he spoke.

Nero turned to us. "She hasn't been here. He says to try the Merceria or the Rialto. Tomorrow is Christmas Eve. He suggests that she may have gone shopping."

Christmas Eve. It seemed impossible that time could have passed so quickly. More than that, it seemed incongruous that there could be anything happening beyond the events in the Basilio, that there could be people shopping and preparing, that anyone could care about Christmas now.

"Do you think she may have?" Samuel asked.

Nero shrugged. "I don't know. Perhaps."

"Giulia said she would not have gone alone," I reminded him.

The skin around Nero's nose whitened. "There is much Giulia doesn't know about my aunt."

"Zuan was still there, so she didn't take the gondola."

"Or she hired another," Nero said.

"Why would she have done that?"

"To keep a secret," Samuel suggested. He leaned heavily against the door, easing the weight from his knee. "But if she's gone there, we'll never find her. It's too crowded."

Thoughtfully, Nero said, "She has her favorite shops. They haven't changed in years. I suppose it would not hurt to look."

Father Pietro watched us carefully—well, Samuel, anyway. It was discomfiting, how avidly he stared, as if he wanted nothing more than to wrestle Samuel to the ground and wrench the devil from his chest.

I said quietly, "Zuan's gone after the police. Wouldn't it be better to have them search?"

Nero shook his head. "It will be at least an hour before they come to the palazzo. In that time, we could already be at the Rialto."

"If she's there, she'll finish her shopping and come home," I said hopefully.

Samuel said, "I don't think she'll be coming home, Elena. Neither do you."

Nero bit off a curse. "I can't just sit around and do nothing. Come or not, as you like."

Samuel and I didn't confer; there was no need. I knew we would not abandon Nero now. With an apology and thanks to the priest, we left the Madonna dell' Orto and stepped out into the wet, cold day. There were no gondolas to be hired here, and so Nero led us to the nearest *traghetto* station, where the gondoliers lingered for fares, and we quickly hired one and set off for the Merceria.

It was thronged, so much so that the falling snow never hit the ground, but only seemed to hover above the streets, melting on heads and shoulders and vast piles of goods. The snow lent a greater air of gaiety, so the Merceria had the aspect of a fair, even in the cold, though coughing and sniffling seemed to be the order of the day, and I saw the red sores of chilblains on too many hands and cheeks. Peddlers called out as they pushed through the crowd.

Merchants stood at the doors of their narrow, dark little shops, displaying their goods, their arms full of brightly colored scarves or housewares.

Samuel struggled to keep up, and I put my arm through his and kept closely to him while Nero dodged into one or two shops that had been favorites of his aunt, coming out each time looking grimmer than ever, a short shake of his head, a terse, "He hasn't seen her in days."

I could see the strain in Samuel's eyes as we reached the part of the Merceria that expanded into a campo so filled with stalls overflowing with clothing, Christmas mustard, and boxes of mandorlato that it was a maze. We would follow the flow of the crowd only to come to a dead stop before one and then have to untangle ourselves to join another flowing river of people, only to have the same thing happen again. The campo seemed paved with crockery and glassware.

"Only the fish market left," Nero said, sending an apologetic look to Samuel. "If she's not there, we'll go home."

Fortunately for Samuel, we could not move quickly, or he would have collapsed long before we reached the fish market, where people stood in long lines waiting for eels to be pulled from barrels splashing with their writhing bodies and bled out.

"They're a tradition on Christmas Eve," Nero told me when I grimaced at the pools of blood. "Aunt Valeria buys them every year."

Samuel had gone pale. He licked his chapped lips and said, "We should go back."

"Just one more place," Nero insisted.

But it wasn't just one more place. We followed him from stall to stall as he gestured and shouted his question about his aunt, in return getting only shaking heads and shrugs and short sentences that even I could tell were negative. The day began to feel unreal—crowds and snow and Christmas shopping, that festivity that was at such odds with the three of us that it felt as if I'd entered a dream. With every passing moment, Samuel grew more strained; I grew more afraid; Nero grew more desperate. Whatever he had believed about his aunt's whereabouts before, it was clear he now felt as Samuel and I did—there was something wrong.

"Nero," I said finally. "She's not here. We should return."

He turned to me, his gaze sweeping past, searching the crowd beyond. "One more. Old Gio's—just down there."

Yet, just as he had each other time, Nero didn't stop when Old Gio hadn't seen Madame Basilio either.

"Calderario's," he insisted. "Just there."

I glanced behind at Samuel, who leaned against the post of a stall. "Samuel's going to collapse any moment."

"Then go to a café. Wait for me there. I've only a few more places—"

"She's not here, Nero."

"She is. Somewhere. I'm sure of it." His eyes burned with fear, and obsession now too—I recognized it. Like the patients at Glen Echo, who became trapped in endless cycles of compulsion, he would not stop until I stopped him.

He started to move off. I grabbed him again, pulling him back.

"What is it?" he asked impatiently.

"She's not here. We need to go home."

"Not yet—"

"Nero." I gripped him harder, forcing him to look at me. "Enough. We're only wasting time."

He tried to pull away. "Just the jeweler's—"

"To buy what? With what? Why would she have gone there? No one's seen her. Please."

Nero stilled. I saw when my words hit him, this terrible desolation.

"It's all right," I whispered. "She'll be in her sala. She'll laugh that we were so concerned."

He stared at me searchingly. Then he glanced away, and I saw that his eyes were wet with unshed tears. "She won't be. Giulia's right. She would not have gone on her own." He pulled me close, pressing his forehead to mine. "I'm afraid to return."

"Everything will be fine." I said the words only to comfort; I did not believe them.

His fingers scrabbled at my waist, the barrier of my corset keeping him from anchoring me as hard as he obviously wanted to. "Everything's a disaster. Let's not go back."

"Elena," Samuel groaned.

I turned to look just as he collapsed to the ground.

Chapter 31

Nero and I sprang apart and rushed to Samuel, who lay in a heap at the edge of the stall. Nero reached him first, squatting in a pool of mud and eel blood that spattered his boots—as it had all of Samuel, so he looked bloodied and hurt.

"He's swooned," Nero said.

Even as he pulled Samuel into his arms, Samuel was rousing, blinking, disoriented. He put his hand to his eyes. "Christ."

"Come on, amìgo. Let's get you up." Nero pulled Samuel to his feet, keeping a firm hold, which was good, because Samuel swayed, falling into him.

I dragged Samuel's chin so I could look into his eyes. "What's wrong?"

"Nothing, I'm tired." He jerked his chin from my hand as if he couldn't stand my touch.

"I'm sorry. We should have gone back earlier. I knew you were—"

"That's not it." He pushed away from Nero. "I'm all right. I can stand on my own. Christ, look at me. Fish blood everywhere."

"You look like you came out on the bad end of a knife fight," Nero said.

"A bad end would be dead," Samuel said dryly. "And I fear I'm very much alive."

"Can you get to a gondola?" I asked.

"I'm not helpless."

But he was, mostly. Nero looped Samuel's arm around his neck, and I lodged myself under his other arm, and even so, he was breathing heavily and sagging before we'd got a few yards. It didn't help that the crowd jostled and pushed; none of us could keep our balance well.

Finally, Nero jerked his head toward a small gathering of tables and chairs near the door of a café. "It will take more than me and Elena to get you there. The two of you wait here while I hire a gondola. I'll bring the man back to help."

I was surprised when Samuel didn't protest. We limped over to the café chairs, and he let out a loud sigh of weariness as he sank into one of them. Nero gave me a quick, worried look. "I'll be right back. Don't go anywhere."

"We won't," I assured him.

He hurried off, disappearing almost immediately into the crowd. The moment he was out of sight, Samuel straightened, his exhausted expression disappearing. He looked perfectly well, so much so that I exclaimed, "There's nothing wrong with you at all! You swooned deliberately."

He wiped at the eel blood on his trousers. "I think I ruined these."

"I don't understand. Why?"

"I wanted to talk to you alone."

"You could have done that back at the Basilio."

"Could I have? Since he's crawled into your bed?" He glanced away as if to assure himself that Nero was nowhere near. "He's been stalling."

"Not stalling," I corrected. "He's worried. He thinks something terrible has happened, and he's afraid of returning to bad news."

Samuel looked thoughtful. "Perhaps. He didn't seem too worried about his aunt until Giulia said she was sending for the police. Do you believe him when he says he doesn't believe in the ghost?"

"I think he's afraid to believe in her. Otherwise he would have to acknowledge that she's still unhappy. It would be painful for him. He cared for her very much."

"Perhaps too much." Samuel reached out, flicking a loosened tendril of my hair meaningfully, and I understood. My chestnut hair, so like Laura's. "I think I should tell you something."

My stomach tightened. "Please don't."

"You need to know this, Elena. That lover of Laura's . . . she wanted to marry him, but her mother wouldn't let her break her engagement to Nero."

"There was a duel," I said, irritated that he was telling me nothing new after all his intrigue. This was a waste of time. "He killed the man when he didn't have to."

Samuel looked surprised. "He told you? Well then, it seems my little act was all for naught, given how fully you know each other. And I've ruined my trousers for nothing."

He lifted his face to the sky. Snowflakes splashed his cheekbones, his nose, melting into droplets. He blinked away one that landed on his eyelashes. "But you're right about how much he cared for her, and you should remember it. When he returned from Venice to the news that Laura was dead, I thought I might lose him. I tried to cheer him up with every diversion I could find in Paris, but his despondency lasted for weeks. He told me he hadn't the courage to take his own life, but the life he was living was suicide of a sort. Too many women, too much wine . . . but he took no pleasure from any of it. I thought he was punishing himself. I still think it."

Something in what he said jarred. "You think that's why he chose me, you mean? To punish himself?"

"I can promise that you remind him of Laura, Elena. I don't want to think that's the reason he's pursued you, but you know I do."

We fell into silence. I was angry with him for doubting Nero's feelings for me, and sorry too, that he felt as he did. I was relieved when Nero pushed through the crowd a few minutes later, bringing with him a tall, muscled gondolier.

"Do you feel any better?" Nero asked Samuel, who had allowed his shoulders to roll forward, his chin to sink.

"A bit," Samuel said.

Nero gestured to the gondolier, and the two of them lifted Samuel from the chair, and Samuel made a show of grunting with pain and limping as we all went to the gondola.

Nero was nothing but tension as we headed back. I reached for his hand, weaving my fingers through his, and he gave me a grateful look and brought my hand to his mouth, kissing it, drawing me closer into his side.

The very air in the cabin felt heavy with dread; hard to breathe in. We were all aware, I think, that we were heading to a place where the news could not be good, no matter how much we wished for this feeling to be nothing but imaginations run rampant, a dream that had somehow followed us through the day, nothing but a dream.

And so I was not surprised when we disembarked to see the police boat moored before the palazzo, black with a green box of a cabin.

Zuan met us at the door; he had obviously been waiting. He had been crying, and I knew.

Nero stopped short, tripping Samuel, who was close behind him. I grabbed Samuel's arm to steady him. Zuan spoke. It was very short.

Nero staggered. He looked over his shoulder, searching for me. "They've found her." His voice was only a harsh whisper. "She's dead."

After that, the rest of the evening passed in a daze. The police were waiting in the courtyard, gathered around a body covered with a sheet that was so damp with melting snow it molded to her contours, making her look like a statue carved of marble—how exquisitely the artist had managed the cloth; she seemed to be wearing a veil, so beautifully diaphanous, how had he done it?—while all about her were gathered puddles from melting snow. I wondered why they'd put her on the cold, wet stones rather than somewhere dry and sheltered, and then I realized that it wasn't just the snow that made the sheet cling that way, but the fact that she was soaking wet; she had been found floating in the canal between the Madonna dell' Orto and the Basilio, caught beneath the bridge we had crossed so hastily hours before—had she been there then? How had we not seen her?—and all I could think was how glad I was that she had not drowned in the dyer's canal, where her daughter had died.

"They think she slipped from the bridge on her way to see Father Pietro," Samuel told me after a quick conferral with Nero, who was now secreted away on the piano nobile with the police. One could see their figures through the windows, silhouettes against the drawn curtains, pacing and gesturing. It made it hard to leave the courtyard, because I could watch him from where I stood. He might need me; at any moment he could pull aside the curtain and look out to see me standing there, the reassuring presence I hoped to be.

"Planning another exorcism attempt, no doubt," Samuel went on.

"I don't think that's what it was," I said. "I saw her face that day. Whatever she saw gave her the answer she was looking for."

"What answer could that be?"

"I don't know. I planned to ask her that this morning."

Samuel glanced up at the window and frowned. "Come. Let's go somewhere warm."

"There's no place warm here."

"Someplace else then. There's a café in the campo."

"We can't leave. The police asked us to stay."

"Then the kitchen." Samuel took my arm. "You're shivering, Elena. They can find us there if they need us."

"But Nero—"

"He'll know to find you there too."

Gently he pulled me with him, and I had to admit I was glad once we stepped into the warmth of the kitchen. I had not realized just how cold I was. My hair was wet too, from the snow, dripping down my neck and into my collar.

Samuel sat on the bench with a sigh, but I could not be still. I pulled my cloak more tightly about me and paced. "Do you remember anything from the exorcism?"

"I barely remember the day."

"I want to know what Madame Basilio understood. I want to know what she saw. Tell me what Laura's ghost has shown you. Everything you remember."

"Umm . . . the woman drinking and falling. The man with the pistol. Blood on the walls . . . Christ, will you stop pacing? It's too hard to concentrate when you're playing Lady Macbeth."

"What else? What do you remember about Laura?"

"She's angry," he said, rubbing his eyes. "But you know that."

"When she possessed you, I saw jealousy too."

"Perhaps she knew what would happen between the two of you when Nero showed up," Samuel said. "It wasn't so hard to predict."

"She didn't love him anymore. Why would she care? There's something more. Something we're not seeing."

"I don't know what else that could be."

"Anger seems odd for a suicide, don't you think? Sadness I would expect, and hopelessness. Regret, perhaps. But I don't feel those things from her, and neither do you. Not really. When you woke from your seizure the other night, you thought you'd drowned. You were certain of it. You remembered falling, and that you were angry and afraid. These are all her memories. What is she trying to tell us?"

Samuel stilled.

I went on, "When you were choking yourself—when you were choking me—you spoke in Venetian. Whatever you said meant something to Nero's aunt."

"Elena, be careful what you're considering." Samuel's voice was very low.

"I don't even know what I'm considering," I said, but that wasn't true. I did know. I felt it like a clenched fist in my chest, in my stomach.

"You think Laura's spirit returned for vengeance," he said. "You think it wasn't a suicide, but murder."

"I don't think that," I said anxiously. "I don't know anything. Who could have murdered her? Why?"

Samuel's gaze locked to mine. He said nothing. He didn't have to.

"No," I whispered. "He wasn't here. He was in Milan."

"He was," Samuel said. "And then he wasn't."

I remembered what Samuel had said: *When he returned from Venice to the news that Laura was dead, I thought I might lose him.* The thing that had jarred. Dully, I said, "He told me he went straight to Paris from Milan."

"Then he lied to you," Samuel said bleakly. "Or he's forgotten. He went to Venice in between. He brought me that book. *The Nunnery Tales.* We'd talked about it and he wanted to show me. He'd left it here, and he told me he'd stopped to get it. I didn't think anything of it. By then, his anger with her was past. It never occurred to me that he would hurt her."

"Because he didn't. He wouldn't have."

"He'd taken care of his rival, so I thought it was over."

"It was," I insisted. "It had to be."

He paused. "I think I understand."

"Samuel, it can't be. He can't have done such a thing."

"She's showing me what happened, Elena," Samuel persisted woodenly. "She's demonstrating through me. You're *her* in all these scenarios. I'm *him*. The jealousy, the anger . . . it's what she saw in him. It all makes sense."

"It doesn't make any sense at all!" I could not bear to hear his words, each of which felt to be a blow, sinking deep and true. "You said he was despondent when he heard she'd died."

"I also said I thought he was punishing himself."

"I won't believe it. I suppose next you'll tell me that he's responsible for his aunt's death."

"I don't know."

"You saw him, Samuel. He was beside himself."

"He didn't want to return. You're the one who said that. He knew it would be bad news. He knew the police would be here."

I felt sick with fear that it was true. "I don't believe it. I can't."

"It makes sense though, doesn't it?" he pointed out reasonably. "You say his aunt understood something. Perhaps she realized what had happened and she confronted him with it. He went to talk to her that night. The next morning, she's gone."

"But I heard her." I grasped at anything, everything. "That night, when he came to bed, I heard her in the courtyard talking to Giulia. She was alive then, and he didn't leave me the rest of the night. It couldn't have been him."

"Are you certain he didn't leave you?"

"I'm certain. We . . . I'm certain."

Samuel said thoughtfully, "Then perhaps it's true that she slipped. But it seems coincidental, don't you think?"

I felt near tears. "It can't be him. He hasn't lied to me. I know he hasn't."

Samuel looked down at his hands. "I don't want to believe it either, Elena. He's my closest friend. I trust him. But I know him too."

"He loved Laura."

"He was angry with her. You didn't see him. I did. He was jealous and furious. He loved her and he felt betrayed. It was as if she'd crushed his whole life into nothing."

What was it he'd said? That Laura had been something certain in a sea of uncertainty. One thing to cling to when everything else was falling apart around him.

But to kill her . . . it was so at odds with what I knew of him. His gentleness and his depth of emotion. A man who wasn't afraid to show how upset he was at his aunt's disappearance. Who wasn't afraid to say "*save me*."

Save me. From what? "*I'm not a good man.*"

I tried to swallow the lump in my throat. "I won't believe it of him."

Samuel looked as distraught as I felt. "We may not have a choice."

The kitchen door opened; we both turned to see Nero come inside. My heart seemed to swell; I felt thick with love and longing. But then it all slammed into a nauseating, horrible knot. He looked ravaged with grief, face drawn, dark circles beneath his eyes, his hair looking as if he'd run his hands through it dozens of times.

"There you are," he said. "I've been—what is it? Why are you looking at me that way?"

"It's nothing," I said. "What happened with the police?"

He frowned, but thankfully he was too distracted to pursue it. "I've told them everything I know. They're talking to Giulia now, and I'm to send the two of you up. It's a lot of bother for an accident, if you ask me, but it seems they've nothing else to do today. Do you mind? I've told them about the exorcism and Padre Pietro already, but they have some other questions."

"Like what?" Samuel asked.

"They aren't sharing them with me." A quick, forced smile. He sat on the end of the bench near Samuel. "I've no idea what they expect to find. But if I were you, I wouldn't say anything about a ghost. They already think everyone here is mad."

I did not let myself look at Samuel. Instead I stared at Nero, soaking him in, those laughing eyes that weren't laughing now, the question mark of a curl near his ear, the blade of his collarbone beneath the open collar of his shirt.

"What is it?" He asked me, bemused. "Have I something on my face?"

"No. It's just that . . . I love you."

His eyes warmed; his smile was answer enough, soft and quiet and real despite his obvious strain and grief. He turned to Samuel. "You won't say anything about hauntings, will you? They're already half inclined to take you away. The whole Satan thing troubles them—well, how could it not? A ghost would send them over the edge, I'm afraid. I don't really relish the thought of arguing with four hundred Venetian officials about where they've taken you."

It could not be him. Look at him there. How could it possibly be him?

Samuel said, "What do you think, Elena?"

I knew he wasn't just asking me about whether or not to tell the police about the ghost. "We'll say nothing," I said firmly.

He nodded, but he was so somber it ached.

"You'd best go up," Nero said. "They're waiting."

Samuel rose and opened the door. The damp, chill air rushed in, along with a few snowflakes, bigger now, and wetter, more slush than snow. He stood back, waiting for me to precede him, but Nero caught my arm, rising and pulling me to him in one motion. He whispered in my ear, "I love you too, cara," and gave me a quick kiss, and I wanted nothing more than to throw myself into his arms, to believe completely in his innocence, and yet . . . there it was, that little prick of conscience and suspicion. Oh, how I hated it.

I kept hating it as he let me go, and I followed Samuel out into the courtyard, leaving Nero behind.

Chapter 32

Neither Samuel nor I spoke as we went up. Giulia opened the door, her face swollen and streaked with tears, and I remembered Nero saying how Madame Basilio had rescued Giulia and Zuan from the street when they were children. As we followed her bowed, grief-stricken steps to the sala where the police waited, I wondered what Giulia thought, if she suspected Nero in this at all. They'd been lovers, and I could not help but wonder how recently.

I pushed away the thought, which was unfair and unworthy. He said he loved me; I would know if he was lying. I would know. I knew just what to look for. The brief shift of a glance, the too ardent protestations, the wheedling manipulation. *"If you do this for me, we'll be free. We can go away. We can be together. Come away with me."*

The memory pressed as if to torment me: *"You and I can leave all this behind. We'll make love in every city on the Continent . . ."* Nero next to a barrel of wriggling, splashing eels. Pressing his forehead to mine. *"Let's not go back."*

It wasn't the same. Nothing about him was the same as it had been with Joshua Lockwood. He was not lying to me.

Inside the salon, two police officers spoke to each other in low voices. When we paused at the doorway, and Giulia said in a choked voice, "Mamzelle Spira and M'sieur Farber," they stepped apart. They'd seen us already in the courtyard, but now they studied us as if for the first time, and I felt them measuring; I felt their questions and suspicions as if they'd voiced them, particularly when they looked at Samuel.

I put my hand on his arm, the only support I could offer, and I saw how they noticed that too, how every movement we made seemed full of gravitas and import, a clue for them to follow.

Giulia withdrew; one of the officers gestured to a settee. Samuel's limp seemed to become more pronounced, the sala too large to cross, as we went and sat.

One—tall and handsome, with a lovingly tended mustache, long and waxed at the tips to hold its smiling shape—introduced himself as da Cola, and his fellow—broad shouldered and thick, like a fit battering ram, with a face that looked as if he'd served as one—as Pasqualigo.

Da Cola said in French, "When did you last see Madame Basilio?"

I answered in kind, "Yesterday afternoon. But I heard her, last night. In the courtyard."

"You're certain it was her?"

"She was calling to the housekeeper. Yes, it was her."

"What time was this?"

"I don't know. I'd been sleeping. Perhaps midnight? It had just started to snow."

Da Cola frowned. "Where were you?"

"In my bedroom."

"You were looking out the window?"

"No, I—" I felt myself redden. "I was in bed. As I said, I'd just awakened."

"How do you know it had just begun to snow?"

There was no way to avoid it. "When M'sieur Basilio came in, he said it."

"He came into your bedroom?"

I felt Samuel tense beside me as I said, "Yes."

"You're lovers?"

"Is this necessary?" Samuel asked.

Da Cola glanced at Pasqualigo. "Yes, I'm afraid so, m'sieur. Mademoiselle Spira, answer the question please."

I stared down at my hands. "Yes, we are."

"Was he with you all night?"

I nodded.

"You're certain? Perhaps you fell asleep and he snuck out?"

"I would have known," I said. "And . . . it would have been a very long time later."

"Ah." Da Cola's smile was knowing and a bit obscene. He leaned back on his heels. "Very good. And you, m'sieur? When did you last see Madame Basilio?"

"Yesterday afternoon."

"At what time?"

"I don't remember."

Pasqualigo said, "She was here with the priest, yes? For the exorcism?"

"She was."

"She stayed for the entire rite, yes?"

Samuel looked uncomfortable. "I don't know."

"You don't know?" Pasqualigo crossed his arms over his burly chest. "You were the subject of the rite, were you not? You were there."

"I don't remember any of it."

"Because the devil had you in his hands, yes?" da Cola asked. "I would very much like you to tell me how it is, m'sieur. I have heard of such things, but I have never seen it myself. I'm quite curious. When Padre Pietro called the demon forward, were you there as well, watching? Your . . . soul . . . or conscious mind . . . whatever one calls it? Were you aware of what was happening?" He sounded genuinely curious, but I could not be certain. It required all my skill to translate.

"I don't know how an exorcism usually is," Samuel replied steadily, though I saw how tense he was. "But no, I was not aware."

"Is it like slipping into sleep? Or perhaps . . . swooning?"

"No," Samuel said tightly.

"But you have no agency, yes? So the devil could make you do . . . well, anything, and you would not know it or remember it?"

"I don't think it had anything to do with the devil."

"You are not possessed? Then why call the priest?"

"It wasn't my idea—"

"But you allowed it, yes? So there was a part of you that believed it may be true that a demon resided within you?"

"No, I—"

"The housekeeper says you convulsed and screamed. She said she had never seen such a thing. She believed the devil was inside you."

I could not help myself. "That isn't what happened at all."

Da Cola didn't even glance my way. He raked Samuel with a razorlike gaze. "Those bruises around Mademoiselle Spira's throat. Who made those?"

I felt something within Samuel surrender. "I did."

"And around your own throat?"

"I did that as well."

"Do you remember doing this?"

"No."

"Did it happen during this exorcism?"

"Yes."

"So it was the devil, then, working through you? Would this same devil have, do you suppose, followed Madame Basilio into the early morning? Perhaps onto a bridge?"

I gasped. "No! No, that's not what happened at all! Samuel's an epileptic. The exorcism caused him to have a seizure. He didn't know what he was doing. It's not uncommon for them not to remember afterward—"

"Elena," Samuel warned.

"—and I never thought it was a demon. That was Father Pietro's idea. I just wanted to know if there really was a ghost, and what she wanted. Then she possessed Samuel and made him strangle me—"

"Elena!"

Samuel's voice called me to myself. I broke off, horrified at what I'd said.

"What ghost?" da Cola asked.

"Laura Basilio's," I said lamely.

Da Cola threw a questioning look at his partner, who said, "The daughter of the old woman. She died two years ago. Three, maybe. Drowned in the rio."

"Just like her mother?"

Pasqualigo's grin was a thin line. "Bad luck."

"Who is seeing this ghost?" da Cola asked.

Samuel and I were both quiet. I dared not look at him.

"Let me guess. M'sieur Farber, yes? A ghost that possesses him and makes him strangle people? Perhaps like . . . a demon?"

Again, we were silent. The sick churn in my stomach worsened.

Da Cola said, "We spoke to Father Pietro earlier. He told us that M'sieur Farber became violent enough that he had to be restrained."

"He was unconscious by then. There was no need," I said angrily.

"Was this exorcism successful?" da Cola asked Samuel, who shrugged.

"Don't ask me. I don't remember."

"Nothing?"

Samuel shook his head.

"When is your next memory?"

"From later, when I woke up. I was in bed. Buckled in. Elena was there. I asked her to take off the restraints."

"Did she?"

"Yes."

"So you were free to go anywhere?"

"He asked me to tie him again," I rushed in. "I tied him to the bedpost."

"He asked this why? Because he feared he might hurt you again? Did you fear that too?"

"No, I didn't." It was a lie.

I saw that da Cola noted it. "Do you think he was capable of hurting someone, mademoiselle?"

"He was very weak."

"But still you tied him. So you believed there was a threat."

"He insisted on it."

Da Cola's gaze slid to Samuel. "Did you ask to be tied because you believed the devil was still inside you? Did you believe you would hurt someone again?"

Samuel bowed his head; I felt him sag. "Yes." The word was a breath.

Da Cola looked back at me. "Did he remain tied the entire night?"

"He would not have followed Madame Basilio. He was far too weak."

"Was he tied, mademoiselle?" the officer persisted.

"He was deeply asleep. You don't understand. After such seizures, patients are exhausted. They can barely move. He slept for hours."

"Was he tied?"

"No," I admitted reluctantly. "But he had nothing to do with Madame Basilio's death."

"And how do you know this, mamzelle, if you were safe in your own bed all night with M'sieur Basilio? Unless—" he gestured between Samuel and me and jiggled his brows insinuatingly. Pasqualigo laughed.

Samuel started to rise. "If you're finished here . . ."

Pasqualigo's laughter died abruptly. "Sit down. We are not finished with you, m'sieur. But Mademoiselle Spira can leave. We have no more questions for her."

I didn't like what I was hearing. I hoped it was only that my French was inadequate. "I'd rather stay," I said.

"We are not offering a choice," Pasqualigo said. "We know where to find you if we need to."

Samuel sighed heavily. "Go, Elena. It's no good. Just go."

"I can't just leave you to this," I said quietly.

"It's all right." He looked exhausted, and when he raised his eyes to mine I knew what he was thinking. I knew he was afraid and why. I hadn't realized until that moment how much I feared Nero had somehow sneaked out in the night, that he was lying to me. But now . . . if Samuel had done this, it could not be Nero.

I saw the pain in Samuel's eyes, and I knew he'd seen what I felt. "Go on, Elena."

I whispered, "You didn't do this."

He leaned close, his lips against my ear. "Can you say for certain that I didn't? Because I cannot." He drew away. "Please go. It only hurts me that you stay."

It was only the knowledge that I might hurt him more that allowed me to rise, to walk out of that room, past Giulia sitting blank-faced and silent in the receiving hall, to the third floor. But when I closed the door behind me, I knew the rooms were not empty; I did not feel alone. I hated the twinge of fear that came with the thought. I did not want to feel it.

"Nero?" I called softly.

"In here." His voice came from my bedroom.

The door was open. Nero sat on my bed, holding a black Carnivale mask in his hand. The trunk that had been beneath was pulled out, the lid open to reveal the black-and-white cloaks and tricornered hats of dominos. Two other masks—one checked red and white on half, black-and-white on the other half; another painted bronze, with sharply defined brows and a spadelike nose and a broad mustache—lay on top.

Nero looked up as I came inside. His eyes were red from tears, his face sharp with grief. I found myself searching for cunning, for guile, for Samuel's suspicions and my own, which I did not want to have. I saw none of it. I saw only sorrow and desolation. "This used to be my room in the summers. Did I ever tell you that?"

I shook my head.

He rolled the mask in hands. It had a large nose, pointed and sloping. "This was mine," he said. "Pulcinello. I wore it every year for Carnivale. He's a trickster, and he can be vicious. You can't trust him at all. He's very smart, though he pretends to be too stupid to know what's going on."

I went cold. Softly, I asked, "Is that what you think of yourself?"

He exhaled heavily. "Every Carnivale, yes. It was a license for bad behavior, though Carnivale is not what it was. Those days were gone long before I was born. Still . . . there were parties enough, and I took advantage. Laura too. The Harlequin was hers."

"And the other?"

"Brighella. The crafty old man. My father's. My aunt declined to participate." Again tears started. He blinked them away. "She thought Carnivale depraved. She didn't want to see it brought back after the unification. *Chi comincia mal, finisse pezo.*"

I had heard those words before. *No, not the same ones. No.* I could barely force myself to ask. "What does that mean?"

He searched for words. "Ah . . . I guess you would say, a bad beginning makes a bad end. My aunt thought Carnivale belonged to another world and had no place in a civilized society. Mostly I think she worried for Laura and for me. Hard to believe, isn't it? That she once worried for me? When she's dedicated the last years to thwarting me at every damned turn? I should be glad she's dead. I expected to be. I've been waiting for it long enough."

"I know you loved her."

"Did I?" He raised questioning eyes to me. "I don't know what I felt for her."

"Nero—"

"I want to feel relief, but I don't." He put the mask on his head, pulling it down over his face, that beaklike nose, only his mouth showing, eyes darkening, suddenly nothing but cunning and guile, the face I'd been looking for, the one I'd been afraid to find.

"Take it off," I breathed.

"You don't like it? You don't think I look dashing?" He rose, coming toward me, black and devilish, smiling so his upper lip nearly disappeared.

"I don't like it. Take it off."

"Come, Elena. Let us be joyous. Let us be gay. Let us celebrate my aunt's passing by doing everything she disdained." His voice rose, an edge of hysteria that only frightened me more. He made a quick gesture, a flick of his fingers, *come here.*

Instead, I found myself backing away, my breath coming fast and my heart pounding, all my suspicions gathering painfully in my chest, a knowing I did not want to have. *No, no, no,* this was not what I wanted. He was not Nero, he was not the man I loved, and I saw in him now what I didn't want to see.

"Elena?" He reached for me.

My panic surged. I ran.

"Elena?" He was right behind me. "Elena, stop!"

I was in the receiving hall when he grabbed my arm.

"Are you afraid of me, Elena? Afraid of *me*?"

"Take it off." I felt near tears.

"It's just a mask." He tore the mask off, throwing it to the floor, where it skidded across the speckled stone. "There, it's off. Better?" He looked stricken, forlorn, alone in a way that I couldn't stand to see, as if he saw only futility where once before he'd seen hope, and I knew I'd done that. I was to blame.

But without the mask, I saw no tricks in him, no secrets and no lies. Only concern and distress, as if he hoped to call back what had been lost and was afraid he could not. I felt that too, this desperate wish to unsee what I'd seen, to be innocent again, and when he leaned close—no force at all, ready to be stopped, allowing me to stop him if I would—my elbow bowed to let him in, my hand against him no barrier at all. I said, "I'm sorry. That was stupid. You frightened me."

"I've never known a woman to have that reaction before." His eyes were sad; the tease had no weight. "Usually they're intrigued."

"I know. I know. It's just . . . the police . . . and Samuel . . ."

"What happened? What did they say?"

"They think Samuel murdered your aunt," I said. "It doesn't help that he doesn't remember."

Nero stepped back, stunned. "But . . . you told them about his epilepsy?"

"Yes, but it doesn't make any difference. Giulia told them about how he tried to strangle me, and . . . well, you can see how it must be. I think he even believes it too."

"What do you mean?"

"He knows Laura's spirit can make him do whatever she wants—how can he not believe that perhaps he followed your aunt to the bridge? Did Laura hate her mother enough to want her dead?"

"A ghost made Samuel push my aunt into the rio?" Nero took my arms, caressing, soothing, reassuring. "You're trying to make sense of things that don't make sense, Elena. This house could make you believe anything. When I have you far away from here, you'll realize how absurd you were to think it." He laughed lightly. "You almost had me believing it too, I'll admit. But then I saw that seizure, and . . . it is the simplest explanation."

I felt confused, assaulted on all sides. I did not want to believe this of Samuel, just as I did not want to believe the suspicions of Nero that flitted like moths in my head, panicking against the light, drawing back into darkness where it was safe, where I did not have to ask, where I did not have to think. How was it that I was so caught between the two of them? How was it that I could not look at either and know the truth?

You've never been good at that, have you? I thought of Joshua Lockwood's intense blue eyes, the kisses that fooled me, the desire that said only what I wanted it to say.

I took Nero's face hard between my hands. "You were with me all night, weren't you? You never left the bed."

His hands came to my wrists as if he meant to pull me away, but his fingers only wrapped around, holding me in place. He was frowning. "You think I killed her?"

I swallowed hard. "Tell me where you were."

He closed his eyes briefly. When he opened them again, I saw only a deep, endless well of grief and misery. "I was with you. I never left the bed."

My relief was dizzying, though how that could be, I didn't know, because I had never really believed this of him. I had heard Madame Basilio in the courtyard as he came inside. She was still alive when he came to me, and then he had stayed. The other questions burned on my tongue, but I could not bring myself to ask them.

I dropped my hands, and buried my face in his chest, wrapping my arms around him. I felt his hesitation, but then his arms came around me too. His voice was deep, rumbling against my ear as he said, "What is it you want me to say, Elena?"

"I hardly know you and yet I feel I know you all too well. I couldn't bear it if I was wrong."

"You're not wrong," he said. "I love you."

I made myself say, "There are things . . . questions I have—"

"I would bare my soul to you if you asked it."

Wasn't that proof enough that he could not be the man I was afraid he was? I tightened my hold on him. I pressed my mouth against his shirt.

"Ask it," he said—the barest whisper. I heard the suffering within it. His hand was in my hair, dislodging pins. I heard them fall to the floor, skittering like roaches. "I'll tell you anything you want, so long as you promise to love me after."

What else mattered? He was here and he loved me, and I loved him. I didn't want to ask. I didn't want to know.

He kissed me, and it was ravenous and hard, as if he could not take me deeply enough. I tasted the fear and misery within it. We were right next to the door, anyone could come in, but I stopped caring the moment Nero's hands pulled up my skirts, sliding up my thighs. He lifted me, and I wrapped my legs around him and his hand was between us, undoing my drawers and his trousers, and then we were crashing against each other like waves upon the rocks, battering and tempestuous, and we were falling to the floor, rough and heedless of whether we hurt one another, even worse, as if that hurting was necessary, as if it could somehow make everything right. My head and my hips cracked against the floor as he ground himself into me; I dug my nails into his back, through his shirt, feeling a piercing satisfaction at his grunts of pain, and then we were both gasping, crying out, shudders of completion, spent and throbbing.

It had taken two minutes, perhaps three, and it was the most devastating pleasure I had ever known, and the most wrenching. My heart ached, and I wanted to cry, but instead I ran my fingers through his hair and listened to his breathing fall into a steady rhythm again as his fingers clutched my thigh convulsively.

I heard voices in the courtyard, some words muffled, others carrying in that strangely twisting way of Venice, and I realized they were taking Madame Basilio's body away. Nero froze as if he realized it too, and then he was pulling himself from me, rising, buttoning his trousers with an expression of such tormented sorrow that I wanted to pull him down again, to make him forget whatever it was that caused that look with my mouth and my hands.

And then I thought: *What makes him look that way?*

Was his aunt's body in the courtyard not enough cause? His whole family was gone now, only himself left, and every one of the others a victim of tragedy. I told myself it didn't matter how much of that tragedy was his fault.

He reached for me, pulling me to my feet, to him, burying his face in my throat, kissing the bruises there with what sounded like a sob, and when he drew away, sorrow had given way to bleakness, to a purpose I didn't understand and felt in my bones was wrong and wrong and wrong.

Nothing could be undone, I reminded myself. It was all past. It didn't matter.

But then a sudden frigid blast of preternatural cold made me shiver, and with it the wafting scent of vanilla and canal water, telling me that I was lying to myself. It did matter. I felt the peril of her, and her determination, and dread filled my lungs until I was drowning in it, and I knew: she was going to force me to understand, whether I wanted to or not.

Chapter 33

I heard the step on the stair just as Nero did, and Samuel came inside, looking inestimably weary. He shuddered, gaze dodging to the corners of the room, and I knew he felt her there, just as I did. Watching, waiting. Expectant. I thought of what had just happened between Nero and me, and I felt guilty and embarrassed, and then I noted the way Samuel glanced at us, and I wondered if he saw it too. But all he said was, "They're taking your aunt's body to the coroner."

Nero nodded and started for the door. "I should go—"

Samuel stopped him. "There's no need. Da Cola and Pasqualigo will be here any moment, and I need to speak with the both of you first."

"Why?" I asked in alarm. "What happened?"

He said nothing, but went down the hall toward the sala. When he reached the mask, he bent to pick it up. "What's this?"

"Pulcinello," Nero said shortly.

Samuel fingered it wistfully. "Carnivale? I've read about it. I suppose I'll never see it now."

"Why do you say that?" Nero sounded as wary as I felt. There was something in Samuel that discomfited, something else wrong.

Samuel gestured for us to follow him. When we reached the sala, he went to the balcony doors, staring out at the lights glimmering in the snowy twilight. He was quiet for a moment, and then he said, "They're arresting me. I'll need to telegraph New York. Could you send someone to the office for me, Nero? It might be closed so late, but . . ."

"Yes, of course." Nero's voice was a rough whisper.

"Arresting you?" I repeated. "But . . . how can they do this? You didn't kill her."

"She was strangled," he said. "And as I have a reputation for such things, I seem the most obvious choice, don't you think?"

"Strangled? They said she slipped off the bridge, or was pushed . . ."

"That isn't how she died. They were saving that bit of news for after you left. They had me targeted from the start, once they spoke to Father Pietro, and he told them what happened at the exorcism. And then of course, they saw your bruises."

I collapsed onto the settee. "You would not have done this. Not of your own accord. Her ghost—"

"Perhaps," Samuel said. "It does seem that strangulation is the order of the day here, doesn't it? Madame Basilio, you, me. Laura."

I looked up.

Nero had gone still where he stood.

Samuel turned to me. "It seems clear that one of us has done this. Either him or me. Which would you prefer it to be, Elena? Tell me so I can fall on my sword for you."

I was horrified. "Samuel, no."

"I don't mind it so much. What have I to go home to? A fiancée who will likely hate me within the year? Seizures that won't go away, whatever I do? I suppose I can look forward to imbecility by the time I'm fifty. Or complete madness. Having got a taste of it lately, I can say it's . . . bearable. Especially if you don't remember."

"What are you talking about?" Nero asked tightly.

"I'm talking about murder," Samuel said. "Your aunt's, yes, but Laura's too."

"Laura slipped and fell."

"No, that's the story you tell everyone. Keep it straight, Nero, will you? It's your aunt who slipped and fell. Supposedly. Laura jumped into a canal dyed red. Isn't that it?"

Her presence gathered strength; I thought I saw her at the corner of my vision, that floating shroud, a wisp of movement, but when I turned to look it was gone. The air grew icy. A cold shiver went down my spine.

Nero had gone white. "Yes. She jumped."

"Samuel," I said, wanting to stop him, afraid to stop him.

He ignored me. "Did you know you meant to do it from the start? When you left for Milan, meaning to kill her lover, did you mean to come here after too? Or was it just a whim?"

"I didn't come here from Milan." Nero's voice was rough. "I went to meet you in Paris. You know that. You were with me when I got the telegram about her death."

"I think you've forgotten," Samuel said. "You brought *The Nunnery Tales* from here. Do you remember? You told me you'd gone to get it, as you were so close."

They were both so tense it seemed a strong breath might crack them. My heart pounded. My dread was overwhelming, the only thing I could feel. I could not bear to look at either of them; I could not bear to look away.

Samuel prodded, "Did your aunt know you meant to kill her? Or was that just a whim too?"

Nero said nothing, but I saw the trapped look in his eyes.

"You weren't so careful to keep from making marks on her throat this time. Or perhaps you didn't bother with Laura either, and it was only that the eels and the crabs ate them away. They didn't find her for two days. Long enough for that, I think. How lucky for you."

"Samuel," I managed. "His aunt . . . he didn't—"

I broke off when I saw Nero's expression. The closed eyes, the swallow—everything in him spoke of something past cure, irretrievable. I could not breathe. "Nero. No. Please. Say something. Deny it. Please."

He opened his eyes and looked at me, beseeching, plaintive. "You know already, Elena."

"The question is, can she bear it?" Samuel asked. "I'll take the blame for Madame Basilio, all Elena has to do is say the word. I'll give her a life with you if that's what she wants. But you'll tell us the truth now. You'll tell her what she needs to hear."

I made a sound, a whimper; I felt everything falling away. And Laura's spirit seemed to gain strength with my every pain, gathering it to herself, letting it coalesce and grow into something horrible, something mean. I felt her vindictiveness and her anger. "Nero, please don't."

He ignored me. "It was my aunt's fault. If she had let Laura marry Polani, none of it would have happened. But no, I had to bear these . . . these letters full of hate and . . . and bitterness. As if it were my fault. I'm not the one who betrayed her. I loved her. I never stopped. Even when . . ." He took a deep breath.

"Even when you killed her," Samuel provided.

Still that pleading gaze. I felt all of Nero reaching for me, begging me to understand. He said, "She could not stop nattering about Laura's ghost. I never thought anything of it—who could believe it? Then Giulia wrote me to say that my aunt thought Laura might be speaking through Samuel. Aunt Valeria believed his illness made him susceptible. She was doing things to make him worse so the spirit could gain hold."

"Giulia wrote you?" My voice did not sound like my own.

"It was a warning," he said, looking sick and sad. "She told me to stay away. You can thank past affections. She was my first. She was always a bit . . . maternal after. But when I realized that my aunt was hurting Samuel for this . . . obsession . . . of hers, I had to come. I couldn't leave him to her, could I? Could I, Elena?"

I could not answer his pleading glance. I felt numb.

The loneliness in his eyes . . . the heartache . . . and all the time her glee growing, the cold taking on an acid, unsavory edge. I felt her urging him on. *Now, yes, now.*

He went on, "It was a mistake to return. I only settled my aunt's suspicions more firmly. She'd heard Laura shouting that night. I thought no one knew I was there, but Aunt Valeria heard me in my bedroom getting that cursed book. And then the exorcism confirmed what she thought she knew already. You said Laura's nickname for me. *Lasagnone.* She used to call me her pretty lazy boy. Aunt Valeria told me she was going to Padre Pietro with her accusations early in the morning. All I had to do was wait for her to go."

"But . . . but you were with me," I said.

"You were exhausted," he said in a pained voice, heavy with contrition. "I made sure of it."

He'd lied to me. The realization was a blow, but what was worse was knowing how well I'd believed him, how certain I'd been that he was telling me the truth about not leaving my bed—the one thing that had given me the strength to repel the rest, to ignore it. The thing that had given me the will to save him. "All your protestations. The church. All of that searching at the market and . . . and you knew. It was all a lie."

"It was. I'm sorry. If you only knew how sorry I am . . ."

"I don't want to hear it."

"Elena, please. I never lied to you about what kind of man I was. I told you—"

"You told me about a man you killed in a duel. You said you were jealous. That you had a temper. Not that you'd murdered Laura."

"It wasn't like that. Not really—"

"No? You didn't put your hands around her throat? You didn't push her into the canal?"

He came to me, falling to his knees before me. "It was an accident. I never meant to . . . I meant only to talk to her. But she goaded me. She hated me. My aunt made sure of it. It caught me by surprise. I went to tell her I would still marry her, but . . . I couldn't reason with her." He reached for my hands.

I recoiled sharply, and his expression changed, just that fast, from fear and desperation to anger. Laura's spirit wavered like reflections behind him, gathering force.

"You said you loved me," he accused. "Only a few minutes ago you said it. And you knew the truth then. I saw it in your eyes."

"I wanted to pretend." My vision blurred with tears. "I wanted to believe you."

"Elena, please." He grabbed my hands, yanking me to him.

Samuel cried, "Don't touch her!" at the same moment cold air blasted through the room, so frigid and strong that our breaths turned immediately to frost. Nero started, jerking around to look, and his eyes went wide. I smelled her perfume, canal water and algae; I felt her anger as a force, that wall of air shifting as if the river of light on the ceiling and the walls had come between us. Colder than anything I'd ever felt. It seemed to freeze me from the inside out. Then the dim lamplight went red. Red as the walls in the receiving court with their bloody shadows. Red as a canal colored scarlet from a dyer's vat.

Samuel was there, beside us, but he was no longer himself. His brown eyes had gone to black, and she was in them. I saw her rage and her hate and the pure gleam of vengeance in her eyes, and Nero gasped. "Laura."

Samuel wrenched him away from me, spinning him, forcing him across the room, up against the wall.

"Samuel, no!" I cried, but when I rose I felt thrown back as if a giant hand had slapped me. The scene seemed to grow dim before me, as if she'd doused the light. I saw Samuel slamming Nero, once and again, the same way he'd slammed me. I heard the thud of his skull against the wall.

Again I tried to go to them. Again, that force pressing me back. I fought it, desperate to get there—Samuel was going to kill him; no, it was Laura. Laura was going to kill him, but it would be blood on Samuel's hands, a horror he would have to live with, and I could not bear that, even now, after everything.

Nero gained hold, pushing Samuel away, his foot behind Samuel's bad knee, jerking, and Samuel fell to the ground, scrambled up, grabbing Nero's arm, and they grappled, up again, but this time it was Nero who had Samuel against the wall. Nero with his hands around Samuel's throat, squeezing, Samuel prying at his hands, just as he had at the exorcism, just as terrible, wheezing and gasping, and I felt her fury and her resistance, fighting him, hating him, all her strength gone to that battle, none left for me, none to keep me from racing toward them, none to keep me back.

I grabbed the knife from my pocket, the Basilio blade, without thinking, wanting only to end it. I came up beside Nero and pressed the blade to his throat.

He froze.

I said quietly, "Let him go."

He didn't drop his hands. Samuel pried at Nero's fingers, which hadn't eased.

I heard footsteps. They seemed to come from far away. I heard the quick knock on the door; I heard it open. Da Cola and Pasqualigo. I heard them come into the room and stop as they took in the scene. "Signor," one of them said, appeasing, and then a stream of Venetian that Nero did not seem to hear.

"You don't want to do this, Nero," I pleaded. "I won't let you do this. Please, Nero. You wanted me to save you. Let me."

I don't know what I meant by the words. I don't know if I meant to try. I don't know if it was forgiveness or redemption I was offering, or something else. I said them because he had wanted it so badly. I wanted only to make him stop.

And he did. He dropped his hands from Samuel's throat, and Samuel fell to his knees, gasping. But before I could lower the knife, Nero's hands curled around mine on the hilt, holding it in place. He looked at me, that endless depth of pain in his eyes, a pain that I felt with every part of me.

"I killed my aunt," he said loudly, for the police who stood in the doorway. "Samuel had nothing to do with it." And then, to me, a whisper, mine alone, "I love you, Elena. But you can't save me."

Samuel cried, "No!"

Nero twisted the knife in my hands, plunging the blade into his throat just as he'd once shown me it could be done, a quick twist and blood spurting everywhere, blinding, warm as it coursed over my hand. I heard a gurgling rasp, a short cry of such relief it staggered, and he collapsed against me, a last grasp at my hips before he fell helplessly to the ground, a pool of blood spreading at my feet, over the floor. I stared in horror and disbelief, frozen in place in the moment before I realized what had happened, what he had done.

Then I fell to my knees beside him, heedless of the blood, gathering him in my arms, whispering, "No, no, no." Over and over again, because there were no other words; I could think of nothing else to say, not even when the light died in his eyes and he was gone, and I felt her all around us, a release of grief and pain and anger like ice shattering, and along with that a sense of satisfaction that I could not bear, that made me hate her. She had her vengeance, and I could not forgive her for it, nor could I forgive my part in it. I had not wanted it this way.

I buried my face in his chest, blood sticky on his shirt, on my skin, and my heart simply broke.

Samuel's hand was on my shoulder, cupping, gently pulling. "Let him go, Elena," he said softly, voice raw from choking, heavy with grief. "Let him go."

I did. I let him go. I went, bloody and bereft, into Samuel's arms, and I let him comfort me as the police took Nero away. I cried into his shirt and streaked us both with Nero's blood, until there were no tears left, until there was nothing left at all.

Chapter 34

In the days after, I waited to feel her presence. I paused at every movement I caught from the corner of my eye. I waited for the uncanny cold, the whiff of her perfume. But her revenge had been complete, her unfinished business finished now and done. Laura was gone. It wasn't as if the despair or sadness that was the palazzo's history had disappeared, but now it felt old and distant, patinaed like copper in moist air, corroded but somehow inert and soft, tinged not with anger but with acceptance.

"If it's any comfort, I was wrong," Samuel told me. "He did truly love you. I saw it at the end."

The world felt as if it should stop, but it didn't, of course. It only started again, inexorable, unmoved, and yet . . . forever changed. The funerals had been brief, the mourners few—Giulia and Zuan and the Nardis; Father Pietro and another priest from the Madonna dell' Orto. Samuel had taken charge, and as there was no family left, no one cared enough to question him. He was still not well, and the effort of arrangements left him exhausted often, headachy and collapsing into bed. But at least now his health was something I knew how to manage—healing ribs and knee and epilepsy, and if I sometimes saw shadows in his eyes, I think that it helped him that they were in mine too, that I had borne witness, that I understood.

We had kept everything very quiet; what friends of Nero's might have come to the service were only told once it was over. Madame Basilio's body was borne in a red gondola—the traditional Venetian color of mourning—to the island cemetery near Murano. The only funeral procession was the gondola following that carried me and Samuel, Giulia and Zuan. Nero could not be buried on consecrated ground, so his body was burned, his ashes scattered into the dyer's canal—we waited until the water was blue, the color he'd loved.

"If there's something you want to remind you of him, you should take it before they do the inventory," Samuel told me. "No one will know."

But there was nothing. The most personal things I had of him were the Basilio knife I'd carried for weeks that had killed him, and the Pulcinello mask that had revealed the truth to me. I wanted neither of these; the burden of them was too great. What I wanted was the man he'd been to me before I'd suspected anything, that first night; his gentleness and ardor, his laughing eyes and his tease, his body next to mine, my fingers in his curls. How did one keep hold of such ephemeral things? How could one live without them?

And yet . . . how could I have lived with them once I'd known the truth? How long would I have been able to pretend, because it was only by pretending that I could have him?

I suspected I could have done so for a very long time.

"*You can save me*," he'd said, and I think I would have tried.

I didn't know who I was anymore. I didn't know what I wanted, and as the days went by, and the decision of what to do drew ever closer, I knew there must be a reckoning. I saw the way Samuel watched me too; measuring, thoughtful, and I remembered what he had said so many months ago—no, not that long, it only seemed that way. One of us would have to make a sacrifice for the other. I could not forget what he had offered in the sala. To go to prison, to take the blame, so that I might turn my head and live with a lie.

It seemed only fair that I should offer my own sacrifice in return. There was the redemption I'd wanted so desperately, and I wanted to save my father too, his reputation, his life. The truth was that I no longer knew how, or even if I could. Nero's regret and misery had taught me that. He had not been able to live with the things he'd done, and perhaps in the end, that choice was all we had, the only redemption left to us—to live or not with the consequences we made, hoping we could do better, knowing that perhaps we could not.

I sent a letter to my father, and prepared myself to return.

I didn't tell Samuel. I wanted what little time was left to me, and I didn't want to give him the chance to make some heroic gesture. I would wait to say anything until it was too late. It was made easier by the fact that we didn't speak of the future, of life beyond this moment. We spent our days arranging things: the distant branch of the Basilio family must be contacted in Crete, where they'd been for generations, hardly remembering their relations in Venice. Giulia and Zuan must be cared for; Samuel lavished money on them. It seemed Zuan had always wanted to open a cookshop, and it was a simple matter to help him. Samuel bought good will and promises—no, they would never speak of what happened at the Basilio; they would call Madame Basilio's death an accident; they would talk of Nero with affection and respect. Not such hard things to do, it seemed. Giulia had been half in love with him all his life, and Zuan was a docile man who had no interest in angering his new patron.

Even after everything was done, we delayed, a tacit agreement. We had until the end of January, after all, and neither of us was in a hurry to face what must be faced. We spent long hours in cafés, walking the city, getting lost in the narrow streets until Samuel could not go farther because of his knee, which would probably

always be weak, and then hiring gondolas to take us about. Art
and churches, promenading the Riva to take advantage of the sun
in the afternoon, the Public Gardens and the Zattere to watch the
artists at work, both of us thinking of Nero and neither speaking of
him, or the things he might have shown us in this city of his youth,
neither admitting that we were procrastinating.

Then, finally, it was time.

We were sitting in a café on the Riva Schiavoni, in a shaft
of sun that warmed a small slice of the damp cold. The sky was
impossibly blue, the Canal riffled with hundreds of tiny diamond
sparks in a dark chop, gondolas swaying on the waves, the fishing boats in the distance with their ruddy-colored sails decorated
with the black marks of saints. The air smelled of a low tide in the
lagoon—fetid mud and seaweed, the tang of salt—and the bitter
warm aroma of coffee and chocolate; nutty, rich roasted chestnuts
from a peddler just down the way.

Samuel toyed with his tiny cup, swirling and dipping the last
syrupy remains of coffee as if he meant to paint patterns. He said,
"I don't want you to go back to New York."

I looked at him in surprise and dismay.

"I want you to have a Grand Tour, the way you hoped."

"If we could all only have what we want," I said. "You've already
offered too much. I can't watch you go back and marry that woman
and live . . . that way. I couldn't be happy knowing that you'd done
it for me. Don't ask me to."

"Elena—"

"No. I've written my father already. I've told him that I've failed.
No, don't protest—I've already done it, so there's nothing you can
do. Tell your parents you won't marry that woman. I release you
from any obligation to me. You're free to do whatever you like."

He eyed me thoughtfully. "So you'll go home and marry your
cousin?"

I had wanted him to protest, I realized, though I had done all I could to prevent it. I nodded shortly. "It's all right. I don't need a Grand Tour. I've had these last weeks, after all. They've been lovely. Mostly."

"But you miss him, despite everything."

That ache behind my eyes, the quick blur of vision. "Yes. I miss him."

"So do I." Samuel sighed heavily. "I don't know what to do without him, to be honest. I feel . . . adrift. I was angry with him half the time. He was intemperate. He took foolish risks. He got into trouble constantly . . . but I loved him. I wish . . . well, I suppose we all keep secrets. I didn't want to believe things about him that I knew in my heart were true."

"I believed him," I said.

"We always want to think the best of those we love," he said gently. "But he was right in the end, Elena. You couldn't save him."

My quick laugh turned into a sob. "I haven't been able to save anyone, it seems."

"Nero made a choice. So did your father. So did I. Everyone does what they must to survive. You can't save people from themselves. No one can. You can only save yourself."

I blinked through my tears, dashing them away with the back of my hand. "I mean to at least try to save you."

"By giving up your life."

"You were willing to give up yours."

"Well, mine is worthless, isn't it?" His smile was grim. "I told you: madness and idiocy. There's my future."

"I don't believe that," I said. "I don't think it's worthless."

"Neither is yours." He paused, looking down into that cup, swirling it again. "I'm going to go back. I'm going to talk to my parents. My mother will listen to me. My father . . . well, perhaps I can make him see reason. In any case, I won't marry this woman and make her life miserable, or my own. I'm done with that. It's time to find something new. Some other way to live."

Dryly, I said, "A return to decadence and debauchery? Drinking yourself into unconsciousness?"

"I was thinking perhaps I might hire myself a nurse. Someone to make me take my medicine. Cold baths. Burning liniments. Things like that. In return, I thought I could show her the world. There's a place in Paris that caters to contortionists and dwarves, you know. It might be entertaining. I don't suppose you know anyone who'd be interested in the job?"

"Oh, Samuel. I can't. You know I can't. My parents . . . my father."

His full lips thinned. "I won't press you for more than friendship, if that's what worries you. I've no wish to compete with him for your affections."

"That's not it," I said.

He said nothing more. He didn't try to persuade, and I was glad. I was afraid I would give in, just when I'd accepted what must happen. I was ready to take my punishment. I even wanted it, in a way, my own hair shirt, something to make me feel better for every mistake I'd made, my own inability to see the truth of things, the longing for something more that had blinded me when I wanted to be blind.

Samuel left the next morning. My ticket was for a week later, bought long ago, before I could know how I would feel to see him board that gondola and disappear from my life forever, the only one who knew what we had been through, who understood how deeply burrowed grief and remorse and impossibility. It was something we could never explain to anyone—how could we? How did one say that a ghost and a murderer had brought us together and tempered us in ways we never thought to know?

He only tipped his hat to me, a smile, and then he was gone, and I was left to wander the rooms of the Basilio—not eerie now, only quiet, resting, as if it waited for something to bring it to life again. Something to erase the sorrow in these walls. I hoped the new owners could do so, and I packed my things and waited for the day I was to leave. I avoided Samuel's room. There was too much I didn't want to be reminded of, though the urge to go in there pressed every day, wheedling, coaxing, and every day I resisted it. They were both gone, and I didn't want to remember, but neither did I expect my missing of Samuel to lodge so firmly in my heart. I had not known until he left how much he meant to me.

My father's letter came two days later.

> *My Dearest Elena,*
>
> *Your letter arrived 15th January, and your mother and I will be happy to see you returned to us, as will your cousin be. I know you are not overjoyed at the prospect of marriage, but we believe you will come to know it as a blessing and a delight, as we do. Michael is a good man, who is anxious to do well by you. I think he is a bit nervous at the idea of having a wife from the city who does not know how to milk a cow, but I have assured him you are an adept learner. You have always been a joy to me in our work together, and you know that I would love nothing better than to have you return to my side, if that were possible. I would like to think it will be someday, when there is time for the rumors and innuendo to die away, but by then I have hopes you will be concerned with children of your own, and will have no time for me!*
>
> *You should have no worry for myself and your mother. I have managed to secure a position at a small hospital upstate. They know of my circumstances, but are in dire need of a physician, and I have assured them that I shall be more vigilant than ever. Your mother is in no trifling way dismayed at our living in a village, but I think too that she*

is looking forward to a respite from her travels in society,
and will appreciate the peace. At last, she will have time to
devote herself to her silly novels.

We expect you in mid-February, and look forward to
seeing you and hearing about your time in Venice—don't
forget to bring back some token for your mother, who, as you
know, enjoys such mementos.

I am, as always,
Your Loving Father

I was glad. Truly I was glad. To see him in such good spirits even as he must start over again in a small town, his prodigious talents turned to agues and coughs instead of the latest techniques for treating hysteria or catatonia or epilepsy. I wanted to cry at his optimism, at the need for it.

And I'll admit that I also felt resentment about that optimism, a resistance I told myself not to fight, as if all of me strained to avoid that ticket home, that narrow room with no doors waiting, my cousin Michael and a marriage built on what was expected, mutual respect and friendliness instead of the love and passion I'd hoped for.

But I'd had that once, hadn't I? How often did most people experience that in a lifetime? Wasn't I luckier than most? I'd known even as I'd fallen into bed with Nero that it could not last, that it was a memory I was harvesting, a secret of my own to hold tight, something to take out to help me weather weary, endless days, to know that once I'd held a bright jewel that still shone, even with the tarnish of its setting.

I resigned myself. I packed my bags. I said good-bye to these rooms. The sala, where I could hardly stand to be. The bedroom that was mine that had once been his. I looked upon the bed and remembered what he'd looked like lying there that morning, all grays and blacks and whites, a drawing that even now seemed unreal, an artist's rendering, a portrait only, but mine.

"Good-bye," I whispered. "I'm sorry. I love you."

He was not there. Not even a murmur in response, though I listened for that. I supposed it was best. I did not want his spirit lingering, unhappy, looking for vengeance or redemption, something undone. I wanted peace for him.

I paused in the hall, glancing toward Samuel's room, and felt that urge to go inside again, gently pressing, but insistent, and I thought, *why not? One last time. Pay it the courtesy of a farewell.*

I stepped inside, and the memories flooded back, my arrival and Giulia's insolence. And then Samuel, huddled in the bed, racked and ruined, staring at me through a laudanum haze as if I were a ghost come to tend him.

Then I saw the envelope on the bed. His writing in broad, looping strokes on the outside. *Elena.*

It was lucky I'd seen it. I could have left without even coming to this room. What had he been thinking to leave it here? I picked it up, curious, puzzled—what more was there to say that hadn't already been said?

I tore it open. Something fluttered to the bed, and I ignored it for the moment to read the words he'd written, short and to the point:

Save yourself.

I glanced down at the paper that had fallen. It was a train ticket to Rome. Attached to it was another piece of paper, a scrap, Samuel's writing again. *Albergo Rosina*, and a reservation for rooms in my name, and below that: *3:30, Café Tacchi. I'll be there as soon as I can. Wait for me.*

My heart jumped. The ticket was for tonight—two hours from now. If I'd come here even an hour later, it would have been too late; I would miss it.

And perhaps I still should.

I took a deep breath, not knowing what to do. A life waited for me in New York. The life my parents wanted for me, the life I'd accepted. My penance and my atonement.

Save yourself.

"What should I do?" I whispered, feeling foolish as I said it, expecting to hear an answer, expecting to hear Nero's voice, his soul clinging to mine still, profoundly set. I heard nothing, but . . . the urge to go to the balcony had me crossing the room almost before I knew it, his words ringing in my head, *"we often left the day's fortunes to the dyer . . . is the rio green or blue?"* and I told myself that was what would decide me. I would go if it was Nero's favorite color. I would go if it was blue.

I rushed to the door, opening it, stepping out. All of it settled on a color, the caprice of a dyer. *Please*, I prayed, still not certain what I prayed for. *Please.*

I was almost afraid to look, but finally I did, and everything in me sagged in disappointment. The canal was no color at all. Not blue, not red, not yellow. No dye in it today, just its usual, dull olivey brown. Just a shallow canal stinking in the winter sun.

I'd left it to Fate, and Fate had answered. Tear up the ticket Samuel had bought. Forget the Café Tacchi and an appointment for three thirty every afternoon. Forget looking up from a table to see him cross the room, a smile on his face, relief in his eyes.

I started to turn away. But then . . . no, a faint touch, a gentle nudging, the same press that had set upon me every day as I looked toward Samuel's room, as if someone brushed my shoulder, urging me to wait, to turn. *"Look."* His voice in my ear, that same breathless whisper from the day he'd shown me the purple canal, that dreamcast voice, and I found myself obeying, twisting back to see.

Nothing at first, and then . . . yes, there it was, barely there, so slight as to be an illusion, a thread of color, a ribbon unfurling through the murk, dodging and spinning in the current, and then growing, a stream, and then a river, spreading and spreading beneath a misty Venetian sun.

Vibrant, stunning blue.

ACKNOWLEDGMENTS

Many, many thanks to my wonderful, sharp-eyed, and lovely editors Jodi Warshaw and Heather Lazare, whose insightful comments truly opened up some doors and made the novel better. Also thanks must go to my author team at Lake Union—Thom Kephart, Gabriella VandenHeuvel, Maggie Sivon, among others—for their wonderful support—you really make this all so much easier. Thank you once more to Kim Witherspoon, Allison Hunter, Nathaniel Jacks, and the staff at Inkwell Management, for their continued encouragement and attention, and to Kristin Hannah, who has not only been a creative and personal lifesaver, but an inspiration as well. Jan Berlin generously provided a crucial Venetian translation for me (not all of them—blame me for errors!), for which, among many of her other generosities, I am eternally grateful. Last, but never least of course, I could not do this without Kany, Maggie, and Cleo, who weather everything with equanimity (sometimes), patience (mostly), and love (always).

ABOUT THE AUTHOR

Megan Chance is a critically acclaimed, award-winning author of historical fiction. Her novels have been chosen for the Borders Original Voices and Book Sense programs. A former television news photographer and graduate of Western Washington University, Chance lives in the Pacific Northwest with her husband and two daughters.